Dedalus Original Fiction in Paperback

The Great Chain of Unbeing

Andrew Crumey was born in Glasgow in 1961. He read theoretical physics and mathematics at St Andrews University and Imperial College in London, before doing post-doctoral research at Leeds University on nonlinear dynamics. After six years as the literary editor at *Scotland on Sunday* he now lectures in creative writing at Northumbria University.

He is the author of seven novels: *Music, in a Foreign Language* (1994), *Pfitz* (1995), *D'Alembert's Principle* (1996), *Mr Mee* (2000, Dedalus edition 2014), *Mobius Dick* (2004, Dedalus edition 2014) *Sputnik Caledonia* (2008, Dedalus edition 2015) and *The Secret Knowledge* (2013). Andrew Crumey's novels have been translated into fourteen languages.

D1563616

Andrew Crumey

The Great Chain of Unbeing

Dedalus

Supported using public funding by
**ARTS COUNCIL
ENGLAND**

Published in the UK by Dedalus Limited
24-26, St Judith's Lane, Sawtry, Cambs, PE28 5XE
email: info@dedalusbooks.com
www.dedalusbooks.com

ISBN printed book   978 1 910213 77 3
ISBN ebook 978 1 910213 87 2

Dedalus is distributed in the USA & Canada by SCB Distributors
15608 South New Century Drive, Gardena, CA 90248
email: info@scbdistributors.com   web: www.scbdistributors.com

Dedalus is distributed in Australia by Peribo Pty Ltd
58, Beaumont Road, Mount Kuring-gai, N.S.W. 2080
email: info@peribo.com.au

First published by Dedalus in 2018
The Great Chain of Unbeing © Andrew Crumey 2018

Printed and bound in Great Britain by Clays Ltd, St Ives plc
Typeset by Marie Lane

Contents

The Unbeginning

When my father was around twenty years old, doing compulsory national service with the British Army, he found himself posted to Christmas Island in the South Pacific. While his former schoolmates back home were square-bashing in the rain, he was spear fishing in the Blue Lagoon or watching land-crabs scuttle across burning sands. He was an avid stargazer, and at night he trained his binoculars on treasures of the southern sky – the Magellanic Clouds, the Jewel Box – which he described to me years afterwards, instilling in me a fascination that was to form the basis of my adult career.

Along with his fellow conscripts, my father was one day ordered to stand on the beach, close his eyes as tightly as he could, and hold his clenched fists over them. He knew what was about to happen. As a safety measure, the men had all been instructed to wear long trousers that morning, rather than shorts. It was a beautiful, calm day, my father told me. They all stood there, heard the countdown, and 30 miles behind them, a hydrogen bomb exploded.

My father said that even with his back to the fireball, and

with his eyes closed, he could see the bones of his own hands. A few seconds later, he turned and saw the rising mushroom cloud; a ball of incinerated air convected so swiftly into the upper atmosphere that sparks of lightning flashed around its rolling flanks.

Then the sound arrived: a shockwave that knocked the young soldiers to the ground. As the spectacle continued to unfold, the disrupted air above them curdled into black rain clouds, drenching them with viscous bullets of water. When it was all over, they showered and changed, got on with their daily duties, and later enjoyed a laugh and a pint at the regimental club's tombola night.

As soon as my father was released from the army he married the girl in Glasgow he'd been writing to every week since he was called up. A year later they had a plump and healthy son, my brother Ken, who now works as a civil engineer. After another two years, I came into the world; but at first the midwife wouldn't hand me to my mother. Instead she called for a male doctor who had a look at the little bundle he was presented with, took it away for closer inspection, then came back to report his findings to my anxious and exhausted mother.

"It's a little boy," the doctor told her. "Unfortunately he's blind." My mother asked how he could possibly be so sure, and he told her that since I had no eyes there really couldn't be much doubt about it, could there?

That's how my life began: I told the new girl about it today. She's called Jagoda and says the hours and money are fine; she'll clean and iron, do a bit of cooking if need be, read the mail. She comes from what used to be the other side of the geo-political divide that caused my father to be soaked in fall-out. The bomb he witnessed was meant to damage people like her, but instead made me. Since then the lines have shifted, the arguments have changed. Best not discuss politics, I thought, recounting to her my nuclear beginning.

"Are you sad about it?" she asked in accented but perfect English, and I laughed, for how could I ever regret being born? I was a love-child, after all. Had my father not been so passionate about the stars, he would never have applied for a posting where clear nights and southern constellations attracted him more than puffer fish or gooney birds. Had a high-energy photon from the blast not severed a chemical bond inside his body, sending a free radical on its hungry, damaging course, then I might have been born sighted, and perhaps I would have been unmoved by the stories he told me about the mythical beasts and heroes that wheel above our heads each night and go unnoticed by people for whom the flicker of a television screen is more compelling than the glimmer of distant worlds. I might never have become a cosmologist – and Jagoda would have needed a different employer.

"Let me show you around," I offered, then led her on a quick inspection of the flat. "The only rule," I said, "is that you don't move things, otherwise I never know where to find them. So no tidying. Otherwise treat it like any other place. And by the way, it's John. Not even my students call me Dr Wood."

"What about the lights?" she asked. I didn't know what she meant. "They're switched on, though it's the middle of the day. Do you leave them on constantly?"

I realised there must be something wrong with the timer; the lights are meant to come on at night to reassure callers and deter burglars, but perhaps my young nephew had fiddled with the control at the weekend when my sister-in-law came to visit.

"Come and I'll show you how to adjust them." As she

followed me along the passageway I heard her bump against my side table, prompting a clatter of framed photographs.

"I'm sorry," she exclaimed. "I'll put them back the same way."

"Don't worry," I said, checking their positions. "They have different frames. This is me with Ken when I was about ten years old. I'd just learned to ride a bike. Here are my parents."

"You look like your father. And this is your graduation?"

"Yes, sweating in our gowns on a very hot day. The fellow on the left is Roy Jones, I think he went on to do a PhD in tribology. The other was some musician friend of Roy's."

"Very interesting," she conceded, though without asking me the meaning of tribology, a term which floated up like vapour to join the hovering cloud of other unspoken words.

"Do you wonder why I have these pictures?" I asked.

"Same reason as the lights?"

"They're precious to me, that's all." Then I showed her the panel for the timer. "The really stupid thing is the digital display, but as long as nobody changes it we're fine. You see how much trouble I have to go to?" I said with a laugh. "It costs me money to keep you folk from being in the dark."

Resuming our brief tour, Jagoda said, "I heard of a restaurant with no lights. Everyone eats in complete darkness."

"Yes, in Paris, I think."

"To make people think how it is to be blind."

"I'm not so sure about that," I said, displaying the bedroom with a wave of my hand and taking her back to the living room so we could finish our tea. "There's no darkness in my life." She thought I was being metaphorical; I was merely stating a fact. "What's behind you right now?" I asked once we were seated.

I heard her turn to look. "A door, some bookshelves." Her

voice echoed against the far wall.

"Now face me again. How does the bookcase look to you?"

"It doesn't look like anything – I can't see it."

"Exactly, and that's how everything looks to me: neither dark nor light, but invisible. I'm sure you've never felt you were missing out by not having eyes in the back of your head; I feel that way about eyes in front. I've never needed them and don't want them. I only wear these artificial things so that I won't frighten people."

Throughout my childhood I had to go to hospital regularly to have new eyes fitted. They prevented my sockets from closing up, but couldn't keep pace with my growth; so on countless unpleasant occasions I sat stoically while gel was squirted into each empty orbit and left to set, providing a cast for my next pair of custom-made eyes. In a medical school drawer somewhere, I expect my youth is still mapped by a forgotten array of ancient discarded blobs staring blankly in every direction.

In the old days, the world's false eyes were crafted by German glass-blowers renowned for their unmatchable skill. The one-eyed Prince Christian of Schleswig-Holstein, maimed in a shooting accident, had a different eye made for every occasion: proud, lascivious, sleepy, hung-over. A man's soul, it is said, is written in his eyes, so I share with Prince Christian the opportunity for self-creation; but my eyes are not glass, because the Second World War cut the supply line, and when Spitfire pilots fell from burning, shattered cockpits into the safety of military hospitals, there was nothing to plug their ruined faces. It was the Perspex shards embedded in their flesh that saved them. Found to be biologically inert, the plastic proved a perfect substitute for glass, and henceforth the nation's artificial eyes were moulded in a workshop in

Blackpool, which is where mine came from, made to simulate real eyes, with matching irises and pupils, so that I can look relatively "normal".

"They're very realistic," Jagoda told me. "When you came to the door to let me in, I thought at first that you were someone else, because you'd told me on the phone that you were blind. It took a few moments to see there was something different about your eyes."

"They don't move or blink – you can only do so much with two lumps of plastic."

"I think they make you look very distinguished," she said tactfully. Perhaps mine came from the same design catalogue as Prince Christian's. Posing as a child for successive generations of these impostors meant sitting patiently in a leather chair, holding my mother's hand while the gel went firm in my sockets. When the casts were ready, the cheerful doctor would extract them delicately, but never without some of the gel adhering to my own tissue – like stripping an Elastoplast from under the tongue. There were consolations of the usual hospital kind: a chair I could swing in as much as I liked; a stethoscope with which to probe my beating heart; inscrutable gadgets of cold, smooth steel, drawn randomly, it seemed, from the doctor's menagerie of disposable spares. None of these, however, could counterbalance the ominous sense of dread I felt whenever we walked down the echoing hospital corridor with its sickly smell of undefined despair; its heavy swing doors; its stock of conversational snippets, momentarily caught from passers-by as Mum and I marched to the eye clinic. Those fragments of unknown lives, falling into my ears like fluttering relics, seemed all the more poignant by virtue of their sheer triviality. This was a place where absolutely no one wanted to be – even the doctors would doubtless rather have been in the pub. And this was the place where I had to come and have false eyes pushed into my head so that to sighted people I would not appear too monstrous. And like any child, I accepted it.

My escape was to think. In the doctor's leather chair I would avoid the discomfort by fixing my mind on an idea, a memory, a hope. I would hold it with the same tenacious grip that kept my comforting mother close beside me.

"Did you ever wonder what it would be like to see?" Jagoda asked.

"Of course, just as I've wondered what it must be like to be a goldfish or Napoleon. Or a woman, though I'd never undergo surgery to find out. I don't suppose you'd want to go round wearing Perspex testicles, would you?"

She laughed. "Horrible thought!"

"False eyes are about as much use to me, and real ones appeal even less. Certainly, I'm curious about sight, but only if I could have the experience for a very short time, and be sure it was reversible. More tea?" She'd drained her cup with a slurp and chink, and accepted a top-up.

What's it like to see? No poet has ever explained it, though accounts abound of what things look like, for the benefit of those who know already. There was even a congenitally blind poet, Thomas Blacklock, who impressed eighteenth-century sighted contemporaries with striking visual evocations of a natural world he never saw. Aristotle offered something more useful in his theory of how the eye works. Rays fly out of it, he claimed, strike distant objects, and in this way give the sensation of vision, so that sight is really a form of touch: a beautiful confirmation of what any blind person suspects. Uncontaminated by the later knowledge that light is a wave flowing into people's eyes, Aristotle constructed a theory based only on what he truly felt.

As a child I sought my own conception of that mysterious ability to perceive what is beyond reach. Embraced by the leather hospital chair whose smell and texture I still recall, I urged my thoughts to probe the limits of their own extension, as with my fingernails I explored the cracks and crumbs beneath me, finding ever new and imponderable questions. Why did I exist? Because my parents made me. But why did they exist? Because of a great chain of causes stretching back... to what? To nothing? Out of the succession of dead and unknown ancestors, and of yet-unborn descendants, here I was, a pattern of raised dots in a Braille text visible only to God whose moving finger made this moment "now", the rest written unalterably in eternity. It made me dizzy, this thought of being alive, the improbable sensation of existence, devoid of any name I knew.

I wonder if Dad felt it when the bomb exploded behind his back, its light strong enough to crowd straight through his head. He could see the bones of his own hands, he told me, even with his eyes shut; and as a child this didn't strike me as extraordinary because the bones of my own small hands made an equally clear impression when I held them to my face. But I noticed the strange pleasure he took in recounting the scene of beauty and destruction he attended: the scorching flash; the momentary, all-embracing burst of creation; the rising pillar of involuting cloud that was a brain, a tree, or a thousand other resemblances to the awed onlookers watching from many miles away through smoked glass, irradiated by human ingenuity.

I was in the back garden with my father one night, holding his star map for him while his binoculars licked the cold sky, when he explained to me how it all worked: the fusion of hydrogen atoms, releasing so much energy that for a brief moment the fireball was like a piece of the sun brought down to earth. He was an engineer by trade, and the universe he described to me was one of machine-like intricacy and perfection. A hoarder of spare parts encountered in his work, he had filled a cupboard in our house with knurled cogs, bits of clocks, greasy gears and tangled wires terminating in sandwiches of plastic and solder that smelled of unknown factories as romantic to my mind as Ursa Major, Canes Venatici, and those other unreachable territories far above our heads. Dad was a hoarder of useless knowledge too: the workings of bombs and stars lay heaped in the reckless jumble he shared so eagerly with me.

We are all made of atoms, he told me, whose centres are like little jack-in-the-boxes. The lids are held down by nuclear force; the electrical repulsion of protons inside the atom pushes against this restraint like a pent-up spring. To close a jack-in-the-box, you need to push down hard on the spring until the box shuts with a click. Squeeze lots of hydrogen atoms together and the force makes a trillion clicks: fusion's thunderous roar.

It was enough to knock my father to the ground, this energy from mating particles carried through seared air into his youthful body. Yet only a single click – on a Geiger counter as he emerged from the shower afterwards – was enough to decide my future and his. For me, it was the blessing of being who I am. For him, it was the cancer that killed him three years ago.

I didn't tell all of this to Jagoda; she'd come to offer domestic help, not hear my life story. But she wanted to know what I do for a living, so I explained how one thing had followed another, like particles communicating their quantity of motion, or the harmonious interlocking of a succession of toothed wheels. I was born from a nuclear reaction and so is everyone, since the sun or any other star is a bottomless ocean of hydrogen whose atoms, compressed by their own sheer weight, fuse unavoidably, sending parcels of light burrowing haphazardly through the thick and perilous mantle, out into space, across distances of unimaginable emptiness, traversing the cosmos without incident until at last a few of them might fall, like unexpected snowflakes, upon the innocent lens a human aims towards the site of their conception.

"But how did everything begin?" she asked. "What caused the Big Bang?"

Like a child again I was at the limit of expression, wishing to resort by way of explanation to a certain metric of general relativity, yet aware that the response would be inadequate, and that calculation is not the same sort of understanding as experience. Instead I said, "You can try to describe to me what it's like to see, and I'll never really know. When I speak of my own invisible reality where neither light nor dark exist, that's equally hard for you to grasp. What neither of us can imagine is a universe without space and time. A kind of unbeginning. We lack sufficient sense, or have too much, or the wrong kind."

"I like philosophy," she said. "It's what we need in this crazy world. But the bomb... it's scary."

She starts next week; there'll be plenty for her to do. I shall ask her to keep a check on the timer. I wonder what ever happened to Roy Jones?

Tribology
(or *The Truth about my Wife*)

Arriving at Moscow airport, Roy Jones passed through the customs channel and emerged into the public concourse to see a row of impoverished-looking taxi drivers, mournfully waiting for their pre-booked customers.

Russia, his wife had warned him, is a wild and unruly place. The taxi drivers are in some instances muggers in disguise. She'd seen it on a TV documentary. They lure Westerners into their cars, drive them to remote and shabby neighbourhoods, then allow their passengers to escape with their lives only if they first hand over their every valuable. Even their Berghaus fleeces.

But among the drivers Roy Jones saw as he emerged stood one, sallow-faced in a fur hat and battered black leather jacket, bearing a sign saying *Mr Jones*. How reassuring. Though surely the organisers of the Thirteenth International Congress of Tribology should have remembered that Roy Jones was Doctor, not Mister.

They went outside to a grimy white car. Roy Jones felt brave enough to place himself in the passenger seat, holding his briefcase, while the driver casually fitted the larger suitcase into the boot. Roy Jones had just about figured out the seat belt when the driver got in beside him and started the car.

"Do you know where you're going?" Roy Jones asked.

The driver gave a thin smile. "Yes. Do you?"

Roy Jones didn't know the name of the hotel. The conference organiser had e-mailed it to him last week, but it was a funny Russian word that meant nothing to him: a possible hotel, nothing more. Now the driver was taking him there.

Roy Jones watched the unfolding succession of slab-like buildings and strangely quiet roads, punctuated by advertising hoardings whose enthusiasm was almost touching in its futility. The sky was grey and overcast; the air was filled with swirling powder-snow, whipped by the slipstreams of the ancient, fuming lorries they overtook.

"Do you live in Moscow?" Roy Jones asked. It was all the small-talk he could think of. Long silences were as discomforting to him, even with insignificant foreigners, as long periods without going to the bathroom.

The driver nodded. "I live in Moscow," he said. "All my life, I live in Moscow. Except for one year, I live in London."

So when he said he lived all his life in Moscow, Roy Jones reasoned, the driver was in fact lying. It was good for Roy Jones to know exactly where he stood. Or rather, sat, with his briefcase clutched tightly on his lap.

"What were you doing in London?" Roy Jones asked.

"A girl," said the driver enigmatically. He looked the kind of man no woman could ever fall for. At least, no woman that Roy Jones could think of. Like his wife, for instance. Or Dorothy, the departmental secretary at the university. But what about the students? Those female ones, who'd sit on the lawn beneath his office window in the summer term? Roy Jones knew nothing about those young and dangerously carefree girls. None of them were tribologists.

"I love London," said the driver, turning towards Roy Jones with a sudden obliviousness to the road ahead. "And I hate it."

It must be a Russian thing, Roy Jones decided: this tendency towards inconsistency. Not to mention a tendency to ignore the road. He said, "Do you love Moscow, or do you hate it?"

The driver nodded. "Yes. That's it exactly, my friend."

The car took a bend, and a dignified building appeared on their left, adorned with a hammer and sickle. Roy Jones thought they would have got rid of all that long ago, but apparently not.

"What I really love," said the driver, "is the taiga."

Roy Jones was puzzled. "You love the tiger?"

The driver nodded.

"Which tiger is that?"

"The taiga," the driver repeated. "You know, the forest."

From the depths of his memory, Roy Jones recalled a wildlife programme he'd watched one Sunday evening with his wife. The taiga: a great expanse of dense woodland, between grassy steppe to the south and frozen tundra to the north. So at once, Roy Jones knew exactly where he was with the driver. Lots and lots of trees, the odd bear or eagle, and the soothing voice of David Attenborough, while his wife got up and asked if he wanted more tea.

"Of course, the taiga," said Roy Jones. "Well, I'm sure it must be very nice. A bit like the New Forest, perhaps?"

"I hate it," said the driver. "The taiga, it is beautiful, and it is hell."

Roy Jones could not recall, in at least twenty years of attendance at international conferences on industrial lubricants, any conversation with a local taxi driver quite like the one that was now evolving. "Tell me," he said, "have you always been a taxi driver?"

His companion shook his head. "I am not a taxi driver." Roy Jones felt a shiver of fear; was this the moment when the hidden plan would make itself known, as the driver pulled up in a side street far from any hotel or officer of the local law?

The driver repeated, "I am not a driver, not a teacher, not a husband, not a writer." Roy Jones was struggling to find the point of all these negatives. Apart from husband and teacher (or rather, lecturer), Roy Jones was none of these things either. "No," said the driver. "I am a man. That is all I am. You go to taiga, you find this for yourself. You find what you are. Then perhaps you love yourself. Or perhaps you hate."

"I see," said Roy Jones. Clearly this taiga place wasn't like the New Forest after all. "Do you go there often?"

"Not since many years," said the driver sorrowfully. "Last time, it was enough for me." Still the car followed its steady route through streets Roy Jones began to notice less and less, intrigued instead by the driver's words.

"Twelve years ago," the driver said, "or maybe more, I can't remember. My cousin and I, we like to hunt. We go to taiga with our rifles. The big black bird, what do you call it?"

"Crow?"

"No."

"Eagle?"

"No, big black bird, kind of a grouse. What beautiful meat! And the one with the tail like this..." The driver drew a curve with his finger.

"Lyre bird?"

"Of course not."

Roy Jones had seen lyre birds on David Attenborough, but

obviously it wasn't taiga week then.

The driver drew the bird's tail again, this time taking both hands from the wheel in order to express himself more accurately, and Roy Jones realised that his life possibly depended right now on his own neglected skills in ornithology.

"Quail? Ptarmigan?"

"No, no. Quail is with the feathers on his head..." The driver was more interested in doing bird impressions than in watching Moscow traffic. Roy Jones was shrinking into his seat, wondering if his briefcase would have the protective qualities of an airbag, as random bird names continued to spill from his mind.

"Partridge?"

"Yes! yes!" The driver clapped and gripped the wheel once more. Roy Jones breathed a sigh of relief. A partridge had saved his life.

"That's a good bird," said the driver. "We hunt it, in the taiga. And another one..."

"Alright, never mind," said Roy Jones.

The driver was hurt. "I bore you?"

Roy Jones was sheepish. For all his consumptive appearance, the driver could still probably kick the shit out of him if he cared to, judging by the deft way he'd handled Roy Jones's suitcase. "I only meant to ask you what else you hunted. Bears?"

The driver shook his head. "Bears, you leave them alone, they leave you. But the pig, with the tusks..."

"Wild boar?" Roy Jones said swiftly, before the driver could bring his hands up and make little tusks out of them that would have sent the car careering off the road into what Roy Jones noticed to be a passing McDonalds.

"Yes, the wild boar. We shot one, cooked it on a fire."

"That's most interesting," Roy Jones said politely. "And you're allowed to light fires in the taiga?" Yes, it really wasn't like the New Forest at all.

"You do whatever you want," said the driver. "In the taiga, no one can see you. In the taiga, nearest village is maybe a thousand kilometres away. You see another man in the taiga, first thing you do, you reach for your rifle."

Roy Jones swallowed. "Well. Fascinating. And you went there with your cousin?"

The driver nodded. "We camp; we stay in huts. They open all the time; if nobody there you go in, light the fire, live there as long as you wish."

"And if somebody's in the hut when you arrive?"

"Then you no go near. You keep your rifle close by your side."

All in all, this taiga place sounded a lot less inviting than when David Attenborough did it on the television. Roy Jones's wife had made a fresh pot of tea, and there on the screen was a big cuddly bear, reaching into a tree and mucking up a beehive, just like an outsized Winnie the Pooh. "Come and look at this, dear," Roy Jones called to his wife in the kitchen, as the bear slopped bee-studded honey into its hungry mouth. "Really, these creatures are so comical, don't you think?"

But now the driver had totally spoiled it all. The taiga, it seemed, was just as lawless as the rest of this huge, unfathomable country.

"We go in boat," he explained.

"You and your cousin?"

The driver nodded. "Some supplies, a tent, essential things. Our rifles, of course. We go up the river, two hundred kilometres from road where we leave the car. Takes us a few days. We hear there's good place for the... for the..."

"Partridges? Grouse?"

"No, the black one. Never mind. We think there's a hut not far away, nobody is there probably. So, on the third day, we wake up in our tent, wash ourselves in the river, we have some fish to eat. In the taiga, very good fish."

Roy Jones could almost see it: the smouldering campfire beside the broad, cool waters. And all around, nothing but trees, impenetrably dense.

"We get the boat ready, and my cousin, he say to me suddenly, did you hear that? What, I say. A noise, he tell me. Sound like a gun. I say to him, I hear nothing – you hear a branch breaking. It might be a bear, he say, we better be careful, and I say, never mind about the bear, we make the boat ready, we go to the hut today and we find a nice bed tonight, have everything we need. He laugh – everything except a woman of course. Yes, in the taiga you have everything except that."

Roy Jones could at least relate to this aspect of the adventure. While the resemblance with the New Forest had dwindled out of existence, the taiga nevertheless had something in common with the field of international tribology research.

"My cousin, he say, let's check the rifles. He not like the sound he heard. In the taiga, you meet another man, he's either mad or he's escaped from a prison."

"What about you two?"

"We were hunters. That's the other kind you meet. And hunters, they like to hunt. So you not want to meet other hunter. Otherwise, maybe he hunt you."

The driver slowed up, but it was not a hotel they had arrived at, only a set of traffic lights that soon changed.

"Well, we check the rifles, we get the boat ready, we set off. Beautiful morning. In the taiga, clear days like you see nowhere else. The air is like... like..." Roy Jones quietly prayed that

23

the fresh air of the taiga bore no resemblance to anything that would mean the driver lifting his hands from the wheel again. "Like honey," he said at last. "Air like honey." All ready for a big bear to come and steal, and without signalling, the driver took a sudden left in front of an oncoming lorry. Roy Jones braced himself, but the taxi easily avoided the approaching vehicle, whose horn blared as they left it rushing behind them.

"And the water," the driver continued, "it's like glass. Only few small waves on the wide river, it flows so slow. And the boat cutting through when we start the engine." He breathed in, as if tasting the honeyed air of the taiga; Roy Jones watched the driver breathe deeply, exhaling noisily before repeating the gesture, and then finally the driver's sickly face darkened. "Shit!" he murmured. "The air, to me, it's like a shit."

Roy Jones wasn't sure if this was Russian contradiction again, or else a comparison between the taiga and the city; but he didn't really care. "Then you took the boat to the hut?" he said, wishing to move things along to their conclusion, as if this might somehow bring them more quickly to his hotel.

The driver slowly shook his head. "No," he said. "We not make it to the hut. We not make it any place. The boat, it goes fine, engine run smoothly, and then my cousin, he says suddenly: Listen! So I listened, and I hear nothing. My cousin, he leans towards me in the boat and he says, it was another gunshot, you didn't hear it? Me, I reckon he's dreaming. But then, across the water, in front of the boat, there it was: pat-pat-pat-pat-pat!" The driver, using only one hand, made a motion like a flat stone skimming over the waves.

"My cousin, he get hold of me while I watch, he grab me and pull me down in the boat. I raise my head to look, and there it is again, in front of us: pat-pat-pat-pat-pat! Line of bullets hitting the water. A machine gun. Some guys in trees, they want a little fun, little sport. Maybe they sink the boat first, then they kill us. Or else they want the boat. My cousin and me, we're lying in the boat, terrified, and we hear bullets flying over our head: zip-zip-zip-zip!" A zooming finger illustrated this new torment for the benefit of Roy Jones. "We not steering the boat – I try to hold with my foot. And then: kaa-kaa-kaa-kaa-kaa! Little pieces of wood splintering all over us – a line of holes in the side of the boat. They getting serious. My cousin, he say to me: we gotta do something! And he reach the... the... what do you call the handle on motor you steer with?"

Roy Jones couldn't remember. "The rudder?"

"No, not rudder I think."

"Let's just call it the handle," Roy Jones suggested. "Tell me what happened next."

"My cousin, he get the handle between his feet and he go THIS WAY and THIS WAY." The swerving of the boat was perfectly imitated by the driver's sudden lurching of his body to left and right, some of which was in turn transmitted to the taxi. "He make the boat spin all around."

"No need to illustrate," said Roy Jones. "I get the idea."

"And for a moment, I think we gonna turn over in the water, maybe we hide under the boat or something – I dunno, it's crazy, but when a man's firing at you – pa-pa-pa-pa! – you gotta do anything you can. And the boat, it's going everywhere. My cousin can't control it. And then: bang! The boat's grounded at the side of the river. We gotta get out and run for it, while the bullets keep coming at us: za-za-za-za-za-za-za-za! I'm running into the trees, and I see a line of them right beside me, like a rabbit I'm chasing – only I'm the rabbit, and the bullets are chasing me. And I get behind a tree and look round to see the river bank. And there's my cousin lying on the ground, my own cousin in front of my eyes. My poor cousin."

The driver at this point kissed his fingertips, touched the small faded icon affixed to the car's battered dashboard, and crossed himself.

"Was he dead?" Roy Jones asked. Being a tribologist of international eminence, he was by nature a man of exactitude.

The driver shook his head. "My cousin not dead. Not quite. His leg was moving – he was trying to push himself along the ground. No bullets now, no sound anywhere, except my cousin, on the ground, trying to get himself to safety, and this kind of gurgling sound he make. Ah – shit!" The driver suddenly stopped the car. "Here is your hotel."

Roy Jones looked out and saw a huge building in which, right now, he had absolutely no interest. "I'd really like to hear the rest of your story," he said.

The driver glanced at his watch. "I have another delegate to meet from airport in forty minutes."

"Well, that gives you plenty of time to get to the end," Roy Jones suggested; but already the driver had got out and walked round to open the boot. Roy Jones also stepped out of the car, and took charge of the wheeled suitcase that was handed to him. The cab had been arranged by the conference organisers; there was nothing to pay, no more to be said. During much of the preceding story about the taiga, Roy Jones had been quietly wondering whether a tip would be expected; but he had no Russian money, and it seemed that this little episode was about to end and be forgotten – as such episodes always are – without any further resolution.

However, with a sudden burst of initiative, Roy Jones said, "Do you think you could help me inside with the suitcase?" The driver looked sceptical. Roy Jones said, "I could even buy you a drink."

"A drink?"

"Well, a coffee, I suppose. And you could tell me a little more about the taiga."

The driver smiled. "I help you, then," he said, taking the suitcase by the carrying handle on its long side, rather than the extendible one for less muscular travellers such as Roy Jones who rely on trolley wheels, and the driver ascended the hotel steps, easily bearing the suitcase while Roy Jones made do with his briefcase which contained the precious presentation – "Mixed-phase lubricants: a top-down approach" – that was still his reason for being here, and almost entirely the reason why he left the driver settling comfortably in the hotel bar while he went to check in.

The girl behind the desk was perfectly groomed but imperfectly trained. It all took a lot longer than Roy Jones would have preferred, and as he handed over his passport, he looked at his watch, wondering if it had really been such a good idea to invite the driver in. Roy Jones was a sucker for a good story, that was his problem. He was simply too impulsive, as his wife told him the other week, when he suddenly changed the habit of a lifetime and decided that their next car would not be a Rover after all.

"Enjoy your stay," the desk girl finally announced with a smile that clearly had had too much prior use. Roy Jones took his key and his luggage and went straight back to the bar, where the driver was sitting silently over a cup of coffee. Roy Jones sat down opposite him at the small wooden table and thought it best to get to the point.

"What did you do about your cousin?" Roy Jones asked.

"What would any man do?" said the driver with a shrug. "He was lying there in the dirt, trailing blood as he pushed himself along the ground with one foot, trying to reach the trees. At the other side of the river, a man with a machine gun, or two men, or a whole army, were waiting for me to make my move. As soon as I ran out to save my cousin, they would finish both of us."

"I see," said Roy Jones. Put in such straightforward terms, the whole matter became as clear as the most elementary problem of engineering. "So you left your cousin to die?"

The driver's eyebrows shot up. "To die! You think I'm a monster! No, I never leave any man to die. I take a deep breath, I say a prayer, I kiss the picture of my mother I carry here in my own head, and then I run – yes, I run out from behind the tree, faster than ever I run in my life. And the bullets, they come BA! BA! BA! BA! BA! BA!" The driver's hand chopped salami slices across the table, so loudly that heads turned in response. "The bullets tear the sleeves of my coat, they chew the leather of my boots. BA! BA! BA! BA! BA! BA! They rip my cousin's back to pieces, and right before my eyes his head explodes – SHAAH!"

Roy Jones gave a jump and clutched the room key in his hand.

"My cousin, there was no hope. And I never make it back to the trees. So I run to the boat in the water, I jump inside the boat, and the bullets are like crazy. And in all those thousand bullets, not one of them hits my body. I think to myself, I am like a saint. God has chosen this. As many bullets as there are leaves on a tree – as many bullets as there are trees in the forest. They've torn my sleeve, my boot. But not my flesh. And I throw myself in the boat – they can perhaps even see me there, but it was the closest place, closer than the trees where I was already safe. I land in the boat, and my head, it hits the wooden seat, real hard. So here I am, a bulletproof saint. And a piece of wood knocks me unconscious."

The driver raised his coffee cup and took a sip. "How long

I lie there? I don't know: a minute, an hour, a day. Next thing, I realise I'm awake, and there's no shooting. They must have decided I was dead. No guns anywhere, except the two loaded rifles there beside me in the boat. I wake up, and I remember that my cousin is dead. I can't raise my head to look: I can't risk it. Perhaps only a minute has passed since I landed here – who knows? So I lie and wait. All I hear is the gentle wind in the trees, the river lapping against the boat, sometimes the birds. And then, after a while, I hear another boat, far away. A motor boat, slowly it get louder, nearer. And now I know what happens. They come to see what they done. They find me, they shoot me – how can I play dead, when they go through my pockets looking for my wallet? How can I lie still, with my heart pounding and not a drop of blood on my body? I think to myself, this is the final test. I hear the motor boat get closer, and I reach for the rifles, very slowly. I'm working it out in my head: one rifle or two? And I figure, I start with two, then I drop one when I got something to aim at. First, I'll get up and fire both of them at once, blindly. At least, if nothing else, I'll die shooting."

The driver drained his cup and stared into it. "Now perhaps a little vodka, my friend?"

"For you? But you're driving."

"Only a little one," he said soothingly. "And I have some mints that will clear my breath before I drive, so it's okay." He looked round towards the barman and called out his order, then said to Roy Jones, "The other motor boat, it's so near now. I hear the motor revving down, idling while it steers closer. I hear someone moving in the boat, sounds like walking on planks. I reckon any moment I'll hear a splash as he jumps into the shallow water and then it'll be my moment. I wait and then... and then..."

A glass of vodka materialised on the table.

"SPLASH!" the driver cried, instantly getting to his feet and, from both arms, spraying with imaginary gunfire the hotel bar and the startled, retreating barman. "GA-GA-GA-GA-GA-GA! And now I could see them, I dropped the rifle in my left hand and took good aim with the one remaining. The man in the water was on his knees – GA! – I finished him. In the boat, a younger guy with a fur hat who was still trying to cock his rifle when I got him – GA! GA! GA!" The driver sat down.

Roy Jones was shaken. "You killed them both?"

The driver nodded. "The one in the water, he was face down, his chest caught on stones on the shallow river bed and his arms and legs swaying like reeds in the current. I went and turned him over, looked at his face. A man in his forties, perhaps. He had no gun. And in the boat, maybe this other one was his son. That boy, I don't know how old. I got him in the face. All they had between them was their two rifles, same as my cousin and me. The boy's was in his hand, where he'd been trying to cock it. The father's rifle was lying with their fishing gear, unloaded. I checked it all afterwards. So you see, these weren't the ones who had fired at me."

Roy Jones's mouth was hanging open. "You killed two innocent men!"

The driver nodded. "And on the river bank, my cousin lay in a terrible mess. And our boat was ruined by the gunfire – I congratulated myself that at least now I had a usable boat, thanks to the men I shot."

Roy Jones was horrified. "But they were innocent! Hunters like you, out on a trip."

The driver again nodded, drained his glass in one shot, exhaled vodka in his breath and said, "We too, my cousin and me, we were innocent men. But in the taiga, there is no law except survival. When I lay in the boat and heard them coming, what was I supposed to do? Was I to lie there like a frightened doe and let them shoot me dead? Was I supposed to be a good citizen and stand up, raise my arms in the air, and say, kill me now please? No. In the taiga, you live by the law of the taiga. The father and son in the motor boat, they knew that too. Or they should have known. A wild boar, it can kill you. A bear, it can kill you. A damned mushroom, it can kill you. And a man, he will certainly kill you, if he thinks that this is what he has to do. So, my friend, I regret nothing, except that I ran a little too fast towards the trees, like a cotton-assed rabbit, when I should have been saving my cousin. But in the taiga, we are not asked to make choices, only to act."

It seemed to Roy Jones that the story had now come to its dreadful end. "What about the ones with the machine gun?"

The driver shrugged. "They went away. They watched me lying in the boat for an hour or a day, and they got bored. I don't know. Perhaps the father and son really were the killers, and left their machine gun on the opposite bank of the river while they came to take some trophies. Who cares? You kill a bear, you don't go asking afterwards what it had for dinner. You shoot, you kill, you go to sleep and you move on. This is law of the taiga. And you see, my friend, I am a man of the law."

The driver reached inside his coat; Roy Jones wondered if a gun might emerge, or perhaps a photograph of the lost cousin. It was only a packet of cigarettes that came out, and a cheap lighter. "Relax," the driver said with a smile. "It was all a long time ago."

"Did you bury those people? Did you tell the police?"

"Relax." The driver lit a cigarette. "The dead are in Heaven,

31

it's we who have to live on Earth. I am a husband, a father. I drive a taxi, I write poetry."

"You're a poet?"

The driver nodded. "I've published books, won a few prizes. Perhaps you think I demean my art by driving a taxi. But I have to earn a living. This is law of the city. And I promise you, since the last time in the taiga, I kill no more people." He chuckled. "Killing, it's bad for you, like smoking. A pity I can't give up smoking like the doctor says I should, and the vodka. Doctor says I have a heart attack in next two years. He can see it like a clock. I say to him, okay." The driver looked down at his empty vodka glass, and the empty cup beside it. "Thank you," he said to Roy Jones.

"Like another?"

"No, I die soon enough in any case." He stood up to leave. "Enjoy your stay," he said to Roy Jones. The two men shook hands, then the taxi driver walked briskly across the hotel foyer, giving a final friendly wave before disappearing out through the heavy revolving door.

Two hours later, Roy Jones was in his room, and having showered and changed, he now felt sufficiently refreshed to begin the next part of the day. It was still only lunchtime: he understood that he was due to be collected by someone from the conference, who would presumably also take care of feeding him. He was at the mercy of whoever should happen to appear.

The telephone rang. Roy Jones went to the chipped wooden desk where it sat, and lifted the receiver.

"Mr Jones?"

"Speaking."

"I am here to take you to the conference."

"Splendid."

"You had a safe trip?"

"Absolutely."

"Good. Please be in the foyer in five minutes."

"Of course." Roy Jones hung up. His briefcase was ready, and he checked once again that the text of "Mixed-phase lubricants: a top-down approach" was safely stored there. He put on his coat, then took the elevator to the lobby where a man in a long grey coat paced conspicuously to and fro.

"I'm Dr Jones." He reached out his hand for the other to shake.

"Hello sir. Now let us go." And he led Roy Jones outside to his car.

This was to be a journey of the strictly no-nonsense kind, in contrast to the earlier taxi ride. Attempting to make conversation out of his habitual sense of politeness, Roy Jones asked, "Are you a tribologist yourself?" The driver merely gave him a look of incomprehension, remaining silent until they reached their destination.

"Here is conference centre," said the driver, suddenly pulling up. They both got out, and Roy Jones followed him inside. Everything seemed so colourless in comparison with the earlier taxi driver's story of the taiga. That alone had been real: the wrong men, shot dead for daring to approach a damaged boat.

Roy Jones followed his escort upstairs, where he was deposited at a desk whose occupant smiled and gave him a badge with his name on it: Mr N Jones. They hadn't even got his initial right this time, never mind his title. A bearded man came over, and the next thing Roy Jones knew, he was being shaken by the hand; embraced, even.

"It is so good to meet you, Mr Jones – we are delighted that you will be speaking at the seminar – and you are just in time!

We were a little nervous that you would not be here!"

Roy Jones's stomach rumbled as he was swiftly introduced to four or five people whose names came from the impenetrably unmemorable world of Tolstoy. One was a woman whose handshake was like touching polished ivory, and whose curved and slanting eyes suggested a message from a distant wilderness. She certainly didn't look like your average tribologist.

Barely able to take in his surroundings, Roy Jones was then led to the seminar room, where rows of chairs, mostly filled, faced a desk with a microphone on it, and an empty seat behind. As Roy Jones took his place to speak it occurred to him that it was just as well he'd brought a print-out of his talk along with the PowerPoint file, since there wasn't a projector or screen in sight.

And so there he was at last, sitting with the text laid neatly before him, ready to embark on a voyage of discovery through the multi-faceted world of mixed-phase lubricants. His bearded host intended first to say a few words in Russian. Some of the audience members, Roy Jones now observed, were wearing headsets, of the kind a diplomat might sport in a United Nations debate. There was one lying on Roy Jones's desk; and at the back of the room he could see a well-dressed woman neatly encased in a glass-walled booth, whose role was evidently that of interpreter. Roy Jones put on his headset and immediately heard the woman's smooth, authoritative voice as she translated what the Russian was saying.

"Mr Jones' work repeatedly poses the question: what is true, what is false?"

Roy Jones weighed this comment up. Yes, his work on mixed-phase lubricants had questioned some of the most familiar assumptions of the subject. Still a pity about the "mister", though.

"As Richard Sand has put it, Jones contests the territory between being and non-being..."

Richard Sand? There was no significant tribologist by that name. Possibly an error of the over-zealous interpreter, translating a conference organiser's name that happened to be the Russian word for sand.

"Consider for example his comments regarding Fragments of Behring..."

A garbled reference to Roy Jones' work on compliant foil bearings?

"Or Jones' striking remark that the greatest adventure one can undertake is to cease to be oneself..."

When would Roy Jones ever say anything so utterly ridiculous?

"In his most recent book, The Truth about my Wife, *Nick Jones exposes the dilemma of people trapped by convention, who long to live a more spiritual life, but can find this only through the most terrible acts of depravity..."*

Suddenly it all began to make terrible sense to Dr Roy Jones, tribologist. Listening to the translated words of the portly, bearded intellectual as he described the literary works of Nick Jones, novelist, his hapless namesake realised why the audience so little resembled the international congregations of engineers whom it was his life's work to address, and with luck impress. This array of Russian poets, dramatists, literary critics and assorted book-lovers hadn't come here to listen to a story about forces in mixed-phase fluids. And somewhere, in some other conference centre in Moscow right now, a poor bastard called Nick Jones was being introduced to a bunch of structural scientists, having made the same mistake as Roy when he got off the plane and saw a taxi driver holding a sign reading *Jones*. This great writer – winner of all sorts of prizes, according to the introduction being offered in his absence – was the other half of a glorious mix-up, and now would be preparing to sell his wares to an assembly of engineers. Would he pull it off? Would he be able to stand up in the boat with a gun in each hand, and save the day?

Roy Jones would. With growing confidence, he listened to the eulogy being offered him. He was wise, far-sighted, profound in moral perception, deft in linguistic invention. He was shocking, at times even disgusting, yet always pure. And above all, said his host, invariably surprising. Yes, he'd surprise them all right.

The audience were applauding. The bearded intellectual had said enough about the glory and importance of Nick Jones. Now it was Roy's turn to preserve the reputation of his ancient tribe. All fell silent: the interpreter was waiting for his words, ready to convey them in Russian to those unable to comprehend him directly.

"Ladies and gentlemen," he began. "I want to tell you a story. It's up to you whether or not you want to believe it. Some years ago, my cousin and I went on an expedition to the taiga..."

Introduction

Introductions are usually self-conscious affairs so when Richard Sand arrives for our interview things might be a bit stiff at first. We've agreed to meet at the recently opened Cafe Mozart, formerly known as The Dolphin until it got a complete make-over and the waitresses took to wearing what appear to be imitation eighteenth-century smocks. I wonder if this really is the best place for us to discuss his book, leafing through it after nervously ordering my Mozart Mocha.

Richard Sand should enjoy this place though, given that imitation is one of his major themes and provides the title of his essay collection. He calls imitation the most fundamental human impulse, but regrets that where once it was seen as essential in any artist's training, now it is too often condemned as plagiarism or pastiche.

Elsewhere he comments on introductions: self-conscious affairs, he says, citing Nabokov's forewords to his own novels as an example. Pride, ambition, doubt; these are characteristics made particularly obvious in those awkward opening moments when the right effect is being sought; and this is why

I resolve that when Richard Sand appears at the glass door of Cafe Mozart, looking just like the photograph on the back of *Imitations: Essays on Style and Substance*, I shall try and imagine that really he's a waiter come to take my order, not someone I need to impress.

Walter Scott by contrast, Richard Sand says (sitting down casually and looking at a menu) is an author whose prefaces are frequently better than the novels that follow. Richard Sand regards Scott's foreword to *Guy Mannering* as his masterpiece, and orders an ice cream.

When Richard Sand comes to the door, therefore, I'll aim for an introduction in the manner of Scott, rather than one in the Nabokov style. I won't, for example, say that the conversation we're about to have will be one of my more "attractive" ones, explaining for him the delicate pleasure I took in choosing our meeting place, arranging the time; nor shall I say I could supply additional information about rejected alternative venues "if I took myself more seriously" (Foreword to *The Luzhin Defense*).

No, I shall tell Richard Sand that three weeks ago I was walking along the street on my way to pick up a programme from the local art house cinema (because their website is hopeless) when I saw on the other side of the road that The Dolphin had had a make-over. "That'd be a good place to conduct an interview," I decided. I'd just split with Pam.

But Richard Sand will care for none of this. "Häagen-Dazs," he says, examining the tub he's been brought. "Where do you suppose that name comes from?"

I toy with Norwegian, Danish; he shakes his head. Still teased by the conjunction of double-A with umlaut I suggest Finnish, then Turkish. Richard Sand smiles and says nothing. I resort to the Ural-Altaic complex, possibly one of the less obvious dialects of Samoyed, though the suggestion is admittedly made in desperation. Richard Sand says calmly, "Some marketing people in America made the whole thing up. Everybody knows that."

The ice cream was created in an instant, like the universe itself, and meant to suggest a past that wasn't there; spurious influences, a false history. Apparently everyone knew about it except me. It's like the dead tramp whose body was used in a piece of wartime counter-intelligence, discussed at some length by Richard Sand. The allied invasion had been booked for Normandy, the beaches had been carefully studied. It was necessary to make the Germans think the attack was to come from elsewhere, unexpected as a sudden waitress.

"Mozart Mocha," she declares. I make sure the cup stays well clear of *Imitations: Essays on Style and Substance*, in which Richard Sand explains how the corpse was given an invented identity, clothed in a military uniform he never wore in life, supplied with false papers. As a final touching detail, a love letter from a non-existent girl was written out, folded carefully and carried in someone's pocket for days until it looked authentic. Then it was put inside the dead man's clothes and he was fired from the torpedo tube of a submarine to be washed up on a beach. His real name was not disclosed; his heroic action remained as hidden from his relatives as it was from himself. The Germans were fooled, they looked the wrong way while Normandy was invaded, etc etc. I told Pam all about it, but she already knew.

What if some maniac were to walk into Cafe Mozart while I'm talking to Richard Sand? What if Richard Sand is just about to speak of Heinrich Behring or Alfredo Galli when a guy pushes his way through the glass door, brings out a machine gun and sprays bullets everywhere in the room? Holes and gashes appear in the recently repainted walls, the marbling effect is ruined, the Gaggia machine becomes punctured and sprays a jet of hissing steam during the otherwise silent moment of terrible calm that follows, when ten or twenty people lie motionless on the tiled floor?

That'd really show Pam.

But Richard Sand is a busy man, and every now and then he glances at his watch. Richard Sand considers Borges the most perfect writer since all his best works seem like introductions and also imitations. Richard Sand cites Kafka's "Great Wall Of China" and Conrad's introduction to *Nostromo* as the sources of most of what we call "Borgesian", in the same way that a few brown smocks and the name Mozart can evoke, for the average coffee drinker, eighteenth-century Vienna; or Häagen-Dazs can equal in Transatlantic minds and wallets a continent as unreal and vivid as the misruled world of Don José Avellanos.

By now I was wishing that a crazed madman would come in and kill us all (except me). Just to show her.

I was walking along the street three weeks ago, on my way to pick up a cinema programme. I've been to see lots of films since we split. It's good to have the freedom.

"We live in a world of ideas," Richard Sand continues. "Language is more crucial than ever."

This hardly seems a radical observation, but it needn't interfere with the cooling of my Mozart Mocha.

"Ultimately it's not what we say that counts, but the difference between what we actually say and what we could have said otherwise. This idea is made explicit in algorithms for transferring video signals, where changes of image alone are conveyed, as a way of saving bandwidth."

All this is in *Imitations*. I was reading it while breaking up with Pam.

"It's precisely because we live in the age of imitation," says Richard Sand, "that imitation is what we most despise. We describe everything in terms of its similarity or difference compared to something else; a new movie is a cross between *Star Wars* and *12 Years a Slave*; a new book is *Cloud Atlas* meets *Fifty Shades Of Grey*. We reduce the world to erroneous etymologies of our own invention."

Toying with the ice cream tub he ordered, whose remaining contents liquefy before our view, he then takes my hand.

"Hey," he says. "Forget Pam. She wasn't worth it. Believe me, I'm an expert in everything, and I know."

Richard Sand has had many affairs but says the best are those that never happened, those which exist only as suggestive prefaces. All our affairs are prefigured in ones that have already been done far better by other people before us. This ought to comfort me, but right now it doesn't.

Three weeks ago I phoned my friend James in London and he said the easiest way to get yourself in print is to interview somebody interesting. Now that's what I call advice.

"Think of Pam as being somewhat like Flaubert's *Temptation of Saint Antony*; a necessary mistake," Richard Sand provokes. Right now, I want him to piss off. Pam gave me *Imitations* for my birthday; by the time I got to the end we'd split. So thanks a bloody lot, Richard Sand.

The day after my conversation with James I was walking along the street on my way to get a cinema programme when I saw the gleaming new Cafe Mozart, formerly called The Dolphin. "That'd be a good place to interview somebody and get myself in print," I thought.

There the matter might have rested but for the chance conjunction two days later of a piece of dog shit and a shower of rain. The dog shit passed under my shoe while I was walking in the direction of Topman, having decided that a change of wardrobe would suit my new state of freedom. I had resolved to become a "top man". Interrupted by canine faeces, I was scraping the turd from my shoe on the kerb when I noticed that the rain had started. I could furnish further details about this incident "if I took myself more seriously", but shall say only that I decided instead to shelter in Waterstones, the bookshop where Pam had bought me *Imitations: Essays on Style and Substance*. The fact that she left the receipt inside the book before giving it to me was a sign, I now realise, that already by then her mind was on someone else.

I hoped I didn't smell of dog shit. Being suddenly and unexpectedly single can make you feel strangely self-conscious, I've noticed; perhaps because every encounter becomes a potential introduction. In the bookshop I saw a poster advertising a forthcoming reading and talk (with complimentary glass of wine) by Richard Sand.

The man who'll soon appear at the door of Cafe Mozart, invited here by me.

The man whose thoughts I already know (I've read his book after all), and which I'll describe in an article the local paper has more or less promised to run.

The man who represents my first step on the ladder. Though he isn't here yet.

"Forget her," Richard Sand insists. "Forget me, forget everything. Forgetting is the sweetest thing. When Odysseus went on his voyage he forgot all about Penelope. Nostalgia isn't a Greek idea, it's a German one. They simply gave it a Greek name to make it sound more classy. A bit like Häagen-Dazs."

Once my article gets published, Pam will come across it in

the local paper. She'll have left her lover asleep in bed, gone to the newsagent on a lazy Saturday morning, and when she returns and sits at the breakfast bar in her kitchen, sipping orange juice while her risen lover blandly inserts the slender nozzle of a miniature espresso machine into a jug of milk (a jug that I bloody well bought her, incidentally), she'll suddenly say:

"Christ! *Interview with Richard Sand. By...*"

She nearly chokes on her croissant. In fact I hope she does choke, Richard, I tell him.

"Forget her," Richard Sand repeats, placing his hand upon my knee. "You're constructing a false etymology of your own life. Free yourself of her influence. Learn to imitate yourself once more."

Borges imitated Conrad and Conrad imitated Flaubert, says Richard Sand. I told Pam about it and she yawned and asked if we could switch off the bedside light now please. I told her about Häagen-Dazs, the allied invasion of Normandy, and she said she already knew.

"How come you know so much?" I challenged. I was sure she was bluffing.

"I know lots of things. A lot more than you realise."

What she was really telling me was that for the last two months she'd been in love with someone called Martin. He's in management consultancy, for fuck's sake.

"It doesn't matter," says Richard Sand, stroking my knee soothingly. "You and me, that's what counts. We could make a great team."

The waitress comes and asks if I'd like anything else.

"Do you have any chocolate ice cream?" I gamble.

"We've got Midnight Rhapsody, Chocolate Chip and Belgian White Chocolate." She says it with her arms folded.

Like it's some kind of snub.

"What's Midnight Rhapsody?" I ask.

"It's basically just chocolate."

"I'll have that then, please." She writes something down and walks away. Will I be equally sheepish with Richard Sand when he arrives? My freedom from Pam, for all its advantages, has also left me with an occasional sense of inadequacy during social interactions.

"Do you ever suffer from a sense of inadequacy?" I ask Richard Sand, preparing to write down his response. Since I don't yet know if I'll be able to write quickly enough I've also brought with me a mini voice recorder purchased in John Lewis.

I didn't buy it for the interview. It was a month ago, and I had finally begun to suspect Pam. I'd been alerted by one of the essays in *Imitations*, I explain to Richard Sand, in which he describes the correspondences between Flaubert's *"Un coeur simple"* and the death of Bergotte in *À la recherche du temps perdu*. To be honest I wasn't really following the essay; it just happened to be what I was reading at the time.

"A sense of inadequacy is something I've never suffered from," says Richard Sand. "Unreality, yes; inadequacy never."

Richard Sand's essay also went on about Nietzsche and Wittgenstein and God knows what else, asserting that literature only becomes possible when we learn how to say one thing while thinking about something else entirely. And as I read, my eyes would skip briefly over the top of the page every so often, like a soldier's in a trench, and I'd watch Pam gathering up items for the laundry.

It became clear to me from Richard Sand's essay that during times when I was out she was meeting someone else in our flat. The mini voice recorder, subsequently obtained at a reasonable price from John Lewis, seemed like a good way to settle the issue.

I quickly encountered technical problems, however. The manufacturer's claim that when fully charged the device could give ten hours of continuous use proved to be an exaggeration. I was out for six, but only the first four had been preserved when I got back. The sound beneath the bed during all that time had been nothing but a low, distant rumble of traffic, increased in pitch but not in content when I ran it through on fast forward.

So I went back to John Lewis and bought an AC adapter with built-in timer. This handy device enables any household appliance to be automatically switched on or off for up to four separate periods in a twenty-four hour cycle.

"What on earth did you buy this for?" Pam asked, poking her nose into the carrier bag I'd rashly left unattended next to our stained-pine CD rack.

I told her it'd come in handy if we went on holiday and wanted it to look as though we were still at home. We could set lights to come on every evening.

"But what about the curtains?" says Richard Sand.

I agree with him that my excuse had certain inconsistencies that must have aroused Pam's suspicions.

Then the waitress brings me my Midnight Rhapsody. "Enjoy," she says curtly as though it's a command.

Richard Sand can guess the rest. The voice recorder, playing itself back to me in secrecy one evening when Pam had gone out with friends, created its own kind of nocturnal rhapsody; one made not of frozen milk, eggs and sugar, but rather of grunts, moans, and a reminder to be careful.

"So that's why I'm here," I tell Richard Sand. "I've now explained to you all the tiny accidents and absurdities that have conspired to bring about this conversation. My introduction is complete."

"If you don't mind," says Richard Sand, "I'll go and take a piss."

He stands and walks confidently towards the far side of the room. He doesn't have to ask the way or look around with a "please tell me where the toilets are" expression. Christ, how I wish that I was Richard Sand.

He's left his jacket hanging over his steel-framed chair. I lift the jacket and put it on. There's a wallet in the inside pocket containing driving licence, credit card and other identifying material of Richard Sand. I'm wearing his entire existence; it fits perfectly. In another pocket there's even a handwritten letter, scented and neatly folded. I open it and discover, without any sense of surprise, that it's from Pam. *I love you, Richard Sand*, she writes.

Suddenly he arrives at last. The crazed gunman.

Wearing a face-mask and dressed in combat gear he bursts through the glass door of Cafe Mozart and raises his weapon to unleash a blazing volley that quickly rips to shreds all the work that's been done on this place, tearing away the fake Mozartian elements, shattering the mirrors to reveal little bits of Dolphin decor underneath. Screams everywhere, panic, the sort of thing you don't expect on an ordinary day in an unremarkable town that nobody would otherwise have heard of, but which will briefly become an item of morbid curiosity to anyone glancing at the news while flicking through a hundred channels on a remote control. At least I'll get myself in print now. In the following day's newspaper my face is shown alongside an account of the tragedy, explaining that I was found dead beside some melted ice cream and a copy of *Imitations*, wearing the bloodstained Marks and Spencer jacket by which I was mistakenly identified. And Pam, silently swallowing her croissant while tears gather in her eyes, finally understands the heroic nature of my sacrifice, when for a single glorious moment I truly became Richard Sand, serving as the selfless decoy whom his would-be assassin killed in error.

An hour later and still no sign of the fucker. The waitress hands me the bill.

Fragments of Behring
(Four historical sketches)

Silk

Do you remember, brother, when they took us into the silk factory? A low, simple building, and yet it housed the mystery we had longed to discover. Do you remember the trays, row upon row, of crisp fresh mulberry leaves and the sound, the gentle crackling like fine rain on a forest; the only sound to be heard in the broad, quiet room? Then looking down into one of the trays we could see the cause: the thousands, millions of caterpillars, tearing methodically at the leaves. The whole room was filled only with the sound of caterpillars eating.

We did not dare speak, not only for fear of disturbing the strange calm of the place, but also – am I not right, brother – because at that moment the only sound we could have made would have been a cry of joy which would have brought the guard running. We had found the secret at last, you and I, of how the silk was made.

Of course, we had known of the accounts of others: it was some kind of worm, they all said; some unique and fabulous species which could weave silk. A fantastic story, brother, and one which you had doubted, yet there they were all around us, grazing contentedly on the mulberry leaves. All the stories were true. And we both knew then, did we not, that something of that secret would have to return to Europe with us. Was it not our duty in God's name to share this wonder with the Christian world? And did you not also dare to think of our monastery rebuilt and repaired, thriving on the only production of silk outside China?

They had taken us there, the Imperial Chamberlain and his guard, eager to show us what we had asked to see; anxious to pay us every form of hospitality. They had brought us there just as they had led us around the tea plantations of Fukien, and the porcelain factories of Ching-te-chen, where the huge kilns were so numerous that at night the whole city glowed under a red sky, illuminated by the flames of a thousand fires and bright enough to read a book by.

And had we not been good guests, brother? Had we not told them of the wonders of our land, and brought them the word of God? We should not regret what we did; put all such thoughts from your mind. How can you call it theft, to bring one of God's greatest miracles into Christendom?

I remember the look on your face as we stood there in the silk factory, in that great calm room, you and I alone with as many precious caterpillars around us as there are grains of sand on a beach. We would only remain unattended for a moment or two while our guide discussed some matters with the factory owner outside. I saw your face, brother, and I could see the thoughts turning rapidly in your mind. But where might we hide the prize? We had no purse, no pockets. And still you were trying hurriedly to think while I acted; you gave a start as I reached out, swiftly and decisively, plunging my hand into the tray beside me. And you gave a faint gasp when I pulled up a handful of leaves and silkworms then put them into the only possible hiding place: my own mouth.

The Chamberlain returned, accompanied as ever by the silent Imperial guardsman who stood by the door, the curving blade of his sword lying across his chest in readiness to protect us, and then we were led from tray to tray. You translated, I smiled, and in my mouth I could taste the bitter leaves and the soft, pliant forms of the grubs; a dozen or so, trying still to eat the mulberry and finding sometimes instead a piece of tongue. I had heard of insects which carry deadly poison, but at that moment I thought only of the lives of the silkworms, since theirs were of greater value.

What were your thoughts then, brother, as you calmly interpreted the words of our guide? Did it seem then a crime, while you were telling me how in its first month a single caterpillar would increase in weight a thousand-fold, and you looked round and saw my smiling face full of the things? Were you praying for forgiveness then? Or were you, like me, eager only to get out of there and make sure our priceless sample was undamaged?

And it was you, do you not remember, who brought the delicate porcelain bowl we put them in after we left the factory and you asked leave for us to go alone together to pray. Out they all fell into the white bowl; seven alive and wriggling, a few dead, and a mass of soggy leaf and mulberry spittle. We kept them hidden in our cell, reared them as if they were our own children, and brought them back to Europe in a piece of bamboo. Was there ever a creature on this Earth which has received such care?

Put all these guilty thoughts aside, brother. The monastery is doing well, God be thanked. Would you rather we lived by making wine? And I hear that the Abbot is very favourably disposed towards your plans concerning the expansion of the library.

But since you are in the mood for confession, let me also admit to one slightly unholy thought that has sometimes entered my mind. Do you realise, brother, that for the next hundred, the next thousand years, whenever a woman puts a piece of European silk upon her body she will be wearing the spittle that has come from the descendants of the worms which were in my mouth that day?

A Room in Delft

Begin not with the room itself, but rather with the light which inhabits it. Consider that pattern of reflections; the suggestions of forms, textures, the appearance of solidity. The possibly illusory appearance of solidity. All of this will fade. The light will fade.

My eye is a shore upon which the conflicting waves of light find their rest. If my eye were not here, the rays would pass further; reaching the wall, undergoing subsequent reflection on its white plastered surface, or perhaps upon the mirror behind my head. My eye is a trap for the light. My eye kills the light. Is fed by it.

I hear Catharina's footsteps above me. I hear her moving from one room to the next. Her movement sends other waves. My ears, also, are a kind of shoreline. My sense of hearing another kind of death. If I were a composer rather than painter, in what way might the sound strike me differently? Yet I am a painter; and when I hear, I naturally see something in my mind. The waves of sound reach that point in imagination where all things are rendered visible. I see Catharina. And I see that other figure standing beside her. I do not even need to hear his footsteps in order to behold him.

All is light. The four elements – earth, air, fire, water – are themselves made of it. The world is a curtain of light and shade. This room, its patterns, textures. The tiles on the floor: a chequerboard of blue and white, cobalt and cream. Not square from this angle, but a network of lozenges, asking to be painted once again. I shall choose the colours differently this time.

I hear her footsteps in the room above. Her narrow feet. A speculative pattern of surfaces: shoe, garter, skin. How I would love to paint her leg.

All made of light, first act of creation. Pure illumination determining objects enshrouded or evaded. I hear her footsteps. Soon I shall hear the tuning of the harpsichord.

To paint a thing is to lose it forever. Having pursued, one is left with an effigy. Canvas and dissatisfaction. This room: the sunlight entering at an angle. Waves, so he tells me. An endless sea of light, an infinite ocean offering the drowning man, myself, no hope of rescue or salvation.

A note! A low key being struck, now also a higher one. Playing the octave, bending the offender into tune, its sagging tone curving upwards into place. When the harmony becomes true they seem to unite, different yet equivalent. He tried to explain it to me, waves again, another ocean. Could light be tuned like a harpsichord?

He's up there with her. I don't need to hear his tread to know. Her flesh and his, tuned like an octave. Myself, a discord. Catharina understands nothing about painting.

Begin not with the room, but with the light which gives it

form and life. This room is more alive than I am. Painting it once again renders me a little less dead. The canvas is primed and ready. I love that smell reminiscent of stale spittle, the odour of a thing about to be created. A blank canvas has never been a cause of anxiety for me, no more than the sight of a meal waiting to be eaten. My hands can't wait to digest what my eyes have already tasted: this chamber, scene of so many paintings. If the world is nothing but light, what difference does it make whether I choose the light of the street, or reflected on the waters of a canal, or within these walls of my private universe?

Some chords now, coming from upstairs. She will pretend to play for a while. Perhaps she will even continue, while he...

Now. All is ready. And the light is strong enough. He was the one who showed me how; the partition forming something like a cupboard at the end of the room, large enough to work in. A single small hole in the front. Camera obscura: dark room. Inside, the image of the remaining space projected upside-down onto the canvas at the back. A world reversed. He explained it to me; drew a diagram of a man standing, then further along, a vertical line to represent the wall, pierced in the middle. Rays from the head and foot of the man, converging on that aperture, emerging and forming their final image, their ultimate resting place. The man inverted like a slaughtered pig. He doesn't draw well; he's a philosopher, not an artist. At the time, I thought I understood it. But now I wonder why, if our own eyes are lenses, we don't see everything up-ended. Unless we actually do, yet somehow ignore it. A very special talent.

I hear another note. How long it takes them to tune the instrument! Gentle application of pigment in my dark cupboard, my camera obscura. At the top of the canvas, the tiled floor's network of lozenges. I don't recognize this melody they begin;

he must be teaching her a new one. Sometimes he chooses to play the viol to her accompaniment; but not today, it seems. When I paint the figures in, I shall include the viol, untouched.

She thinks she loves him, I can tell. A philosopher, musician; and most of all, he is not me. This is what she loves most, seeing him as if from behind the bars of a prison. She forgets that I too am a prisoner.

This room will take some time to paint. Though I work swiftly, I still cannot keep up with the changing of the light. All it takes is for a cloud to hide the sun and everything is transformed; the fall of colour from the leaded windows, its play upon the tiles. If I am lucky with the weather then three or four days might do it. Then the real business will begin. I have already decided where the figures will stand; in my mind I see them, just as I can hear the sounds of that infernal harpsichord upstairs. Gaps on the canvas which the two of them will fill. While in life it is her very presence that fills me with emptiness.

Whose hand is it upon the keyboard? Smoothly done but easy enough for her to manage. And suddenly the music stops. All is silent. At the far end of my quiet room, the virginal keyboard whose image her painted shape will partly obscure. This silence, my tacit complicity, is what I must record. Why condemn a friend for loving her as I once did? He showed me his discoveries and has rediscovered mine. But it nags me, the scene I imagine, if I were to go upstairs during their fictitious music lesson. Slowly, quietly. Difficult to avoid letting a wooden step creak beneath my feet; but eventually reaching the closed door and pausing at it, kneeling as if in prayer, trying to quell my breath and beating heart as I put my eye to the keyhole.

Three days, if I'm lucky, to complete the stage-set of our drama. And I know how the finished painting will look. In the foreground, a table heavily draped, a white jug upon it, the neglected viol beside a vacant chair. The figures beyond are unaware of the hidden eye that watches them; she at the untouched virginal with her back to the viewer; he beside, pretending to instruct. She will not refuse to pose for me, she never does. In the other role: myself. Yet I am also where he will be, and you, looking through the secret aperture that connects silence with eternity. The lesson of unplayed music. Emptiness redeemed by art.

Parable

Let us suppose, pampered child, that you were raised from sleep by the sound of a clavichord brought beside your bed each morning so that you might be born again into thoughts of beauty. Let us believe that your noble father, your only parent, proudly and wisely instructed that your first language should be Latin, so that the French and Gascon of your native land would be the tongues of foreigners whom you would live and grow amongst, educated according to your privilege and birth; taught verse by worthy Buchanan; made to learn the arts of warfare which you would practise while that beautiful country you were born into each day fought itself, tearing at its own mediaeval entrails. Let us presume that you took a wife, sired children, lost the closest of friends, and as tribute to the father you loved and whose title you inherited, translated from your first language the work of a certain theologian who had brought comfort to the dying man. And after this, let us suppose that you would retire to the estate from which your name was taken, would suffer terrible pain caused within your body by bright crystals no bigger than a grain of sand, would feel the sorrowful effects of burnt black bile in your bloodstream, and would know all this to be an indication that you must begin your long and patient preparation for death.

Therefore, we imagine, you would seek solitude in your library, that heart within an indolent tower, where you would read once more, and more closely, those authors on whom you were raised: Plutarch, Seneca, Cicero; a few poets, a few travel books; marking out certain passages – increasingly frequent in their appearance, like gathering snow – which referred to a person you slowly came to recognise, seen vaguely at first but then with growing familiarity; a common author and subject found fitfully yet more densely as he emerged among your predecessors. A darkening shadow whose voice the world would know as Michel de Montaigne.

He was to be found, this relic who shared your name, dismembered and neglected within the satires of Juvenal, the epigrams of Martial; a figure who had always existed but had never been apparent; a broken pedestal, the carved articulation of a future limb, scattered among classical rubble, awaiting only the patient process of discovery, collection and assembly which you were born to perform, and by means of which you could also begin to discern the outlines of the temple that was to be his memorial and yours, built upon a labyrinth whose only guiding thread would be the accidental course of a man's life, revealed in the chapters of a book soon to be recomposed from all those gathered pieces.

He was apt, this man, to eat too quickly; had seen a hanging and quartering in Rome; declared himself to be, at fifty, too old for sex in an upright position. He, a fiction linked by coincidence to a fine estate and the authorship of the work which made him, had once doubted Aristotle's assertion that crippled women make more exciting lovers (the starvation of their limbs provoking a correspondingly excessive hunger in their genitals), and had put the matter to the test, deciding to the contrary that it is no more than an act of imagination to turn any woman into a Cleopatra. He had found that the authority of ancient wisdom was not infallible, and had realised that love and happiness are dreams among many, accompanying us only briefly as we rise out of sleep. These dreams belonged, for a little while, to the architect of Montaigne, and for him the memory of a woman or a clavichord, the prospect of a lyre, need be no more authentic than a passage in Lucretius or Catullus, or some other example by means of which a further stone could be laid, the labyrinth traced. He was a man, finally, who need not exist, except to the extent that he could be written by himself. The eventual moment, calm and unhurried, of his death, was discovered to have existed, recorded already long ago, among certain lines of Horace.

A Lesson for Carl

Ten years old, walking with his father to the street in Vienna where they were to find his new piano teacher: the best in the city. No one else would do for young Carl, such a prodigy, with his miraculous fingers curling in the pockets of his coat as the two of them made their way down the cobbled lane. They walked quietly, too nervous for conversation. Both had heard so much about the man they were to visit.

Their silence was interrupted by a clatter of horse's hooves behind them; Wenzel Czerny gently pushed his son away from the edge of the road as a wagon passed, spattering mud from a puddle while taking its cargo of old furniture along the narrow residential street and then around a bend, out of sight. "Be sure to play your best today, Carl."

"I will," Carl promised. Already at that moment, his destiny was mapped, though neither knew it. Fifty-six years later, on his death bed, people would still want to know only one thing. What was he really like, this man they were about to visit?

There, on a corner, stood old Krumpholz, smiling when he saw them approach.

"Are we late?" Wenzel Czerny asked anxiously, being one who loved good discipline in life as much as in music. He considered punctuality a matter of honour, lack of it a disgrace.

"Never fear," Krumpholz reassured him. "I got here early. But now we should go and see Ludwig." He glanced down at Carl. "Did you bring your scores?"

Terror flashed across Carl's face; the unbounded fear of a child who thinks he might have forgotten something vital, finding himself at the mercy of his elders.

"He doesn't need them," Herr Czerny interjected. "He will play from memory."

"Very good," said Krumpholz, pointing the way and then starting to walk with his two companions. "Ludwig prefers it like that. He learns a piece in no more time than it takes him to play through it at sight. Though I have to admit," he lowered his voice, and his face, addressing Carl with a twinkle in his eye, "Beethoven is somewhat apt to make mistakes."

"He permits false notes?" Herr Czerny said incredulously. "Even before an audience?"

"Certainly," said Krumpholz, softly taking hold of Carl's arm, and then of the boy's hand when the lad freed it from the pocket where it had tightened with the same dread that afflicted his stomach. With his leathery thumb, Krumpholz coaxed the boy's fingers until they unfolded and surrendered to his comforting, grandfatherly grasp.

"You see, Carl," Krumpholz added, "even a virtuoso can play in error, and all is forgiven. I heard Ludwig play one of his own concertos, and there were many passages that lacked the polish a good student would apply. No, to hear the real musician in Beethoven you need to listen to him improvise. Then, my boy, you will be taken to another world; one you will never forget."

As he lay dying, old and venerated, Carl would recall the accuracy of this prophecy.

"Now, here we are," said Krumpholz. "This is the street where he lodges."

They were at Tiefer Graben, a name that to Carl's mind suggested troubling images of dirt, of the grave. Things you can spend a lifetime trying to avoid, perhaps through the liberating qualities of music. In all the concerts that lay ahead of him, in the great career on which, at ten years old, he was already embarking, Carl would never escape the "deep ditch" where it all began.

Krumpholz was leading them across the road, then through the open doorway of a tall apartment building. "I hope you don't mind if we take our time," he said, indicating the stairwell. "Beethoven unfortunately lodges on the sixth floor. Not a problem for you, young Carl, if he takes you as his student. But I do wish he'd find lodgings in a place where an old man like me could visit him more easily!"

Slowly they began to ascend. It was Krumpholz who had first told Carl's father about Beethoven, Vienna's new musical genius. Krumpholz played violin in one of the city's theatres; he knew all the local figures, and had made Beethoven's acquaintance almost as soon as the young virtuoso arrived from Bonn. That was a decade ago – around the time when Carl Czerny was born. And his father Wenzel, seeing the swaddled baby helplessly burbling, had resolved that he too, this child blessed with the infinite potential of life's beginning, would make his own equal mark in the world.

What had happened in those ten years? In Beethoven's case, some concerts and publications, and the making of a name. Anyone who knew about musical life in Vienna was familiar with Beethoven's work. To admirers like Krumpholz he was a miracle; the true successor to Mozart and Haydn. To others his chamber compositions were merely a random outpouring of fragmentary themes, lacking in discipline. He was said to be working on his first symphony now: perhaps that would make more sense.

And what about Carl? These ten years had made not his name, but something infinitely greater: his soul, his entire being. The previous decade, the 1790s, had been his whole lifetime, and Carl's father had watched the boy's development with the patient satisfaction of a gardener seeing the spreading limbs of a tree. Already Carl could play Beethoven's sonatas from memory. What else might he be capable of, in another ten years?

Above all, Herr Czerny knew the importance of starting early. Beethoven was twelve when he gave his first concert. It was, Krumpholz once suggested, perhaps a little late: hence those mistakes Beethoven was apt to make in concert. And contrary to what Krumpholz claimed, Herr Czerny knew there are always those among the impassive faces of an audience who do not forgive; there are those who remember, take note, and arm themselves with the latent ammunition that will eventually topple a career. Ten years from now, where would Beethoven be? Forgotten, perhaps, and replaced by a new generation of surer hands, more dexterous fingers, quicker minds. Young Carl, his father felt sure, would be at the vanguard of that generation.

Having slowly ascended the gloomy staircase they had now reached Beethoven's door, its green paint cracked and peeling. Krumpholz knocked, and a moment later a man opened it. Was this the master? Carl's immediate impression was of someone too scruffy, too humble in appearance. But no, this was not Beethoven. "Come," the shabby servant said curtly, allowing them inside.

They were shown to a room that was like an inanimate version of the servant; equally untidy and neglected, and just as inhospitable. Several men stood waiting, but Carl dared not stare at them, instead finding his gaze traversing the papered walls, stained in places with damp, lacking any picture or mirror. The striped, faded wallpaper was torn and in need of replacing.

Then there were the trunks and boxes carelessly arranged beside the far wall, as if the lodger had only lately arrived, or expected to leave soon in a hurry. And the piles of paper: Carl saw printed music and manuscript pages, many of them strewn where only the soles of visitors' feet could have anything to do with them. If he ran out of sheets of paper, it seemed Beethoven would resort to any other surface. Even a dirty tablecloth, Carl noticed, bore a scribbled memorandum.

He saw broken quills, spilled inkwells; and as Carl took in more and more of the scene, its squalor only deepened. Was he to come here as pupil? Would his father leave him undefended in this place on whose floor the occupant had thought fit to toss a soiled shirt and discarded coat?

Despite the clutter, there were few real furnishings in the room; the shortage of chairs explained why everyone was standing, though after ascending so many stairs they all could probably have done with a rest. One item alone lent a redeeming air of civilisation to the proceedings. In the very centre of the room was the piano on which Carl would shortly be tested. He stared at its open keyboard, a sight as unsettling to him right now as a tooth-puller's pliers.

"The best there is," Krumpholz whispered to him, momentarily breaking away from the round of adult greetings and introductions which their arrival had prompted. "Made by Walther; a lovely thing. I do hope it's properly tuned. Ludwig isn't always kind to his instruments, you know."

Carl was too young to fathom the delicate financial equation that had placed such an item of luxury in a setting of virtual poverty. A less magnificent piano would have equalled more chairs, a polished table and other costly surfaces upon which the assembled company, if they had wished, could have seen reflected the bourgeois tastes that gave them all a living. But they were here for only one reason: the same reason that the piano was here. They were musicians, scraping a living in a world that valued them simply as a soothing background to genteel conversation. Here at least, in Beethoven's lodgings, their art was treated with respect.

Krumpholz was tactfully offering Carl's father, whom he had drawn aside, a hushed synopsis of all the social information with which Wenzel Czerny had too swiftly been bombarded during the initial handshakes.

"That's Ludwig's brother," Krumpholz explained in a whisper loud enough for Carl to hear. "He takes care of Ludwig's business arrangements; and does so very competently, I believe. You see, genius is all very well, but there has to be a commercial brain too. And that man – yes, the portly one – no, not him; I mean the one who's really fat. That's Schuppanzigh, the violinist. He and Ludwig admire one another artistically; but to be perfectly honest, I don't think they really get on. And that one there, Süssmayr, he was Mozart's pupil. Yes, that's right – it was he who completed the Requiem. So you see what an audience has been assembled for your son!"

Overheard by Carl, whom all the men ignored, these words were hardly reassuring. Like any child, he had to remain silent until the moment when they would want to listen to him. Then at last something happened. "Here he is," someone said. And Carl saw a new figure enter the room; someone straight out of the book he had been reading that morning. It was Robinson Crusoe.

The newcomer was stocky, strong looking, with the snub nose of a fighter. His complexion was darkened by the sun, his chin unshaved, and the thick black stubble made him look like a savage. He had come from the dangerous wilderness of Carl's imagination, and now he was standing close in front of the lad, towering over him, placing a hand on his shoulder by way of greeting.

"Say hello to Herr Beethoven," Carl's father instructed. Carl tried to form a greeting but found his throat dry. The nervous crackle that emerged drew laughter from the adults.

"Ssh!" Beethoven raised a finger, silencing them. The back of his hand was hairy; his whole body must have a pelt like a bear's, Carl imagined. The locks on Beethoven's head, black as coal, were thick and uncombed. Strangest of all, though, was the detail Carl would still recall vividly many years later. There was something sticking out of Beethoven's ears. Wads of cotton, steeped in yellowish fluid. Was it perhaps a joke designed to make Carl laugh? Or was it a way of avoiding sounds the composer didn't wish to hear? Whatever the reason, nobody else appeared to notice these silly cotton ears. Nobody knew, in fact, that the thirty-year-old composer had recently begun to experience problems with his hearing.

Carl saw kindness on the face of this swarthy Crusoe, as if the lonely man recognised in his young visitor a new companion, a pet, who would share his island domain. But Beethoven's face grew harder, more determined, as his gaze rose from son to father. "Let's not waste time," he said in a deep voice with an accent which, to Carl, sounded foreign and mildly ridiculous. "Show us what the boy can do."

Beethoven went and stood with the others while Carl sat himself at the keyboard. Then Carl launched into the piece he had prepared: a Mozart concerto. As he began playing, his nervousness left him; everyone else in the room quickly disappeared. The stained walls, the soiled clothing, the discarded pages: all were magically washed away by the waves of music that came from beneath Carl's fingers. The instrument was perfect; the finest he had ever touched. It stood on a tropical beach, and behind him was Robinson Crusoe, picking the remains of a freshly caught fish from his teeth.

The wild man softly drew up a chair beside Carl as the boy embarked on a series of intricate arpeggios. There was no orchestra in this island paradise; instead, Carl's companion began to touch the keyboard with his own shaggy hand, his fingers blunt as chisels yet infinitely delicate. Beethoven was filling out the harmonies of the concerto with his left hand while Carl continued the solo part.

All the burden of his father's ambitions were lifted from Carl's shoulders as he moved effortlessly through the concerto, swimming aloft while Beethoven continued to accompany him, tugging gently with notes and chords that kept Carl anchored to a steady beat. When it ended there was silence. Carl felt his bodily weight return, and with it he experienced the swift restoration of all his anxieties.

Beethoven stood up and addressed himself to Carl's father.

"He plays well, but I want to hear him in a solo piece. Make him give us a sonata."

Carl looked up at his father who nodded in confirmation of their prearranged plan. Then a moment later, Carl struck the opening chords of a work that had only just been published. It was Beethoven's own *Pathétique* sonata. Carl felt a murmur of surprise and approval from the onlookers, then silence again as they let him perform the first movement from beginning to end. This time there was no desert island, no Robinson Crusoe. Instead Carl was on stage before hundreds of people, a grown man, showing everyone exactly how the piece should be played.

All great art is a vision of the future, and Carl was being granted such a vision; an ineffable foretaste of his destiny. Ten years from now, Beethoven would be the most famous composer in the world, and Carl Czerny his most famous pupil. Another twenty years and Beethoven would be dead, while Carl would be revered. The decades rush on until Carl himself lies dying, sixty-six years old, his mind clearing for a moment as he looks from his bed towards the light of the window, a pale drizzle, the memory of his first visit to the master who gave his life its greatest meaning.

When the boy finished playing, Beethoven spoke once more in that rustic accent of his, brought from his native Bonn. Addressing Carl's father, he said, "I shall take him."

Carl had passed the test. He saw his father beaming broadly and felt profoundly relieved. His mother, too, would be smiling when they told her, equally grateful to have been spared the calamity of failure.

"Well done," Krumpholz was saying, shaking Carl's father by the hand. The other men joined in: all congratulated Herr Czerny on the triumph of having produced such a son.

Beethoven interrupted, concerned only with practicalities. "Be sure that when he comes to me next week he has C.P.E. Bach's book on keyboard playing. We'll start with the positioning of the hand." Wenzel Czerny promised that they would buy the book at once. "And another thing," Beethoven added. "Don't make him practise too much. Let him be a child. He'll grow up soon enough." He looked at Carl, speaking properly to him for the first time. "You're lucky to have so kind a father," Beethoven told him.

"Yes, sir," Carl said, wondering what sort of childhood Beethoven must have had.

"Now we must leave," Herr Czerny instructed. "Come along, Carl, we need to go to Sterner's bookshop."

Carl saw that the music-making in Beethoven's lodgings was set to continue. Schuppanzigh was tuning a violin and Beethoven was seating himself at the piano. Carl longed to stay and listen, but his father drew him by the hand, outside onto the cold stairwell, where the servant closed the door on them without a word.

"What did you think of Herr Beethoven?" Carl's father asked him as they began to descend the stairs.

"He's too hairy, he's got a funny voice, and I don't know why he has to stick things in his ears."

Wenzel Czerny laughed. "I agree he's an eccentric character. But they say he's the best teacher in Vienna. You did well, Carl. One day perhaps we'll look back on this moment and see it as the most important in shaping your career. Doesn't the future look marvellous?"

Above them, the music was beginning. Carl could clearly hear the violin; the piano was softer, with only a few booming notes drifting down the stairwell. While Carl had played, the future had indeed seemed wonderful. Now, hearing fading music from behind a closed door, he was less sure. His life, he suspected, would be an endless, arduous climb; and at every moment he would fear falling to his doom.

They came out onto the street where fine rain had begun to fall from the grey sky above. A coal wagon was trundling past; the grown-up world was going about its business. His father was eager to get to the bookshop to put in an order for Bach's manual: Carl's homework for the next year or so. And suddenly, from above the clouds, it was not rain Carl felt dropping onto his face, but notes of music. They were Beethoven's: little black notes melting on his face, moistening his coat, gradually puddling on the ground, slowly drenching the street.

That's what he saw at the window now. Not the drizzle he had thought, but those notes of music that fell on him as a boy. He felt the urge to say something; but as with his greeting to Beethoven more than half a century earlier, old Carl Czerny found his throat to be dry and voiceless. He couldn't call the maid, or his wife. Nor could he move the arms and fingers that had been taught by the master and premiered his works. At the age of sixty-six, Carl Czerny was about to die alone.

Yes, he was revered: but as a teacher and performer, not as a composer of the highest rank, as Beethoven ultimately was. Carl had never lived up to his father's aspirations, had never outgrown his famous master but had instead been supplanted by his own pupils; people like Franz Liszt. Too disciplined, they called him; too polite, too shy. His destiny was already fully scored when Robinson Crusoe patted his ten-year-old head.

The notes were tumbling out of an infinite sky; they were dripping through the ceiling onto the bed where Carl lay dying, and he opened his mouth to taste the black notes falling on his tongue. It was what he had spent his whole life trying to avoid: falling into the deep, dark ditch. Stumbling, playing a note that was false. Yet there they were, millions of them carelessly cascading over the entire world. Krumpholz had been right all those years ago. Clumsy Beethoven was forgiven. It was Carl Czerny who was damned for his accuracy, his modest fidelity. Rising into the sky, he thought for a moment of how he might have done it differently. But Beethoven's first lesson to him was also his most accurate. Don't practise too much. Let the child be a child.

Singularity

"You might suddenly feel like you're wetting yourself," Patrick heard her say, and he gave a start.

"I beg your pardon?"

"Just a side effect, not everyone gets it." The nurse was prodding the pit of his elbow in search of a vein while he lay prostrate awaiting the start of the scan. Her companion had already retreated to the neighbouring control room; looking past his feet from where he lay, Patrick could see the radiographer through a glass window, like a producer in a recording studio, though no instructions were coming from the white-coated young man who hadn't even offered his name when Patrick first walked in. Instead it was the nurse who took care of the talking, the human stuff that right now Patrick needed. She was called Rose and was from the Philippines, hadn't been back in the last three years. "Sharp scratch," she said lightly as the needle bored into Patrick's arm. He swung his gaze away, pondering the space-age curves of the CT scanner. "You may get a hot flush as the dye goes through your body," Rose warned. "Only for a moment."

She went to join the nameless radiographer next door, and soon the machine began to fire up, a sleek metal O that Patrick's body was to be slid through, his organs sliced by penetrating X-rays. Conveyed like an item at a supermarket checkout, Patrick felt himself being transported into the scanner's benevolent view. He wondered what it would find.

He'd thought about postponing his lecture, or shifting the hospital appointment, but both were equally important. So here was the first stressful event of the day; the other would come at five o'clock when colleagues, friends and interested members of the public would assemble at the university to hear about the beginning and end of the universe.

The scanner had revved itself fully into operation, light panels within its arc were changing colour, sequencing through purples and greens. They were only there for soothing decoration, Patrick supposed, like the false window in the ceiling of the scanner room that showed an image of blue sky and treetops. The machine put him in mind him of a teleportation device from a sci-fi movie, it had probably been designed by someone who grew up on *Star Trek* and *Doctor Who*, dreaming of flights to the stars. Someone much like Patrick, in fact.

"Hold your breath," he heard a voice say over the intercom. It was Rose, who he suspected was the real string-puller around here. Always so hard to work out who's who in a hospital.

And there it was, the sudden hot flush she'd mentioned. As if a furnace door had opened next to him, though just as quickly it was gone again. No feeling of wetting himself, thank God. Strange, though, to think of that dye coursing through his bloodstream, its image tracing curlicue shadows on the monitor screen next door. Patrick had spent a career looking at pictures of gigantic galaxies far away. Maybe he should have paid more attention to the little things inside.

Rose came over the intercom again to announce they were going to do another pass; the moving bed slid back to the start position so they could repeat the imaging. It would only take a further minute or two. He'd cleared his morning schedule, expecting to be kept waiting for hours at the hospital, but at this rate he'd soon be out of here and would have time to kill before meeting Lucy. Perhaps she could manage an early lunch. He wondered what frequency of X-rays the scanner was emitting, and how their intensity might compare with the background flux from cosmological sources; the faint but ubiquitous ripples from matter swirling into distant black holes. At every moment something dying somewhere, unnoticed.

"All done," Rose announced, then came in to help him off the bed. The radiographer remained sequestered in his control booth while Rose escorted Patrick to a small room where she checked his blood pressure. "Any plans for later?" she asked.

"Meeting my daughter," said Patrick. "She graduated recently. History of art. Tough finding a job."

Rose nodded sympathetically, but the time for small-talk was over, the readings had been taken. "Go whenever you're ready," she said, and left him to put his jacket on. Walking back along the corridor he brought out his phone to text Lucy, and as he reached the radiology unit's small waiting area he sat to type it, opposite a smartly dressed older man with head bowed over his own phone.

Finished already. Can you get to bistro sooner? 15 min? x

Looking up, Patrick met the eyes of the other man. The two of them in the same uncomfortable predicament. Neither spoke. The man's gaze instead moved up to something behind Patrick's shoulder.

Rose re-appeared. "Jack Fisher?" she called out, as if there

71

could be any doubt, and the man got up to follow her. Patrick rose too, and as he turned to leave he saw what had been behind him: a picture on the wall of an idyllic sea view. The Med, perhaps, or Greece. Somewhere very far away.

Lucy's reply came as Patrick walked out. *OK*. When he arrived at the restaurant she was already seated at a table.

"Hi, Dad!"

She got up to kiss him, and he noticed the clothes-store carrier bag on the floor beside her chair.

"Been shopping?"

"Just a top. It was a third off. How's work?"

He hadn't told Lucy about the scan, or anything else. Best not to worry her, he reckoned. "Work? Oh, the usual. You ready to eat?"

They thumbed menus and after a moment Lucy said, "About later. I won't be able to get to your lecture, hope you don't mind."

"Of course not."

"I promised Mum and Geoff..."

"It's alright, no excuse necessary. I wasn't expecting you to come."

"I'm sure I wouldn't understand it anyway. I mean, you know what I'm like with anything scientific."

She had a way of gesturing that was exactly like her mother. "You forever underestimate yourself," Patrick told her. "It's a talk for the general public, bit of PR for the university. Nothing technical."

"You'll be brilliant," Lucy affirmed, then decided on the tempura tiger prawns. Her signal that they should change the subject.

"Any progress on the job front?"

Lucy looked up narrowly from her menu. "Don't start on

72

that. Getting enough grief off Mum as it is."

"I know it's hard for you," said Patrick. And for an instant he saw her as a six-year old in McDonalds, legs swinging above the sticky floor. He'd spent a lifetime mastering general relativity but a familiar cliché summed it up well enough. Time goes faster as you get older.

Much later, as she ate the last of her tempura tiger prawns, Lucy finally got to the topic that must have been on her mind all along. She'd split from her boyfriend.

"Paul? The window man?"

"That was ages ago, Dad. I mean Conor. I told you about him."

"Ah, yes. Amicable?"

Lucy shrugged. "He started to bore me."

Fifty per cent amicable, then, as far as Patrick could make out. Though "dating", as it seemed to be called now, American style, was a set of principles as mysterious to Patrick as the workings or otherwise of his own internal organs. When it came to the laws of the universe he knew the limits of his expertise, which was why he wouldn't presume now to offer his daughter any advice on a situation he frankly didn't understand. How enviable, though, to have the luxury of being bored. She was staring towards the restaurant window, momentarily diverted by something outside. Patrick looked at his watch, and she must have registered the gesture in her peripheral vision since she immediately asked, "Do you need to go?"

"Not yet."

She hesitated. "Perhaps I should though." She stood up.

"I haven't paid yet," Patrick reminded her.

"Alright, I'll leave you to it. Thanks for a lovely lunch, Dad." She leaned to kiss him on the cheek. "Love you."

"You too, sweetheart."

The waiter came as she was walking out, made the standard suggestion of coffee or dessert despite Patrick's half-hearted mime of scribbling a bill, and so Patrick decided that yes, why not treat himself to a latte and a few more minutes of being here. He felt fine, he reminded himself. No one seeing him would think there might be anything wrong with his health. Though for all he knew, in a few months or a couple of years he might be dead. He'd already googled the survival rate before even receiving any diagnosis.

He brought out his smartphone and checked his emails. The usual redundant admin messages, plus good wishes for the lecture from his colleague John Wood who unfortunately had to be elsewhere. Patrick's coffee arrived and he gazed at its cooling froth. One of his slides that evening would show the distribution of galaxies, clusters of galaxies, clusters of clusters. At its largest scale, the universe is like a tenuous foam, matter stretched thinly around enormous voids. We're a speck on the surface of a single bubble among a host too numerous to count, too remote to contemplate. And here he was, thinking about whether he'd still be alive by Christmas. A star could vanish from the sky and no one would mind.

He walked to the university, gradually noticing and even enjoying the fine weather. The natural sciences block where he worked was on the far side of a small public park. On a bench in the middle, a man who looked like a down-and-out was, incongruously to Patrick's mind, engrossed in a book. The man looked up as Patrick passed and in his sun-worn face Patrick suddenly saw what looked like a flicker of recognition or an intention to speak, which unnerved Patrick and made him quicken his step, expecting to hear from behind his shoulder a request for some ridiculously precise sum for a non-existent bus fare. But the man said nothing, and soon Patrick was back in the safety of his office surrounded by familiar things: the textbooks and monographs on his shelves, the posters for conferences he'd attended or in some cases organised, and the paintings done by a far younger Lucy, that he'd never taken down. Now, for a few hours, he could resume the comforting routine of work.

It all began with a singularity. This was the paradox he had to explain, the sudden leap from nothing to everything, the infant universe appearing in an instant, stretching and unfolding in hyper-acceleration. He had to address the question that people always ask: what caused the Big Bang? His answer: no one knows. Perhaps there doesn't need to be a reason. Some things just happen, a matter of chance. A universe comes into existence; a cell becomes cancerous. And that, Patrick thought, was simultaneously the most reassuring and most devastating insight. Whatever was to happen to him didn't matter, really, because nothing does. Best to forget enormities, focus on the trivial and mundane. For instance, all those stupid emails he needed to answer.

At five o'clock he was standing at the front of the large lecture hall, looking up at the sparsely filled tiers of seats. He recognised some of his students, the keen ones. The head of department was there, fulfilling professional obligation, along with some other staff members. Yet the number of familiar faces was gratifyingly low. To Patrick's satisfaction, most people appeared to be outsiders who had simply noticed a poster and decided to come and hear the show. As he scanned the audience his gaze alighted on a man sitting alone, and Patrick realised it was the fellow he'd seen in the park. What had brought him here? He still looked like a down-and-out, shabbily dressed and in need of a haircut, a shave and a bath. The empty seats around him were almost like a cordon. But he had as much right to be here as anyone else. This was his universe too.

Patrick's nerves eased as soon as the first slide went up on the screen. His script now was dictated by astronomical fact, empirical evidence. Over the next fifty minutes he explained how the clusters of galaxies will continue to separate at ever greater speed, and matter within them will gradually be swallowed by black holes until eventually there will be nothing except cold, empty space. "All things are finite," he concluded. "Every life must have an end, even the life of the universe." Then it was time for questions from the audience, and the first hand to rise was the down-and-out's. With some apprehension, Patrick invited him to speak.

His voice was not what Patrick expected: an American accent, possibly Canadian. Gentle, thoughtful, intelligent. "Professor, when you think of the vastness of space, and all the countless stars and planets, surely we can't be the only one with intelligent living creatures. So wouldn't you agree with me that we can't possibly be alone?"

Patrick had heard the point made many times. "You're right," he answered. "It seems inconceivable. But how do we connect with anyone else out there? What if they're always too distant from us? Whether or not we really are alone, it certainly feels that way. Whatever we have to face, we face it alone."

There were a couple more questions, then it was time to bring proceedings to an end. After the applause subsided and as the audience began to leave, Patrick waited in case anyone wanted to speak to him individually. And once again it was the dishevelled man who took the opportunity. Patrick expected to hear from him some pet theory, his personal solution to the cosmic riddle. But as the man approached he reached out, and to Patrick's surprise took him by the arm, with a grip whose strength was momentarily unsettling. In the man's eyes Patrick could see a glimmer that might indicate madness or inspiration. And he said to Patrick, with a voice that seemed almost urgent. "You're not alone."

"Pardon?"

"Not alone. No matter how it feels."

Then he left. Patrick never saw him again, but in the coming months he would sometimes think about those words. I hear he's doing alright.

The Assumption

Tired after her long journey, Anna Fisher prepared to disembark. For most of her fellow passengers the island was merely an unwanted delay before the ferry could sail onward to its final destination; some heavily burdened Greeks and a couple of Dutch or German tourists were the only others caring to alight on the quiet quayside where a straggle of people stood waiting in the afternoon heat. Anna's father had emailed promising she'd be met on arrival but there was no sign of him or his wife, no text on her phone. Typical, really. Anna wheeled her suitcase past two local women holding handwritten cardboard signs offering *Rooms* and went instead towards a line of cars parked in shade before the whitewashed wall of a shabby taverna, hoping one might be for her. They were all empty. A glance through the cafe's open doorway revealed two labourers playing backgammon, while at the single rickety table outside an old man in a battered suit silently ignored the small half-filled glass at his elbow. Anna stationed herself some yards away on the pavement and watched as the ferry was made ready to move on, while the tourists concluded hand-waving negotiations with the ladies, and the other arrivals gradually dispersed.

Her father, in brief emails responding to Anna's suggestion that she come and stay at his villa, had invariably referred to her visit as a holiday, failing to perceive that what she sought was escape and respite. Any time spent with him and Fi was no holiday, nor done out of family duty, but only from economic necessity. At some point there would have to be a "proper talk" as Dad would put it, but that should be near the end of her fortnight, not the start.

A voice called to her. "Hello stranger!" It was Fi in straw hat, oversized sunglasses, and a blouse that would have seemed too young on someone of Anna's age, never mind one in her late fifties. "I'm parked around the corner, you look wonderful darling, how was your trip?" Before Anna could answer she was receiving a motherly hug and a double-cheek kiss. Anna had only seen her a couple of times since the wedding nearly two years ago.

Fi led the way to her car, a little red two-door hatchback. "Ex-hire, got it through our neighbour Yiorgos's brother, perfect for nipping round the island whenever we're here..." The boot was too small for Anna's case; she heaved it onto the back seat after managing to move the front one, whose upholstery felt uncomfortably hot when she settled in it and fastened her seatbelt.

"How's Dad?"

"Perfectly splendid." A twist of the key sent the car juddering to a stall; Fi had inadvertently left it in gear. She tried again and they set off.

"He didn't feel like coming too?"

"Bit tired, that's all." Driving away from the town they were soon ascending a high corniche: on one side, patchy scrub clinging to the parched slope; on the other, the glittering sea crested by tiny white waves. "Gorgeous, isn't it? I keep telling Jack we should get a boat."

"And what does he say?"

"Oh, he grumbles about winter storms when we aren't here, says we might come and find it smashed to matchwood."

"Does the weather really get so bad?"

"I wouldn't know." A pause. "Bring your camera?"

"Did you see something?"

"I mean to do your artistic stuff."

"I graduated from the course."

"But you still make pictures, don't you? Whole point's to become something, not give it up."

"Let's not discuss all that now, Fi."

"Sorry I mentioned it."

A longer pause: a kilometre of silence. A few goats, a whitewashed roadside chapel, a swim-suited couple speeding past on a moped.

"Your father got some new test results. He told you, didn't he?"

"No."

"I expect he will, then."

A glimpse of a sandy beach below.

"What were the results?"

"Best if he tells you."

"Not now that you've brought it up, Fi. Has it come back?"

"He'll tell you when he wants to."

"So I pretend I don't know anything?"

"You do what you want, Anna. I've told you because there's no way I couldn't. It's stressful."

"Stress? Tell me. Reason I came all the way out here."

"Well, whatever your reason... at least..."

Fi didn't finish her sentence but broke off with a barely concealed snort. Anna always knew this trip was going to be an effort but hadn't expected things to turn awkward so quickly. She reached for the radio and the car became filled with Greek pop music, a woman's melancholy voice backed by bouzoukis.

"Sorry if I'm too tense," Fi said eventually. "Jack's been really looking forward to seeing you."

Through her side window Anna watched the shrinking olive groves and isolated houses as they drove to the rugged, sparsely inhabited plateau of the island's interior. Here, she assumed, was an area devoid of interest to tourists and with little benefit to locals, hence affordably undesirable. The last place on Earth you'd want to be if you were sick.

"Home stretch now," Fi said jauntily as if trying to erase all thought of their prior journey, and she steered off the road onto an unsurfaced track. Jostled in her seat, Anna noticed in her wing mirror the great cloud of dust that now rose in the car's wake. Fi showed no sign of slowing, instead treating the little car more like the four-by-fours she was probably used to in England. "Look, he's waiting for us."

From a small white building ahead, a figure had emerged that Anna now recognised as her father, perhaps alerted by the car's plaintive whine or the billowing dry dirt it had kicked up. By some strange paradox of perspective he seemed to diminish rather than enlarge as they approached, the man of childhood memory and imagination being replaced by others seen more recently until finally they pulled up beside the present reality, an old man in white shirt and linen slacks, thinner than when Anna had last seen him at the party for his seventieth, and with a suntan that accentuated the liver spots on his bare scalp. She quickly got out and went to hug him. "You're looking great, Dad."

"You too, mouse."

Fi remained at the car, pulling the front seat down to retrieve Anna's suitcase.

"Let's sort it later," Jack called.

"I've started now..."

Jack said they should go to the terrace, leading Anna round the side of the house to a concrete patio beneath a corrugated plastic shade. An over-turned wheelbarrow and a pile of builder's sand adjoined the upcycled wooden table and chairs where Jack invited his daughter to sit while they waited for Fi to join them.

"Looks like you've been busy, Dad."

"We're getting the place ship-shape, little by little. Out here you need to do everything at the locals' pace. *Mañana* and all that."

"Wrong country but I know what you mean."

He chuckled. "Fi told me a phrase but I forget it now. She wants us both to learn the lingo, reckon I'm a bit long in the tooth for it."

"Never too old to try."

"Ha, *touché*."

The terrace overlooked an expanse of stony ochre soil where some kind of crop struggled to exist. A dusty lorry stood parked or abandoned, and beyond it the roofless shell of a half-finished house.

A glass-panelled door opened onto the terrace; Fi emerged. "Still a bit hot to sit out."

"Getting cooler now. Anna, what'll you have, G&T? No? Sprite? Bird, be a love and do the honours." Fi disappeared back inside.

"Great to sit down at last," Anna said.

"Must be." Jack reached across and patted her knee

tenderly. "So what do you think?"

"The house? Lovely."

"We'll give you a tour shortly. Isn't exactly picture-postcard but in this weather, well... And it's not so far to the beach. Couple of great tavernas in the town. Why the serious look?"

"Tired."

"Long trip, I know. That's the downside. Not the sort of place where you pop over for the weekend, but that's the whole idea, of course. A few months here, rest of the time in England."

Fi returned with drinks: lemonade for Anna, gin and tonic for Jack who wanted his wife to join them for what he jovially called an early sundowner, but Fi decided she'd go and rest while the two of them caught up.

Jack raised his glass to toast his daughter. "Congratulations."

"What?"

"Your graduation."

"Thanks."

"Only sorry we couldn't be there."

"I didn't even go to the ceremony myself."

"Your show, I mean. I hear it was great."

"Who told you?"

"Tim Kennaway. You know, the critic."

"He was there?"

"Surprised he didn't say hello – he's known you since you were a baby."

"Not really known, Dad."

Jack used the word in a different way from Anna: to him, knowing meant meeting, and a career in stage management and theatre reviewing had let him meet a great many people. Anna had no idea what Tim Kennaway looked like: she only knew he was a reactionary old tosser whose opinions on art had fossilised somewhere around 1979. She decided to change the subject.

"Have Bob and Claire been?" Anna had no genuine interest in her doltish older step-brother from Jack's first marriage, or his simpering wife.

"Came for a fortnight. And how are you set up these days, Anna?"

"What?"

Jack raised and rubbed his fingers. "You know, filthy lucre."

"I'm managing."

"Temping," he said with what sounded almost like derision. "I hear they call it the gig economy now."

"You were freelance, it's no different."

"I wouldn't agree. Didn't they have you on some zero-hours contract at the sports shop?"

"That was for a few weeks after I left school."

"Keep up with networking. We could try Camilla and her gallery people again. Bond Street, serious stuff. Or even here, little shop in town does framed prints..."

"Fi said you had some tests."

Jack took a sip. "Did she? Well, what do bloody doctors know, eh?"

"Has it come back?"

"Nothing to be alarmed about. And whatever Fi said, ignore it. She's worried, upset. She cares about me, that's all, and I'm lucky to have her. So lucky. I'd pretty much given up, you know. After we lost your mother. I thought, that's it, I've had two cracks at this lark and I'm not going to balls things up again."

It was much the same speech he'd made at the wedding, when it had sounded even more tasteless than it did now. "Why don't we do the tour?"

"Good idea. Come on, mouse, let's show you the mansion."

It took about ten minutes. Jack said the place had once been a farm house but it was impossible to discern any kind of prototype or timeline for something that had been bodged and adjusted by a succession of owners, each in search of something the property refused to yield, some charm beyond functionality. It was a white-walled concrete box divided into a few sparsely furnished sub-boxes, and the only art Anna could see was whatever had come out of that little shop in town. Fi had left Anna's suitcase at the front entrance and was now resting behind the closed door of what Jack, without a trace of irony, called the "master bedroom". Anna wheeled her case into "guest room one", a space of spartan simplicity containing a small wooden desk and chair, bare clothes rail, low bookcase and a double bed with an electric fan on the floor beside it.

"Beautiful place, Dad."

"We love it here. Our oasis of calm. But now I think you need a siesta. What time were you up this morning? Four? Five?"

"Actually I've sort of woken up. Adrenaline, I suppose."

"Fi and I would both have slept earlier if we hadn't been waiting. Let's have a lie down, won't we? Regroup at five."

So that was that. Anna retired to her allotted cell and switched on the fan whose caged propeller sent itself into a loud whirr. There were half a dozen hangers on the clothes rail so she opened her case and made use of them, then lay on the bed looking towards the bookcase with its crazily varied stock of curled and sun-bleached paperbacks, most likely donated by other visitors. She imagined Bob and Claire, with their Grisham and Rowling, acting out the sweaty rituals of a stereotypical holiday that would have revolved around beach trips, drinks on the terrace and discreet copulation with the same clattering monotony as the spinning blades of the nearby fan. How sweet and simple to be so dull, with nothing more complicated to consider than what to order in the taverna, whether to buy the tacky vase they'd have spotted in the art shop, or what factor sun cream. How wonderful to have ticked the empty boxes of unfulfilled destiny – answered all the questions of career, relationship, identity – then to relax in comfortable banality. Perhaps Bob got the vanilla gene from his mother Sally, whom Anna knew only from a couple of photographs and her father's dismissive summary. Anna's own mother was Jack's great, mad passion, the one he left Sally for, the real love of his life. He'd hurt so many people, was going to leave Fi a widow, not even a particularly wealthy one. But he had character, the spark of life, and that was what Anna hoped to have drawn from him, perhaps to pass on.

She was more tired than she realised, didn't notice herself falling asleep and was surprised to be woken by a knock at her door, Fi announcing plans to go to town for the evening. It was nearly seven o'clock and the room seemed twilit, long-shadowed with the descending sun. The fan was still spinning and Anna's neck had grown stiff. She sat up and flexed, called in reply to Fi and soon emerged to find Jack pacing in a pale blue blazer while adjusting his tie, looking ready for dinner and smelling of a woody aftershave that instantly reminded Anna of distant times.

"Sleep well, mouse?"

"Like a log."

"How does fish sound? Super place in the town."

"Anything."

"Let's sit out while Fi gets ready. Fancy a Scotch?"

She opted for beer and while he fetched it she went ahead

to the terrace. It was cool now, the landscape looking gentler. Even the randomly parked lorry seemed picturesque in the reddening light. If she'd come here a year or two ago, she reflected, she'd have photographed it. Now the desire was gone, she was content to sit and look.

Jack came out and handed her a chilled can. "Local stuff, I never drink it but hear it's acceptable." His was whisky, the ice cubes rattling as he placed his well filled tumbler on the table and sat down beside her to admire the view. She popped open her beer, took a welcome gulp of foam then wiped her lip and savoured the evening calm as the constant chirp of countless cicadas formed a kind of harmony with the fragrant air.

"Best time of the day," said Jack. "Good to be sharing it with you."

"Thanks."

He gave his glass a contemplative shake, gazing at its swirling contents. "Seeing it while there's still a chance, eh?"

"What?"

"But I'm afraid I'll likely not be dying any time soon."

"Dad..."

"I expect they'll poke around, do the same rigmarole over again. At my age these things grow slowly."

"I didn't come here on a mercy mission. You wouldn't deserve one."

"Well said."

"I'm here for me."

"Glad to hear it. Only reason any of us ever do anything, isn't it? Except most people pretend otherwise. At least that's something you've learned."

Fi came out. "Ah, aperitifs. Don't get too relaxed, Jack."

"No rush, bird."

"You want me to drive, darling?"

"I'll be fine," he insisted, taking another sip of whisky. "Grab yourself a G&T and join us."

"Would be nice to show Anna the town before it gets dark. We could watch the sunset from the promenade."

He shrugged, looked at his remaining alcohol, then at Anna. "What do you reckon?"

"Sure, let's go." No point watching him drink here when she could do the same in more sociable surroundings.

Tipping back his head he drained his glass, ice clattering against his lip. He nodded at her beer. "Bring?"

"I'll wait for the restaurant, thanks." She could see his childlike eagerness for a drinking companion and realised that whatever roles Fi played in his life, enabler wasn't one of them. When the three of them went around the house to the car, Fi again suggested she should drive, but Jack put himself at the wheel while Anna stooped into the back.

"Do be careful with the bends, darling," Fi said as they set off. "Remember we've a passenger."

"How could I forget?" he said with a forced chuckle that failed to hide a degree of impatience. At the first sharp turn they reached, he slowed with exaggerated care and pointed to a shrine at the roadside, a concrete church in miniature. "Some bugger went too fast," he said as they swung past.

"The kids drive like maniacs here," his wife complained.

"Not only the kids. Greek spirit, eh?"

"Don't go catching it, darling. Remember you're a sensible Brit."

"Sensible?" He called back over his shoulder to Anna. "When was I ever that?" She gave no answer. The drive to town was a chance to let her mind wander while Jack and Fi exchanged mundane marital banter, and the same unspectacular scenery she'd seen earlier unrolled in reverse under the falling twilight.

Approaching the town, Fi asked, "Are we going straight to the Swordfish?" Jack nodded, steering into a narrow street that took them down to the waterfront where evening strollers were savouring the air. The taverna stood alone at the end of the bay, a simple building with only a few customers populating its large terrace. The sign at the entrance was in Greek but the creature Fi had named was shown in a cheerful cartoon-like representation. "It's still early," she observed as Jack led them past unoccupied white plastic tables to one at the sea wall where waves could be heard lapping a few metres below.

"Let's have a drink first," he said, and as they sat down a grey-haired, casually dressed waiter emerged, smiling broadly and coming towards them with a small wicker bread basket.

"Welcome," he said in a heavy accent, quickly covering the table with a paper sheet he clipped in place, and depositing the basket that held three sets of cutlery. "English menus?"

"Yes, please," said Fi.

Anna was bemused, trying to decide whether in the waiter's eyes Fi and Jack were anonymous tourists or regulars who'd never bother to learn the language.

"I'll have a Scotch," Jack said to no one in particular. "Not too much ice. Girls?"

"Only some water for me," Fi told the waiter. Anna said she'd have the same.

The waiter retreated and Jack turned his chair to admire the remnants of daylight still glowing on the horizon. He rested his arm on the table and drummed his fingers softly, as if in time to some melody in his mind.

"Do you come here much?" Anna asked.

"Been a few times," Jack told her without taking his eyes from the sea or his elbow from the table.

"They do lovely fish," Fi explained. "Best we've found so far, I'd say."

Anna's seat gave her a view past her father to the rocky shoreline they'd driven along and the harbour where she'd arrived. The promenade was becoming busy with people of all ages; among the distant, tiny figures she could make out a child on a scooter. "I'd like to explore the town."

"Won't take you long," Jack said with a laugh. "Not exactly guidebook material. Though it's a nice enough way to pass a bit of time."

"There's a lovely old church," said Fi.

The waiter returned, placing a large whisky at Jack's elbow and pouring iced water into two glasses from the jug he left beside three laminated menus and a wine list. Anna lifted a menu; her father reached for his drink.

"Any recommendations?" Anna asked Fi.

"I couldn't really say."

Jack commented, "When the fellow comes back I'll ask about specials. No rush." He took another sip.

"I'd like to see that church."

"Good idea, mouse."

"Now, I mean."

Jack turned and looked quizzically at her. "What's up?"

"Nothing. But if we're only killing time until we eat I'd rather not do it here."

Fi's expression signalled weariness and irritation; Jack merely smiled and said, "Off you go, then. Be back in an hour and there'll be something to eat. I'll choose."

Fi said, "She doesn't know where the church is, darling."

Anna rose from her seat. "I'll find it, thanks." As she walked away she could feel behind her the beginning of the conversation they'd now conduct about her rudeness:

something to occupy them for the next sixty minutes. Leaving the taverna she headed for the promenade which she took at a slow pace, enjoying the light sea breeze, and in less than ten minutes she was at a paved area on the waterfront where children were playing while on surrounding benches elderly locals gossiped. Across the road she could see a small building in Byzantine style, the excuse she'd come in search of, and may as well visit. She found it open and empty, save for an unsmiling old lady in black who was seated just inside the entrance and said nothing when Anna nodded and went past to inspect the gilded interior that glowed by lamplight. Anna had no idea what she was looking at; the church might have been fifty or a thousand years old, an architectural jewel or a wholly typical place of prayer. An ornately decorated screen hid what she guessed to be the high altar; above her, on the domed ceiling, angels and saints crowded around the dominating image of a solemn Christ. Pillars on either side of her bore icons; the one on the right was the largest and most elaborate, a great slab of silver propped firmly on a stone shelf showing in relief the Madonna and Child. Their faces were painted on flat inlaid wood, delicately drawn but expressionless, both of them looking out at the viewer rather than each other and comically reminiscent to Anna of the head-through-hole stall of a bygone seaside photographer. Jesus was a tiny man on Mary's lap, vaguely military in appearance with a tunic resembling the sort of Roman costume Anna once coloured with crayons in primary school.

She was startled by a voice at her shoulder; the old lady had approached and was saying something unintelligible. Anna wondered if it was a warning not to touch or perhaps an instruction to make an offering; two small, thin candles burned on the shelf supporting the icon beside a box containing unlit ones and a tin for donations. She didn't know the going rate; one euro, probably, but she had no change and in any case the gesture would be meaningless. Anna shrugged, the lady said something else then tottered back to her chair near the entrance. Might it have been some information or explanation that she had offered? A warning of the approach of closing time? There was no way of comprehending how the huddled arthritic figure fitted into the incense-scented world Anna had intruded upon; whether as official guardian or rootless soul in search of shelter and occasional company.

Anna came out and followed the adjoining street uphill, past a line of gift shops still open but devoid of customers. She reached a junction marked by a decades-old statue of some great statesman or public figure from whose marble plinth jutted a metal spout, green and dented, trickling water into a smooth stone bowl where she dipped her hand, feeling its coolness. Here must be the town centre, she presumed, offering little charm and serving mainly as a hub for functional business premises: a bank, a car-hire firm, an electrical goods shop. In front of the single cafe young Greeks were sipping milk shakes or iced coffee from tall glasses, laughing and gesticulating as they conversed. It only made Anna feel more alone.

She returned to the seafront square, now thronged with people of all ages. On the ground at the first corner she reached, a slim and dark-skinned man was sitting with an assortment of leather belts and bags laid out on a striped rug. "Handmade, twenty euro," he said, looking up at her as she passed and raising in his palm a tan-coloured purse. She didn't take it but paused to look at the other goods, none of which took her fancy.

"Ten euro," he said, pointing at a woven belt. "Fine leather, very good."

"Where are you from?" she asked.

"Senegal." He smiled broadly, but Anna noticed the stare she now received from a middle-aged lady walking her small dog on a lead, the animal having paused to sniff at the rug. As the woman tugged at her pet, her stern expression conveyed disapproval of the hawker and his over-priced wares.

"Good quality," he insisted to Anna.

"No thanks."

"Another time. Best price."

A full circuit of the square seemed sufficient delay before beginning to walk back along the promenade. Then, approaching the taverna, she noticed more diners on the terrace, Jack and Fi sitting in silence when she eventually reached their table where a dew-moistened bottle of white wine stood open between them, with two stemmed glasses half-filled and a third still empty, beside a dish of olives and a basket of bread.

"Grilled swordfish," Jack said when he saw her.

"He assumed you'd want it," Fi explained.

Jack then looked towards the kitchen door from where the waiter nodded back. "I told him to hold it until you showed up. I'm starving."

"You needn't have waited for me."

"I said we would, though." He filled her glass.

"I've been less than an hour."

"Bravo to that."

Fi asked if she'd found the church. "Pretty, isn't it?"

Anna nodded and the three sat in silence until Jack said, "Shall I order a second bottle?"

"Only if you and Anna need it, darling." Fi was gazing at the dark moonless sky over the sea where myriad lights twinkled. Eventually she said, "I wonder, do they have the same ones here?"

"What do you mean?"

"Stars."

Jack snorted. "How can they be different? They're in space, aren't they?"

"We saw the Southern Cross in Kruger Park, don't you remember? They have different constellations in the southern hemisphere."

"We're still in the north, though."

"I suppose. But look, there's a cross there." She pointed at it, hanging like a great dagger.

"Maybe it's the Northern Cross."

"Is there such a thing?"

Jack laughed. "We're looking at the bloody thing, aren't we? Expect there's twenty different names for it, half of them Latin or Greek or what-have-you. Can't say I've ever noticed it in England."

"They'd have to switch over somewhere, wouldn't they, between north and south stars?"

"Equator."

"So what do they see there? We should go, Jack. A cruise. They do something with a bowl of water when you cross the line, water goes a different way down a plughole."

Anna felt like screaming at this connubial inanity but fortunately the waiter arrived with their food. Jack ordered that second bottle. Anna's swordfish steak looked juicy and appetising; a heart-shaped section through the creature's middle, centred on a pearly vertebra, with soft white flesh specked and blackened from the grill. She squeezed a halved lemon over it.

Fi peered at Jack's plate. "They gave yours a good old roasting."

His fish, whole and deeply charred, lay proudly with its garnish. "Jealous?" he teased.

She'd opted for a lamb and onion stew in a clay dish. "Jack went in to choose and weigh it," she explained to Anna who began cutting into hers. "I can't be bothered with that rigmarole. At the end of the day it's only fish. And not cheap, mind."

"Doing my bit to support the local economy. They do have a crisis, after all."

"Haven't seen much evidence of it," said Anna.

"Greek spirit," he replied. "Carry on regardless. Life is for living." He raised his wine. "Cheers to all of us." The women joined the toast, the three glasses almost touching as they came together over the table. "How do you like the vino, Anna?"

She gave a noncommittal shrug. The label looked expensive. Her father was trying to be grand, as usual. He'd had a career dining out on others' expenses and wanted to keep up the appearance, if only for his latest partner and his own precarious ego. Anna asked them both, "Have there been refugees here?"

"We're too far from Turkey," said Jack. "They'd have to miss Samos to wind up here."

"But there were a couple of tragedies, weren't there?" Fi interrupted. "That boat they found drifting with everyone dead or dying on it."

"Oh yes, gone off course or something."

"Even small children. Syrian, Afghan..."

"I spoke to someone from Senegal in the town."

Jack nodded. "They've been coming for years, Athens is full of them. Don't think they've got a war though."

"Who'd want to stay in Africa?" Fi wondered. "Can't blame them. Refugees, migrants, they're all people like us, doing their best."

"And nobody gives a shit about us," Jack said sardonically. "How good we are for caring about them. But you know what I find strange, Anna? This island used to be mostly Muslim. Greek-speaking Muslims. And there were places in Turkey full of Turkish Christians and Jews."

"Ottoman," Fi interjected.

"That's right. Bloody great caliphate running the whole show from Istanbul. Here, Middle East, the lot. They said: it's fine for you to be whatever you want, you can have your own Jewish or Christian schools and laws and so on, only we'll tax you and treat you as second-class citizens. Called it the millet system. Then the empire fell apart, Britain and France carved up the last of it after the First World War and we've had problems ever since."

"Sounds like it wasn't very fair before," said Anna.

"Makes you wonder, though."

"We saw a good documentary," Fi mentioned, and Jack looked somehow displeased by the interruption, saying he'd read about the population exchange in a book. Fi asked Anna, "Do you like documentaries?"

The question seemed a lame attempt at emotionally neutral conversation. "Not really."

"Jack and I watch a lot. We've got decent wifi at the villa."

"Really?" Anna said with ironic interest.

"Amazing what you can find online, so informative. And a real tragedy, that population swap. Nineteen twenty something."

"Twenty-three," Jack said authoritatively, moving the first, now-empty wine bottle to the side of the table and refilling his glass from the second.

"Ethnic cleansing, that's what it was."

Andrew Crumey

"Palestine was meant to be the same sort of game and look at that balls-up. Even Ireland." Jack sipped, looked dreamily at the ocean and began quietly singing, *"What we need is a great big melting pot..."*

"You're getting merry, darling."

Anna was finishing her swordfish, oblivious to its flavour and in no mood to watch her father get increasingly drunk. "I think I might phone for a taxi."

"I only had half a glass," Fi said reassuringly.

"Oh mouse, you party pooper, the night is young. Indulge your old man. Price you pay. No such thing as a free holiday."

"So you're going to pay my air fare too?"

"If you want. I know times are hard for you and if there's any way I can help..."

"Bit late in the day for that, Dad."

Fi put down her fork with an air of finality. Her face tightened. "Anna, we know you're having a hard time..."

"You don't know anything."

"Some of us have got bigger things to think about than money."

"Oh really? So you've got cancer too?"

Fi was speechless, aghast, unable to respond, so she looked towards Jack who however appeared unperturbed and after taking another large sip said, "I'm so glad, Anna, that you've turned out as big a shit as me."

"Thanks a lot."

"We're survivors. Sure, I could be dead in a year."

"So could anyone your age."

"And so could you."

"If this is going to be a live-for-the-moment bucket-list speech..."

Fi snapped. "Oh shut up."

Anna moved to rise from her chair but Jack waved her down. "Both of you, hold it. Anna, if this isn't going to work I can find you a place in town. Or we simply agree to keep apart at the villa. Or we have it out now. I honestly don't give a fuck, one road or the next. Just because we don't all like each other doesn't mean we can't have a pleasant time."

Fi was shaking her head. "Jack, I don't know how you put up with this."

"I want to go now," said Anna.

"Let's then, I only need to settle with mine host. You can both toddle to the car if you like." He brought the key from his pocket and put it on the table, then waved to attract attention, scribbling a finger on his palm when he was noticed.

Fi slid the key towards Anna and said, "I'll wait here." Anna sat silently.

The waiter soon came with their bill; Jack took the slip from its dish, peered at it through his reading glasses and nodded with satisfaction, handing over his credit card. He asked the waiter if he was from the island originally.

"No, Bulgaria."

"Ah." Then once the waiter had left Jack brought some cash from his wallet to leave as a tip. He tilted the half-full wine bottle.

"Bring it," Fi suggested.

"No need."

They all rose and walked to the car, silently like strangers. Jack quickly fell asleep once they set off, Fi drove with fixed concentration along the twisting unlit road out of town and Anna sat hunched in the cramped back seat wondering how she was going to get through the rest of her stay. Eventually the villa swung into view in the headlight beams. When they halted, Fi gave Jack a nudge and got out, letting Anna exit.

And as if she had been preparing her words beforehand, Fi said to her, "I'm sorry about earlier."

"Let's forget it."

Jack had stirred and climbed out stiffly, then they went into the house whose air was stuffy and warm. "Night all," he said simply, going to the bedroom, followed by his wife.

"Night, Dad," Anna said to their closing door.

Next morning when Anna rose she found Fi sitting in shade on the terrace, reading a book and with a small cup of coffee on the table beside her.

"Dad up?"

"Not yet," Fi said without looking, and turned a page.

Anna drew a chair at the other side of the table, sat down and tried to find satisfaction in the view. The lorry was still there.

"I can drive you somewhere if you like," said Fi, continuing to study her book. "I'd let you take the car yourself but I don't think we're insured for it. The roads can be tricky."

Anna couldn't decide what she might prefer, so remained silent.

"Town or beach?" Fi eventually prompted.

"I suppose a swim would be good."

"Twenty minutes?"

"Sure."

"Just want to finish this chapter."

Anna stepped back inside, to the small kitchen where she found a loaf of bread and jar of jam in the fridge, made herself a cup of instant coffee and had her breakfast standing at the window, staring at the unmade track that led to the main road; a view as stark as the one from the terrace. Her prior imagining of this place had been a collage made from travel programmes and tourism websites; a place she could escape to. Yet it was as if she had gone nowhere, the world having simply moved under her feet, bringing something different to gaze at but no new thought to replace the ones that troubled her.

She went and filled her shoulder bag with everything she'd need for the beach, and found Fi waiting for her, in sunhat and dark glasses and with the car key in her hand.

"Good chapter?"

"Yes."

They had reached an unspoken agreement to remain civil with each other, a truce sustained during the twenty-minute drive that ended with Fi halting beside a couple of parked mopeds and a shabby four-by-four. They were on a dusty brow beside low dunes patched with coarse marram grass, sloping gently to a beach visible a hundred or more metres away, specked with a handful of prostrate sunbathers.

"If you wish to have lunch at ours I'll come and collect you at half past one."

"Sounds fine."

"Text me if you change your mind."

"I didn't bring my phone."

"Oh. Half past one, then."

Anna got out, saw a foot-beaten track to the sea and heard the car rev and turn behind her. Reaching the beach she selected a place far from the other people, close to the water's edge where a cool breeze was raising foamy breakers. She laid out her towel, trapping its corners under items from her bag, then stripped down to her swimsuit and applied suncream that had already liquified in the rising heat. She stepped into the water, cold at first against her skin, then flinched and gasped with masochistic pleasure when she launched herself against an incoming wave. She swam and felt the power of the buffeting ocean, plunging her head down so that the world became a muffled ringing and a green haze through which a couple of fish could be seen beneath her, silvery blurs picking at the sandy bed.

Raising her eyes and turning, she saw the beach's expanse to be enclosed within rocky headlands at either end. One looked close enough to swim to, a convenient exercise target, so she made towards it with a leisurely breast stroke whose steady rhythm soon prompted a flow of random thoughts. How long had her father got, she wondered. Wrong to bother about money, but what if Fi made him disinherit his own daughter out of sheer greed and spite? Or leave some token amount to Anna and Bob with Fi taking the lioness's share? To hell with it, Anna didn't need anybody's handouts.

Rounding the headland, she saw sitting on the rocks a grey-haired man, topless in faded denim shorts, possibly as old as her father but in better shape, burned dark brown by the sun. He met her gaze briefly and peacefully swung his head to look elsewhere, revealing a short pony tail that made him appear like an old rocker or hippie, the antithesis of Jack. She swam past, wondering why her dad should have chosen a laid-back place like Greece for a summer home when he could instead have been posing in white linen suit at the wineries of Tuscany or the Dordogne. Fi's decision, surely, or the only place she told him they could afford.

Anna could now see that the shore beyond the headland was an inhospitable shingle margin beneath red cliffs. She considered swimming onwards but the sea was choppier here and her breath was feeling shorter. Better turn before she got too tired. As she did so she felt something brush against her leg, startling her. Sudden fright was immediately followed by scorching pain, an intense burning that made her scream. Some creature had attacked her and might be about to strike again. She thrashed to the nearest rock, pulled herself out of the water and sat sobbing. Her leg had only a small red patch on it but the wound felt larger, deeper.

"You alright?" He must have heard her scream, the tanned old man coming round to look.

"I got stung."

He clambered nimbly over and crouched beside her, the hairs of his bare legs looking starkly white against his leathery skin. "Jellyfish?"

"I don't know. It hurts."

"Hey, don't cry, we'll get you sorted." He sounded American, calm, and had the reassuring air of an expert, inspecting the wound with dispassionate interest. "Medusa alright. Usually don't get them till later in the season. You were unlucky."

"Will it get any worse?" It was as if boiling water had been splashed on her.

"There's a standard way of treating it but you're not gonna want me to do that."

"You mean piss on it?"

"You've heard? Neutralises the poison. Or else I can get you some lotion, that'd help."

"I'll take the lotion."

He rubbed his stubbly chin. "My place is only a five-minute drive but it's ten to walk to the car. How about we get you back round to the beach and you wait there?"

He helped her up and steadied her. "Here, you can wear my flip-flops, my feet are tough enough without."

"Thanks." She limped beside him over the rocks.

"Name's Conrad."

"I'm Anna."

"You here with friends?"

"No, visiting my dad, he lives here."

"Me too."

"Visiting your dad?"

He laughed. "I mean I live here. Never knew my dad. What's yours called, I might know him."

"Jack Fisher. His wife's Fi. They're at some place I don't know the name of. Up a big hill."

"Jack and Fi, huh? Yeah, I painted some window frames for them." They rounded the promontory bringing the beach and road back into view. "You leave anything over there? I can run along and pick up your stuff."

"It can wait."

"How about I give you a ride to my place, get you mended, drop you off at your dad's?"

"That's very kind."

When they reached sand she offered Conrad his flip-flops back. He said no, it was a tad warm underfoot, he was used to it. "Even tried fire walking, there's a knack."

"You mean run like hell?"

"I had a guru taught me a really important thing. Pain is inevitable, suffering isn't."

"Easier said than done."

"Still hurting?"

"Easing a bit." They made their way up a track across the dunes towards the road. "How long have you lived here?"

"Twenty years, off and on. Plenty enough to know those rocks aren't a great place to swim. When I saw you go past I figured best keep a lookout. Lucky I was around, huh?"

His vehicle was the four-by-four, dented and caked in dust. He'd screened the windows so the interior wasn't too hot when they got inside, but Anna could feel grit on the seat beneath her. There were old cassette tapes strewn at her feet, while from the overhead mirror a dangling charm began dancing as the vehicle reversed across the dirt then set off along the crumbled tarmac.

"Does that mean something special here?" She nodded at the swinging charm, a ringed disc of blue glass.

"That's a *mataki*. Wards off evil."

Its concentric circles formed a stylised eye; a pale iris surrounding a black pupil. Anna thought it spooky. "People here are very religious."

"I guess."

"There are churches and shrines all over the place. I went in one last night, in the town near the seafront."

"Oh yeah, that's pretty. Think it used to be a mosque."

He turned off the road onto a rough track and Anna grabbed the handle above her door to steady herself.

"Still hurting? Nearly there." Ahead stood a low stone building with peeling whitewash and a small side terrace shrouded by a thick overhanging vine. It looked like the poorest kind of farm cottage but had an honest simplicity Jack's place lacked. "Home sweet home," he said, the car halting awkwardly. He jumped out, went and opened the unlocked front door. Anna followed and found herself in a dark, sweltering room where it took a moment for her eyes to adjust and begin taking in the crowded contents. A sink and a table at one end, an iron bed at the other. A battered old chest of drawers, a cooking stove. A further interior doorway showed some kind of space beyond but it seemed as if the house consisted almost entirely of this single long room. The roughly finished walls bore shelves bowed with age; Conrad began rummaging on one near the sink that held pots and jars of varying sizes. On the shelf beside Anna lay an assortment of what he presumably considered ornaments or curios: a rusted cog from a car or machine; an old shoe, its red leather cracked and twisted; a partly melted plastic container with a faded logo of a chicken and some writing that looked like Chinese; a little blue and white toy boat.

"Here's that lotion." He came over to her holding a brown glass bottle, unlabelled and unmarked, and a piece of cloth.

"What's in it?"

"Stuff that'll take away the pain."

"I mean, where did you get it?"

Conrad smiled. "Made it. And don't worry, no piss." He motioned her to sit on a stool decorated with crudely painted stars. She angled herself so he could dab the thick liquid onto the reddened skin of her leg.

"Ow!"

"It'll help, believe me."

He was right: her wound quickly felt cooler.

"You should sell that stuff."

"I'm not a businessman. I see someone who needs help, I give it for free." He took the bottle back to its shelf.

"Very noble of you."

"It's how I choose to live. Like some juice?" He reached down to a steel bucket on the floor and from out of it began lifting fruits that Anna couldn't recognise, dropping them into a heavy metal hopper on the bench beside the sink whose handle he turned, sending squirts of yellow liquid into a jug placed in readiness. He poured out two glassfuls, came and handed one to her. She scrutinised the thick pulpy liquid and cautiously sipped. It was delicious.

"What is this?"

"I just call it juice. Better than any you'll ever get in a store."

"I admire your self-sufficiency."

"I take what I need and give back what I can. You heard of karma?"

"Sure."

"Then you understand. Let's go sit out."

He was still barefoot as well as bare chested, indifferent to some spiky looking dried plant heads that crunched beneath Anna's sandalled feet when she followed behind him holding her glass. On the terrace stood a rickety wooden table and two chairs, shaded by the dense vine above. "You've been living in this house for twenty years?"

He shook his head. "This place four or five. When I first came here there were a few of us, thought we could have ourselves a kind of community, didn't really work out. Others've all moved on, I guess. But this island seemed like it was my destiny, place where I was meant to be." They both sat down.

"So you're alone?"

"You say it like it's bad."

"No... I mean..."

"Sure, I'm alone. We're all of us alone, one way or another. Some more obvious than others. Your dad say much about his illness?"

She gave a start. "What do you know about it?"

"Anyone can see it in his face, don't need to be a doctor. He's a sick man."

"He might be dying."

Conrad nodded. "We're all doing that." He pointed to his tanned midriff. "See there?" His finger indicated the pale ridge of an old scar that had been surgically stitched. "Fellow stabbed me, left me for dead."

"When?"

"Long time ago, forty years I guess, give or take. An

alleyway in Amsterdam.

"You lived there?"

"I've lived everywhere. This kid was bad and I was in his way. So he killed me."

"Only you didn't die."

"Sure I died. But we get more than one life. That's karma."

Anna was prepared to accept the hazy metaphors of an old hippie. "You reckon my dad might get another chance, same as you did?"

Conrad shrugged. "Up to him. Most people think they only got one life, that's the problem. They want to hold on to everything when really they need to let go. After that shit in Amsterdam I got the hell out of there. I was a husband for a while, got a grown-up son some place. I've been a farmer and an actor and Lord knows what else."

"What are you now?"

"A healer."

"Not a decorator?"

"That too."

He was old and rootless and a bit sad, but because she felt sorry for him, and grateful, and because his was a world completely unlike her own, Anna felt a connection with Conrad. Pensively she rubbed the sun-bleached surface of the table. Then she said, "I got pregnant."

"Hmm." He took a sip of juice and looked up at the bunches of ripening grapes hanging from the trellis above. Either he was inviting her to say more or else had nothing to say.

She decided not to elaborate. "You've had quite a life, by the sound of it."

He levelled his gaze and returned his chipped glass to the table. "One time in Turin I was with this girl, she gave me something to drink, said it was a cocktail. I couldn't even get the stuff to my lips, it was like my arm was stuck. Guess she was trying to poison me, but my body knew better. What I'm saying, we do too much thinking inside our heads. Should listen to the spirit, huh?"

"I suppose so."

"The body knows what to do. Looks after the soul. I was with a bunch of friends, we had ourselves some mushrooms and I got real bad, worse trip I ever had. Collapsed and my heart stopped beating, like I really did die that time. Only my body wasn't ready for it. So I woke up as if nothing happened. Everything has its time and place. Mine's gonna be on this island, I knew first moment I set foot here. You ever hear of a band called Linden?"

"No."

"They had this song, line in it goes, *Paradise is where we are, it's on the other side*."

"And what does that mean?"

"It means, like, we're already on the other side."

"That's very profound." Really she thought it new-age bullshit.

"My guru, Daido, he taught me a lot of good stuff."

"Were you in Tibet or something?"

"Manchester. Daido was English."

"Not his real name, then."

"No name is real, it's only a word we attach to something. Let go of attachment and life gets simpler. Like when you were stung in the water, you were attached to the pain."

She looked at her leg where there was still a small mark, faded and no longer hurting. "What I just told you, I'm wondering if I should tell my father."

"It's such a big deal?"

"Well, yes."

"What all happened, exactly?"

"I..." She stopped herself. "No, let's not talk about it. Look, you've been really kind but I ought to get back."

"Sure," he said, calmly draining his glass. "Let's go to the car."

They walked round and she saw he'd left the driver door open, for ventilation or out of sheer indifference. When they got inside she kicked off his sandals and sat back realising how pleasantly tired she was feeling. He put a CD in the player.

"Is this the band you told me about?"

"I've no idea who this is. Car's not mine, I borrow it off a lady lives the other side of the island. Cool track, huh?"

He remembered the way to Jack and Fi's pretty well, hesitating only once at a crossroads. They were soon approaching the house where Anna saw the car to be away, perhaps Fi had already left for the beach. "Any idea what time it is?"

Conrad twisted to look at the sky. "Well past noon for sure." They pulled up.

"Want to come in and say hello to Dad?"

"You go fix yourself. See you again perhaps."

"Thanks."

He drove off behind her as she pushed open the front door, calling out for her father but without response. The house was empty, nor was anyone on the terrace, now baking in full sunlight. The kitchen wall clock showed it was already after two, they must have gone out for lunch. Nothing to do here but grab a bite, shower, lie down.

She was woken later by the sound of their return, Fi at the open bedroom doorway looking outraged.

"Anna, what the devil!"

Drowsily lifting herself to explain about the jellyfish, the kind man, her poor sense of time.

"We've been worried sick! Thought you'd drowned!"

"Now, now," Jack soothed, appearing behind his wife. "Told you she'd be here." He looked flushed, sated by whatever he'd drunk.

Anna got up from the bed while Fi continued complaining angrily. "All your things left lying on the beach!"

"My sun-lotion and a cheap pair of shades."

"Your clothes. Our towel!"

"Conrad offered..."

"Who?"

"Said he painted your window frames."

Fi looked quizzically at Jack who simply shrugged. She glared at Anna, then pointed to where she'd deposited the recovered beach bag on the floor next to the front door. "Take your phone next time."

"Or take the car," Jack suggested, swaying.

"She's not insured."

"Bugger that." He left to lie down.

Anna went to the entrance, picked up the bag and turned to see Fi continuing to stare at her, arms crossed. "Well?" said Anna. "What do you want me to say?"

"Sorry would do."

"For what? Getting stung? Wasn't my fault."

"No, never is." Fi marched crossly away to join her husband.

"Fuck you," Anna hissed quietly after her.

A couple of hours later, she found her father awake and ready for further refreshment outside, where sufficient shade had slid across the seating area. Pulling up a chair beside him, Anna had already decided what she wanted to say.

"I'll find a hotel in town."

"No need for that."

Fi looked out, she'd overheard. "Nobody's forcing you." She retreated back inside.

Jack looked pensively at the waste ground before them, the lorry that seemed fixed forever on it. "Really can't see why you two don't get on," he said without turning to face his daughter. "Fi's not the awkward type."

"You mean I am?"

"Today was unlucky. Fi was mightily pissed off but she's fine now."

"I'd really prefer to stay somewhere else. Actually I'd fly home if I could change my ticket."

"Is it all about money, then? Shall I book you on the earliest flight I can get? Or do you want me to book the hotel?"

"Oh Dad, don't turn it into that. Look, it's great that you've got Fi, she's so... right for you. We clash, that's all."

Fi came out with drinks on a tray. "Two G&Ts and one beer. You would like a beer, wouldn't you, Anna?"

It was some kind of peace offering or victory celebration. Anna took the opened bottle, touched its cold glass against her lips then drank a mouthful and felt the alcohol wash into her.

Fi sat down and looked at Jack, then Anna, and at Jack again. "Well?"

"Well what, love? Are you two going to bury the hatchet?"

"I think I have already," said Fi.

Anna laughed derisively. "Takes two to do that. Dad, maybe the phrase you're looking for is sweeping things under the carpet."

Fi's eyes rolled. "Here we go again."

Jack was unperturbed. "Then let's have it out. A damn good row, clear the air, and I'll get you that hotel or flight or whatever."

111

"Dad..."

"You've never accepted the way I moved on after your mother died."

"It's not that."

Fi interrupted. "Then what is it? Why did you even think to come here?"

Anna took a breath, gathered her thoughts and said, "That guy who helped me today, Conrad. I told him exactly what's been on my mind. A total stranger. So easy."

"Then tell us," said Fi. "Because you know we've got things on our mind too. Very serious things."

Anna shook her head. "It's no use."

Jack swatted away a fly that had begun to disturb him and when it landed on the table he took an unsuccessful swipe at it. "Ha, devil got away."

Anna gazed pityingly at him, her old father who surely couldn't have long to live, no matter how the latest scare turned out. If it wasn't cancer it would be his heart from too much booze. "I had to have an abortion," she said.

Jack and Fi both looked momentarily stunned. "What do you mean, had to?" Fi asked.

It was such a such a stupid question. "I got pregnant," Anna said, as if explaining to a small child.

Jack nodded, his face sorrowful and sympathetic, struggling to find what to say. "Could have helped you out, though."

"Dad, for God's sake, this is not about money."

Fi bridled. "So now we know. Thanks for sharing."

Jack silenced her with a wave of his hand, a slower version of the way he'd dismissed the fly, only this time with an air of defeat. "When did this happen, Anna? Are you still involved with the father?"

"I don't want to talk about it now."

"No," said Fi, "just lob in the grenade."

"Oh, go to hell," Anna snapped, standing up. "Dad, if you can give me a lift to town I'd appreciate it. Otherwise I'll get a taxi."

"He's had a drink..."

"I'm fine," said Jack, also getting to his feet. "Go and pack, we'll leave whenever you're ready. Think I'll put on a clean shirt."

Anna retreated to her room, emerging twenty minutes later to see Jack through the open bathroom doorway, straightening his tie in front of the mirror, slicking back the thin strands on his scalp as if getting ready for a date. He must have caught sight of her reflection, for he turned to her. "Fi's still outside." Unclear why he felt necessary to say it, as though Anna could care. "I'll tell her we're leaving. Do you want to say goodbye?"

"Say it for me."

When he went to the terrace Anna could hear only his side of the conversation.

"We're off... Yes... I shall. Oh, and if you get hungry... No... I don't know, perhaps... Yes, it's fully charged."

He came back in, took hold of Anna's case and they went together to the car where the two of them quietly struggled to fit her luggage neatly within the confined space. Turning the key to set off, Jack said, "Too bad, isn't it?"

"Yes."

"And such a beautiful evening." He was right, the late afternoon sun was exerting its habitual calming effect on the dry landscape. "I know a place we could try," he said as they drove.

"I'm sure it won't be hard to get a room," said Anna. "There were a few people when I arrived, wanting guests. Not many tourists."

He sighed. "Are you going to tell me any more about it?"

"You don't need to know, it's over. Left me upset, that's all."

"Of course it would."

Reaching the town they parked next to the square at the seafront where some elderly locals sat on the green-painted benches gossiping, perhaps exactly the same folk Anna had seen last night. The African hawker was there too, with his rug of goods. From his seat in the car Jack pointed across the road to a balconied three-storey building that stood inconspicuously between similarly old-looking residential ones on either side, the interloper distinguished only by a small sign above the door: *Hotel Lena.*

"Not exactly the Ritz," said Jack. "But we can give it a go."

They walked across and entered the small reception area whose wood panelling and kitsch decor evoked some earlier decade. The desk was unattended; Jack rang the bell on it and a plump, dark-haired woman in her forties soon appeared, immediately greeting them in accented English.

"You want a room?" She was formal and unsmiling, her gaze flicking from Anna to Jack as if trying to assess the relationship between them.

"A single for my daughter."

"Only double or twin."

"Whatever you can offer."

The woman opened the ledger on her desk and without look-ing up from its sparsely filled page said, "How many nights?"

Jack and Anna looked at each other, neither knowing what to say until Jack suggested, "Only one for now, then we'll see."

"Sixty-five euro per night. Sixty if book three in advance."

He said to Anna, "We ought to see the room first."

"I'm sure it'll be fine."

"Alright," he told the woman, bringing out his wallet and

extracting his credit card. "We'll take it."

"Passport?" she said to Anna.

"We'll bring everything shortly," Jack explained, and they exited to fetch her luggage. Walking together back across the road, he said, "Are you really sure you want to do this? You know you don't have to."

Anna didn't reply; surely he could see there was no other sensible option. Opening the car, he wanted to retrieve her heavy case himself, but she moved him aside. "I can manage."

"I want to help, mouse."

"I know you do. Sometimes better not to try." She stood the case on its wheels beside the car, slung her bag on her shoulder, and there was a moment of wordless awkwardness that Jack eventually broke. "What if I give you some time to settle in, then we go and have dinner?"

She knew he would have planned this in his mind, told Fi not to wait, dressed himself for whichever restaurant he had in mind. "Give me half an hour."

"More if you need it."

"Should take less."

"I'll sit in the square. With the oldies," he said with a laugh.

"Perfect."

The room proved to be basic but adequate. The wardrobe and side table were like relics from a house clearance. The deep mattress of the wooden-framed double bed didn't sag too much when she tested its edge. She went to open the full-length white-painted window shutters and was pleased to discover a view of the seafront; she could see her father's car, and a moment later spotted Jack on a bench. The double-door window was latched ajar for ventilation; she unhooked and pulled it open. The balcony wasn't large enough for a chair but she could stand here looking out to the calm sea and the softening glow of the early evening sky. Her mind was made up: she would stay here and forget Fi, forget everything.

A movement in the square caught her attention: the African hawker was in an argument with a young Greek-looking man, the two of them standing nose to nose and gesticulating with arm-swings that might at any moment become blows. Heads were turning, bystanders edging away. At this distance, and with the intruding sound of traffic, she couldn't hear if they were shouting; their mime was a confrontation in microcosm, a battle of competing insects. Her father hadn't noticed; Jack's bench gave him a view in another direction, out of earshot. Suddenly they were throwing punches; the Greek man lunged, the African fell to the ground, cowering there as if in expectation of being kicked, but instead it seemed the battle was now over, all the violent energy quickly released. The Greek turned and walked away, the hawker got to his feet, dusted himself down and paced around his rug, restoring its arrangement and his own dignity, then sat beside it again as though nothing had happened.

Anna came back inside her room, closed the shutters and wondered if she should change, but decided instead merely to unpack and hang a few items from her case, put her washbag in the small en suite shower room, and brush her hair. It was only dinner with her dad, after all.

She found him still sitting on the bench, lost in thought when she tapped his shoulder.

"Did you notice what happened over there?" She knew he hadn't, explaining it to him and pointing out the hawker.

Jack's brow furrowed. "Trouble with these low-life types. Hungry yet? Or do we have an aperitif?"

She'd resolved that it would have to be an early and alcohol-free meal if her father was to get home safely. She could see the plastic awning of a taverna not far off along the seafront road; Jack said he'd never tried it, suspecting the place to be too touristic, but Anna suggested they give it a go. "I can be your guinea pig, save Fi the effort." They found it already busy but got themselves a free table that had upon it a photographic menu in German.

"*Tintenfisch*, eh?" said Jack, squinting at the legend beside what Anna took to be a syndicated library image showing a perfectly arranged plate of fried squid. "Ought to mean haddock, don't you think?"

"Why? I don't get it."

"Tintin, Captain Haddock."

She couldn't help smiling. "Got any more gems like that?"

His head was still bowed over the menu. "They've also got Hanchen. But no Gretel, apparently."

"Sounds even worse." She leaned to look. "Is it chicken?"

"God knows. Here comes *garçon*."

The waiter offered them English menus but Jack instead pointed to a few items and ordered two beers, for which Anna chided him as soon as the waiter walked away.

Jack was unrepentant. "Beer doesn't count as alcohol. Well, hardly." Then he said, "You remember Tintin, don't you?"

She nodded. "Sure. I always found him a bit creepy though."

"You never said that when I used to read the books to you. If I'd known you were scared..."

"No, not like that. I just thought Tintin looked freaky. That quiff. And his trousers too short."

Jack appeared disappointed, as if a precious memory had suddenly become tainted. "I loved him when I was a kid."

"They're boys' stories, though. I can't remember a single woman."

"You copied the pictures. That was how I first realised what an amazing talent you had."

She was surprised by the compliment. "Really?"

"I've told you that before. Many times, I'm sure."

She could recall two figures, identical walrus-moustached men in black suits and bowler hats, mirror images of one another in a drawing fixed to the wall above her bed. "I liked the Thompson Twins."

"But they weren't twins," Jack said knowingly. "They were Thomson and Thompson."

Anna indulged her father's desire to appear knowledgeable, letting him say something while her attention drifted past his shoulder, beyond the painted wooden pillar of the taverna's awning to the street and in the further distance a row of trees planted alongside the promenade, everything in deepening evening light. How much better to be alone here.

Her father was singing, not loudly but as a way of explaining some point he must have decided to make. *"Hold me now, warm my heart..."* He was swaying with the tune, his hands beginning to rise at his sides as though he might soon begin snapping his fingers.

She laughed. "Dad-dancing looks even better when you do it sitting down."

"You do remember, though?"

"Before my time."

"The party? You would have been eight or nine."

"I suppose." She looked towards the restaurant interior. "You were probably right about this place."

"Never mind. A chance to spend some time together."

Her gaze swung back to her father who looked tired but contented. The beers arrived, the waiter placing two brown bottles on the table, removing the glass tumblers lodged on each and popping their caps.

"Efkaristo," said Jack.

"Parakaló," the waiter responded then departed.

"Well done," Anna said, filling her glass. "Got any more phrases? How about cheers?"

He began offering something in reply but quickly stopped, doubting himself. "It was on the tip of my tongue."

"Yammas, I think."

"That's the one." He clinked his bottle against her glass. *"Yammas,* mouse. Here's to health and happiness."

She couldn't tell if he was being ironic or sentimental. She didn't care for either. "That man who helped me today, Conrad. He did some painting for you."

Jack shook his head. "There's a fellow called Spiros who did everything for us. As a contractor, I mean. Must have hired this Conrad chap."

"He knows you, though. Said he could tell you're not well."

Her father gave a start. "What the devil's he on about? Thinking of someone else, I expect. I can't be the only Englishman on the island."

"He remembered the way to your house."

Jack rubbed his chin, suspicion growing. "I wonder if he saw a photo while he was doing whatever job it was that Spiros had given him. Good thing we don't have any items of value here, Fi wanted to bring a little sculpture she bought in Paris but I told her, people going in and out when we're away..."

"He spoke as if he really knew you."

"Then what exactly did he say, apart from my being ill, which must be plain enough to anyone?"

Anna couldn't recall anything specific. "I just felt it."

Jack swigged from his bottle then wiped his lip with the back of his hand. He'd grown cross. "I don't like the sound of him."

"He helped me."

"Did he make a pass at you?"

"Oh for God's sake."

"How old is he?"

"Let's leave it. He saw a photo in your house, he's a con artist, whatever, who cares. At least I didn't drown when that thing stung me."

"What did you tell him about me? Or about Fi?"

"Nothing."

"It seems you were discussing my health, though."

"No. I don't remember. Maybe I've got it wrong, he didn't say you looked sick. Please can we drop it, I wish I hadn't mentioned him, some old bum who painted your door."

"Did he say when?"

Anna could hold her patience no longer. "Dad, enough."

They fell into an uncomfortable silence; Anna could see the thoughts turning in her father's head, his groundless suspicion of someone who'd shown only kindness and concern. He was staring at the table, his palm upon it next to his unused glass and already half-empty beer bottle. She said softly, "Pain is inevitable, suffering isn't."

He looked up. "What?"

"I read it somewhere."

Their food arrived, bearing little resemblance to the images on the menu. The plates were smaller, the arrangements on them less neat. Jack pushed each dish towards her, encouraging her to select and taste first so as to decide what she preferred.

"I don't mind," she said. "This one's fine." The rubbery fried squid had probably come from a supermarket freezer.

Jack took a lamb cutlet. "Should I book three nights for you at the hotel?"

"I'll pay you back for tonight."

"I don't care about that. I'm asking if I'm likely to have the pleasure of your company again *chez moi*."

"Don't say it like that. Like you're hurt."

"But I am."

"No need to be. Fi's the problem, we know that."

"Fi isn't a problem, Anna. She's my wife. I love her. And I love you."

"Well. Thanks for that." She took a few mouthfuls then laid down her fork. "Did you really mean what you said before? About amazing talent?"

"Of course."

"But you meant when I was little. Do you think it now? Have I still got talent?"

He raised an eyebrow, sat back and steepled his hands thoughtfully. "I've no way of telling. If you'd invited me to your degree show, and if I'd come, and if I knew enough about art, then perhaps I'd have been impressed and would have told you so. But you didn't, I don't and I won't."

The old bastard, smart-arsed as ever. Anna got up from her chair. "I've had enough. Thanks for the meal."

He stared at her as if waiting for a follow-up or challenging her to depart without further comment. Finally he gave a shrug and with a dismissive flick of his fingers said, "Too bad but thanks for coming."

Anna turned and walked swiftly away, crossing the road to reach the waterfront with rage deepening inside her. She stood on the promenade watching the indifferent sea, wondering if Jack could see her from his seat, wondering if he cared, or perhaps was ordering the bottle of wine he'd have preferred to his beer. She refused to look back at the taverna, instead following the promenade to the square where she found an empty bench. Damn them both, she thought. Now she was free, a lone tourist answerable to no one, able to sit here for as long as she chose, idly admiring the view or discreetly scrutinising the people passing by. It first calmed, then gradually excited her, the thought of this liberty she'd been a fool not to embrace from the start. Why did she even come to Greece, when she could have gone alone to any place within reach of her limited budget? Her father was a useful resource, she needn't feel guilty about admitting it to herself, but there was also a cost for that resource, and it had proved too high. Still, she ought to have eaten more. Some pieces of squid and a few chips wouldn't keep her filled for long. She could find another taverna later. Or a supermarket.

She got up to stroll and soon found herself approaching the crouching hawker. Should she say anything to him about the fight she'd witnessed from her balcony? She paused to inspect the wares on his rug.

"All fine leather," he said robotically. "This fifteen euro, best quality."

He didn't remember her, she was only another white westerner, a possible customer. "Are you alright?"

He grinned up at her. "Yeah, cool. You like handbags?"

"I saw you getting hit."

He waved away the comment. "No trouble."

"It looked serious. He knocked you down."

"I lose balance," he said with a laugh. "Not hurt. He my friend."

In his sleeveless basketball shirt and blue shorts he looked lean but athletic, with muscular limbs that surely could have hit back powerfully. It might only have been play-fighting after all. It didn't look it but how was she to know?

"These ones very best. For you good price."

She wasn't looking at the bags he was indicating but at his

arm, his shoulder, the sweat beaded on his bare neck. What would it be like to have sex with this man she knew nothing about? And where did he say he was from? Some part of Africa she wouldn't be able to point to on a map. What language did he speak, what was his religion? It didn't matter, that was the beauty of it.

"Do you make these yourself?"

He rocked his head evasively. "Some." Then he looked up at her again. "You here alone?"

They were at a precipice of possibility, yet somehow his comment sullied it, made too imperative the decision that would bring it into being. How could she ever sleep with someone like him?

"Yes, I'm on my own."

"We go to a bar, I know one, nice place."

"No thanks."

"I show you the island. Any time. You ride my bike. We have fun."

It was another sales pitch, offering her an illusory bargain. "I have a boyfriend."

"Ha, but he no here. No treat you right. You beautiful, why he no here?"

"Long story."

He laughed. "We go for drink, you tell me."

His persistence was beginning to irritate. With a cordial but dismissive gesture she turned to walk on, hearing him call after her.

"'Nother time baby."

She headed away from the seafront, crossing the road to take the street uphill towards the more modern part of town she'd seen the previous night. She reached the square with its bland shop fronts, the place devoid of traffic and deserted apart from the cafe with its clientele of young locals on the small pavement terrace. She chose an empty table at the edge, wondering if it was waiter or counter service. Some minutes passed and she found herself observing a nearby couple seated side by side with arms around one another, foamy frappes half-finished in tall glasses before them, angled straws jutting in opposite directions like mirror images. Eighteen or nineteen years old, perhaps, in love or playing at being in love. That's the thing, Anna thought: it's not enough to love, you've also got to be in love with loving, in love with being in love: an infinite self-reflection, a mutual absorption. And that, she told herself as she watched them, is what you will never have: such puppy-dog devotion. When the thing stung her in the water: that was real, immediate, no thought necessary. How could she ever feel stung by love? Instead it was more like deciding what to order, trying to imagine what would satisfy her, and at what cost. She wasn't even thirsty.

A girl came out carrying drinks on a tray, must be the waitress, same age as most of the customers and casually dressed in a white tee-shirt and jeans, wearing thick-framed glasses that didn't suit her. Summer job possibly, Anna could imagine her studying engineering or biology. The girl served a group at the far side, turned and came unbidden towards Anna who was still undecided when the waitress arrived and said something in Greek.

"Brandy," Anna announced flatly. The girl nodded and without a word retreated to attend another table. Anna didn't particularly like brandy but what the hell.

A bus drove noisily into the square, an old and dirty looking vehicle she guessed must be some local service. It stopped at the far side and its pneumatic doors hissed open, depositing a handful of mostly elderly passengers but also a young guy in green cargo shorts and red scoop-neck tee shirt who looked like a tourist, sunglasses still propped on his forehead though it was well after nightfall. As the bus moved off he came across the square and reached the cafe where he paused to choose a table. His vision met Anna's and a brief smile seemed to flicker involuntarily on his face before he selected a seat a few yards from her that happened to be roughly in the direction of the teenagers she'd been watching. Now if she continued to observe the couple it would amount to looking at the guy. His view as he settled himself was towards the empty square where only an occasional motorbike or passing figure might further intrude upon whatever drink he was soon ordering from the spectacled waitress who quickly came to serve him. He was English, attempting to say something in Greek but finishing with laughter and a thank-you to the girl that had a note of flirtatiousness, and as she went inside his head swung so that he was glancing again at Anna while behind his shoulder the teenage couple were whispering their vain promises to each other, everything suddenly floating in Anna's imagination, this empty moment where only possibility or its exclusion could exist. With a sudden defiance she held his gaze, returned its beam as if picking out of darkness the startled eyes of a creature about to be shot. It was a decision as arbitrary as the drink she'd ordered.

"British?" she called to him.

"Yes. You too?"

That was all it took to initiate the trivial exchange of hometowns, the bartering of verbal beads and shells cementing first contact and establishing the lingua franca of the middle class abroad. She invited him to join her and he rose as the waitress strode out with their drinks on a tray; she looked unduly surprised by the new seating arrangement, this sudden friendship hatched under her watch. Flipping down two paper mats she deposited the identical tall glasses that held their drinks, each with a printed bill. His was beer; as the waitress departed he looked at Anna's in puzzlement. "What have you got there?"

"I asked for brandy."

"Well then, cheers." He clinked it where it stood. "You like your spirits?"

"In the right moment." She raised and sipped, felt the liquor's heat on her tongue and passing into her throat.

"I'm Matt."

"Lucy." Not the first lie she'd told that day.

"Pleased to meet you, Lucy."

He started talking about the trip he'd made to the other side of the island, something about a ruined temple, turned out to be no more than a few bits of rubble. She wasn't really listening, instead she was being Lucy, feeling new. He was on a sailing holiday with friends, she saw a yacht or HMS Victory but it couldn't be like that, sailing needn't mean sails, she supposed his group had hired something with an engine and a guy who knew how to steer it, they'd lie sunbathing on the deck all day.

"Where are your friends?" she asked, interrupting him.

Bit of a fall-out, he explained, cooped up on board, frayed tempers. "I asked to be dropped off for a couple of days. This happened to be the nearest place."

"Well, fancy that." Another burning sip of alcohol.

"So, what about you, Lucy?"

She said she was an artist and this intrigued him; he leaned closer as she spoke about her most recent exhibition, and with sudden inspiration she brought out her phone and laid it on the table having summoned an image of a framed canvas.

He was impressed. "That's fantastic." A clash of intense

fiery red and marine turquoise, a prominent strip of black, and on closest inspection the emergence of what might be a figure, a tree. He asked her, "What's it called?" and on registering her pause added, "Is that a stupid question?"

"Not at all. But names are tricky, sometimes a help and other times a distraction."

"That's so right."

He moved back for another mouthful of beer then looked again at the image of Lucy's painting. One that Anna could never have made.

"What would you call it?" she asked.

He laughed. "I don't know anything about art!"

"You don't need to."

"Alright. How about 'Storm at Sea'?"

That amused her, his philistine literalism. She'd got the measure of him by now. "And what do you do back home?"

He called it media relations, a term as abstract as Lucy's painting but made more specific when he explained that he worked at the House of Commons.

"How did you get into that?"

"I did some student journalism, edited the college newspaper."

"You studied politics?"

"PPE." He registered her puzzlement. "Philosophy, politics and economics."

"Oh. So you'll be Prime Minister some day?"

"Ha, who knows?" He moved his glass towards hers to propose another toast. "To future success. I expect you'll be carrying off the Turner Prize."

Her phone screen had timed out, she removed it from the table. "We can all dream."

"Thing is to make them real. Tell me," he said earnestly,

"as an artist what matters more to you, the commercial or the critical aspect?"

"You mean making wall decorations for rich clients or getting good reviews for stuff that nobody buys?"

"Right. Which is it?"

"Neither. It's about making meaning."

He nodded. "Expressing yourself."

"Making meaning," she repeated.

He pursed his mouth in a gesture of polite acquiescence and his eyes slipped briefly though not for the first time towards her breasts. Then at her half-finished drink. "Don't know how you can stomach that stuff."

She pushed it away. "Me neither. Not the time for it after all."

"Shall I get you something else?"

"No. I need to eat." She fixed him with her eyes and he understood.

"I know a good place. Not far from here." His bill lay moistened by dew from his glass. He lifted it, and her's, briefly considering the amounts then bringing out his wallet, soft-looking brown leather. As he opened it she saw the edge of a wad from which he drew a twenty euro note that he tossed onto the table.

"Let's go, then," she said, and as she rose from the table she felt the brandy hit her, a pleasant wave of mild intoxication. She had no idea how much her drink had actually cost, how much of a tip she was making Matt leave, but this was now a date and they both knew the rules.

"It's this way," he said, indicating a narrow pedestrian street leading uphill from the square they walked across. "Nothing remarkable but more authentic than the tourist places on the seafront."

"You've explored this town better than me. Or did Trip Advisor help you out?"

He laughed. "It's near my hotel, the proprietor suggested it. Expect the chef is his brother or something."

"No harm in a bit of nepotism."

"Indeed."

He hadn't taken her point; she was wondering how he'd landed his job in the Commons.

"The Greeks invented it, after all," he said.

"Nepotism? How so?"

"It's a Greek word surely."

"Or maybe Latin."

"Well, plenty there too."

The sloping street they ascended was mostly lined by old residential buildings with wrought-iron balconies. There was a small bakery, and a cake shop from which a smartly dressed lady emerged holding a large white box tied with ribbon.

"Must be someone's birthday," Anna said in a low voice as they passed. She wondered when her own new birthday should be, now that she was Lucy.

"The cake might be for tomorrow," Matt suggested. "It's a big day, apparently. National holiday."

That sounded like an inconvenience: shop closures and disruption; but Matt said it was a religious festival, some important day in the Orthodox calendar that would be worth seeing.

"Is that another thing they told you at your hotel? More helpful there than mine."

"There was a lady at the harbour when I arrived, fixed me up with a room. I expect I could have got something cheaper if I'd shopped around but it's only for a couple of nights until I get picked up."

She admired his indifference. "What if your friends don't want you back on board?"

"Oh, they will. Everyone needed a bit of space, that's all."

Did he really mean that the others needed space from him? This wasn't the time to find out as they'd now reached the restaurant, which appeared to be a substantial house standing discreetly away from the street behind iron railings, with a long outdoor eating area.

"This looks promising," she said as they passed through the gate and made their way to a table beside an olive tree with a white-painted trunk. Lanterns gave the terrace a softly romantic glow; the other diners were mostly couples, at tables spaced thinly around the ample garden.

"It'll do," Matt said, pulling a chair for her as a smart, handsome waiter arrived, gave her a broad smile of perfectly white teeth, and responded in fluent English to Matt's questioning about the day's specials. Was Lucy vegetarian? Did she have any special preferences? She decided not, and let Matt order a selection of small dishes for them to share. The waiter left; Matt looked up at the dark sky where stars were visible, then at her. "Do you like holidaying alone?"

She sensed a subtext. "I think of it as a working visit."

"Are you painting here? Sketching?"

She hesitated. "It doesn't happen like that. I'm looking. Getting ideas but not thinking too hard."

"Looking at, not looking for?"

"That's a good way to put it." It sounded like he understood Lucy better than she did.

"Then when you get home you'll work it all out on canvas?"

"Exactly."

He nodded appreciatively. "Must be a wonderful life." Pushing a finger on the smooth wooden table top, he asked,

"You prefer not to bring your significant other?"
    "What makes you think I have one?"
    "Don't you?"
    "No. You?"
    "Too busy."
    The waiter brought the white wine they'd ordered, pouring for both of them. She thought the brandy must have lost all effect by now but when they toasted, and she sipped the cool liquid, she felt a quick and welcome return of giddiness. She knew that Matt and Lucy would sleep together, there was no doubt or tension, instead a sense of dispassionately watching it unfold as if on a screen. She decided to throw Matt's previous question back at him. "Do you prefer holidaying alone? Is that why you left the boat?"
    "I suppose. I like both. Having people around is... convenient. Not all the time, though."
    "I feel the same way."
    She didn't like him, nor find him as attractive as the waiter, but he interested her, and that would be reason enough to spend the night with him at his hotel, as was sure to happen. Over the next hour they spoke of places they had seen, films and music, while a succession of dishes arrived providing unobtrusive punctuation. Having finished the first bottle they started a second. She was enjoying this holiday away from being Anna.
    He spoke about his family; she wasn't too attentive but gathered that his father was an academic, his mother something medical. He touched on politics; testing her out, she supposed. He said he'd voted Remain.
    "My side won," she said.
    "You voted for Brexit?"
    "Sure."
    He looked suddenly disappointed, crestfallen, as if this

arbitrary polarity were going to rob him of the sex he expected. "Why?" he asked.

"Why not?"

Now he was puzzled, almost on the verge of anger. He quaffed his wine, took the last piece of fried courgette and quickly swallowed it, then said, "It's a decision that'll resonate for the rest of the century."

"Yes, because it's change."

"For the better though?"

"Who knows?" It was like pulling the wing off a fly, she could see him squirming. How often did they ever hear this sort of thing in the House of Commons media team? She said, "Do you hate me now?"

"Of course not." He laughed, nervously. "I'm a bit surprised, that's all. But then, you're an artist." He attempted another toast. *"Vive la révolution."* His glass stayed poised mid-air in his grasp, unmet by hers; so he sipped, returned it to the table and fell silent.

"Yes, I'm an artist," she said. "I like randomness, chance. People think they can control things but how much choice do any of us really have? We can't decide the weather or when we'll die or if people like us."

"We can have an influence though. Maybe not the weather. Unless you count global warming."

She tipped back her head and looked up at the clear sky. "Are they the same in Greece?"

"What?"

"The stars. I heard someone say they're different."

"They can't be. Stars are stars, wherever you are."

"But they look different."

He too was gazing upwards. "I thought you meant are they actually different stars from British ones."

"Ha! I'm not stupid."

"Of course not." Another wing tugged from his body.

"Where's Senegal?"

"What?"

"I met someone from Senegal."

"Is that who said about the stars?"

"Maybe. So where is it?"

He told her it was in west Africa, a former French colony, its capital the coastal city of Dakar which he'd never visited but would like to. They were both still looking at the sky.

"I think they'd be different stars in Senegal," she said.

"I'll go and see some day."

"When you're Prime Minister?"

"Before then. When I can still be a tourist, strike out on my own..."

"And pick up unsuspecting defenceless women."

"Exactly."

It was time to move on. He rose to go to the toilet, settle the bill, whatever. She suddenly thought of her father and wondered which of the two of them, Jack or herself, had drunk more this evening. Had he driven home? She might have trouble standing. She looked towards the restaurant doorway and could see Matt at the desk handing over something, cash or his card, couldn't tell at this distance and with her vision now a little blurry. Then disappearing further inside. He had his future mapped out like a motorway, not a career in politics as such, he'd said, she couldn't remember what. Only knew that it sounded so certain, as if it had already happened and he was giving her the summary. And her? Fuck knows, she thought.

He came back out, walking confidently towards their table, steadily, as if the wine hadn't touched him, or had all evaporated from his system.

"Thanks for a lovely meal," she said as he approached. "Now I'm tired."

"Me too," he said, and hesitated. She stood, which proved easier than she'd expected, and somehow found herself walking arm in arm with him, bumping against his shoulder as she tottered occasionally.

"Drunk enough yet?" he asked jovially.

"Maybe not yet."

"How about a nightcap?"

His hotel was just around the corner, a bright foyer more modern and up-market, to her inebriated vision, than her own place, though nothing too fancy. He guided her upstairs, rattled his key in the door to his room and then they were inside, bed looked enormous, a double uncovered except by a thin sheet. He closed the door, there were a couple of chairs but she stood waiting, leaning against a desk strewn with small items as he turned from the entrance then took hold of her and they were kissing. Hadn't expected anything quite so abrupt. It felt good.

He released her, kicked off his sandals and sat on the edge of the bed, his bare right leg extending like an invitation. His shorts bulging. He patted his hand on the mattress, gesturing her to join him.

"What about that nightcap?" she asked.

"I almost forgot." Calmly he stepped to the other side of the bed and opened the dark brown wooden cabinet there, bringing out a bottle. "Duty free on the way out," he said, coming and placing it on the desk, then he went to the en suite where he said he'd get glasses. She heard the rush of its extractor fan as he entered and switched on the light. A half-full litre of whisky, twelve-year old single malt, looked expensive. On the desk a couple of pairs of sunglasses, one wayfarer style, the other aviator. A small, plain brown leather money purse with a long strap, from the African hawker or someone like him. A paperback book, she angled her head enough to see that it was by someone she'd never heard of. Thriller, maybe. She heard him taking a piss. Some loose change, British coins. A black notebook, his diary she expected, and heard the toilet flushing. She lifted the diary, opened and found that only the first few pages were filled, a record of places where the boat had landed. There really was a boat, then. He was running the tap, too long for handwashing, must be rinsing glasses. She put down the logbook, didn't much care where he'd been or where he was going. Turned and saw him emerge with the glasses held high in each hand, no tee shirt now, only his shorts.

"Bring the bottle," he said, sitting on the bed.

She unscrewed it, came and poured two generous measures then put the bottle on the floor and took her glass. She sat beside him, her turn now to propose the toast. "Cheers, Mr Politician."

"Ha, I told you already, I'm in media."

"Whatever."

He kissed her, she withdrew her lips but let him keep his arm round her, she liked the feel of it. She took two mouthfuls of Scotch, hardly noticing the second, then they were lying on the bed, must have put their drinks on the floor or somewhere, he was moving on top of her and fondling her breast like a teenager. They were going to have sex, she didn't care particularly but thought how funny it all was and did her best not to laugh, especially at the way he sheathed himself so fastidiously. The alcohol made her head pound, the satisfaction she felt was in having chosen to be here, in making all of this happen. When he got up this morning he didn't know it was going to be his lucky day.

He finished, rolled off her and she went to the bathroom,

again that intrusive roar of its extractor fan and the harsh light in her eyes. Then they were lying beside each other and maybe they talked, she couldn't remember when she woke up and found herself in daylight alone on the bed, naked beneath the thin sheet.

"Fuck."

She lay on her back running her hands through her hair, a dull ache pulsing in her skull. Looking towards the en suite she could see that its door was open, no light or sound within, he wasn't there. She sat up, pulled the sheet aside, saw her panties on the floor, reached them with her foot and dragged them closer, lifted and put them on. She needed a glass of water, the one on the bedside table still had whisky in it. Taking it to the bathroom she poured it down the sink, refilled, then watched herself in the mirror while she quenched her thirst.

"God, I look like shit."

She was Anna again. And what about Matt, had he maybe checked out, left her to settle the room bill? No, she emerged from the bathroom and there was his crap still lying on the desk, jacket hanging from the door, all his things in place. She went to the desk and saw on it a hotel notepad on whose top page he'd scrawled a message. *Gone for breakfast. Join me if you can!* A couple of x's and a smiley.

No, Lucy wouldn't be sharing his pot of coffee and basket of bread. Anna could grab something later when she felt less queasy. She lifted her remaining clothes from the floor and quickly dressed, then looked again at the desk, his note with its childish handwriting. And that paperback, thought it was a thriller but perhaps not. There was something wedged inside as bookmark, she found it to be a postcard, white buildings overlooking a perfect blue sea, the other side written and addressed, awaiting a stamp. Who the hell still sends postcards?

Dear Gran – Thought you'd like this lovely view. Trip is wonderful, boat very comfortable. Losing track of where we've been! Will tell you everything when I see you. Love from Megan xxx (Matt sends his too!).

So that was the fall-out. Maybe the book was in his bag by mistake when he landed here for his couple of days of girlfriend-free R&R. Her curiosity aroused, Anna thought to inspect the blue cotton jacket on the door, but the pockets were empty. She tried the wardrobe and found at the bottom of it a suitcase and a small gym bag, unzipped with only a few items inside. She pulled out a black cloth-covered wallet and opened it. Here were his passport, House of Commons pass, a couple of other documents of no interest except to confirm the identity of the man she could barely recall fucking. And a wad of euros, lots of twenties, maybe a grand or two in all, held together by an elastic band. This was a moment of genuine decision at last. She ran her finger along the bundle's edge and selected where to pinch, not thick enough that he'd miss anything without actually counting, in fact hardly anything at all, couldn't be more than a dozen notes that she rolled in her fist while hurriedly returning the wallet, restoring everything to order. Five minutes later she was walking quickly past the dining room entrance without looking round, through the lobby, seeing the door ahead of her and the bright sunshine of freedom as she stepped into the street and away, smiling.

He was a cheat and so was she: they were quits. He'd go back to the room and see she'd scarpered, most likely think nothing of it but maybe check, find nothing amiss. Anna headed downhill, past the restaurant where they'd eaten, its garden looking stark and unromantic in daylight, then to the square where the cafe terrace was empty. She suddenly wondered if at some point they'd exchanged phone numbers. Surely not, but didn't he ask for it when they were having dinner? Or did she only show him that photo of the painting? She stopped, brought out her phone and saw no new contacts, no messages except one from her father. *Good seeing you. Hope the hotel works out.* She carried on down towards the seafront, the taverna where she'd been with Jack last night was open and offering "Fuel English Brekfast". She chose the same pavement table as before, ordered black coffee and an omelette, and looked towards the sea. A few old men were fishing from the promenade, their long rods rooted to the ground and prodding skywards while they smoked and talked, waiting for good luck. A banal way to pass the time but Anna couldn't imagine what else those blokes might do with their time except perhaps shout at their wives. Somebody was setting up a stall, looked like toys he was selling, cheap coloured whirly things, but she couldn't see the African. What did he say his name was? Did he tell her? She thought of the night she didn't have, with him instead of Matt. Those two events, one real but past, the other still a possibility, felt equally weightless in her mind. There is only now, she thought. Nothing else has any existence.

The waiter arrived, tried to engage her in conversation but she didn't feel like small-talk, said everything was fine though the omelette looked like rubber and the bread when she touched it felt stale. At least her coffee appeared acceptable, dribbling at the lip of its steel pot after she'd filled her cup. It was hot and bitter and exactly what she needed.

Matt would have realised by now that she'd gone. Anna saw him opening the wardrobe, reaching into the gym bag, counting his cash and calling her a fucking bitch whore while out at sea his girlfriend is already sunbathing on the deck in her bikini. Matt won't go to the police, Anna decided. Too much hassle for the sake of a few euros and not worth the risk that his girl would find out. Megan, Anna remembered, writing to her Gran and putting it in a book she might not even have missed, on Matt's desk where he can see that it's been moved and is saying to himself: I'll fucking find her and kill her. Or laughing, that's what Anna would have done in his shoes. She'd have admired the chutzpah, acknowledged the transactional nature of everything that happened between them. By taking his money, she was reassuring him that he'd never hear from her again; that if she was to see him here on the island with Megan and his mates there would be no flicker of recognition, no moment of awkwardness. She'd sent him a message and done him a favour. Some food and drink and a little cash: he'd had a cheap night.

Let's just suppose, though, that he reported her. How many young English women answering her description must there be on this island right now, she wondered. Too many for the police to try searching, surely. They had better things to do, even if it was only playing backgammon at their silly little station, wherever it was. Still, Anna would need to keep her head down, at least for a day or two until Matt got picked up to sail away over the horizon with his golden friends, tomorrow's politicians and captains of industry. Some day he might be making his speech outside Ten Downing Street with frumpy Megan at his side and he'd be silently wishing he could be back here on this island in that one night that was his moment of freedom.

"Hey, Anna."

Nearly choked on her coffee, male voice making her take the cup from her lip and turn her head to see who'd seen her while passing, not Matt thank God but that old hippie, name took a moment to come back to her.

"Conrad, hey."

"Good breakfast?" Nodding at the omelette she'd barely touched.

"So-so." A thought in her mind. "Want to join me?"

"Only if you're not just being polite."

"I owe you one. For what you did."

He came and pulled a chair opposite her. "You don't owe a thing." He sat and turned the laminated menu that lay on the table. "Can't say I've ever tried this place."

"That doesn't surprise me."

The waiter came out and Conrad spoke to him in what sounded like fluent Greek, presumably asking what they had, specifying exactly what he wanted; or maybe the two of them were merely having a chat, Conrad looking younger, more intelligent than she'd remembered. She guessed he was in his fifties. The waiter left them.

"So, Anna, how's your holiday going?"

She described the fall-out with Jack and Fi. "I stayed in a hotel last night."

"Any good?"

"Over-priced."

"Hmm." He pondered the situation as the waiter returned and placed a glass of water before him, and there was a further short exchange. Then Conrad said to Anna, "I could find you a place, pretty basic of course."

"I only need a roof over my head."

"At this time of year, not even that. But if you want, I'll get you something. Probably not here in the town, if that's alright."

She readily agreed, and Conrad said it would take little effort to arrange. "Meet me back here at noon," he said, took a sip of his water then stood up. "See you later."

He walked away and Anna pushed at the remaining pieces

of omelette on her plate, lifting a forkful and judging it even less appetising now that it had cooled. Some coffee remained in her cup, she dipped a piece of bread in it and ate that, satisfied by its softness. When the waiter emerged to attend to new customers at another table she caught his attention and gestured for the bill. He came over. "It's all okay."

"Paid?"

"Finish okay."

She'd seen no money change hands but Conrad had fixed it and she didn't need to understand how. Her phone showed it to be nearly ten o'clock, she didn't know what time she'd need to check out of her hotel but didn't want to risk being charged for another night. She went straight there and found a teenage boy behind the desk who looked puzzled when she asked and he inspected the register.

"Miss, you're booked for tonight."

She was sure her father had only paid for one night and wondered who was mistaken, herself or the youth, but said nothing while he pulled a couple of memos from the spike where they'd been skewered and examined the messages on them. "It's booked," he confirmed. "There was a phone call earlier."

Must be karma, she decided. After all the shit she'd endured, the world was now rewarding her through the actions of intermediaries: her dad who owed her anyway, Conrad who didn't lose anything by helping her, and Matt who could afford to lose what he would never miss. "Thanks," she said and went up to her room that she had only seen briefly last night. She'd left the shutters open, the interior was bright and stark, and she dropped onto the unused bed, feeling her head spin with sleeplessness.

A few minutes later her phone sounded; it was a text from Jack, wanting to know if she would stay longer at the hotel.

She tossed the phone aside, sat up and looked towards the full-length windows that were casting pure white light onto the wall. She remembered that the balcony outside was too small for sitting, but she could position herself just inside and sunbathe. She got up and drew the desk chair then opened the windows wide, blinking in the glare. Her sunglasses and lotion were in her bag, soon she was fully equipped for idleness, seated with a view of the seafront. The promenade seemed busy, she remembered that Matt had said it was a holiday, and there as always sat the African man displaying his leather goods, his patience and optimism outstripping any chance of genuine success. There, too, was the toy seller, and some kind of snack stand, and beyond the morning crowd the calm, indifferent sea.

Her eyelids had drooped when a car horn woke her and she saw that a man was talking to the African. She was sure it was the one who'd argued with him before. Dark curly hair, smartly dressed in a long-sleeved white shirt and light-brown chinos. The African had called him his friend but he was clearly the boss, pointing this way and that, explaining or giving orders while the hawker stayed crouching beside his rug of goods. The boss became more agitated, wringing his hands impatiently then suddenly kicking at the rug, sending items flying that the African scurried to gather while his master calmly walked away and eventually out of view.

"Poor bastard."

Her ringtone played from the bed. She considered ignoring it but rose from her chair, saw that it was some unknown number calling and responded before it had quite occurred to her that it could be Matt, the police or anyone else she wouldn't want to speak to. It was Fi, her voice clipped. "Did you get Jack's text? He's wondering about your plans."

"My plans?"

"The hotel."

"Oh. Yes, it's fine."

"You want him to pay for another night? Probably cheaper if he can book the rest of the week. Though I don't suppose that makes a difference to you."

"I don't know about the rest of the week."

"Have you heard about the boat?"

"What boat?"

Fi explained that a group of refugees had got into difficulty that morning, most had been rescued, not all. "I think they might be putting them in hotels so it'd be as well to book ahead in case."

"I don't think that's necessary."

"Please yourself, Anna, I'm only the messenger."

She hung up, and Anna wondered why her father hadn't rung instead. Too afraid of his own daughter, perhaps? Too hungover? And the refugee story, Fi's tactic to force Anna to commit to staying at the hotel. Probably bollocks. "Screw you," she said to the phone.

Further rest was impossible. She got herself ready and went downstairs, her sandals flapping on the marble tiles as she passed the reception desk where the teenage boy had been replaced by an elderly man she ignored. Crossing the street to the seafront she bought herself a cheese pie and stood eating it, flakes of pastry blowing from her hand. She looked across and saw the hawker still in place, he hadn't noticed her but was tending his wares, so once she'd finished the pie and thrown its tissue into the litter bin beside the stall she walked over, and as she approached he looked up.

"Hey," he said with a broad smile.

"How's business?"

"Good, man, very good. You want a drink? Bar near here."

"Not today."

"Ha, 'nother time baby." He waved a hand over his display of goods. "For you best price. This ten euro, I give you for five."

She pointed instead to a handbag. "How much is that one?"

He rolled his head. "Best quality, twenty."

"You can't do me a deal?"

"Already best deal."

"And how much of that do you keep after your boss gets paid?"

The hawker looked puzzled, startled or defensive: it was hard to tell which. "No have boss."

"The guy who shouted at you, kicked your stuff."

"Michaelis? He my friend. Lose temper sometime. No harm." His expression grew earnest. "You see him, no speak. Is private."

"Does he run this business?"

"Private, baby." He grinned again. "You and me we go for ride, maybe I tell you."

She shook her head and brought out her purse. "I'll buy the bag." From Matt's money she extracted twenty euros and handed it to him.

"You make good choice. And a belt? She matching."

"No thanks." She tried to remember whatever Matt had told her about Senegal; they spoke some other language there, French perhaps? The guy's accent was sort of French sounding. "Do you like doing this?" she asked him.

"It's the life."

"I suppose so."

Yesterday she'd imagined having sex with him; now the fantasy that struck her was of reaching back into her purse,

144

pulling out another twenty euro note and giving it as a present. She hesitated, challenged by his continuing smile and then defeated by it.

"Bye," she said, and went back across the road to her hotel. It was nearly time to meet Conrad and she had to make ready to quit her room. She said nothing to the elderly desk clerk: if there was a change of plan she might still need to fulfil her booking tonight. Instead she quickly packed and walked back out wheeling her case with a swift confidence that drew no comment.

She reached the taverna a little before twelve, sat at what already seemed her usual table on the pavement terrace, and ordered a coffee. Over at the promenade there appeared to be some sort of preparation going on, people gathering around a small platform beneath a white tented pavilion where a sound system was issuing music of an old-fashioned kind, a song from an earlier generation rising and falling in volume as it carried through the warm air, over the voices of people and the raucous traffic. A traditional folk ballad, Anna guessed, perhaps a national favourite, patriotic or religious. The crackling tannoy and sinuous, exotic melody brought to mind the Muslim call to prayer as she'd heard it in so many news reports from places torn by violence, though here all was peaceful. The waiter came with her coffee and she asked him what was going on.

"Holiday today."

"Sure, but why?"

"August fifteen."

"What's so special about the date?"

All he could offer were some Greek words that meant nothing to her; he didn't know how to explain it in English. With a friendly shrug he left her, and a few minutes later a crowd appeared on the promenade, walking slowly and surrounding some object held aloft as it was carried. She couldn't see from such a distance what it might be, only that it caught the sunlight every so often, a bright metallic gleam. The procession reached the pavilion where the object was then positioned on a plinth. She was still observing the inscrutable preparations when Conrad arrived and sat down with her.

"Do you know what's happening over there?" she said. He repeated exactly what the waiter had told her, August fifteen, then explained it was a religious day.

"Something to do with the Virgin Mary, they bring an icon from the church and set it up beside the sea. Good luck for fishermen, they reckon."

It must be the same precious icon she'd seen on her first night. "You mean they're going to have a service?"

"Oh, I expect there'll be a bit of chanting and incense-waving, but it's more like a party. The Greeks know how to do these things in the right style. Anyway, I've got a place for you to stay, I'll drive you over, we'll stop at mine first. I see you've got your case, I guess you're all set."

"Ready if you are," she said, pushing away her coffee then rising to go inside where she paid and visited the toilet. She came back out into the bright daylight, dropping her sunglasses over her eyes, and saw Conrad's dusty battered car revving at the kerbside, the motor still running as he got back out to help her with her case which had to be wedged in with an assortment of scrap metal, wood, household junk.

"Having a clear-out?" she asked.

"It's others doing that. I can use all this." As they drove he told her about the accommodation he proposed, a house he'd been decorating. "Belongs to a guy on the island who I guess plans renting it to tourists, been standing empty a while. Pretty sure no one's likely to bother you there."

"What if the owner shows up?"

"House is one more business deal, he's got plenty others to occupy him. Still, if you do get rumbled, you obviously don't say anything about me."

"Obviously."

Conrad laughed. "Just run."

They first reached his dilapidated cottage where she helped carry some of his worthless booty inside, and she wondered why he hadn't offered her his floor to sleep on. After all, he appeared completely unembarrassed by the squalor of his existence. What mattered more to him, it seemed, was his solitude.

"What'll you do with this?" she asked, depositing a broken wooden chair beside a small collection of dented metal pots and tubs.

"Come and I'll show you."

She followed him back out and around the house to a yard she hadn't seen previously, a patch of bare hard ground dotted with sculptural assemblages. They were crude, abstract, amateurish – little more than an exercise in creative recycling – but she respected his effort.

"Didn't realise you're an artist."

"Isn't everyone?"

"Do you sell any?"

"Don't need to."

She paced among them, trying to decide what she thought. The largest was as tall as herself, an intricate tangle involving a twisted iron bed frame rising from a pair of rusted, tireless car wheels, and impregnated with an assortment of small bottles, wooden fragments, plastic cartons, held together with glue or wire or gravity or maybe simply faith, she couldn't tell.

"What would you call this one?" she asked. "If you had to give it a name."

He shook his head. "Wouldn't make a difference to me, whatever I called it. Want to suggest?"

She stroked her chin pensively. "It makes me think of a family." Snared among the bedsprings she could see broken dolls, items of cheap jewellery. "Or a tree."

"There you go: family tree."

"I'm not good with names." She paused, then said, "Is Conrad your real name?"

"It's the one I use. That's as real as any name gets."

"I was thinking of that guru you mentioned."

"Daido in Manchester?"

"That's the one. Suppose I was wondering if you decided at some point to be a new person."

"I do that every day. Whole world keeps remaking itself. Can't stand in the same river twice, doesn't matter a damn what you call it."

She nodded slowly, thinking how sad it was that the only way to reach enlightenment, apparently, was to drop out and live like a tramp, alone in a junkyard.

He said, "How's your leg, by the way?"

"That? Oh, fine. Your lotion fixed it straight away." She moved to another sculpture which involved pieces of broken ceramic tiles, circuit boards and wires, light bulbs. "Everything's subjective, isn't it?"

"Sure is."

"People pay thousands for things like this, if they're by the right person. Someone with a name."

The yard was in full sunshine; Conrad suggested they move to the covered terrace where he left her sitting while he went inside to fetch them both some juice. Anna gazed up at the thick vine overhead and when Conrad came back out, placing two glasses on the flimsy table, he said, "Any wasps?"

"None that I can see."

He sat down and took a sip. "Why do you think it happened? That thing in the sea."

"Getting stung? I don't know; wrong place, wrong time."

"Stuff happens for a reason. We don't know you were stung."

She was peeved. "You think I imagined it?"

"Of course not. Something happened. It hurt." He left the comment hanging for a while. "That's what you told me yesterday."

She knew what he meant. "And that's why I got stung?"

"Who knows? But now we're here." He paused again. "Want to tell me about it?"

She toyed with her phone, rubbing its edge pensively. "My life's complicated."

"Is there a way to simplify?"

"I suppose coming here was a way of trying, though it isn't working too well."

He nodded sympathetically. "Maybe you need to let go of something. You know, have a clear-out, discard things you no longer need. It's what I do."

"I was thinking more of feelings."

"Me too."

"Like in your sculptures? Are they how you let go?"

"Sometimes." He ruminated, and Anna looked again at her phone. She unlocked the screen and brought up the image she'd shown Matt last night.

"What do you make of this painting?" she asked. He peered but found it hard to see, even under the shade of the veranda, so she cupped her hand to make it more visible. "Reckon it's any good?"

He laughed. "Eggs and fish are good or bad, not art."

"But do you like it?"

"If it helps me out, sure. Don't see how, though. I think what you're saying is that you made it and if I say it's good and I like it then it means that you're good and I like you. Is that right?"

"I didn't paint it. Just wondering."

"Or maybe testing me a different way. Well, it doesn't much matter if I think you're a good egg or a bad fish. I like you. If painting makes you happy, then paint."

"What about all the unhappy artists in the world? What if I was Van Gogh?"

Conrad rocked his head, considering the question. "He was troubled alright. That time I got stabbed in Amsterdam, they took me to the hospital and I remember being wheeled in, there was this picture on the wall, one of his paintings, lots of yellow in it. Made me realise it wasn't my time yet. I guess he might have thought that when he painted it: not yet, not quite. But some day."

"Everyone thought he was mad."

"Now everyone thinks he was a genius, even people who only know his name and haven't seen anything he painted. But who cares what people think?"

She still felt irritation over the doubt he'd expressed. "What you say is easy enough as long as you live like a hermit. Anyone can be a saint that way."

Conrad agreed. "Who'd want to be a saint? And that thing they do in monasteries, hitting themselves. There's a word for it..."

"Flagellation?"

"That's the one. Bad idea. Don't you think there's a lot

150

of folks beat themselves up? And over what? I sure used to, especially when Pierre was little. My son, cute little fellow. Thought I was going to be in this perfect happy family forever. Then things change, of course. As Pierre grew I gradually came to realise he didn't like me as much as I thought. His mother and I, we were no longer living together though we still got on well enough. But this boy I'd loved so much, now he was becoming a person, his own self... Well, he hated me, pure and simple. Yeah, I really beat myself up over it."

"Where is he now?"

"No idea."

"That's sad."

"No, it's life."

She watched him drain the rest of his juice. "Are we leaving now for the other place?"

He shook his head and returned his empty glass to the table. "Something I'd like to do first. Come inside." They both rose and entered. The cluttered interior was dark, cool and oddly refreshing, despite resembling a scrap merchant's storeroom. "I'd like you to take something."

"A souvenir?"

"If you want to call it that."

She looked around and spotted an item she'd seen previously, a blue and white plastic toy boat. "I'll have this. Thanks."

He was lifting a couple of objects; a square metal box and something else. "Let's go back to the yard."

They returned to his sculpture collection where she realised that what he was holding was a can of liquid and a cigarette lighter. "What are you going to do?" she said.

Conrad waved an arm towards his works. "Pick one."

"What are you going to do?"

He was perfectly calm, as if about to carry out some unremarkable task that formed part of his daily routine. "The universe is a circle," he said. "A great chain of living and dying, giving and taking. Every moment is a link."

"Is that what Daido taught you?"

"It's what I learned from Pierre. Daido taught me there is only One, not Many. No Difference, only Alike. Which shall we burn?"

Choice was irrelevant; she pointed randomly and Conrad walked to the place she indicated, a monstrosity fashioned from broken chairs and a car bumper. He opened the can and poured, carefully and generously distributing the fuel like salad dressing, shaking out the final drop then standing back and crouching, his arm stretched along the ground to the bottom edge of the sculpture. As soon as he sparked the lighter the pile erupted and he leapt back. Even in the intense sunshine she could feel heat from the pyre's blue and yellow flames. He came and stood with her.

"You do this often?"

"Not particularly."

"Better be careful not to let it spread."

"It won't, not over bare earth."

"If pieces blow..."

"It happens how it's meant to."

Both watched as the heap consumed itself, sending up black smoke, gradually collapsing. Anna found it thrilling at first, tedious after a couple of minutes, but eventually – kneeling with the toy boat in her hands as she watched – soothing.

"Think of what you'd like to throw there," said Conrad. She visualised multiple immolations. "Will you give away something today?" he added.

"I already did."

"Then everything's balanced."

When it had burned low enough he went to fetch some water and a dirty rug that he used to smother and quench the flames, stamping the charred fragments flat and forcing billows of steam and ash from beneath the carpet's frayed edges. Satisfied that it was finished, he declared it time to go to the car and set off.

The boat was on her lap as they drove. He'd found it on one of the beaches, some tourist kid must have lost it. "Or maybe it got washed up," he suggested. "You know, wreckage."

"Refugees?"

"It happens."

Jostled by the uneven road and with the wind beating her face through the open side window, she imagined the child who'd played with the battered toy. A hypothetical human being, neither alive nor dead. It disturbed her. "I don't think I want to keep this."

"Toss it away, then."

In her mind she saw it fly out of the car and smash onto the hot asphalt. "I'll leave it with you."

"I asked you to take something."

"Do you mind if I don't?"

"No, why should I?"

Again he had annoyed her, and they were both silent for a few minutes, journeying inland to the higher, more barren part of the island, occasionally passing roadside shrines like the one her father had indicated. She hoped they weren't going to arrive anywhere near Jack and Fi's place.

"Who exactly is this guy you're working for?" she asked.

"The house owner?"

"He's Greek isn't he?"

"Sure, grew up here as far as I know. Car hire business,

other interests, like they do." He tapped his nose with a laugh.
"All about making a buck and dodging the tax man."

"And you're fixing up his house?"

"One of them. Don't ask me how he came by it or what
he'll do with it. I'm assuming it'll be a holiday let but for all I
know he might have some babe he's going to install there for
whenever he's bored with his wife."

"He sounds like a gangster."

"Just a regular guy. Don't know if he has a wife. His
brother owns that taverna we were at. In this place everyone's
connected, one way or another. Like it or not."

"It would drive me nuts."

"Sometimes drives them crazy too. At least I get to choose
my connections." He swung onto a side-road and soon
afterwards in the distance a hillside village came into view.
"That's our place over there, Pyrgos."

It made her think of pyres, purging. "Does the name mean
anything?"

"Tower. There's a ruined one, think it was a minaret."

"And you're certain I'll be okay staying at that man's
house?"

"All the time I've been working there, I've never seen him.
Only in the town. I've slept there a couple times and had no
issue, he knows I do a good job. No reason for him to come
looking before I'm finished."

They entered the village: a few unattractive buildings
strung either side of a street where an old men's cafe was the
only sign of activity. Up a bend into a steep narrow lane of
houses whose plastered walls looked grey and cracked. Conrad
stopped the engine, his vehicle almost filling the lane's width.
They'd parked beside a door of frosted glass and painted
wrought iron. Conrad got out, went to the door and opened

it, unlocked. Anna followed after retrieving her suitcase and found herself in a white, empty room smelling of fresh paint.

"Is it still wet anywhere?" she asked, approaching the window and tentatively reaching towards its frame.

"All dry now. Come and I'll show you where to sleep."

There were two rooms; the back one was cluttered with Conrad's decorating materials and a bare mattress.

"That's it?" she asked.

"Kitchen through there, taps work. Toilet behind, works too. Out the rear door there's a place to sit. Even got a seat." He gave her a moment to consider. "Want to stay, or do I drive you back to the town?"

She gathered her thoughts. "Fine, yes it's fine. Thanks." Then brought out her phone.

"You might not get a connection inside the house. Street maybe."

"Can I call you if there's a problem?"

"Nope." He smiled. "I don't have one of those gadgets. I'll drop by tomorrow, give you a ride somewhere if you need. Otherwise people here could help you out, say if you're hitching to town. Might even be a bus."

Anna bit at her lower lip, wondering if she'd been right to sacrifice a hotel room for this. Her phone showed no signal.

"See you tomorrow, then?" he asked, walking back through the apartment to the front door, still ajar.

"Yes, expect so. Oh, is there a key?"

He raised his eyebrows quizzically. "Think you'll need one?"

"I suppose not. If anyone asks me what I'm doing... If the owner..."

"Don't worry," Conrad insisted, stepping outside. "People here look after each other but they also know when not to interfere. And I told you, Michaelis has plenty other things to keep him occupied."

She stood watching from the doorway as Conrad drove up the lane and away round its bend, the strains of his engine remaining long within earshot while he circuited and eventually left the village's tight maze. She pondered whether to unpack but realised it would only mean moving objects from one featureless box into a larger one. The mattress had looked mercifully clean and any odour from it would be masked by the pervasive aroma of solvents. Still, the thought of it made her queasy, in fact all of this was a mistake. Why did she have such an uncanny knack for making bad choices?

A walk seemed the best way to avoid claustrophobia. The village proved every bit as dead as it had first looked from the car; a path took her uphill between patches of low thorny shrub and coarse red earth, finally to a bare and flat-topped stony crag with a view of the distant sea. Where was the tower Conrad mentioned? She could see no sign of it among the houses below, and wondered if it might have stood here on the hilltop, commanding everything around. But you surely couldn't put any kind of building on the smooth, weather-polished rock beneath her sandalled feet. Marble, she guessed, or was it limestone? Perhaps in ancient times there'd been a temple here, a little local Parthenon. Vanished people, long dead and forgotten as we all eventually are. So it didn't matter diddly-squat about that money, or anything else. Whether you're a saint or a bastard, it's all the same in the end; and it consoled her, the merciless equality that also gave meaning to the hours before and after this moment. Time that could be as densely full as her unopened suitcase or as vacuous as the unlocked apartment where she'd left it: time that was like money, to be spent this way or that but ultimately without any value except possibility of exchange.

Her stomach rumbled as she descended. She went to the cafe she'd seen, entering to find a faded, brown-panelled room hung with large black and white photographs of heroic-looking elderly men who might have been politicians or former proprietors. The present one understood no English, however sign language was sufficient to procure some bread and salad with a tin flask of wine which infused Anna with a sense that she was enjoying herself.

The sunlight made her head throb when she emerged. It was mid-afternoon, the hottest time of day. Returning to the apartment, she found the atmosphere stuffy, the smell of paint oppressive. There was shade in the back yard; a square of cracked concrete, high-walled on either side, with an old wooden chair as its only adornment. The yard's open end looked towards an olive grove beyond the empty road. The chair creaked and wobbled when she sat but appeared strong enough, painted blue long ago, worn and peeling now after untold days. Anna couldn't imagine this place attracting many tourists; holiday-let was the sort of hare-brained scheme someone like Fi would dream up. Perhaps the flat had been inherited from a dead relative. Or won in a card game at the cafe, if the owner was instead the gangster she'd imagined, who'd use it as hideout or love nest.

The seat made her feel too upright, as if she were waiting for a dental appointment rather than relaxing. It would help if she could at least raise her legs, and it occurred to her to bring her suitcase as a footrest. That operation gave her the satisfaction of purposeful activity but resulted in only partial success; if she leaned too heavily against the back of the chair she feared breaking it. She did find a way to slouch that appeared structurally safe but it was not particularly comfortable. And there was nothing to look at except those olive trees. Yet she was still, she reminded herself, happy.

After a while she needed to pee and went back inside. The shower cubicle, washbasin and WC looked completely new; she guessed Conrad must have done all the plumbing as well as neatly tiling the small room, the most appealing in the apartment. She left the door partly open as she sat on the toilet; if she stretched her leg she would be able to kick it even wider. Hearing her waters run she stared past the door's edge at the featureless passageway. The apartment was a possibility waiting to happen; an attractive thought. She envied those who could afford the luxury of choosing to live anywhere, in any way.

A flicker caught her attention; a sudden change of lighting on the wall of the passageway, as if a shadow had passed. Then a voice, a man outside in the lane. A vehicle arriving, the heavy sound of its engine idling. She craned forward until she could see round the doorway towards the apartment entrance.

"Oh fuck!"

Through the front window she could see a van or minibus, someone edged past it then came back into view long enough for her to recognise him. That guy she'd seen in town kicking the African. The gangster. She wanted to throw up. Suddenly it seemed overwhelmingly hard, just to stand and pull up her panties. The front door was opening and without thinking she pulled the toilet door shut on herself, then saw there was no lock. Would it have helped at all if Conrad had fitted one? She teetered back until she found herself sitting again on the toilet.

People were entering the apartment, she had no idea how many. The bumps and footsteps made her imagine a crowd yet there were no voices except one calling from the street, the gangster she supposed, barking orders. She was shaking, it was stupid, she was only a dumb English tourist squatting in a flat she'd found unlocked. She'd say she was lost. She'd been robbed. It was all a mistake. No, she'd tell him about Conrad. She'd have to. And then it opened: the toilet door.

In front of Anna stood a woman, dark-skinned, perhaps around thirty years old, looking as shocked as Anna herself but not screaming or even saying anything to the intruder she'd chanced upon. For a few seconds the two of them stared at each other, frozen in confusion, too startled to move. Was this the gangster's lover? His cleaner? Anna's attention dwelt on the woman's eyes and found in them an unexpected sympathy. Some kind of understanding.

The woman closed the door. Anna felt herself release a breath, she could hear movement continuing in the apartment, the gangster still shouting outside. She leapt forward, deciding to make a run for it, and in the instant of her flight saw the scene in the front room: half a dozen men and women, one or two kids, a couple of bags. Swiftly to the back door before any of them could even work out what was happening, grabbing her suitcase and knocking over the wooden chair in her haste to reach the road, somehow managing to trot with the case wheeling and rocking behind her, not daring to look back, past the other houses with yards of their own. A woman watering pot plants with a hose. A shirtless man, standing immobile in private contemplation of his universe. When she found herself stopping, exhausted, she realised she was alone, ignored, with no one pursuing her. She then walked, regaining her breath and composure, went back to the cafe and took a seat inside. The patron looked surprised but pleased; she ordered a coffee to calm herself, brought out her phone and called her father. The ring tone seemed to go on for a long time. It was Fi who answered.

"Anna?"

"Where's Dad?"

"Lying down. He's not feeling well."

"Look, I need some help." She'd been given a ride out of town, she explained, there'd been a misunderstanding and she was stranded.

"Where are you?"

Anna struggled to remember the name of the town. "It means tower. There's a tower."

"Doesn't sound familiar."

"Wait a minute." She brought up the GPS map on her phone. "It's called Pyrgos."

"Oh yes."

"Can you come and pick me up?"

A pause at the other end. One gladiator standing over another. "I suppose so."

They both hung up. Drinking her bitter coffee, Anna re-created in imagination what she had seen as she burst out of the toilet: the refugees a tableau vivant of helpless confusion, epitome of exploitation. Anna had evaded what they could not. She was refugee too, but more cunning. Beside the tragic mental portrait a second picture: the African hawker, not clever enough to escape the gangster's boot but a survivor nonetheless, like Anna. Keep ducking and diving, she thought, taking another sip. Honesty gets you nowhere. It's everyone for themself.

It was another half hour until the text came: Fi was in Pyrgos, parked directly outside the cafe as it turned out, standing beside the vehicle wearing her oversize dark glasses and broad sunhat when Anna emerged trundling her case. She asked Fi about Jack.

"A little groggy, that's all."

"Too many whiskies?"

"Something he ate, I expect. Took you to some tourist

place, didn't he?"

They got in; the seat was hot beneath the exposed part of Anna's legs. "I've felt fine all day."

"Well, you would," said Fi, setting off with a judder.

"What does that mean?"

"You're young. In good health." They were silent for the short time it took to exit the village, deferring to the roar of the air-conditioning that Fi temporarily raised to full strength, lowering it again once the atmosphere seemed sufficiently cooled. "Has he spoken much about it?" she said eventually. "The tests?"

"Not a word."

"You do know he's dying?"

Through the side window, Anna watched the sweep of vegetation that was accustomed to dry heat. Cactus-like things, branched and spiny. "We've all got to go eventually. Dad's been dying for about as long as I can remember."

"I'm serious, Anna. We're probably talking months." She took a breath and said, "This is the last time..." and then quickly stopped, holding back a sob.

"Shit."

"Yup. That's life, eh?"

It meant, of course, that Fi and Jack were immune to criticism or hostility: angelic icons for Anna to worship. "When you say he's not feeling well..."

Fi cut in, displaying the expertise her partner's misfortune had given her. "His immune system's weakened. Could have been the food or a dirty glass or anything."

An image in the gallery of Anna's mind: his body an island, invaded and defenceless. Hers resistant. Then sitting again in that same polluted taverna, the same table, with Conrad looking sleek, tanned, fit for all his years and squalid existence. It's a

161

lottery. So fuck it.

"I'm taking you to the town," Fi announced.

"My hotel's near the sea front."

"To see the festival, I mean. You do know?"

"Think I saw it starting."

"Jack and I were both planning to go. Says I shouldn't miss it. Pity he won't... But anyway, it'll be nice for you."

"Bit of local colour."

"Exactly. National holiday today but they have their own custom here, we saw it last year." She stopped herself again and Anna heard the unspoken completion of her sentence. Jack was never again to witness the routine village fete that Fi now venerated.

"What's it for?" Anna asked eventually. Fi didn't seem to catch Anna's drift, her mind elsewhere. "The holiday?" Anna reminded her.

"Feast of the Assumption. When the Virgin Mary went to heaven." Fi spoke with the confidence of someone who had read it all five minutes ago in a travel magazine. She wasn't at all religious, Anna knew that since the wedding. "Maybe the Orthodox Church does it on a different date from us, like Easter, I don't know. But over here it's a very big day."

"And what are they assuming?" Anna asked. "That she really went there? Like they're not sure?"

Fi gave something approaching a chuckle. "It's more like assuming office, assuming a title."

"You mean taking? I hadn't thought of assumptions that way."

"Assuming command, assuming an attitude."

They pondered the issue, each aware of being on the verge of some kind of linguistic paradox they couldn't quite grasp.

"Let's say I assume I'll have dinner later," Anna proposed.

162

"What am I taking? It's more like I'm guessing."

"Maybe guessing is a sort of taking."

"But I haven't taken anything yet. Not until I have dinner."

"You take the idea into your head," said Fi.

"No I don't, it comes out of my head. I don't understand it."

"You assumed you knew what the word meant," Fi said with a wry smile. "You took it upon yourself."

"You think I'm stupid?" Anna said coolly.

"Of course not."

"Everyone knows what an assumption is; it just had a different meaning when they wrote the Bible."

Fi managed a laugh. "I suppose you're right. Things change, don't they?"

The topic was exhausted and none came to replace it until they reached the town and encountered a sign in Greek, a tape across the road, people milling densely in the pedestrianised street beyond.

"Is this what they did last year?" Anna asked.

"We came from the other side that time, I'll have to back up and go round." The diversion took them to a yard enclosed by ugly corrugated iron, its tall gates open and offering service as a car park. An elderly man with a stubbled chin stood directing traffic, his dark blue cap as creased and crumpled as his face. "Wonder if I have to pay him?" Fi muttered to herself.

"Doesn't look like it. Think he's just trying to make himself useful."

"Assuming control of the situation," Fi ventured.

Anna wasn't going to take that one up again. Fi parked awkwardly beside a brash Mercedes, both got out and when they passed the man at the gate he said something with a wave of his hand. Fi paused, uncertain how to respond, and Anna thought: go on, stupid cow, give him your money. She didn't, though. Instead Anna intervened, responding to the old fellow's gesture by wishing him a nice day, gently pushing Fi's arm to hasten their exit. "Which way?" she asked Fi, who pointed right.

It took them no more than five minutes to reach the sea front, densely crowded and pervaded with a sense of expectation, even if no one seemed entirely clear what was going on. Making their way slowly along the busy promenade, Anna and Fi approached the pavilion where the icon stood serenely on its plinth, flanked by two burly men. Anna saw an old woman kiss the Virgin's image and cross herself; another followed. There was no queue but instead what appeared to be a constant flow of passing worshippers, accompanied by curious tourists eager to share the experience.

"Shall we?" Fi asked.

"What's the point?"

Fi joined the moving mass and Anna watched as she reached the image, crossed herself and kissed it, exactly as the locals were doing. No doubt praying for Jack, hoping for a miracle. Then Fi jostled her way back to Anna, smiling as if some transformation really had occurred.

"Let's go to a quieter spot," Anna suggested.

"Not too far, though. They do a performance in honour of Mary, some old custom about blessing the fishing boats. It'll be right down there on the beach in that bit they've roped off.

"Nothing happening yet, though."

"It's worth having a good view."

Fi was like a small child afraid of missing an animal at the zoo. Anna said, "Why don't I meet you back here when it starts?"

"Fine."

Anna made her way along the promenade. The sun was lower now, the air pleasantly warm. She reached the square where the toy sellers and hawkers were in their usual spots. The African looked like he was doing good business; she went instead to the other side of the square to peruse jewellery laid out on a table by a slim, well-tanned man in a beige nylon shirt. "Nine-two-five silver," he said in a monotone as she touched a pendant. She ignored him, overhearing British accents at a neighbouring stall that made her turn to glance. There to her right was Matt with a woman. Anna felt herself go rigid with surprise, caught between dread and curiosity. This must be postcard girl, whatever her name was, pretty in an unexceptional way, her dark hair tied back in a ponytail, sunglasses perched on her forehead while she stooped to examine tacky souvenirs, something for granny perhaps. Matt was standing at her further side, watching and speaking to her while she dithered. Some nonsense about how to roast meat on a spit. But then he happened to raise his eyes so that Anna found herself directly in his line of sight, discovered by him. And on his face there was no ripple of altered emotion, only a momentary hesitation before he continued talking to his girlfriend about meat and juice. An awkward situation for everyone, Anna reasoned, best ended quickly. Postcard girl straightened, becoming an inch or two taller than Matt who put an arm round her waist to encourage her away from the rejected souvenir while his gaze stayed fixed on Anna like a rifle sight. But before disengaging and turning, unexpectedly, he winked. Then they moved off. Anna wondered what it meant, that parting gesture, and decided it was a signal of truce, the kind of surrender that the defeated party calls a victory of sorts. She was glad she'd taken his spare cash.

They seemed to be heading back towards where the ceremony would take place; Anna slowly toured the busy square and when she reached the leather seller squatting beside his rug he looked up and nodded in recognition.

"Hey baby, I got good belt for you."

"Maybe not today."

"When we have that drink?"

People were jostling behind her, there was an announcement being made on the distant tannoy. She said, "Have you seen him today?"

"Who?"

"You know. Your boss."

He shook his head. "Not my boss."

"I know what's going on. Trafficking, isn't it? How you got here."

"How? From Athens, no problem."

"He's got a bunch of refugees in a village, I saw them."

Suspicion clouded his expression. "You aid worker? Red cross?"

"He's taken them to his safe house. Boat people, right?"

"Yeah, I hear about that boat. Many drowned. Others here in hotels, houses. Give them food. Look after everyone."

"And this guy's behind it all."

"Why you want to know about this? He done nothing wrong. Get angry some time if I owe money, but then we cool again. You say he give his house to boat people? Then he good man. Michaelis good friend."

"Yet you have to sit here every day to pay Michaelis back?"

He looked cross. "Bullshit, I make good work. Only one time he fix my bike, hard for me to pay. Who you anyway, girl?"

Tension was growing. "Look, it doesn't bother me if you got here illegally."

"Hey, I legal! Four year in Athens, work in my uncle's restaurant. What you want, eh? See my papers? What you fucking want?"

She was startled. She didn't know what she wanted, or if she wanted anything at all. "Sorry," she said quietly, and hurried away from him, pushing along the promenade in the direction of the ceremony that was now commencing. There seemed no chance of finding Fi so instead Anna positioned herself among people gathered expectantly at a spot from where they could see the area of smooth sandy beach that had been cordoned off, and the distant pavilion under whose white canopy a robed priest was chanting, his amplified voice carrying over the loud chatter of the hundreds of onlookers. Gradually the chant became melodic, others were joining in and a great slow song began to unfold itself, some kind of hymn or anthem that many in the crowd seemed to know, even the family directly beside Anna, where the father sang heartily while holding aloft his small son. They were looking towards the sea; Anna saw there a number of small boats assembled just off shore, men standing in them and beginning to cast – what was it – flowers, scraps of paper? Then suddenly the blast of a klaxon, and from out of the water in the midst of the boats an object emerging, the father speaking excitedly to his child and explaining it in words Anna had no hope of understanding, except she was sure she caught something that sounded a bit like Poseidon. And here he was, rising out of the water: a living person in the costume of a sea god. How had he managed to stay underwater without anyone noticing? What was lifting him up? And what did Greek mythology have to do with the Virgin Mary? It was completely baffling but everyone loved it, a great wave of cheers and applause greeting the enigmatic figure who came wading towards the shore and then onto the flat sand where he stood in sodden robes with pitchfork in hand, a spiked crown upon his head, and posed for the mass of raised phones that were being aimed at him.

Next it was the pavilion that became the centre of attention, for now the icon was being lifted on its bier by men in naval uniform who began slowly carrying it down to the beach followed by the priest and other bearded black-robed men whom Anna supposed must be monks, unless they too were costumed actors like Poseidon who waited at the water's edge. When the icon reached the god there was some inaudible transaction, the swinging of a censer and Poseidon lobbing his pitchfork across the bare sand with the strength of an athlete, an attendant running to mark its landing spot and retrieve the weapon while the god kneeled and was blessed. Then he rose, turned seawards and waded out again into the water, finally submerging to more cheers and applause.

"What the fuck?" Anna murmured to herself, watching the place in the sea where the man had disappeared, waiting for him to surface again and draw breath, yet failing to see him. It was as if he'd really gone back to his own kingdom – or drowned. Everyone around her understood what was happening, no one was surprised or alarmed by the stunt, instead delighted. Another song was starting up, with greater audience response this time. The tune was of an exotic kind that Anna might have called Indian or Arabic if she hadn't known it must be Greek, its slowly twisting line distinctly mournful in quality, though the people singing it seemed joyful and uplifted when they finished and cheered again, acknowledging the end of the ceremony.

Gradually everyone resumed milling about the promenade. Anna watched the water a little longer in case Poseidon might reappear but eventually lost interest, instead staring at the bobbing blue and white boats while her thoughts wandered. She was interrupted by a touch on her arm.

"Found you!" It was Fi, looking more friendly and relaxed than Anna could remember. "Did you see it?" she asked excitedly. "Wasn't it lovely?"

Anna could do nothing but agree. Fi asked if she'd like to go for a drink, perhaps a bite to eat, away from the busy sea front. She was making an effort.

"Do you have anywhere in mind?"

Fi nodded. "A place I noticed the other day, let's give it a try."

It was in a side street not far from the church Anna had visited. The church was decorated with banners to celebrate the festival; smartly dressed worshippers were entering or leaving it in steady succession now that sunset was approaching, but the narrow lane that housed the taverna was quiet, the tables set out there mostly empty. It was still too early for the Greeks, Fi explained, pulling a red-painted metal chair and waving Anna to sit opposite. "Did you notice the lady a moment ago carrying presents? I expect she's called Maria; it's her name day."

"Wonder when mine would be."

"They'll certainly have a Saint Anna's day. Fiona's trickier. I suppose there must be something like All Saints' Day for awkward cases. Lovely custom, don't you think?"

A young white-shirted waiter came out and gave them menus in English.

"It's like birthdays, I suppose," said Anna.

"But no one knows your birthday unless you tell them. Everyone clocks your name day. And no worrying about age."

The ceremony had done something to Fi, mellowed or perhaps inspired her. She even looked different, Anna thought. Or was she only imagining it? In any case it made Anna feel more at ease. "I liked the show, would have been a shame to miss it. Thanks for bringing me."

"Could hardly have left you stranded."

"Was Dad really unwell, or simply looking for an excuse not to come?"

Fi shrugged. "Bit of both, perhaps."

"Because of me?"

"Certainly not." She swept something from the table, a dried crumb or leaf. "He really cares about you, Anna." Fi fell silent and bit her lip as if wondering whether to say something that had been on her mind.

"What's up?" Anna prompted eventually.

"Do you remember Sally, my sister? She was at the wedding. First time we'd seen each other in about two years, since a fall-out we had. Started with a disagreement about Christmas plans, blew into a row, things were said that maybe shouldn't have been."

"It happens. Did you make up?"

"Not exactly. At the reception she said something that came to strike me as very important. We don't have to like each other. I insisted that I did like her, and she said no, don't kid yourself, you never asked to be my sister. There's no rule that says you have to like your siblings or parents or even your children. You have to accept them as they are, because like it or not, they're your family forever."

Anna felt she understood the point that Fi was moving towards but asked her to clarify it.

"You and I don't like each other," Fi said. "And that's alright."

"You put it very bluntly."

"Wouldn't the world be a happier place if everyone was so honest?"

"Honesty is over-rated."

"If only we could accept that people are allowed not to like us as much as we'd wish? If we could simply give permission, to ourselves as much as them?"

"What you're really saying is that Dad doesn't like me either. I know that already."

The waiter came to take their order; both women hurriedly scanned their menus, made their choice, then when they were alone again Fi resumed. "Jack cares about you. We both do."

Anna was surprised at how little tension or anger she felt, hearing Fi's words. Some strings had been loosened, the notes they sounded had been lowered.

"Now, about Jack's will..."

Anna waved her hand. "Too soon for that."

"No," Fi said, shaking her head decisively "Your father wants everyone to be looked after properly. You'll get a good lump sum. And he'd like you to have the house here. I wouldn't want to keep it, not on my own. It'll be up to you what you do with it. Sell it, let it, or even come and live here until you figure out what to do next."

In Anna's mind a tantalising picture shaped itself, postponed from attaining reality by nothing more than her father's continued existence. "I don't like talking about this."

"Remember," said Fi, "we don't have to like. Only accept."

Her father was going to die. They all were, not immediately but eventually. "What do you want me to do?" Anna asked.

"You don't need to do anything."

"Is Jack expecting me back at your place?"

"No," said Fi. "Stay at your hotel as long as you want. He'll pay."

"How do you feel about that?"

Fi looked at her from across the table with an expression of perfect calm. Something had happened, whether at the house with Jack, or at the ceremony. Something had changed. "I don't have to feel anything," she said.

They ate their meal in an atmosphere of polite indifference. In Anna's mind, Fi had assumed the persona of a rarely seen aunt; someone in respect of whom no opinion was required, only patience. As twilight gathered they talked about places on the island, acquaintances in Britain, the unchanging weather. When the bill came, Fi lifted it immediately, brought a credit card from her purse and placed it silently on the metal dish. A joint account, Anna noticed. Formalities concluded, they stood and said goodbye to the smiling waiter.

"Do you need a lift to your hotel?" Fi asked Anna.

"It's near. I'll take a walk first."

There was no suggestion from either side that they might walk together.

"Goodnight then."

Anna paused to watch Fi head down the lane, then turned to take its exit at the other end. She emerged on to the square she knew, with its central fountain and the cafe where she had met Matt. It was busier tonight, the festival must have brought people from across the island; but there was an empty table near the kerb and when she sat there she was soon attended by the young waitress she'd seen before, with her thick-framed glasses and casual-looking clothes. Anna ordered an Amstel, sat back in her steel chair and thought about the villa; whether she liked it and would keep it. Whether she needed to like it. She still had notes from Matt's wallet, she could spend some here, get drunk on his money. He'd be back on the boat with his girlfriend now, Anna supposed, and with his posh friends, having forgotten about his little onshore indiscretion. If one day he should come back as politician or diplomat, on a little stop-off from some international negotiation, Anna could still be sitting here in this bar, having lived here for years. Of course that stupid boy was never really going to be anything special;

but the other part of the fantasy, well, that was up to Anna.

"Believe it when you see it," she was saying to herself as the waitress returned.

"Pardon me?" said the waitress in English, placing on the table a moist brown beer bottle topped with an upturned glass she removed and positioned beside.

"Nothing," Anna said, then asked her, "How do you like living here?"

The girl shrugged. "It's okay. Summer is busy, winter is dead. Gets windy. But then I'm away at university. You like it here?"

Anna laughed. "I don't know. I don't have to."

"I suppose not."

The waitress went to serve another customer, and Anna considered tossing a coin to decide her own future. Her father could still change his mind, though. Perhaps even recover. The truth of it was that Anna didn't care, felt no stake in it at all. Stuff would happen, she'd find out what. Night was falling, she sipped slowly, her mind wandering drowsily, and was well into a second bottle of Amstel when she heard a screech of brakes, looked up and saw the vehicle that had stopped right in front of her. Conrad called to her through his open side window.

"Hey, Anna, bit of a mix up."

"Sure was." She lifted and shook her bottle by way of invitation. "Join me?"

He got out, his car parked crazily, and dragged up a chair beside Anna's. "I went back to look in on you and realised what was happening. A couple of them speak English."

"This guy, Mickey whatever, he's like a trafficker or something?"

"Michaelis?" Conrad laughed. "No, he offered to house

some of the folk that got rescued from the sinking. They'll get moved to the refugee centre on Samos but who knows how long that'll take."

"What's in it for him? Does he get paid?"

"I guess not. He's never struck me as a charitable type but everyone here's been touched by this stuff. I mean, there were kids got drowned. People have been offering spare rooms, that kind of thing. About fifty or sixty needing accommodation, small island like this in peak holiday season, kind of a crisis. Are you stuck now?"

"Still got my hotel," said Anna.

"Well, I spoke with Michaelis and a woman called Ritsa who's organising. Thing is, we could get you a free place to stay. All you need do is help out at the centre they've set up, you know, serve food, maybe some cleaning, generally smile and make them feel a little better about the mess they're in. You'd get board and lodging." He could see that she was hesitating to answer. "Though if you're cool with the hotel... Guess it's not much of a holiday looking after refugees."

"No," she said, "I'll do it. I'd like to."

He smiled. "Great. Michaelis doesn't know you were in his place, we can keep that quiet."

"Would he be angry?"

Conrad shrugged. "I don't know, perhaps. I've seen him boil over a few times."

Anna laughed caustically. "I saw him kick the shit out of someone. As far as I can tell he's a thug. Can't picture him as an aid worker. Got to be some angle he's found, some pay-off."

"Could well be," Conrad conceded. "But does it matter? Maybe he wants to look like the big generous guy, or a saint. Buy himself a place in heaven. Long as he's doing something good I don't care why he's doing it. And if he was doing bad, I guess I wouldn't care either."

Anna nodded thoughtfully. "I get you. Are you wanting a drink?"

He declined. "I'm taking some food to the centre. If you're fine tonight at your hotel then let's get everything sorted tomorrow. Say I meet you here around eleven?"

Conrad was about to leave but Anna wasn't ready to let him go. She placed a hand on his arm. "Thanks for everything."

"Hey, it's nothing."

"You rescued me from that thing in the sea, did so much else..."

"It's how we all live here," he said. "We look after each other. Wouldn't think this country was getting its balls crushed by international bankers, would you? Place is virtually bankrupt. But people look after each other, like family."

"And you... alone."

"Ha, that's true. Different ways of being family, right? Guess I didn't do so great with my own blood relatives. But if you can help strangers it all counts. Karma, right?"

She remembered about the Buddhist master he'd mentioned, some guy in Manchester, and asked Conrad to remind her of his name: Daido. "He was kind of inspirational to you, wasn't he?"

"Sure, he changed my life. Taught me to listen to the message."

"What message is that?"

"The one you're meant to find. He gave us exercises to do, I'll tell you one. Think of some place you've been to. Pick an object there."

In Anna's mind, the room where she slept with Matt. He'd gone down to breakfast and she was looking at the desk with his wallet, the postcard inside a book.

"You concentrate on that object," Conrad instructed. "You visualise it as clearly as you can. Until it becomes no longer itself."

"What do you mean?"

"Takes a while, needs some practice, but eventually there's this instant when everything changes."

The desk and wooden chair pushed against it; Matt's shirt from the previous day draped over. The wallet, the book.

"The next stage, you'd sit in front of a mirror. We had quite a large one propped on the floor in the ashram. I'd get in a full lotus and stare at it. For maybe like thirty minutes, an hour. And boy, it happens."

"What, exactly?"

"Put it like this: you were a kid and now you're grown. At every moment you become a different you. Things are not equal to themselves. I'm looking at the mirror, the reflection is me and it's not me. I am me and not me."

It was all too mystical, especially after a couple of beers.

"You're tired," he said. "I got to make that delivery. Tomorrow?"

"I'll be here," she confirmed as Conrad rose and strode to his car. She waved him off, looked for the waitress but didn't see her, then checked her purse and brought out a note, more than enough for the drinks and a very generous tip. She left it under her partly-filled glass, got up and felt the tiredness and alcohol in her body. Before returning to the hotel she wanted to look at the sea again, and when she reached the promenade she found it still busy. Instead of revisiting the stalls she'd perused earlier she went down to the beach and walked along the soft sand, past empty sun loungers and folded parasols, to the part where the ceremony had taken place. It was deserted now, lit only by the glow from the town behind her as she looked out towards the dark sea, a pattern of dim masses gradually resolving when her eyes adjusted. She could see boats bobbing; the same that had been used by the performers, she supposed, remembering how those people had thrown petals or confetti on the waves, now all gone. Far beyond lay the barely visible horizon and above it a clear and starry sky, more and more white lights becoming manifest in it as she gazed, stepping slowly to the water's edge. She thought of what had happened, in Greece and before, and of what might yet come. And she said to herself: I accept. Opening her purse, she removed the last of the money – Matt's, hers, no one's – and knew what she had to do. When she'd been swimming, the sea god had sent her a painful message. She understood it now, and was ready to respond. One by one they fluttered from her hand, scraps of paper that were not themselves, and the ocean gently took them, a vanishing line that might gradually connect her with slumbering Poseidon, with islands beyond view and finally with the infinite sky: a great chain of unbeing.

Between the Tones

The Contract

Conroy's phone is ringing. He gazes at the raindrops trailing dirt down the windows of his untidy flat as he lifts the receiver.

"Conroy here."

The voice at the other end is hesitant, uncertain. They always are. An unfaithful wife, a painful debt, somebody the world would be better off without. There are a million ways of being unhappy, and it's Conroy's job to try and raise the collective spirit.

"Is that... Mr Conroy?"

"That's what I said." Two raindrops are sluggishly racing each other. He wonders if they'll reach the bottom of the pane before the guy can even get started.

"There's a job I'd like you to consider," the caller says. "Do you think you might be interested?"

Conroy's tired eyes roam the contours of his small, disordered lounge. The books he'll never read. The photograph of Laura. "If the money's right, I'm interested."

"Oh, you'll be well rewarded."

"Plus expenses," Conroy adds. The guy at the other end is edgy, anxious. Like they always are. Which only makes Conroy all the more relaxed, because he is in control, and whether he says yes or no might amount to nothing more than a question of which raindrop hits the window frame first. Yes, he needs the money; but more than that he needs the power. He lets his gaze move from the photograph, back to the drizzle-spattered window and then, through a confusion of dripping trails, towards the tenement building on the other side of the street. "Well, then," Conroy invites. "Tell me about it."

The voice says, "Naturally I'd leave the details up to you. How you do it, I mean."

"Naturally," Conroy responds, staring out of the window. "That's how I always work." Amidst the intervening raindrops, he can see somebody moving in the flat opposite.

"It'll be our standard rate."

"I can settle for that." It's Conroy's job to make people happy. "But why don't we talk about the sort of thing you need doing. Or more particularly, where you would want me to be doing it."

"At the university," says the voice.

"I see. Interesting. Many people about?"

"Don't worry. And the room is virtually sound-proof."

"I'm glad," says Conroy. "Acoustics can be a problem, especially when the action hasn't been properly checked."

"Oh, we'll take care of all that for you, don't worry."

"We?" says Conroy.

"I," says the voice.

"You know, last job I did, there was a faulty centre-pin. The hammer stuck. I'm sure you realise how serious such an incident can be."

"Yes, I realise of course."

"Oversights like that can cost a professional his career. And you wouldn't want to do that to me, now, would you?"

"No, no, certainly not." Conroy can almost hear the other man's sweat. He's still thinking of turning him down at the last moment. He's going to bring him right to the edge, and then he's going to decide whether to take the job. He imagines the scene at the university. Blank, expressionless faces. A movement of his finger. A sound. And somewhere, an expression alters. That's all there ever is to it. Then slipping away with the cash in his pocket. "Tell me what sort of person I'm dealing with here."

"Educated, sophisticated."

"Not the sort who likes to be fucked around?"

A pause at the other end. "I suppose not. No."

Conroy says, "I've got a new Ruger I've been waiting to try. Nice piece, a real killer. What time of day are we talking about?"

"Lunchtime," the caller affirms. "There'll be a crowd."

"I guessed so." A one-hour job. Just a quick in and out. Yes, the Ruger sonata will do. Conroy looks again at the photograph of Laura and feels his eyes burrowing deep into her smile. "Maybe some Schumann; what do you think?"

"I wouldn't want you taking any risks for my sake," says the caller. "Standard repertoire is all I ask."

Conroy will take the job, he'll do the recital. But he has to make them wait. He has to remind them who's boss. "I'm really not sure I can help you," Conroy says abruptly. "This town's full of pianists; perhaps you've simply got the wrong guy for what you want."

"They say you're the best, Mr Conroy."

"I'm sure they do, but there are some mean people out

there. These days, I'm resting." That faulty centre-pin had affected him more deeply than he first thought. It was in the middle of *Kreisleriana*; the key jammed, an inner voice was left gasping. It was a moment of panic, but he'd gone on. It was only afterwards that Conroy had begun to wonder if he was getting too old for this game. The flea-pit venues, the touring. And always the risk. Yes, maybe he got scared. Maybe that was the true cause of the incident that put his career on ice.

"The Ruger piece sounds interesting," the caller ventures. Somehow the balance of power is shifting now. Conroy wanted to string him along, but the effect has been to talk himself out of it, and now it's the mysterious voice at the other end of the line that is almost daring him to do the lunchtime recital. A recital that could wind up with Conroy dying on stage, betrayed by his own under-rehearsed Ruger. It's almost as if he's being set up. It's starting to get a little confusing.

"I need to think this over," says Conroy. The raindrops have raced themselves past the outside edge of the window frame; new tears of dirt are already pursuing their uneven trails; new pianists are doing Conroy's job better than he ever could. Faster, cleaner, meaner. Some of those kids can eat up the *Transcendental Études* for breakfast and still be hungry for more.

"I need to come and see the venue," says Conroy. "And the instrument."

"Certainly," the voice assures him. "Tell the porter who you are and he'll let you in, you can try it out. Best to phone first, make sure it's free. They have meetings in there sometimes."

It has all slipped out of Conroy's hands. Somehow he's got himself mixed up in this business and there's no backing out. "I'll do that," says Conroy. And the other man hangs up.

Conroy rubs the stubble of his jaw. He hasn't fixed a

date, or even a time when he should visit the venue. Or the programme, or his fee. But the caller has got what he wanted, leaving Conroy to pick up the pieces. He goes to the other side of the room, lifts the photograph of Laura, and hurls it at the wall.

Four hours later it's dark and all he can think about is the Ruger, and those consecutive ninths in the recapitulation that might prove to be his undoing. He's rehearsed the moves on his own machine, but out there things are different. You show up for an engagement, they give you a cupboard for a dressing room and half an hour to warm up on a crate that's not fit for a bordello. "It's just been tuned," they always say, like you're supposed to be grateful, and you look at it and see a chipped ivory no one's ever thought to repair.

Conroy goes out, walks in the rain, and soon finds himself arriving at the university. His hands pushed deep into his pockets, the collar of his overcoat turned up, his hair wet and his eyes and cheeks dripping, he sees a sign for something whose name sounds like an auditorium, goes there and tries the door. It's locked, there's nobody about.

He stalks the building until he finds a side-entrance he can open, and steps inside feeling glad to be free of the relentless downpour. He shakes himself dry like a dog then walks up a flight of stairs since it seems the only way to go. Now he's on a landing, a dim emergency light guides his way until he finds another door that leads him, as he guessed, into the theatre. The same weak lighting is less effective here; he has to let his eyes adjust before making out a space that's small by normal standards. Moveable seating, some areas unused. Room for about eighty, perhaps. The piano's at the far end under a cover. He gropes his way there, lifts the canvas and opens the lid, and from out of the darkness the keyboard gleams beneath him like a hideous grin. He pulls the stool from under the instrument and sits down, adjusting it to suit his height. Then, like the trained professional he is, he begins to play the Ruger.

What happens next is chaotic and swift. Conroy should have known it as soon as he walked in. As soon as he tried the side door. As soon as he left the flat to wander mournfully in the rain, thinking of Laura, beautiful Laura, and the broken glass on the floor after he threw her photograph across the room. He should have known it from the caller's voice, inviting him to come and try the piano, when Conroy suddenly felt as though he was being set up. But none of this was uppermost in his numb and weary mind as he began playing the Ruger, and what with the mezzo forte allegro and his general level of indifference, he didn't hear the opening of the door again – the door he closed behind him at the other end of darkness he now carelessly seeds with semiquavers evaporating from beneath his fingers while a mean and man-sized shadow makes its way through the gloom towards him.

What happens, therefore, is chaotic, swift, and instinctively violent. Conroy hears a click behind his right ear, swings round and feels the shadow falling before he even lands the punch in return. Something long, wooden and damn hard is impacting the side of his face; he grabs hold of it, turns it back on his attacker. The two of them are sprawling; a face connects itself heavily with the keyboard and makes a messy diminished chord two octaves below middle C. There's blood, a loose tooth, notes everywhere and it's all very unpleasant, but that's music, that's the business Conroy chose long ago to get involved in, and if people sometimes have to get hurt then that's too bad, as long as it isn't Conroy himself who winds up with his chin bouncing on the keyboard while specks and spurts of bodily fluid send dark crotchets spraying across the synthetic ivory's palid glimmer.

"Stop! Please."

Conroy pulls the man up by the scruff of his neck. It appears to be some kind of janitor.

"Who sent you?" Conroy snaps, trying not to mess up his own overcoat.

"Nobody," the guy simpers. "I work here. Thought you must have broken in."

"Broken in?" Conroy tightens his grip on the man's neck. Maybe he ought to use the scumbag's broom handle on him again, only this time he'd get serious.

"We... we sometimes get students larking about."

"I see," says Conroy. "And you thought I might be an eighteen-year-old kid 'larking about'? You thought I was some punk not yet old enough to shave, sitting here playing the Allegro from Heinz Ruger's Piano Sonata Number Four? Is that what you thought? Is it?" He's shaking the janitor hard, and in the poor light can see blood all over the guy's mouth, looks like he might faint, in which case Conroy has to make doubly sure of getting the information he wants before leaving this gibbering bundle of rags to sleep it off.

"Yes sir, that's what I thought. Thought you were a student."

"Fucking liar!"

"Please, honest to God, let me go and you can play as long as you like. I'll even turn the lights on."

"Oh no you don't," says Conroy. "One flick of those switches and you'll be wishing you still had a full set of fingers."

"But... but I thought you wanted to play... the piano." Blood and spit and baby tears all mixed up on his dribbling face.

"Never mind what I wanted. Just tell me who sent you."

"Nobody – aaagh! Please don't!"

"Tell me or you're going to start chewing piano lid. And that's a hard piece of mahogany there, you'd better believe me."

"Alright then," gasps the janitor, "Only let me go before you strangle me." When Conroy releases his grip, the man falls like a cast-off piece of sodden clothing. Slumped on the floor, he raises his face.

"Who sent you?" Conroy repeats. The janitor comes out with some shit about wanting to go and put on the lights so they can talk about this sensibly, so Conroy kicks the bastard and asks again. "Was it Sand?"

"Who?"

"Sand. The one who killed Laura."

The janitor is alternately rubbing his face, his back, his knee, and other parts of his body that are in a more moderate state of agony. "I'm really sorry but I don't know anything at all about – aagh! Alright, alright, stop! And please don't kick me again. Specially not my back, I've had a hell of a time with it recently. Yes, it was Mr Sand. Now can I go and turn on the lights?"

The smell of deceit is even worse than the reek of this janitor's piss. "I think you mean Dr Sand, don't you? Dr Richard Sand. Try saying it again while you've still got a working jaw."

"Yes, Dr Sand. He sent me."

"So this was all simply a fancy way of getting me here?"

"That's right sir. Now I'll go and switch on those – AAAARGH! Jesus Christ!"

He's not making it any easier for himself. Conroy has seen this kind of charade on so many occasions. Like the one in the sheet-music section of Thwaite's bookshop, who wouldn't play ball until he pinned her down and threatened her with a rolled up copy of the Schirmer Scarlatti. But that's the way it goes. There's always someone wants to be a hero, wants to make life difficult for themselves. So Conroy gives the janitor another kick, just to make certain of his co-operation.

"Tell Sand I won't be doing the engagement. Not this month, or the next, or any fucking time. If he wants to see me, he knows where to find me. Tell him I'll be waiting for him."

Then Conroy begins to leave, tripping over a couple of chairs in the darkness as he tries to find the door. "And another thing," he says, turning towards the invisible pile of pain that lies moaning somewhere on the floor. "Get that fucking piano tuned."

Flop

Ten months he's been resting, avoiding public performances of even the most squalid kind, aware that any appearance in front of the wrinkled army who've been his twenty-year meal ticket could easily turn into a high velocity duet with an 8mm Walther. Hasn't stopped the bastards coming after him. He's thumbing vinyl in FLOP, the retro-tech shop, figures if he's going to die then it might as well be to the air-conditioned accompaniment of *Nessun dorma*.

Somebody pushing open the thick sound-proof glass door: three people in the lifeless cavern now, because as well as a comatose assistant behind the counter, Conroy can see a teenage boy, baggy jeans, brown hoodie, not your typical Andrea Bocelli appreciator, more your apprentice hoodlum on his first outing kind of guy, room for a baseball bat down that trouser leg of his, moving with conspicuous nonchalance towards the J-K region of the CD section. If this punk thinks he can convince anybody he wants the Janacek *Sinfonietta* for his nana's birthday he really must reckon Conroy's two beats short of a bar. Could just turn out to be the biggest mistake of hoodie's first day at the office.

Yes, Conroy's resting, hiding, on the run, call it whatever the fuck you want, but he's no spineless patsy. So he puts Donizetti back where he found him and saunters over to Mozart, whole side of a display rack, looking right over the top of it at the kid opposite flicking CDs with his snotty fingers like he's wondering where the fuck Jay Z's gone when all he can see is Josquin des Prez. Can't even hire decent hoodlums these days.

Somewhere behind Conroy: a sound, a real one, not imagined, not the smooth easy-spending pap on the PA, but the nylon rustle of the assistant coming out from behind the till, going to the music-proof door and opening it, walking clean out of the fucking classical music section like he doesn't care it exists, like it's his tea-break or something. Like he's part of it. And Conroy thinks, here we go round the fucking mulberry, all over again.

Last night a fake janitor, now a hoodie looks about twelve years old, not even at the stubble stage, islands of untamed darkness on lip and jaw that'll only join up once they can figure out what the hell they're meant to be doing. Still flicking CDs, not looking at any of them, Conroy staring him out, waiting for what has to happen, knowing how all of this has got to end. Punk looks up, blue eyes of a little boy, whole body freezing in the spotlight. Don't even think of it, kid. One false move and you'll be picking jewel-case from your tongue for the rest of the afternoon.

"Hey," punk says with a noncommittal slouch. Must be the way his generation speak on whatever planet hatches them.

"Yo, dude."

Punk doesn't seem to get the irony. That's the thing about irony: you can always count on idiots not getting it. Instead the punk does a kind of false double-take. "Hey..."

"We've done that already."

"You're the pianist, aren't you?"

Conroy dearly hopes the assistant will make his cup of tea a long one, his Hobnob a symphony, his fag a *Götterdammerung*. The janitor was too quick, a mere overture. Conroy really wants a decent stretch of time in which to kick the crap out of this kid before the security people come and spoil the fun.

"Sure, I'm the pianist. Only I'm resting – didn't they tell you? And you, I suppose, must be the next Toscanini?"

Come-crusted fingers drumming on Kodaly or Korngold, either would make an opening frisbee in whatever piss-poor attack the punk reckons he can muster. Face of someone who just doesn't get it. "You're the pianist..." Can't even remember his lines, keeps repeating them. "I saw you on YouTube."

This is unexpected. "You must be mistaking me for Elton John."

"No, no, I saw you. You were doing a concert and somebody's phone went off."

This punk got his script written for him by Enid Blyton. "Funny you should remember me, son."

"You stopped playing and went over and..."

Yes, yes, he didn't need to hear the story of his own life. Couldn't they get on with the violence, please?

"And when his phone was all smashed on the floor everyone applauded and shouted encore. I remember it."

Give him a gold star and a day off school. "You want my autograph or something?"

Punk flinches. "Only saying hello. Like, you're a celebrity

aren't you? Went viral. That's cool."

A better actor than Conroy expected: this is almost convincing. This is almost like he really did see the clip, and not only that, he believed it. Genuinely thought the whole thing was about a ringtone upsetting a few retired schoolteachers who'd paid a tenner to hear the Chopin *Ballades* in a town hall where every breath was an inhalation of dehydrated rat-shit, when actually it was about a guy in the front row, younger than the rest, evidently one of Sand's people, reaching into his pocket just as Conroy hit the presto con fuoco, must have thought he'd be too distracted by the syncopated chords, but Conroy had the bastard there and then, gave him fuoco alright, and if it turned out not to be a mind-control Q-phone after all, only a Samsung with a dickhead MP3 on it because the cunt hadn't figured out how to do silent vibrate, then that was just as well for dickhead since otherwise he'd now be on indefinite leave in his local cemetery.

"I mean, you're sort of a hero. As well as a celebrity."

It briefly made the news: dickhead claiming damages on account of emotional distress and the phone he'd dropped, case thrown out, Conroy trying to avoid the single hungry lens showing up outside court, but failing, resigned to exposure. Every artist's right to defend what matters to him. Next day on the radio, 72 per cent of phone-in poll respondents agreed, though the issue was put a little more simply. Even some sky-pilot on *Thought For The Day* doing a "can violence be justified?" riff.

"That's nice you think I'm a hero, son. But really, all I want is to get on with what I'm doing. I don't like it when people bother me."

"Oh." Baby-blue eyes almost getting it.

"Especially when they bother me for a reason. Like they've

been sent to bother me. In those sorts of instances, it's not only the phone that gets smashed up. You follow me, son?"

Trembling zit-pickers on the ends of his arms wondering if maybe they ought to get on with finding Franz Liszt; eyes sort of following. The uncertainty of the apprentice.

"Don't do it, son."

Eyes back on Conroy, startled. "What?"

"You understand what I'm saying. Let's you and me walk out of here and forget about this. I know what you've got in there."

"Eh?" The laser bead of Conroy's nod and stare leads the punk to his own crotch; he examines it in puzzlement. Not a place he uses often.

"So in case he still hasn't got the message, tell your boss once and for all that I'm out of this."

"I don't have a boss..."

"But guess what, I kind of like you, must be those big puppy eyes making me come over all protective." Kid takes this platter of conversation and flips it over, looking for some sort of liner note on the other side. Doesn't get it. "And it's been good talking to you but now you really need to get back to the one who sent you here."

"Nobody sent me." The punk, uncovered and defeated, aware how vulnerable he is to a demonstration of the Korean art of being drop-kicked in the nuts, moves away from the CD display, hands clear of his body and in full vision, towards the heavy glass door. "Sorry to have bothered you." Turns, pulls it open and departs, admitting a brief waft of rap along with the returning assistant, until the door reseals itself and the middle-age mood music reasserts its command.

Conroy ponders this latest provocation as he examines the retro hi-fi units and music centres shelved along one side of the room. An ancient gramophone with a "not for sale" sign adds dignity to the obsolescence that the pianist shares and which brought him here. He will not be rubbed out.

"Do you need any help?" the assistant asks suddenly from a point too close to Conroy's shoulder and at a pitch that seems unnecessarily high. Glancing at the lanky figure beside him Conroy decides to play along, pointing at what looks like a 1940s Bakelite radio though it might have arrived last week from a factory in India.

"Does that thing work?"

"Sure, as long as there's an analogue signal to pick up."

"Wonder how long that'll be."

Assistant laughs chummily like he's found a new soulmate. "FM won't die, pirates are ready to fill the gap."

It's a coded conversation: Conroy has to keep his wits about him. "You know any of these pirates?"

The boy shrugs it off, evidently perceiving sudden danger since, for all he knows, this respectable customer might really be a snoop. "I mean, with the off-grid movement and so forth."

Conroy nods and in a low voice concurs. "And so forth," he says slowly.

An awkward silence. Until nylon shirt snaps back to retail reality. "Well, if you need anything..."

"Sure," says Conroy. "I'll whistle."

Time to get out of here before the facial recognition software of the CCTV camera trips an alert somewhere. Conroy's exit takes him from the hermetic classical haven through a fog of hip hop and then to the computing section, a junkyard of devices whose only sin was to have been surpassed in speed and capacity by a subsequent generation equally doomed. Conroy pauses to mourn a model he possibly once owned but can't quite remember, and as he tilts and inspects the lifeless slab he notices a spectre at the periphery of his vision. It's the damn punk again. For a few beats and even a couple of bars he ignores the bastard but eventually it's too much, his head swings in acknowledgment of the irritation and the asshole speaks, coughing it up like another apology.

"I maybe should have explained... I'm doing my diploma."

Up until now Conroy hasn't been aware there exist formal qualifications in being a useless piece of shit but this kid's surely heading for top marks. "Diploma?"

"Piano."

A joke in the sense that it's totally ridiculous, though not at all funny.

"I had sort of a disagreement with my teacher and I'm looking for a new one. I was wondering..."

Then it all gets blurred and when Conroy thinks about it later he tries to recall who threw the first punch. Fuck that. Alone in his apartment in the dead of night, staring from his armchair across the darkened living room and through the uncurtained window, he sees a lone rectangle of light on the tenement building at the opposite side of the silent street. Three a.m. and Conroy's only companion, other than the whisky glass in his hand and the music in his mind, is that little patch of yellow.

He's eight years old, playing the piece his teacher Mrs West has given him. A few stumbles at first but soon he's got it pretty much licked, he's what you might call a prodigy. Beethoven wrote it for a little girl he knew, Mrs West says. Most famous piano tune in the whole fucking world and it belonged to some kid, it's playing right now in the elevator – Singapore, Conroy decides – where Richard Sand is going to a meeting with some drug lord, cartel operator, grandmaster or whatever, a syrupy arrangement for string orchestra or alien synthesiser like the voicemail Conroy found himself connecting with when he hoped to speak to a fucking human for a change, an electronic drill inside his head. *Für Elise*, universal anthem of blandness, musical vanilla, thing you put there when you can't think what the fuck else to do.

So get this. That kid Elise, she's wiped, nothing, zilch. Conroy went round her house and shot her dead, put a bullet right between her eyes. He was 14 or 15 at the time, her dad standing there in lederhosen, mother in *Sound of Music* costume screaming her head off. But Conroy had to do it, and the reason is that Elise's a fiction, a fairy tale, a made-up name for a made-up tune. Guy who discovered the manuscript after Beethoven died couldn't make out the dedication so he invented it.

Layers of fiction: kind of thing Richard Sand would understand, stepping out of the elevator and walking along an air-conditioned corridor to his meeting. That little piece Beethoven didn't think good enough to publish and buried in a drawer wound up the biggest hit he ever wrote. Like being a celebrity for something you never know about, the murder victim whose face is in the papers, the unsuspecting bystander, the accidental intruder on history's carpet. On his liquor-warmed tongue Conroy tastes the five-second thrill of a life that never happened.

Richard Sand is being shown into an elegant suite, orchids in a vase lending a feminine touch to the business-like atmosphere of veiled brutality.

"Do you have it?" Blonde-haired gangster in his thirties, Italian suit, Swiss watch, international accent, local bodyguard.

Sand nods. The attache case dangles from his arm.

"Show us."

Sand rests the case on the glass-topped coffee table, spins the combination with his thumb, hinges it open. Blondie looks with satisfaction. "Leave it here," he instructs.

"And Conroy?"

Blondie glances towards the bodyguard whose shades can barely wrap the circumference of his fleshy face. "We'll take care of Conroy."

"But he suspects."

"We know."

Conroy is still staring at the illuminated window across the street, his gaze locked on it until eventually the rectangle of colour unfixes itself from the building and floats in front, a weightless slab of liquid light scorching his eyes, the shape remaining before him even when he blinks.

He used to do this thing called a masterclass, like he was some Zen Jedi priest, kids of nineteen or twenty all wanting a career looking for him to say they were good. Young girl one time playing the finale of the "Moonlight" Sonata, everything in the right place, efficient, like she was typing a letter to her insurance company. Conroy stopped her, said, "Have you any idea how many times Beethoven moved house?" She looked up at him, bovine and sulky, sausage fingers folding on the plate of her lap. "More than thirty," he told her. "Not counting the places he rented in summer." Girl at the piano wondering what the fuck this was all about, not getting any of it. What sort of a guy keeps moving so much? No wife or kids to hold him down, but that's not enough of an answer. Getting into arguments with landlords could be a reason. Girl staring at him, wanting to know when he was going to tell her if she should play it faster or slower, all she could see was marks on a page, shadows on a wall. Or might he have been running away from something? Failed relationship, sinister secret, phobia, paranoia. Criminal activity. Boredom. A million reasons why a man might spend his life on the run. "You know what I think?" Conroy said to the idiot girl. "I reckon it was because his neighbours couldn't stand the noise." Some kid laughed, greasy-haired boy he hadn't liked the look of, moment he walked in. Conroy glowered, kid stopped. "And us?" said Conroy. "We're the ones who need noise. Because you know what music is? You know what art is? Lies and violence."

Girl at the piano said what about feeling, expression, beauty? In other words, faking it for the public. But a piano is something you touch in order that a string may be hit, yes, hit, and even the gentlest pianissimo is like launching a missile against the certainty of oblivion, against the endless silence that has to be delayed. Those kids in the masterclass, what the fuck could they possibly know about it? Only lesson he could teach them was failure, only thing art can ever teach us about is failure. And they'd learn that anyway.

Fact of the matter, he was in FLOP today looking for himself, anything with his name on it. They're out there somewhere, those recordings he made, must be people who've made love to his Schubert, tapped along with Mozart in a traffic jam, picked their noses to his Ives or Busoni. He's washed up, a has-been, a second-rater, even his agent has given up on him, he's no better than Mrs West and her fucking Furry Lisa. He places his empty whisky glass on the low table beside his armchair, next to the empty whisky bottle, and lifts the remote that's been squatting there, an invitation to nowhere. Turns on the television, switches to the comforting blank screen of a radio channel and finds himself in the middle of Schubert's Ninth Symphony.

He's woken by a noise and the morning brightness through his window and as he becomes aware that another circuit of repetition is about to begin he comprehends that the high volume is coming from the radio in his bedroom, tuned to the same station as the television that continues in low accompaniment. "Brandenburg" Number Four from two locations simultaneously but out of phase, the digital TV a fraction of a second behind the old bedside clock radio that must have had its alarm set for... he peers wearily at his watch... nearly eight. But why the fuck would he do that? Senses sharpening as the explanation crystallises in his mind: somebody's been here in his flat, and since nothing was taken it can only mean that something has been left. Couldn't have been Sand who's still in Singapore...

Bach is reaching its duplicated final chord, the announcer's voice has the same displacement, like a 3D picture that only makes sense once you look through red and green glasses. It's what Conroy needs, the right perspective that will make the fragments line up, the image cohere. And now it's the time signal, his watch is a little ahead of the television that's behind the radio as their eight o'clocks arrive and the pips chirp out of synch, the lightbulb moment. The store assistant tried to tell him, maybe even the dickhead at his recital or the janitor, all warning him of the mindfuck being perpetrated on an unsuspecting world. A plot to distort time, exploiting the digital gap. That's what the intruder left behind: something between the tones.

Renewed vigour propels Conroy from the armchair where he slept, his joints are stiff but he ignores their ache and goes in hunt for his laptop, finding it on his unmade bed at whose side the FM clock radio still blasts, sounding now like an anthem of resistance. Lowering its volume he fires up the computer and enters search terms likely to unpeel truths too long hidden from his distracted view.

Andrew Crumey

Radio Daze, by Daniel Franklane III
(www.memoirweb.com/franklane/chapter17.html)

How I finally came upon the realisation that an intelligent civilization in orbit around Sirius is transmitting signals to Earth is the subject of chapter 23 but before that I want to go back to the start of my time at Columbia when I was assistant to Professor Armstrong. What a fine time we had! It was September of 1938 when he agreed to take me on having allowed me to demonstrate to him my ability with vacuum tubes that in those times were often of deficient manufacture requiring regular replacement. You don't want to be using those C37s I told Professor Armstrong when I went to his office where he had agreed to see me.

"Tell me about yourself," said the famous professor.

He was a very distinguished looking man, quite aloof in manner like a lot of scientists, I suppose you could say he was handsome. Maisie has seen pictures of him and she reckons so, like a film star she says though that's going too far. But he was a strong fellow, very fit for his age which was his late forties I believe, able to get right up that broadcasting mast of his that he'd constructed at his research station over in New Jersey. He was sitting behind the biggest desk I'd ever seen in his office at Columbia University he said he had five minutes then he needed to go to a meeting. So I told him about myself.

"My name is Daniel Franklane III."

"I know that already. Tell me something else."

I'd only published one story at this time that I've already discussed in chapter 15 though it was in fact to be the start of the *Mendophore Trilogy* as will be explained in chapter 42. Briefly the Mendophore robots create a super-intelligent race called the Osgrands who do battle against the Kandane Hoard. I told the professor I was good with vacuum tubes and if he needed a lab assistant then I was his man. He said to me I've already got an assistant and I said I bet I'd do a better job for a lower salary. I said to him I haven't met Maisie yet (chapter 31) and you can see I don't eat a lot. He said to me what do you know about super-heterodyne circuits and I told him exactly what I knew which is just about everything you could know in September 1938 unless you were the man who actually invented the darn thing and who was sitting right opposite me smoking his pipe, the greatest radio inventor in the world.

Professor Armstrong said he might be able to get me into the lab on an informal basis and I took that as a yes. I started next day. What I've learned in sixty-eight years is that you get nowhere in life by being shy and modest you've got to push yourself you've got to sell yourself and that's exactly what I did. I told Maisie I sold myself there and then.

There were a lot of Reds and Germans around. It was a tricky time and we all knew it. Hitler and Stalin were allies and if their emissaries got a hold of the American public mind it would be an end of everything. It gave me the idea for the Osgrands. And there was another story I did at this time about a guy who finds he's got this little spot on the back of his hand just a tiny little spot. There was a place on the way between my apartment and the university I used to go in there for a cup of coffee every day and a girl there who was real nice after all I hadn't met Maisie yet and sometimes I'd stand and chat with her or else I'd go sit at a table by the window and I'd think about this guy with a little spot on his hand a tiny little spot. Only one day it starts growing bigger.

Professor Armstrong had already got his experimental FM station running, call-sign W2XMN. Frequency modulation was arguably his greatest contribution to the field of radio communications because it eliminated the static interference found in AM services and caused by common everyday sources such as electrical machinery but with FM it's the frequency rather than the amplitude that is modulated. She was called Dorothy I think and I was telling her about it while she refilled my coffee cup but then I got kind of a bad feeling like I shouldn't be saying all this. The Germans got hold of FM technology and used it in their Panzer tanks which may have cost American lives and I can honestly say I feel very guilty that I might have played some tiny part in helping them get the secret. But America got there first and it won us the war.

Columbia was a very fine place to work. Better than Wernecke's Book Store that's for sure. I got to meet the other people in the Department of Electrical Engineering and they were as varied and lively a bunch as you'd expect interested in everything from power generation to weather insulation! And one time I saw a little notice on the wall it said Columbia Writers. It was for anyone who wrote stories you could go along and see what other people thought of them. They called it a workshop. I wrote down the details and told Dorothy all about it she said I think you should definitely go because then you'll find out if your writing is any good. She said she wasn't an expert and couldn't know and I appreciated that. I took back the manuscript I'd loaned her of *Mendophore Rising* and said I'd take it to the workshop. She said maybe I should try the one about the guy with the little spot on his hand the tiny little spot.

The workshop was in a room in a building in Morningside that was used by something called the Institute for Social Research. First night I show up I see this German he's sitting right there in the lobby only him and me the two of us and I sat down. It was when he nodded and said good evening that I knew he was a German. I said hello and wondered if he was a spy. He looked Jewish and we knew those ones weren't meant to be spies but a lot of them were Reds and I wasn't taking any chances. A couple other people showed up a man and a lady if I remember correctly and then somebody knew where the room was where we were meeting. About a half a dozen of us in the end all sitting around a big table. I did this every week for over a year until they had a rebellion and ordered me out.

I have to tell you that what these people wrote it just stunk. There was a lady who did some quite amusing stories but the rest of them I could tell had no talent and they were never going to get anywhere. That's the trouble with writing people think it's so easy and you make it all up as you go along when as a matter of fact there has to be planning planning planning. I explain this in more detail in chapter 62 when I start discussing the Seven Step Plan and how it can be used to write highly successful science fiction trilogies but already back then I'd read a couple books on writing and I knew the most important things.

First you've got to have action and it's got to be clear-cut. There should be an inciting incident at the beginning and a major plot point a third of the way in another at two-thirds so for a 240-page novel you're talking plot-points at 60 and 120 it's not so hard it's not as if anybody can't learn it really it's no different from knowing the difference between a C130 vacuum tube and a D15. You plug them in and switch on – simple.

And you've got to have believable sympathetic characters. Best way is to do a list of their personality traits like do they have a limp or little round glasses like the German I couldn't stop staring at him all night that first time. His turn came to introduce himself and he said his name was Heinrich Behring and there you go I told Maisie I knew it right away just knew it. Maisie says you've got to be open minded and I tell her not so your brain falls out. He was a German. Ah but he was Jewish wasn't he says Maisie and I tell her he never said that he only said he emigrated and went to Scotland for a while before he got a visa for the United States and what do you make of that? She says to me honey it's not only Jews needed to escape and why bother about the details and I said Maisie my dearest it's the details that find people out. It's like the little spot on the back of the hand that tiny little spot. It gets bigger.

This Heinrich Behring was writing a historical novel we all listened to a chapter it was about Beethoven and it was simply the most boring nonsense I'd ever heard. One thing every professional writer knows is you've got to show not tell. Just take for example this short passage from an early draft of my novel *The Halls Of Engfreed*:

Struck by the blast of the heat-ray Vult staggered and clutched at his chest. He was dying. "Strieg, Amatt," he gasped, "you two go on without me."

In a later draft (the seventeenth) this becomes:

Agonisingly struck by the intense blast of the Norphene heat-ray Vult teetered, spun and clutched frantically at his chest. "Strieg, Amatt," he gasped as blood rushed out of him forming a spreading pool of hideous vivid crimson on the tiled floor at his feet. "You two go on without me."

You can see the difference that the first time I tell you he's dying but the second time I show it. This is so much better. If there could have been more advice like that in the Columbia Writers workshop it would have benefitted everyone especially Heinrich Behring and his boring novel. The others in the group were polite about it but if there's one thing I've learned it's honesty honesty honesty you never get anywhere simply being kind to people it only encourages them to go on making the same mistakes. I said to him it stinks. I could see that the rest of them agreed but didn't want to say.

"I showed it to someone who knows about Beethoven and he liked it," said Herr Behring.

"What about the ninety-nine per cent of us who don't know anything except he was deaf?"

"I suppose I write for the one per cent."

There you have it typical European. Then when they'd all had a turn I read them the one about the guy who's got this tiny little spot on his hand this tiny tiny spot. Boy they loved it.

Next day I told Professor Armstrong but his mind was on something else. His broadcasting station was transmitting a feed from WABC and it was getting picked up on the very few experimental FM radio sets then in existence. This was absolutely new technology and we were all very excited about how clear the reception was without any hiss or pop or whistle. Now I already knew about the natural radio waves that had been detected from the sun and Milky Way that showed low frequency electromagnetic radiation could penetrate the atmosphere and it meant we could send signals into space if we wanted and alien intelligences could do the same. And I told Maisie I said to myself if there's anybody out there trying to communicate with us then you can be darned sure they're doing it with FM. I was nearly saying it to Dorothy when she filled my cup then I glanced across the room and saw two men in dark suits they sort of looked away when I caught their eye.

One day Professor Armstrong said to me have you ever heard of the Radio Research Project I said no he said no I haven't either. There was a fellow working for it who had an office on Columbia campus said he wanted to know more about the FM system. Could we take a receiver over there and demonstrate? And wouldn't you know it but when I saw the address written down of this office of his it was right where I went every week for the writing group same building. He was called Professor Theodor Wiesengrund Adorno. In other words a German.

I said to Professor Armstrong are you sure this is a good idea and he said what do you mean. I said this German how do you know he's on our side and Professor Armstrong said we're not at war are we and I said not officially but we hardly want foreign powers getting hold of FM technology do we. I told Maisie about all those Panzer tanks and she said honey you had nothing to do with it. Professor Armstrong said in a few years every home in America is going to have an FM radio and we're hardly going to be keeping that a secret are we. I've got the patent and that's what counts and I want you to take the receiver over to the Institute for Social Research and let these people hear what a good signal it picks up. So that's what I did.

The receiver was a large pre-production unit and it took two of us to get it over there. And there was no lift. I'd only ever gone to the meeting room on the ground floor where the writing group met there were all sorts of rooms and offices in the place but the one we wanted was up several flights of stairs had his name on the office door Professor Theodor Wiesengrund Adorno. Come in he said through it.

He was sitting at his desk and he looked like some little bald big-eyed German spy that's the truth of it I'll be honest with you. I said we brought the receiver and he was staring at it like he had no idea what we were talking about this big contraption we'd hauled up the stairs that was on the polished floor outside his office door. Bring it in he said and while we set it up he completely ignored us he was busy writing. Had to find a place where we could connect the cable and that wasn't easy there was furniture to move and so on and at one point

I bumped into a pile of papers and some things fell it was a little awkward. He spluttered and waved his hands and said something in German that I expect meant you stupid American idiot you people are all cowboys and football players and you don't know a darned thing. That was sort of his attitude I think.

We switched it on and tuned the dial. There was some dance music. The professor listened quite intently.

"You see how clear it is?" I said.

He looked at the two of us myself and the fellow who'd helped me haul it all the way up here think he was called Tony. The professor said, "Is it possible to hear some real music?"

"What do you mean?"

"Rather than this nonsense."

We explained that so far there was only one station which was W2XMN and it was broadcasting a feed from WABC so no there wasn't anything else.

"Then it is hard for me to judge the quality," the professor said. "But this is potentially very interesting."

The three of us listened to it for a while I quite enjoyed the dance music I'd been wondering about asking Dorothy out. The professor's interest was always greatest between tunes when there was only silence it was the silence that mattered to him. No static.

How does it work he asked so I explained the basic principles of electromagnetic radiation and frequency modulation and mentioned that radio waves are a perfectly natural phenomenon even emitted by the sun and stars. He blinked those big dark eyes of his. "But how can the sun produce radio waves? Surely this is the music of the spheres!"

I told him my idea that alien intelligences might at that very moment be trying to contact us using FM radio as has subsequently been proved beyond doubt but he got that look on his face again that I took to mean he thought I was a stupid American idiot. I said to him, "Professor, what exactly is this radio project of yours all about?"

He shrugged as if he didn't know it himself. He told us how he was persecuted in Germany and went to England for a while then the United States and I thought here we are again I said to Maisie they're all the darned same. You take someone like Professor Armstrong he could be a film star. Or Professor Hubble. Or any of these people. But this Weasel-Grunt Adorno he was no better than Behring he was one of those absent-minded intellectuals who don't make a whole lot of sense and look like they spent all their life shut up in a cave full of books. So I asked him again perfectly straight and simple question what was it all about this radio project.

And now he told us about how in Frankfurt Germany there was an Institute for Social Research and his friend so-and-so and his other friend so-and-so and this philosopher and that philosopher and how he managed to get out and go to Oxford but his dearest friend was still in Europe and had better escape before it's too late. I said hold on professor at least tell us the name of this friend of yours.

"Walter Benjamin," he said.

Now we're at least getting somewhere. So this guy set you up in the Radio Research Project.

No, he said. It was some other professor got him the job. Half-time only, rest of the week he can do other kinds of social research. He began telling us about how it was funded and how he got his visa and the two of us nodded and listened to the next dance tune. I believe he took our point.

He said, "I'd like to hear what Mozart would sound like in FM."

I told him I was sure we could manage it and I thought

there we are it's always classical music with these Europeans
never anything modern like Louis Armstrong he simply
doesn't count as far as their type is concerned. What's so great
about those old composers I said to the professor then told him
about the writing group and Heinrich Behring who he didn't
know but he said the Radio Project sometimes have meetings
in that room too and the professor added that as a matter of fact
he was due to give some lessons on music appreciation and
perhaps I'd be interested. I said sure if there's one thing I've
learned it's that you've always got to keep trying new things
and improving your mind.

The writing group was on Thursdays and music appreciation
was on Tuesday so it filled my week quite nicely apart from
those other five days when I wondered if I should ask Dorothy
out. She served me a donut and said she didn't think she'd
want to hear the professor's lessons because she'd had enough
of all that when she was in high school. And she looked over
my shoulder towards the door where someone was leaving
behind me I glanced round and saw them it was the two men
again. I said to her do you know them? Who she said. Those
men. No she said they're only customers like you.

First week of music appreciation there was a gramophone
had been brought into the room and about fifteen of us come
to listen and Weasel-Grunt paced up and down rubbing his
hands not looking at any of us thinking to himself these
dumb Americans what can I possibly teach them they're all
too stupid. So instead of saying anything at all he started the
record it was Schubert's "Unfinished" Symphony. Sound
was terrible and the record was scratched. At the end of it the
professor looks like he's almost crying and doesn't know what
to say so a lady puts up her hand and tells everyone it reminds
her of when she was a little girl and her father took her to a

concert in Philadelphia she was maybe five or six years old and he said to her before it started the one thing you absolutely do not do is make a noise and wouldn't you know it as soon as it got going she had what you might call an emergency and needed to leave the room we all laughed when she said this it was a very funny story. Another person there a man in a bow-tie he said the music made him think of the sea and he wondered if Schubert knew anything about sailing or possibly marlin fishing because there was something about that music and its power and energy that showed a real understanding of the elements like when you hook a truly large creature. Whaling even. But what we all wanted to know was why the symphony is unfinished we all supposed it must be Schubert's last and he died but no that's not true it turns out he went on to write another. Someone wondered if perhaps he wasn't very happy with this one and gave up and I know I've done that on quite a few novels when they haven't gone exactly how I wanted it's a very necessary part of creativity but the "Unfinished" Symphony is apparently the best thing he wrote so he must have done some more movements that got burned up or something. The rule was that you did four movements but the "Unfinished" Symphony has only two so it's simple arithmetic.

Now I have to say that the professor wasn't much help to us in any of this. He was more interested in how this tune turns into that tune and gets thrown around so that it's on a violin one minute and an oboe the next and that's all very well but it's not the main question. It's like someone opening the back of a radio and saying this part has got a yellow wire and this component is the same shape as this other one here. You won't fix anything that way. So if he wasn't going to tell us why Schubert never finished it, which is the important question, could he at least tell us what it was all supposed to mean? What does it express, what does the music represent? What's its message? You read a story you know what it means. You hear a piece of music and it's all in code. We wanted him to break the code for us. Is it ships at sea, knights in a forest, elephants, what? Schubert must have had something in mind. But Weasel-Grunt couldn't tell us. Instead he kept going on about how this joins to that and the instruments pass it round like a ball game. You go to a ball game there's a winner and a loser that's the point you read a novel there's a story that's the point but the one thing this darned fool German couldn't get to was the point of music except that it's something you play on the radio while you read the newspaper.

A kindly looking man in his seventies with a neatly clipped moustache said he'd been to many lectures on music appreciation and he knew about sonata form and he wondered if the professor could explain sonata form because the gentleman wasn't always clear about the difference between transition and second subject nor was he always able to spot the exact moment of the recapitulation because sometimes he got it wrong and was still really in the development.

The professor said to him there's no such thing as sonata form. I couldn't believe it here was this extremely nice polite civil gentleman who worked forty years in the insurance business and had been to Lord knows how many music appreciation courses and genuinely knew the subject as well as I knew vacuum tubes and the professor was telling him no they got it all wrong and all the things you thought you learned they all mean nothing they don't exist you stupid dumb American. I asked the gentleman to explain sonata form to us and he said it's how Mozart and Beethoven and Schubert and those other composers wrote a lot of their music. You start with a tune called the first subject, then you have to change key until you get to another tune called the second subject, then maybe it all gets repeated. After that you have a development section where the tunes get mixed up until a while later the first subject comes back and then the second only this time in the home key and after that you're pretty much done except for a bit tagged on the end called the coda. That's sonata form.

Now if there's one thing I know it's that when you ask an idiot to explain something they'll make it sound darned complicated but if you ask a truly wise man they'll make it clear as pure water and that's exactly what this gentleman had done. He'd given us the best music appreciation lesson we'd ever had. Classical music, it turns out, is exactly like writing a good novel. Instead of plot points and three-act structure you've got exposition, development and recapitulation, and the reason why Beethoven was great was he was a rebel who broke the rules Mozart and Haydn simply followed, for example he put the second subject in an unusual key, and the reason why Schubert was great was that although he copied Beethoven a lot of the time he had this way of writing really fantastic tunes so you knew exactly whether it was first subject or second. I said to the gentleman this is like a eureka moment sir and I'm so grateful to you because what the professor said was all very well but I understand now that tunes are like characters in a story and the important thing is that they're sympathetic which in this case means you can hum along with them and we both looked at the little bald German so-called expert standing there with his mouth hanging open and he wasn't saying a darned thing. I said you know it's almost like we've got Schubert right here in the room with us it's all so clear to me now and that's all it takes, you've just got to make things simple and accessible to ordinary people with average intelligence, then it's no more complicated than fixing a radio.

Intermezzo

Takes a moment for Conroy to identify the sudden intrusion of sound: his own entry buzzer, rarely heard. He's still in his bedroom, as good a place as any to hide the evidence when they come to search, so he closes the laptop and puts it inside his wardrobe, covering it with a green woollen pullover he can't remember ever having worn. Did they perhaps leave that too? He goes through his flat to the intercom beside the door, presses the button and attempts to stall. "Go away."

A pause at the other end. Then, "I've come for my lesson."

It's risible but Conroy doesn't feel like laughing. "I don't do lessons."

"You agreed."

It's the damn punk, Conroy can recognise his juvenile whine even through the compressed signal of the intercom. Must have a couple of heavies with him that'll try to push their way inside the flat. "We never agreed anything."

"Nine till ten."

"It's nine o'clock now?"

"Nearly. I've got the money."

The three of them down below at the front entrance are probably willing to camp all week until Conroy has to go and buy a loaf of bread. Best get this over with. He presses to unlock and puts his eye to the peephole, waiting to see the aggressors he will have to contend with. Eventually it's the punk whose under-developed form stands distorted in the fish-eye curvature of the lens, the other two presumably positioning themselves out of view with weapons raised. Just hope there

210

aren't any neighbours around to get caught in the cross-fire.

The scrawny hoodlum taps on the door. Calls weakly through it. "Mr Conroy?"

"Really sure you want to do this?"

"I brought my scores." He's holding up a red plastic folder for display, must be a blade in there.

Conroy takes a deep breath. "I'm going to count to three, then open. There's no need for anybody to try anything rash or hasty. Let's all just take our time and do this real nice."

"Sure."

He counts, each number echoing in his mind with the thought of it, and in that space between voice and imagination he reminds himself what this is all about, the insertion of fake time into a distracted world. He reaches three and opens the door waiting for the chaos to start. But the lad simply walks inside and halts in front of Conroy awaiting further instruction. Moment of hesitation. Conroy steps past him into the corridor to confront the others and sees they've gone. Puzzled by the ruse he comes back inside and closes the door. "They want you to do this on your own?"

The silent response is a small white envelope in an outstretched hand. Conroy snatches and opens it.

Dear Mr Curran,

As agreed on phone heres Ryan you said 35 the hour so check for 70 thats two weeks same time.

Thanks, Tracey Blyth

"What the fuck is this?"

"My mum phoned you."

Something resembling a cheque flutters to the floor, failing to release any anthrax spores or polonium dust. Conroy stares again at the punk who is suddenly looking less hoodlum-like. "How old are you?"

"Fourteen."

"A genuine child?" Somehow it hadn't been quite so obvious in FLOP, but now Conroy understands why the natural urge to beat him to mush had been suppressed by an involuntary protectiveness towards those soft-toy eyes. "Still at school?"

Kid nods.

"So why aren't you there now?"

"It's Saturday. I'm missing football for this."

"And I sorted all of this with your mother?"

"You gave me your card and she phoned you."

Propagation of false history: the theorem is proved. "Ryan, eh? Let's get this over with. Know what a piano looks like?"

Kid nods towards the gleaming black upright. "I can play you my diploma pieces."

"Not so fast, son. Park your arse on the stool over there and give me C-major scale, two hands, legato."

What follows is perfectly convincing, from the seat-height adjustment to the smooth thumb rolls and evenly articulated tone. Then without further invitation the boy begins a Brahms intermezzo. Conroy goes to the armchair he slept in, still moulded to his shape as he slumps bewildered onto it. "Slower," he mutters. For all its immaturity the boy's playing is skilful and, far more importantly, shows true musicality. Such polished elegance merely highlights the illusory nature of what purports to be taking place. Conroy lets him play the complete first section before halting him. "Is your mother a musician?"

"No, she works in a sandwich shop. Happy Bun."

Sounds plausible, and the answer came quickly. "Your father?"

"Welder. I don't see him much. But my grandfather could

play, so dad says. He's in a home now."

The information could prove useful. "If I paid your grandfather a visit would he verify these details?"

"You wouldn't get a lot of sense out of him."

Conroy nevertheless gets the name of the care home for reference. He can check it out later. He asks what other pieces the boy can offer and requests Alkan's *Barcarolle*. Soon, gently rolling sextuplets fill the room, a poignant vision of impossible romance. Isn't that, after all, the whole point of art: to give us a fake world better than the shitty real one? Why not simply yield to the mindfuck? Pretend the kid's got a future, indulge the vain hope and give thirty-five quid's worth out of thirty-five years of professional expertise. After Alkan they look at the other items on Ryan's list and Conroy sets him a sight-reading exercise. It's almost enjoyable, nearly a kind of redemption. But it's a false consciousness, an empty interpolation. To be redeemed would be to capitulate.

"Now get out."

"What?"

"Time's up."

"See you next week?"

"If I'm alive."

"Thanks."

Once Ryan's left, Conroy goes to the bedroom, opens the wardrobe and checks that his laptop is still under the green woollen pullover. In his absence the garment's folds appear to have been disturbed. He'd been distracted by the boy's playing; while both of them were looking at the keyboard someone must have come in behind them. Conroy retrieves his laptop, sits on the bed and resumes reading.

Radio Daze (continued)

I was telling Dorothy about Adorno's music appreciation lesson while she poured me a cup of coffee and why are they all so crazy about Schubert or Beethoven I said to her why not Benny Goodman. Dorothy has blonde hair with a very fashionable permanent wave, pale skin like porcelain and a small attractive mole above her lip. I don't mention any of this to make Maisie jealous but only because I know the importance of physical description in good writing. Take for example this sentence from the first draft of *The Martian Protocols*:

Everything seemed calm as Goodman opened the locker-room door and selected a space suit.

Now you might consider this a perfectly good sentence and it would certainly do the job well enough in a great many modern science fiction novels. But thanks to a series of rewrites made according to the Seven Point Plan it became transformed into the following:

The tiny sun had risen in a salmon pink sky beyond the thick plexiglass window of Dome A when Goodman who was still rubbing his sleep-starved eyes went to the polished steel security door and keyed in the code then entered and looked right and left inspecting the hanging spacesuits that were like oversized deflated party balloons on their curved aluminium hooks.

Any fool can see that the second version is a million times better than the first which shows us incidentally why good novels have to be long. Dorothy said to me if the German writer's story is so terrible then why did you go to his talk from which I realised that she hadn't quite understood. At this stage in my career I still needed to learn the important rule of making the facts as clear as possible. Usually this means research research research for example the salmon pink sky in *The Martian Protocols*. When I wrote the first draft in 1960 nobody knew what the sky on Mars looked like and it was not until 1976 that we saw colour pictures and I was able to make my story more accurate. I didn't arrive at the final version until 1980 a full twenty years after starting. There aren't many writers who dedicate themselves so completely to the idea of perfection especially the ones you so often see in print these days who don't bother to check the simplest fact like the orbital period of a planet or its gravitational strength but if there's one thing I know about it's the importance of detail.

So let me get this clear she said there's a fellow in your writing group who's doing a novel about classical music and then there's the professor who gave a talk about classical music and they're two different people don't you think it's a funny coincidence. I said no not really because they're both Germans and those people are all the same. And Dorothy looked past my shoulder in a way that made me turn and see them sitting at a corner table at the far end, the two men in dark suits, one of them glancing away when I met his eyes.

I looked at Dorothy again and said in a low voice who are those people and she said why don't you go over and sit at the table next to theirs. I said are you sure that's a good idea and she said I think they need to talk to you. Funnily enough I had the sudden impression that Dorothy knew exactly who they were and what they were doing and thus reassured I took my coffee cup and selected a seat. It was a fine bright morning outside and the sun had risen into a clear blue sky. Except that it wasn't directly visible from where I sat being occluded by tall buildings. And in any case I had my back to the window and was staring down at the table in front of me.

"May I?"

I looked up and saw one of the two men who had come across and was pointing at the ashtray. I nodded but instead of simply taking it he then reached inside his suit jacket and brought out a packet of cigarettes. "You wouldn't happen to have a light would you?"

"I don't smoke, sir."

"That's unusual."

"I'm asthmatic."

"Smoking is good for clearing the lungs, they've done studies to prove it. Say, don't I know you from somewhere?"

"I don't believe so, sir."

"Columbia?"

"I do work there."

"You're with Professor Armstrong, aren't you?"

"You know him?"

He smiled broadly. "Sure I do. Let me introduce you to my friend, he knows him too. Come and join us."

They called themselves Mike and Bobby though I kept forgetting which was which. Their suits were identical and so I expect was their toothpaste. One had darker hair and a more pronounced shadow on his jaw but in other respects they were pretty much indistinguishable and I soon realised they must be government men.

"Cigarette?" said one.

"He doesn't smoke," said the other.

"How do the two of you gentlemen know Professor Armstrong?"

They said they were interested in the frequency modulation system and were convinced it would revolutionise American life. "And of course there are strategic implications," one of them said with a lowered voice. The three of us moved our heads closer together in an instinctive way.

Andrew Crumey

"Dan – you don't mind if we call you that, do you? Dan, we truly appreciate the contribution you're making to scientific progress in our country. Even a humble laboratory technician has his part to play in the march of technology, and you're playing that part very well."

"Did Professor Armstrong tell you that?"

"You bet. The professor's a great man, isn't he? But you know, there are some people who feel jealous of his greatness. They don't like it that he has the patent on the FM system, so that anybody who wants to set up a station to broadcast it, or manufacture compatible receiving equipment, has to do it under licence from him. Those envious people say that no man should have such a monopoly."

The other joined in. "Imagine if Guttenberg could have patented the printing press, or Galileo the telescope."

"Dan, what we're really concerned about are the strategic implications. When people get jealous they start spying and you wouldn't want that to happen, would you?"

"Certainly not!"

"Especially if the spy was going to take our American technology and export it to some other nation that totally despises our way of life."

"You mean Germany? Russia?"

"Any number of places. We're a free country and freedom has its problems. Wouldn't it all be so simple if we had tyranny?" He laughed, the other laughed too.

I said quietly, "Are you with the government?"

His laugh froze. "Sure, we're with the government."

"I could tell from your suits."

"Then we might as well go straight to the point. You've recently had dealings with a certain Theodor Wiesengrund Adorno."

"I wouldn't exactly call them dealings, sir."

"He splits his time between two employers, the Radio Research Project and the Institute for Social Research. You realise one of those is an organisation of communist sympathisers?"

I swallowed. "Not exactly, sir. Though I'd kind of guessed."

"The other is supposed to come up with recommendations for reform of public broadcasting. A pretty sensitive mix of interests when you consider what a crucial point we've reached, both with television and FM. Our children's future could be decided by a few Reds."

"Can't the government act?"

"We're a land of liberty, Dan, we don't go about things in a heavy-handed way. But look, you already took an FM receiver to Adorno's office, didn't you? Those receivers are still experimental, secret, commercially sensitive..."

"I acted under direct instruction from Professor Armstrong!"

"We know, we know. In fact we were the ones who made the suggestion to Professor Armstrong, though naturally he didn't discuss it with you and in fact would need to deny all knowledge if ever you were to raise the subject with him. You do promise, don't you, never to mention any of this to the professor? It would only complicate matters unnecessarily."

"I give you my word, sir, as a loyal American citizen."

"Good. Here's what we propose next – and I can assure you this is all with Professor Armstrong's full approval. We have another piece of equipment that we want you to collect from the following address." He handed me a printed business card. "The device is smaller, lighter than the ones you've seen. We want you to pick it up this afternoon after you finish work, then take it to Adorno and give him a demonstration."

"Will he be expecting me?"

"No, but he never knows what to expect so it won't be hard for you to convince him that an appointment has been made. Afterwards you'll leave the equipment in his office. It's very important that you do this for us."

He stood up and shook my hand and the other followed his lead. "Very nice talking to you Dan," he said then they both went out. I looked across at Dorothy behind the counter but she had her head down almost as if avoiding me and I realised then that she was a government agent too. It made me feel good knowing our nation's freedom was in such capable hands. It was also kind of exciting to have been allowed into their exclusive secret club.

They had not however mentioned what was really on my mind which was that the FM system could potentially be a way of communicating with space so that not only were Reds and Germans a threat but also Martians and Venusians. Most probably there were already broadcasts from other planets possibly of a propaganda kind and it was only a matter of finding the correct frequency and having an appropriate receiving circuit probably requiring considerable amplification. Now I had often wondered about modifying equipment in Professor Armstrong's laboratory but of course this was not possible however my new role in intelligence might give me valuable opportunities and all in all I would say that this was the most thrilling thing that had happened in my life since the time when the angels spoke to me (chapter 4).

The business card belonged to an organisation called the Rosier Foundation which sounded like some kind of charitable body and as soon as my lab shift finished at three-thirty I headed over to the address and found a smart looking office building with all sorts inside such as an insurance company and an advertising agency and a fur importer and on the eighth floor

I got the place I was looking for where this nice lady told me to wait a moment until Mr O'Yea could see me. I sat watching her type a letter and the clock on the wall ticked slowly behind her and I said to myself Daniel you're really moving up in the world now and you're bound to make contacts here that will be invaluable in your future career.

If there's one thing I know it's the importance of contacts contacts contacts. William Shakespeare would be a forgotten and unknown name if it wasn't for all the handshaking he did in London even with King Charles. Michelangelo worked for the Pope and you can't get a lot better connected than that. Take any of these great artists or writers and they were basically in with the big-shots because that's how it operates. Once in a while you get some complete outsider but it's so rare we might as well forget about it. I knew this even way back I figured the Columbia Writers were a bunch of losers but maybe one night someone important would come along simply to listen and I'd have my break well it came from completely the different direction didn't it. Life's a lottery and we make our own luck.

The phone rang and when the secretary picked it up she said hello this is the Rosier Foundation like it was French, Rosy-A, and that only made it sound all the more classy. It's important to have a good name and I've used quite a few in my writing career for example Herbert Clarence, Dan Zorn, Lincoln C Roberts, Wayne Johnson. All my books have been published by my own Daniel Franklane III Publications Inc but that's because it's important to have continuity and in any case I find that existing publishing houses have never been understanding enough of what is most original and important in my work. I don't need anybody telling me how to write a novel for goodness sake! I get all the advice I need from Maisie my loving wife of forty-one years and from our four Pekinese dogs who bark at anything they don't like and are wiser critics than all of those trumped-up idiots you see in the newspapers not to mention the lunatics that work for publishers and write rejection letters for books they haven't even taken the time to read.

The phone rang again then the secretary said to me, "Mr O'Yea will see you now." She waved towards his door as if to say that's that go ahead so I went inside and there was this little office with shelves nearly empty and no photographs or anything as if he'd only moved in that day and Mr O'Yea sitting at his desk.

"Take a seat, Mr Franklane."

He was maybe thirty-five years old and had a French accent which is so much more pleasant on the ear than German. Light grey business suit, looked expensive. Most noticeable thing was he wore a black eye patch, I guessed it was maybe on account of a war injury until I did the arithmetic.

"I've come for the equipment Mr O'Yea."

"I know." He reached for something on the floor beside him and I noticed the name plate on his desk he was actually called Mr Oeillet but the secretary had said it in a French way. He lifted the thing and put it on the table, a brown leather case with a handle.

"It's in there?"

"That's right."

"How can it be so small?" It looked to be no bigger than a sewing machine. "Is that really an FM radio receiver?"

I saw kind of a twitch in his only eye. "Never mind what it is." He opened the case to reveal what looked pretty much like a conventional receiver except there was no tuning dial only a volume control. "You know what you have to do with it, don't you?" He closed the case and slid it across the desk to me. "Then off you go."

After having waited so long this all seemed too abrupt. "Now hold on sir I'm very happy to help my country but shouldn't you perhaps explain a little more about the operation? For example could it be dangerous? What if the German pulls a gun on me?"

"I promise you he won't."

"But he's a spy, isn't he?"

"That's something we hope to determine."

There was another matter I felt obliged to mention because if there's one thing I know it's that you never get anything in life unless you ask for it. "Will there be any remuneration?"

He opened a drawer in his desk and pulled something out that he tossed onto the surface like it was a piece of rag. It was a wrapped bundle of dollar bills.

"All of this?" I said incredulously, picking up the money and estimating with a flick that it was more than I could earn in a month of lab work.

"Consider it an advance on anything else we ask you to do in the next week or two. Now please get out of here."

I went straight back over to Morningside and smooth-talked my way into the office of Dr Theodor Wiesengrund Adorno who naturally was rather surprised to see me.

"What in heaven's name do you want?"

I raised my arm that held the case with the equipment inside.

"I shall have to check this..."

I assured him it was all arranged and we should get on with the demonstration. "I enjoyed your talk the other night."

"Did you really?"

"But I do think you should consider your method of presentation." I suggested to him an idea I'd had that would make his music appreciation lessons more memorable and entertaining. "Why not do them in historical costume? Pretend you're the actual composer."

"What? You mean dress up as Schubert?"

I'd opened the case and now was sliding the filing cabinet to get at the wall socket behind. "Presentation is very important sir. I think you might not understand just how much it matters to us in this country. You've obviously got a lot of interesting ideas but it's no use simply giving them out as a lecture. What you need is a way of bringing them to life." I plugged it in then turned the knob and switched on the receiver, expecting to hear the feed. Instead there was silence.

The professor stared at the device, and at me, and at the device again. "Well?" he said.

"Let's wait for it to warm up. The vacuum tubes can be a little temperamental. But notice how there's absolutely no hiss, no static."

"In fact nothing at all. We could characterise the experience as wholly negative."

"Two minuses make a plus, professor." I don't quite know why I said it except as a way of gaining time. I gave an encouraging glance at the papers spread before him that he'd been working on until I came in. "How's work going?"

"Well enough."

"You told us your project is all about... let's see... Karl Marx didn't you say?"

He looked at me suspiciously. "It's about monitoring public opinion regarding radio programming."

"Oh yes, sure." Still nothing from the receiver. I figured I must have bumped it too hard on the way and damaged a tube. "But you're not exactly enamoured of the American way of life, are you? Let's be honest sir, you think we're all complete idiots."

"Neither all nor complete," he said slowly.

"But the guy who invented this thing, you'd hardly call him an idiot, would you? We've got the finest scientists and engineers in the entire world."

The professor could do nothing but agree. "It's the condition of the arts that I question, because here they are entirely controlled by the culture industry."

He was going straight back into one of his speeches about how much he resented our freedom to innovate and improve society that only showed him up for the lousy stinking Red he really was and it suddenly dawned on me that this silent equipment I'd switched on wasn't a receiver at all. It was how the G-men could monitor subversives like Adorno.

Yet almost as soon as the thought occurred to me there was a loud pop and then the music started only this time it was a symphony orchestra.

"Ah, this is more useful," the professor said, leaning back in his chair.

"You can hear how little interference..."

"Ssh!"

He was the most rude and arrogant little fellow I'd ever come across this big-eyed bald gnome like an overgrown baby. He wasn't even a whole lot older than me only he acted like he was this big-shot academic or something instead of a guy nobody had ever heard of. He was listening to the music like he was hearing a really deep and complicated message in it though it was only some old tune and I simply stood there watching him and realising that if it truly was a monitoring device then the G-men weren't getting a whole lot on him right now only the sound of his chair creaking occasionally when he moved or else a sigh. It was in all honesty quite tedious and if there's one thing I've learned it's never to be boring which is quite the worst thing a man can do.

After a while the music stopped and the receiver went quiet so I wondered if it had failed again but Adorno appeared happy enough. "The sound quality is quite exceptional," he said. "This really does give me cause to reconsider my views."

I said I was glad to be of help and he could keep the receiver for as long as he needed but he didn't listen to me it was exactly like the scene in the music appreciation lesson he only wanted to follow his own line of thought. He said to me we need to consider the new form that art will take in the age of perfect mechanical reproduction. His point I think was that if everybody can hear a symphony orchestra on the radio then they don't need to go to a concert hall any more and if the radio station can broadcast music from phonograph recordings then all you need is a studio. He appeared to think this a bad thing though I couldn't understand why and in any case they have baseball on the radio but people still pay to see the game. As long as there are conductors who can put on a good show I expect the same thing will happen with concerts and he said that's exactly my point.

More music started on the radio and the professor listened to it every bit as eagerly as before. There was no talking on the transmission or any station announcement or sponsor's message or anything only this classical music with long gaps between each piece. Obviously this wasn't a genuine radio station and the device was no ordinary receiver. But as long as it kept pumping out these old orchestral tunes the professor wasn't going to object. The G-men had found the perfect way of keeping him under control. I expect he'd sit there all day in that creaking chair of his listening to the perfect hiss-free sound and never doing anything to subvert America's children with his godless communistic nonsense.

I said goodbye to him and when I came out and crossed the street a guy came up to me dressed pretty much like the agents I'd spoken to before and asked me if I'd done what was asked. Sure I said he's listening to it now and the G-man said come with me, there was a car parked around the corner and he told me to get in back, driver was kind of a rough-looking type and that made me feel safe knowing we couldn't get attacked by any enemy agents with this great hunk of beef looking after us he was real mean with a big scar down his face. The G-man and myself in back and the car setting off and I'm saying to Maisie I turned to him and said what'll you do to him?

"Who?"

"Adorno of course." Maisie doesn't always follow too well what I tell her and the dogs were barking pretty loud at this point.

"I expect we'll deport him."

"Is that all? You mean you won't shoot him? If you ask me that's what we should do with any spy who comes here upsetting our way of life."

We drive for a bit and wind up in what is frankly not the best neighbourhood of New York City. Car stops at kind of a rundown warehouse looking like it probably used to be a garment plant, G-man says get out and they take me inside. Maisie doesn't believe a word of it but I swear to God this is all true so help me and it's only now I'm old and not afraid of the consequences that I'm prepared to tell the story.

Inside of this place they've set up an electrical workshop but nobody else is there only me and the government man and the driver and they take me to this bench where there's a radio in pieces and the G-man says to me do you think you can make this operational as an FM receiver. I tell him I'll try and so for the next two or three hours I'm working like a madman. They bring me coffee and donuts. At one point we play cards and the driver tells a joke I don't exactly understand. He plays with a switchblade.

The G-man says to me you know Dan you're absolutely right about the aliens and I say to him what do you mean. He says to me we think they're trying to establish contact and if they get through to the Russians first or the Germans or the Japanese or the English then where do you think that'll leave us and I said in the soup that's where. Exactly.

Maisie's never believed any of it but if there's one thing I know it's that the world needs its visionaries even if to the rest of the society they appear eccentric or unusual or completely deluded. They all said Copernicus was mad, Columbus was a nut and Da Vinci was a fruitcake. The world's greatest geniuses have been derided simply because they were so far ahead of their time. I even wonder if my own time has still to come, despite all the proof that has built up over the years showing beyond question that our planet is being watched.

"You're right Dan and we need you to fix this radio because the aliens are certainly using the FM system only it's not Armstrong's version it's another that wouldn't be covered by his patent. We want you to stay here until you can make it work will you do that?"

Sure I said.

After a while longer they needed to go home and see their wives and families. The driver said he had a four-year old daughter who was sweet as Shirley Temple. Didn't take after him in other words. I didn't have any wife or family not even four Pekinese dogs and was perfectly happy to remain in the workshop until morning by which time I was sure I'd have fixed the radio so they left me there alone. I suppose some people might have considered the place spooky or unearthly or downright menacing but to a technician such as myself it was a comfortable and stimulating environment and they left biscuits and milk in case I needed them and there was a side room with a mattress on the floor if I got tired.

The machine looked much like the one I'd taken to the German professor's office about the same size only this had a tuning dial. Must have been around two o'clock in the morning that I finally got it working. Place was so quiet it made me jump when a loud crackle came out from the loudspeaker and my screwdriver almost slipped where I had the back open and was poking around. Maisie still says she doesn't believe a word of it but I sealed the rear panel in place and turned it round and started slowly twisting the dial to see what I could pick up. No markings on it so I hadn't any idea what sort of frequency range I was listening to but I soon hit the signal from Professor Armstrong's transmitter and it was loud and clear. Tried looking for the classical station but of course I couldn't find it because whatever Adorno was listening to was a fake. Sure was a satisfying feeling knowing I'd been of service to my country and then I thought to myself why not look around see what else they've got in this lab. Quite well equipped in spite of the rundown surroundings which only goes to show it truly was a secret experimental facility run on behalf of the government. One cupboard I looked in all it had were these big canisters and when I opened one it was sort of a black powder inside. There was a device nearby started clicking as soon as I put a handful of powder near it. If there's one thing I know about it's nuclear radiation and these boys obviously weren't only interested in radios no sir. Maisie doesn't believe it but how else did I get that thyroid trouble a few years ago? Patriotic service that's how. So what I say is three cheers for

Mr Oeillet and the Rosier Foundation and to hell with the likes of Adorno.

I went back to the radio feeling proud to be an American and turned the dial feeling sure that if I tried hard enough I might even pick up a signal from Venus. Anything's possible if you truly believe. And you know after a while I hit it loud and clear, came out of nowhere this FM station that couldn't be any on Earth because there was only one at the time and I'd heard it already. This was something else. A little faint on account of the great distance but no mistaking it.

"A mighty fine story," says Maisie. "But I do prefer the one about the guy with the tiny spot."

So I tell her that instead, after we've walked the dogs.

Blyth

A famous philosopher wondered how we can be sure the world didn't get made five minutes ago along with all our memories. Something for Conroy to chew over in the day room of Elm View Care Home where amid the subdued chatter of a dozen residents he sits near a window with Mr Blyth, grandfather of Ryan. The folk here all look like cute old-timers with zimmer frames and hearing aids but Conroy's no patsy, he knows things could turn ugly at any moment. So he stays vigilant while trying to get some new lead on the foulest plot in all of creation, the great digital swindle he has to bust if it's the last goddam thing he does. Too bad that Blyth, shrivelled like last week's newspaper and silent as a toy whose battery ran out, is deciding to be uncooperative.

Then across the room Conroy sees her. Tall, sleek, cool. What's a girl like her doing, getting herself mixed up in the geriatric care industry? She's slowly pushing a drinks trolley, kind of half-leaning on its tubular steel frame as though her mind is elsewhere. Conroy rises. "I'll get a coffee." He'll risk running a gauntlet of knitting needles if it means getting a whiff of the hot new chick they've parachuted out of girl-heaven into this asylum of broken dreams and weak bladders.

"A cup of your black magic just might make my day," he tells her, sidling up casually to the trolley where she stands.

"Tea or coffee?" She stares blankly at him.

"Your finest java, make it a double shot."

She proceeds to pour something hot and dark from the smaller of two urns into a polystyrene cup. "50p," she says, handing it to him. "Help yourself to milk and sugar."

This kid doesn't waste her words. Conroy likes that.

"New here?" he says, but instead of answering she only turns her pretty head to an old lady seated nearby who's waving a handful of shrapnel like her over-extended life depends on it.

"Sorry, what did you say?" the girl asks, looking at Conroy again after handing the lady the tea she's ordered. This broad isn't the kind for small-talk, she's a no-nonsense type. The sort who knows how to handle a heavy tubular steel trolley with enough boiling liquid stored up in its great silvery urns to turn that old lady and her friends to mashed potato sooner than you could count the change from a one-pound coin. "Like anything for your uncle?" she asks, nodding towards the window table where Blyth sits drooling.

"Tea," Conroy decides, watching her take another cup and place it beneath the nozzle, then she flips the lever and makes it all pour out, brown as the good earth and steaming gently as it flows, real slow. "I can see you're something of an expert." But once again her ice-blue eyes are on someone else, scrawny guy with dark spots all over his bald scalp, says he wants milk, that's all, cold milk. Looks harmless enough but you never can tell.

She hands Conroy the cup of tea and it's like they've run into some kind of da capo. "50p. Help yourself to milk and sugar."

He takes the two drinks back to Blyth's table, feeling ever so slightly vulnerable, walking across the day room with each of his hands trapped by his own unexpected generosity, clutching the hot drinks that would go flying if one of those old ladies – that one with the magazine, say – were to prove instead to be a young, male, heavily disguised emissary, suddenly pulling off a blue-rinse wig and rubberised wrinkle mask, raising the loaded barrel of a cleverly converted zimmer frame. Conroy would know exactly what to do, throwing the two cups high and to the right where their scorching parabola would fail to intersect with any innocent by-stander. Or rather, by-sitter, since nobody is actually standing except for the chick at the trolley who's more kind of slouching, and Conroy himself, who's made it back to his companion without being attacked.

"A famous philosopher wondered how we can be sure the world didn't get made five minutes ago along with all our memories," Conroy announces as he settles himself. "And you know what he reckoned? We can't. No way."

Blyth is still playing dumb but from the other side of the room there arrives a sound that signals unexpected movement. Conroy freezes, cup in hand as he searches for the distant threat, perceiving a spillage of tabloid newspaper at the feet of a woman he thinks goes by the name of Mrs Tanner, awkward type by the look of her, necklace and cardigan too faux-senile for comfort. She's trying to reach down and pick up the pages she's dropped; the old dear beside her is gazing around mock-casually. They're up to something, and Conroy is on his guard.

Then it's the tea trolley again. The chick, she's part of it, has to be; she's beautiful and that means her presence in this mess must make sense if only he can figure out how, because the world is a system of signs and every sign signifies something. A hyphen on a stave, an innocent fermata: it's in the silences between the notes that things happen. Threat hovers like a hornet around his neck but Conroy doesn't flinch, he can handle himself in a situation. The buzzing fades.

"Ever heard of Edwin Armstrong?" he asks Blyth or the air between them when the coast is clear.

Eventually the old man says something. "They were out in the rain again."

"Frequency modulation," Conroy reminds him, determined to break down his resistance. "Greatest military secret and technological breakthrough of the twentieth century. Know how many lives were sacrificed so that decent ordinary citizens could twiddle a knob on their car radio without fear of static interference?"

"I told you not to let them get wet..." Blyth trails off, eyes glazed. The trolley girl comes over.

"Are we alright today, Mr Blyth? Warm enough? Comfortable there?" Each phrase delivered with a final upswing.

"What do they call you, angel?"

"I'm no angel, pet." This babe sure knows how to look after herself.

Conroy nods towards Blyth. "One day we'll all be like him."

"That's not a nice thing to say." She raises her voice to address the one she's paid to take an interest in. "Not nice at all, is it Mr Blyth?" Mr Blyth blinks but says nothing.

Conroy brings a photograph from his pocket. "Ever seen

this man?"

She squints at it. "He your grandfather or something?"

"Professor Edwin H. Armstrong. A genius with everything to live for. Then one night he took a walk out of a thirteenth-floor window. Official verdict: suicide."

"What a shame." If she knows anything about it she isn't letting on. No, this siren is as cool as a Cornetto, allowing herself to be momentarily distracted by Mrs Tanner calling to her from the other side of the room but in no immediate hurry to respond.

"I want to know what really happened."

"You some kind of detective? Historian?"

"Musician. Sometimes that means being a kind of historian, kind of detective. Armstrong was up against powerful vested interests. FM versus AM, you can imagine what that was like."

"Not really."

"Like Apple versus Microsoft. VHS and Betamax. AC/DC."

"I'm afraid you've lost me. Any more tea or coffee?"

"It goes so much further. This is about good versus evil, freedom against tyranny."

"Well good luck with it, but maybe time to leave your uncle now so he can rest." She's about to go over to Tanner, like it's all planned between them.

"You're beautiful."

"That's what my husband thinks."

"Have dinner with me."

"You have to go now, before I call for assistance. Please let's not make a scene in front of everyone."

All a little too simple: the babe who claims she's never heard of Armstrong, the old man with a trail of drool abseiling from the corner of his mouth. Both in it together. Conroy knows he's lost this round but he'll leave with dignity, returning the photograph to his jacket pocket as he rises. "If you change your mind then let me know."

"I'll do that. Goodbye now and take care."

They're all grinning when he walks out, the actors hired for the charade. The care home itself is no more than a poorly constructed stage set, convincing only if you don't look too carefully at it. Getting into his car Conroy inserts the ignition key and is about to twist it when a vision comes to him of what he knows is about to happen. The key starts the engine and also the radio that was playing when he arrived here, tuned to the classical station on the FM waveband that they know he always listens to, the place where they can insert something. A ball of flame and a rising cloud of thick black smoke interrupt the otherwise peaceful and unremarkable afternoon. The switchover has begun.

Laughing and Fainting, by Richard Sand
(www.memoirweb.com/richard_sand/chapter23.html)

Freud made the observation that melancholia and mourning both stem from a sense of loss, though it is only the mourner who can readily identify what has been taken away. As a therapist I cannot fill holes, only recognise their outline. I think of this in relation to C, a professional musician whose tendency to focus on a theme and perform endless variations upon it led him to confront the silent void, the absence, which lay at the centre of his existence. We might seek to cast our silences into the mouths of others, but their refusal to comply will only reflect our own inability to give voice to emptiness. Jung understood music's symbolic role in this: responding to a hostile letter from Freud he promised to "tune his lyre a few tones lower". I mentioned it to C in one of our sessions. C told me to shut the fuck up.

The angry exchange between Jung and Freud followed a tense lunch they had together in Munich on 24 November 1912. Freud's name had not been mentioned in recent articles Jung had written; Jung's defence was that since everyone knew Freud as the founding father of psychoanalysis no mention was necessary. The conversation moved on to the pharaoh Akhenaton, creator of a new solar cult, who scratched his father's name from all monuments and substituted his own instead. Freud's opinion was that Akhenaton's father-complex was the key to Egyptian monotheism; Jung found this too simplistic and pointed out that all pharaohs erased the names of their predecessors. At this point Freud fainted.

Discussing the case with C, I suggested that Freud took flight in silence, just as Akhenaton had sought to silence his father, and just as Jung had sought to silence Freud by erasing him from academic literature. C called me a pretentious wanker.

Jung picked Freud up and carried him to a sofa; Freud revived while being carried. "In his weakness," Jung later wrote, "he looked at me as if I were his father". Freud wrote to Ernest Jones: "There is some piece of unruly homosexual feeling at the root of the matter." Freud took flight in an orgasmic "little death"; I have seen cases of fugue far more elaborate and extended in form.

I asked C his opinion of Bach; the complexity of his counterpoint and the system of "equal temperament" that is a form of compromise, an acceptance of imperfection. Or Schumann, who wrote compositions supposedly dictated to him by angels. C said he would like to take the long pole

I use to open the high window of my consulting room and shove it up my poncy arse. This lance-pole, I reminded him, with its connotations of medieval jousting, had been a topic of previous conversations. No, he said, he didn't care about mythology, he merely wanted me to shut the fuck up.

The psychiatrist Paul Möbius posthumously diagnosed Schumann as having suffered from dementia praecox, a condition soon renamed by Eugen Bleuler as schizophrenia. Bleuler delivered a paper at the Third Psychoanalytic Congress in 1911, and in the conference photograph we see Jung crouching so as not to overshadow Freud. Relations between the two men were already strained by this point, but by way of rapprochement Freud spent some time after the congress studying mythology. Jung saw myth as representing universal features of the human psyche, and Freud became willing to entertain Jung's concepts. In many myths, the monster that is slain represents the father, while the treasure that is sought is really the umbilical chord whose severing will leave the hero free of his mother and able to find a bride. I suggested to C that by seeing the window pole as a possible tool of sexual violence against me, he was casting me in a parental role; which, of course, is also exactly what Freud was doing when he fainted in front of Jung. Freud saw that Jung sought to usurp him, as Akhenaton erased his father and his father's gods, and Freud's pre-emptive strategy was first to become a convert to Jungian symbolism, then later to collapse in Jung's arms like a child.

C said this was a very pretty story but all he really cared about was the great digital switchover, and if I wasn't going to discuss that with him then he was quite prepared to use the pole in order to give my dentist several months of repair work. Not only was C acting like a child, but he wanted now to silence me, to fill my mouth: a desperate flight from the unspeakable within himself. Some obscure and non-existent conspiracy had been the reason why C initially came to me. Also it was a condition of his probation. To heal such wounds we must sometimes be like Akhenaton and reconsider our own mythologies, the stories by means of which we make sense of the isolated facts of our lives. C imagined some great plot against him: I explained that the word plot originally meant a piece of land, then the map or plan of it, and hence by association any plan, such as that of a novel. C's plot, I suggested, was a fiction. The pole, he replied, was completely real.

C spoke of various traps, such as a rehearsal at a concert venue that led to a violent confrontation. I easily established that there had been no invitation to perform, nor any incident of the kind he described. Trap can mean the mouth, or the gaping void of a trap-door: he wanted me to shut my trap, by which he actually meant he feared his own silence. No, he insisted, he really wished I'd shut my fucking trap and stop spouting smart-arsed bullshit. Clearly we were getting somewhere.

Another element of C's mythology, apparently culled from the internet, was something called the Rosier Foundation, which again can be assumed never to have existed. The choice of the rose was however significant. I reminded C of the story of Beauty and the Beast, in which a man steals a rose from the Beast's garden and must send his daughter as payment. The Beast allows her to return to her dying father, but she then goes back to the Beast, who has also suffered without her, and her kiss liberates him from the spell of a witch. C asked me what the blazes that had to do with anything and I suggested he was behaving like a Beast, roaring fury at me. We had to discover what stolen rose lay at the heart of the matter. C of course resisted my analysis (so often a sign, to the experienced therapist, that the analysis is in fact quite accurate). I didn't come here to talk about sodding roses, he tellingly insisted.

The rose in mythic symbolism can be the female genitalia or the Virgin Mary. It can be the sun; the one true god with whose assistance Akhenaton erased his father. It remains an emblem of love which is understood by everyone; it is also a symbol of secrecy and silence. Carved alike on Roman Catholic confessionals and on the ceilings of banqueting halls, the flower was a reminder that whatever was said *sub rosa* would remain in strictest confidence. The rose, in other words, was everything that Conroy found unspeakable; everything he needed to speak about.

Harpocrates was given a rose by Cupid as a bribe not to betray the sexual adventures of Venus. Represented in Greek sculpture as a naked boy sucking his own finger, Harpocrates became the god of silence. He was the Greek version of Harpa-Khruti, Horus the child, whose adult representation with his four sons influenced the depiction of Christ with his disciples. C's mythology was a cult of silence.

He said, you're fucking dangerous mate, you could really screw up a person's mind with all this bullshit.

At last we were making genuine progress.

Jung, back in Zürich after the meeting where Freud fainted, wrote his colleague a letter which has been analysed countless times, as has Freud's reply. Each offered kind words couched in ambiguities, and their subsequent correspondence became increasingly antagonistic. Jung offered to tune his lyre a few tones lower. Matters reached a climax in a letter from Jung dated 18 December 1912 which denounced Freud as a prophet whose beard no one dared pluck, since Freud used analysis of his pupils as a means of subjugating them. "Instead of aiming continually at their weak spots take a good look at your own for a change," Jung advised. Freud, in reply, proposed that "we abandon our personal relations entirely." Jung accepted, saying, "The rest is silence."

As I told C this, he leapt at me with impressive vigour and placed his hands around my throat. The room spun interestingly as my brain became starved of oxygen, and before losing consciousness I reflected with satisfaction that his behaviour proved conclusively what I had already deduced. I was father, master, pharaoh and god. Quite flattering, really.

Fragments of Sand
(Six little pieces)

The Post Artist

The Postman has learned his art through long experience and practice. The optimisation of routes, the economical management of time. In his journeys through the streets he has had the opportunity to study the diversity and (he reflects with satisfaction) the fundamental simplicity of the world he finds. He has observed that dogs are stimulated to initiate barking by sound and sight as much as by smell, and have an innate response to uniforms of every kind. He has noted that well managed doors attract more mail than those which suffer neglect. He has often considered writing a book based on his rich experience: he knows the addresses of several publishers who might be interested.

The Postman has noted over the years a change – a deepening – in his attitude to the craft. Obsessed initially with brilliance of technique, he sought speedy delivery and a showy flourish. In the early days he was satisfied by power and volume more than tone. His footsteps on the path, the clapping of the letterbox, the flutter and fall of the delivered items: all these had to be well audible, even to the hard of hearing. It was only as his career developed that he began to appreciate the fact known to all the masters, that technique should only be a platform, never an end in itself. He now sought the subtle nuance, the unexpectedly appropriate touch that could raise a good delivery to one sublime. Fundamental to this new (and for him revolutionary) approach was the principle that the mode of delivery should always be in perfect harmony with the subject. Bills and legal notices should arrive to an even, resolute rhythm of footsteps; the entry should be firm, just, merciful – always decisive. Love letters must come with passion; letters of condolence with tenderness and sympathy, untainted by sentimentality. Above all, a postman must never be apologetic. Even the most grovelling of letters can be given some nobility.

In his pursuit of perfection the Postman found himself entering his next phase (his "middle period") when he began the systematic practice of steaming open all mail before delivery so as to prepare himself correctly. Most pieces were relatively undemanding but there were also those few that posed deeper problems. It might be a letter to an aunt or a reply to a newspaper advertisement, yet it would somehow seem to possess a quality of otherness, a hidden depth that would compel the Postman to sit long into the night planning his approach, practising the steps, perfecting the intended movements of the wrist. He would make notes in pencil, draw sketches of the type of drop he desired; endless sketches that he would ponder, cross out. Sometimes he would hold on to a difficult piece for days or weeks while he tried to decide exactly what he wanted. There would be happy flashes of inspiration that would wake him in the night, send shivers through his body, bring forth warm tears. There were also many failures. In the most exceptional cases he would make a preliminary visit to the intended street (out of uniform, naturally) and look carefully at the door of the problem address, mute and imposing. He would study the architecture of the house, take measurements, consider the likely weather. On several occasions he arranged rehearsals in the middle of the night, silently walking barefoot on the path then putting through the letterbox the piece of mail with a string attached. Once, he found that the tape holding it in place had come loose; the letter remained trapped inside when the string was pulled out, and so it was necessary for him to make use of an open kitchen window in order to break in and retrieve the letter before delivering it properly (and most memorably) in the morning.

Now, he knows, he is in his late period, when mastery and habit are one. The transition became discernible in retrospect: no artist can be his own critic, only the curator of his own history, and the Postman thought little at first of what he subsequently understood to have been prophetic symptoms of profound transformation. For a while he put it down to advancing age, being no longer as vigorous in mind or body as when he made those debut rounds decades ago with a delivery sack as full as his youthful and ambitious heart. Gradually, however, the signs multiplied. The weighing scales at the depot betrayed the incontrovertible truth of steady decline. He bumped into people in the street; youngsters at first, but soon pedestrians of any age, faces lowered, their thoughts engaged by texts delivered electronically. An analogous homogenisation, too long ignored, had already infected the envelopes on which he still strove to practise his craft. Handwritten letters, he realised, were becoming as painfully rare as the hairs on his head. In response he gave greater attention to printed bills, discovering that their stark delivery could express a strident modernism; but this, too, proved no more than a cry against the certainty of oblivion. The world was going online, life itself was increasingly virtual and intangible. His art was the solid fossil of an extinct era.

At least the news was given to him in person; made redundant on the very verge, he felt sure, of the masterpiece towards which his entire career had been unconsciously steering itself. It is as Post-Postman that he now undertakes his final magnum opus, his home having become his personal delivery route, a shrine to correspondence. Innumerable letter boxes of every kind crowd the walls, enabling him to exercise virtuosity without limit, sending hand-crafted missives to himself. He sees through his window the couriers with their bland packages and imagines the whirring drone that will one day lift him away to anonymous incineration. But he is happy to have lived for his craft and to have learned its most profound lessons. Art is truth: never lose faith. And post early for Christmas.

Bug

Professor Cimex began by speaking about segmentation, an obscure subject the students found hard to grasp; in any case some (the new ones) were distracted by his appearance, since Professor Cimex is a large insect of the sub-order Heteroptera. From somewhere in the tiered auditorium one student was heard to ask her neighbour naively, "Is it a reference to Kafka?"

The Professor described to us how segmentation is form-giving but external, his bristly appendages ably commanding the keyboard controls that summoned successive slides of his presentation. The Professor's tough brown exoskeleton suggests years of experience but also hides, it is generally agreed, a tender heart. He spoke of many things – mineralogy, optics, silk production – then showed a picture of his enemy, the Assassin Bug.

"When the Assassin feeds he ingests his own poisonous saliva," the Professor declared. "Thus all things taste the same to him, of nothing but himself. His every meal is a preformed experience, he can only dissolve and destroy whatever he encounters, turn it into a homogenous soup, digestible and bland. He acidifies the world in order to comprehend it."

The Professor makes distinctive clicking sounds as he paces; it has never been clear to us where exactly these characteristic noises originate, given the large number of joints and articulations evident both in his body and in his mind. Everyone's a bit surprised at first then gets used to it; not his fault he's an insect, they say, in fact you soon hardly notice. He does have something of a predatory reputation, though, some students finding in his manifest grossness an indefinable attraction.

"Categorial truth procedures are segmentary," he said, returning (we thought) to his opening topic, "but now I must speak of sex." At this point everyone began paying very close attention. "Traumatic insemination is the practice in certain species such as my own where the female, lacking any genital opening, must be hypodermically pierced by the male."

The one who'd mentioned Kafka looked as if she might throw up, and asked to leave the room. Some of us were remembering another student who'd once come to class with her head completely bandaged except for a single tearful eyehole. She was said to be one of his favourites.

"Pre-formed experience is found in the perception of art. It is salivary and segmented. It makes judgments identical; this sameness becomes the body named 'taste'. Trauma is unformed experience, entirely tasteless. Pre-formation is mediated by a dual tube but registers itself as unitary; trauma is single-tubed yet feels dual. 'One becomes two' becomes 'two becomes one'."

Professor Cimex has a foreign accent and some say this is the only reason anyone takes him at all seriously. Others retort that he is an insect and has his own way of expressing things. The girl with the bandaged head never gave us an opinion either way; she disappeared soon after the incident, quietly and mysteriously.

"I want to tell you something very, very important." He told us it was a sentence he'd read in a book and we needed to learn it by heart because we would only be in a position to understand it later on. None of us had a clue what he meant, but that appeared to be the point. One student copied it down as follows:

Hiq lonfa dobrejm pa ssuriud nexa ka heq drodla iodbrem eskrid fo.

Another, however, when asked afterwards, had it thus:

Jetso wenniher ythma kran oriunt sedpi.

A third had drawn some daisies. Of those who had transcribed anything at all, one subsequently gave her version to a friend in the mathematics department, good at crosswords, who suggested it was possibly a coded transcription of a remark by someone we'd never heard of called Deleuze. Could be wrong, though, he added. In any case we all tried to memorise whatever it was we thought Professor Cimex had dictated since that, we reminded ourselves, was the point.

"There are those who understand and those who do not: that is one kind of segmentation, one sort of salivary pre-formation. But what if understanding is actually traumatic insemination? Then it is a wound, and what concerns us is not understanding, but the trace."

There was also that other girl, I recall, who came in one morning with a limp.

"It is under erasure of the trace that fluids are cast into variation: saliva and semen no longer vectors but rather tensors in multiple dimensions."

Holding my phone beneath the writing ledge where I sat, I consulted Wikipedia.

The common bed bug (Cimex lectularius) *lurks inconspicuously by day, typically in crevices such as can be found in bedposts or behind peeling wallpaper. At night it emerges, attracted by the warmth of its sleeping victim as well as by volatile perspiration and exhaled carbon dioxide, finding an appropriate patch of skin where it inserts its needle-like proboscis. The process is a dialectical one, the proboscis containing two tubes, one for extracting the blood that is the bug's meal, another for injecting an anaesthetic to prevent the victim from waking.*

The bed bug is a parasite, benefiting at the expense of a host left alive and potentially reusable. Competition, by contrast, is a battle that can harm either party. What is called competition in market economies is more usually conflict between parasites on a collective body.

The bed bug is a domesticated species, in the sense that it was only able to spread from its native tropical habitat to temperate regions once there were heated houses in which it could thrive. The domestic and anaesthetic are conjoined like the bug's dual proboscis: as it feeds, the bug becomes enhumaned while the human is enbugged, each partaking of the other's fluid.

In the Reduviidae or assassin bugs the rostrum is likewise used for blood-sucking but can be vibrated quickly in order to emit an intimidating hissing sound. Charles Darwin encountered a form of assassin bug in Argentina in 1835, commenting, "It is most disgusting to feel soft wingless insects, about an inch long, crawling over one's body." The type that invaded his bed was a triatomine, or kissing bug.

Evolution has furnished us with a species of assassin commonly called the masked hunter (Reduvius personatus), *whose target is the bed bug. The masked hunter camouflages itself with household dust and in this way is able to stalk its prey, piercing it with a proboscis not unlike the bed bug's own. Yet the saliva of* Reduvius *contains no anaesthetic, instead a poison capable of dissolving its victim's internal organs so that they may be sucked out, a venom as strong and painful as a bee sting. A native European species, it had to make do with other invertebrate food sources until the arrival of bed bugs. A beneficial opportunist, some might say; the acceptable face of evolutionary competition. They are kept in some places as pets and in others as government advisers.*

Darwin (whose long-term illness in later life may have been due to the nocturnal kiss he felt in Argentina) knew that the category "species" is an historical as well as biological index: there were no men in the Triassic though there were dinosaurs. We can however say that there were capitalists in Byzantium, modernists in Renaissance Florence, gays in Ancient Greece; or just as legitimately say the opposite. In a mixed state there can be no historical index, only a juxtaposition of anaesthetics, poisons, anticoagulants, stimulants, hallucinogens, pheromones.

The author of the Wikipedia entry, I discovered, was User:ProfCimex. A pale light had begun to shine across the room; to some of us it had the odour of music, prompting dreams of unsegmented existence without wound or trace. But there can be no true knowledge without trauma. We all knew it was our destiny to be pierced, or else submit to the corroding juices of the Assassin.

"It is in the void left by these excavations that we shall return to our main theme," Cimex declared. "You know what that is. On a bare mattress lies a body we must crawl over, all of us, for I am not the only bug, simply the most visible. We needn't ask why; call it destiny if you like, or duty or play or anything else you want. It is the traversal of space, the invocation of a plane of possibility."

The music was loud enough for everyone to hear, even drowning out the clicking of Professor Cimex's articulations. Someone put up a hand and said, "What is the moral of this story?"

Cimex said nothing, instead only swaying, infused with rhythm.

The Burrows

Is it monument or burden? From somewhere came the urge to replace bulk solidity with weightless void. Our Scottish forebears chose to dig.

The Burrows had their origin in what was considered at the time a combination of impulses: educational, patriotic, artistic, commercial. Nowadays we might think all of them a subset of the philosophical, bracketed within that era's presiding spirit: random curiosity or grandiose boredom. What would they find down there with their excavating machines? What might they add? So many tunnels and passages existed already; mines closed and abandoned, underground railways, nuclear bunkers and silos, entire streets built over and forgotten. A dark, disconnected world of caves, cellars and subways, a labyrinth awaiting the unifying power of thought and the labour that would make it real. A second nation below the surface.

Some saw it primarily as tourist attraction, a well for foreign coin. For others it would be a scientific quest or spiritual journey. At what depth below the Earth's surface do you start to feel the fires of Hell? With the finest equipment available, and with the most supreme effort, might a shaft pierce the planet's soft core? Nationalists asserted Scotland's right to determine its subterranean affairs, opponents pointed out that the size of any country must shrink with increasing depth, the centre is where all borders meet and dissolve, a geo-political singularity. It was rumoured that the Russians had got there already. Why not the sky instead? The area that calls itself Scotland must surely increase with altitude; go far enough and it will embrace numerous stellar systems. But the cash ran out. So down they went.

The initial phase was a linking of existing underground spaces with new passages. The first was meant to run from Mary King's Close to St Ninian's Cave but navigational problems emerged almost as soon as the contractors began tunnelling: they hadn't realised their GPS wouldn't work underground. They had to fall back on traditional surveying techniques, and old digging methods too, when an industrial dispute brought the giant screw-nosed machine to a shuddering halt. In the end it was local schoolchildren who scooped out the last of the earth between Edinburgh and Whithorn, while householders along the entire route took legal action over subsiding homes and disappearing gardens.

It might all have ended there, were it not for a discovery made during the tunnelling. At a location somewhere beneath Sanquhar post office a temporary restroom needed to be installed and a side passage was created. Engineers noticed something strange about the rock they encountered; geologists took soundings, revealing a large chamber of strangely regular proportions. Earth was moved and the unusual rock revealed as ancient building stone, enclosing an empty hall of unknown purpose, devoid of any artefact save a small corroded metal disc.

"What does it mean?" the head of operations was asked by a television news reporter when word leaked out.

"It means we're not the first."

There were suggestions that the submerged room was a nineteenth-century folly but there was no way to prove it. Fantasists were quick to invent outlandish explanations: the metal disc, it was said, had been fashioned from a meteorite. But now there was a new impetus to excavate, and donations came from Scots around the world, or at any rate people who considered themselves Scots. Litigant householders found that their collapsed dwellings had suddenly acquired a new cachet and increased market value. Properties were advertised, offering extensive views of the underground they had fallen into, made attractive by the promise of easy transport connection to the capital just as soon as the tunnel mini-train was finished. In the meantime it was foot or mule, a healthy and environmentally friendly option.

There was another Scotland down there waiting to be dug out, mapped, inhabited. Its discovery and colonisation would entail the linking of every surface entrance: the network was to be as thorough and complete as the road system above ground.

In any cellar there would be a door, some further steps and then the cool passageway that could lead wherever the stroller wished to venture; softly illuminated walkways of pleasantly curved cross-section, ceramically tiled, along which electric cars could hum peacefully at moderate speed. It wasn't long before everyone was calling it the Burrows; or Burghs, for here was a subterranean community in its own right, demanding proper dwellings, services, schools and hospitals, political autonomy, even independence.

Much of the work, it transpired, had been done already, by whoever was there before. The metal discs turned up frequently, assumed to be money, jewellery, religious symbols or gaming tokens. Archaeology was rewritten: the old assumption was that the deeper you dug, the further back in time you went. This stratified view could no longer be sustained. History, it was realised, is an infinite superposition, all times being present at every point. Certainly the excavators unearthed layers of distinct eras, but only down to a certain limit beyond which everything was too jumbled to be worth worrying about. If a new chamber was broken into, no one asked any longer if it was a hundred or a thousand years old, or even if it was one that had been dug the previous year and forgotten about. What mattered was its emptiness, its ability to be entered and imagined.

For many people the Burrows became just another place to shop. The chain stores were quick to move in when the first licences were granted, their rows of premises looking no different from any covered mall, quickly reached by high-speed lifts whose occupants could barely tell whether they were going down or up, transfixed in aluminium compartments by illuminated characters declaring an alphabet of levels, more conducive to throughput and spend-per-head than numbers, it was found. After a strenuous afternoon of retail there would be the relaxation of pub, cinema or restaurant, with no one ever noticing the absence of daylight or the air's particular taste.

Potholers insisted on the benefits of the great below-floors: a popular route started just behind the Marks and Spencers eight hundred and fifty feet beneath Comrie. Guidebooks described how the ramble would soon take you away from the brashly lit shopping centre, past a waterworks, to a dimly lit unsurfaced section requiring sensible footwear and waterproof clothing. Here could be seen glittering stalactites and enough smooth slabs to allow for picnicking if all the benches should happen to be occupied (a frequent occurrence at weekends). But go further, the guides insisted, beyond the realm of day-trippers, carrying with you a torch and spare batteries, and wearing a hard hat in case of bumps. A natural fissure in the rocks, easily managed by all except the most morbidly rotund, would then lead into a cavern so large that no one had ever been able to shine a beam all the way to the other end, or so it was said. Here the air was clear, cool and pure: breathe deeply and you would feel better in an instant. The place was believed to have been a thriving village once, and Robert the Bruce passed through on the way somewhere. Or maybe it was Mary, Queen of Scots. At any rate, that's what it said on the notice that got put up there.

Thanks to its alleged health-giving properties, Burrows water became a bestselling brand above ground. Some international medical authorities insisted that being starved of sunlight would cause long-term health problems but the Scots had been managing like that for centuries and it hadn't done them any harm. Even so, a variety of strange, unique conditions began to appear, attributable to troglodytic life. The Burrovians' skin was pale, their eyes smaller though with larger pupils. Bone density was found to be greater in comparison with surface people. Perhaps a new race was evolving, or an old one had been reborn. The issue was delicate: should one speak of race at all? A sinister underground movement was found to be emerging, whose members claimed to be whiter than white. Comparisons with sheets of paper and Polo mints showed they actually had a point. Given sufficiently many generations, it was claimed, the Burrow-folk would eventually become translucent, with skin like rice paper and internal organs made visible by anything stronger than fluorescent strip lighting. Continue the evolutionary progression and the result would be total transparency, the disappearance of eyes, a complete re-adaptation to underground existence.

There were accidents in the Burrows. The very first casualty was Mr Ian Seggie, inspector of operations on a northern stretch of the early phase of tunnelling, who was supervising a subsea link between the Grain Earth-House at Kirkwall and Shebster Cairn near Thurso. There had been much debate about this particular route which posed extreme technical problems, needing to be carved through difficult rock beneath many fathoms of tempestuous ocean. Quite a few people couldn't see any point in it at all, and were invited to attend free public education classes that helped them understand the error of their ways. Mr Seggie, moreover, is reported to have been a "difficult" type, which would partly explain why progress was so slow, even once his team found a way to stop the tunnel continually flooding with seawater. An official enquiry held after the incident that claimed Seggie's life found that over a period of weeks he had gradually lost all confidence in his workforce, their machinery, and the navigational methods they used. He had, in short, decided that the best way to tunnel from Orkney to Caithness was to drive the excavator himself and use his own judgement about which way to steer. His widow Edith summed him up as being a person who would never ask directions from anyone, no matter how lost he became, which the enquiry panel considered to be no explanation at all since it applied to any man. The report instead highlighted the misfortune of a wrongly aligned burrowing screw that meant the vehicle would rise by one centimetre for every three metres travelled horizontally. This, they decided, was the reason why Mr Seggie, on his lone progress beneath the sea floor, found himself worming out of the dark safety of old red sandstone and into the perils of the Pentland Firth. Death, however, was by no means instantaneous: he was found to be wearing a diving suit, a precaution Edith thought entirely characteristic of her late husband who liked to be prepared for any possibility, no matter how remote. One of his foibles, it emerged at the enquiry, was a lightning conductor built into his folding umbrella, with a wire trailing down to earth, just in case. How ironic, then, that he did not think to take it with him underground. When Seggie bored up into the ocean it was not the water that killed him, but the thirty-three-thousand-volt electricity cable his machine cut through as it roamed along the seabed in search of a good way of getting back down again. Orcadians noticed a brief, inexplicable dimming of their lights, and a trawler skipper who happened to be in the area reported an unusual boiling effect on the sea surface. Such was Seggie's brief mark on history.

There were to be many more fatalities in the Burrows; though when one looks at the statistics, being underground is actually slightly safer than life on the surface. There are, for example, far fewer cases of pneumonia down there. Some attribute this to the lack of rain, though it's more likely due to the lack of pneumonia. One disturbing figure, though, is the suicide rate.

Andrew Crumey

The unfortunate trend began soon after the opening of The Pre-Cambrian Experience, a theme park designed to transport visitors into the geological past long before the emergence of human life. It was not the thought of primordial non-existence that troubled visitors, rather it was the temptation of a dark shaft exposed by construction work, of incalculable depth and unknown origin. Infra-red security cameras revealed that people were showing up at The Pre-Cambrian Experience with the specific intention of throwing themselves down what became known locally as "the plughole".

The solution was obvious: fence it off and cover it up. But doing the obvious has never been the way of the Burrows. A team of investigators decided that covering the hole would treat only the symptom, not the problem. To understand the plughole one needed first of all to know how it came to be there in the first place. Was it a natural feature, a volcanic fissure? Had it been created by those forgotten folk with their metal discs? Or accidentally blasted out while cave-scaping the area to accommodate the rollercoaster in The Pre-Cambrian Experience?

Experienced human resources manager Linda Waddell was tasked with going down to have a look. Her brave effort proved unsuccessful: the rope was only a hundred metres long and left Linda dangling in her hard-hat and orange safety-wear with no sign of solid ground beneath, merely a fine mist revealed by the swinging beam of her head-torch. Her supervisor radioed to say they were going to get another length of rope and tie it on, they'd only be about half an hour, but Linda declared she'd had enough, this was never in her job description.

Two weeks later, underground parachutist Clive Knoll stepped in to help. The sport of hole-diving was at this time still in its early days, with only a few drops known to be large enough to accommodate it. The plughole was an obvious challenge for Clive, who edged to the black unfathomable rim wearing a video camera on his helmet and his life's hopes on his back. The whole thing was sponsored by Sleeptight Bedspreads and relayed live on BurrowVision. Clive gave a thumbs-up to the crowd, pulled his goggles over his eyes, then a moment later launched himself into the void. The feed from his helmet-cam showed near-total obscurity, with maybe a wee bit of the mist they'd seen before from Linda's attempt. But it was the last that anyone saw of Clive Knoll. How the devil did he expect to get back up again? Sleeptight Bedspreads went into liquidation not long afterwards.

It was suggested that the power of the plughole might merely be conceptual: a mental womb. Celebrity philosopher Angus de Mouchoir made it the subject of a four-part mini-series and accompanying book. A highpoint of the Burrows Festival of Ideas was his appearance at the plughole, where he promised to show that the thing existed only in people's minds. And that was the last anyone heard of him too.

A scientific investigation was commissioned, with backing from International Biscuits who apparently thought the shape of the thing could be utilised in their packaging and marketing, or else maybe wondered if the plughole could serve as a convenient means of disposing of all the waste their underground factories produced along with a cloying buttery smell that many Burrovians found appetising but which was widely suspected to be carcinogenic. The scientists lowered various instruments on ropes and cables and decided that none of the ropes and cables were long enough. Robotic probes fell to oblivion. Some commentators reckoned this was worse than the bloody space race, and look where Scotland had ended up over that nonsense (a space station that fell foul of Friday-night rowdiness, best forgotten).

The only way was to send someone climbing down it. A public competition yielded a shortlist of experienced sub-alpinists, skilled in tackling the steepest and most scenically negative of slopes. The contenders all had fine beards and good musculature, the clear winner by phone-in poll being Annie Thromnick, who impressed everyone in the live final by managing to descend two hundred feet with her hands and feet tied together, using only her teeth to hold onto the rope (it was suggested in some less generous quarters that her success was owed in part to a sympathy vote when people saw the friction burns on her lips – her gran's on-air rendition of Burrovian folk-songs may also have generated some sentimental support).

Annie's de-scaling of the plughole proved however to be a muted media event. Everyone expected her to disappear after thirty seconds like the rest had done; even International Biscuits thought it best to remove their corporate banners temporarily from the mouth of the hole. But Annie was a cut below her predecessors, her heart and spirit belonged to the great depths she loved and was determined to plumb. Quickly chewing her way through the CaveBix she was required to consume as preparation for the ordeal, and watched by a few dozen experts, dignitaries, and folk with nothing better to do of an afternoon, she lowered herself down the vertiginous wall, almost glasslike in its smoothness but with just enough unevenness to give purchase to the virtuoso descender.

Five minutes passed and half the people went away (there was a red-carpet event to celebrate the new Library of Comedy, an archive and celebration of everything that had ever made anyone laugh, anywhere). Another five minutes of looking at watches, head-shaking and whistling, and it was generally agreed that Annie was done for. So the rest went too, though by this time the red carpet thing was pretty much done anyway. It was not until three days later that an exhausted Annie heroically lifted herself over the lip of the plughole and was noticed by a wandering Alsatian dog being looked for by Suhindra Wylie, 15, who was caring for it while its owner was on holiday in the Overland. Suhindra told reporters that she thought Annie was a heap of old International Biscuits packaging because of all the signage around her, until the heap smiled, revealing a mouth strangely reshaped by friction burns.

During a full debriefing at Burrows Central Infirmary, Annie revealed the miracle of the plughole. On the first day, she said, it was pretty much a standard descent, until she reached a ledge wide enough to rest on. Allowing herself half a CaveBic and a portion of Deep Spring Water, she accidentally switched off her lamp and was surprised to find that her surroundings remained illuminated. The rock, she said, was exuding a uniform crepuscular luminescence, a bit like what you see if you close your eyes and push on your eyeballs. As she said this, the three scientists at her bedside shut their eyes and tried it for themselves, pleasantly entertained by what they saw. The other scientists were away at the Comedy Library and missed the whole thing.

Dr Phoebe Signorelli of the Institute of Geology asked Annie, "Why did you squeeze your eyeballs when you were down the plughole?"

"I didn't," said Annie. "That's what it looked like."

"You mean someone else squeezed them?"

Professor Vanguard Pym intervened. "Nobody squeezed anything."

"We just did..."

"Tell us more, Annie," the Professor instructed.

So Annie described how she waited on the ledge for a

considerable time, regaining her strength and allowing her vision to adjust more and more to the strange luminosity around her. Eventually it was bright enough for her to read the health warning on the side of her CaveBix packet. Phoebe Signorelli had meanwhile been squeezing her eyeballs so much that she was advised to go away and sit down. She bumped into the door-edge on the way out and needed some medical attention that rather distracted from Annie's gripping account. The other two decided they'd hear the rest of it next day when they were more in the mood.

It was around this time that Dave Vinsky and his wife Shehalagh returned from their holiday and came to collect their Alsatian dog from Suhindra Wylie, 15. They brought with them souvenirs of the Overland, a pair of deeply offensive sun-tans, and news that the folk up there were a bigoted and spiteful lot who never said a word to each other on public transport. Not only that, but a person in the queue for the Ben Nevis Aurora Borealis Stagecoach Monorail had the effrontery to say the Burrows didn't even exist!

"You think it's a hoax or something?" Dave Vinsky challenged.

"I'm saying you're not a separate country, you're part of Scotland."

"But we've got our own laws and education system and football team and everything else."

"Aye, like language," Shehalagh chipped in.

"You talk the same language as me," said the offensive queue-person who was dressed in the internationally recognisable uniform of a lollipop man, must have been his break or something, maybe it was the school holidays.

"What do you call this, then?" said Vinsky, drawing from his wallet a Burrows bank note.

"Piece of paper, still the same currency."

"Worth more underground though."

"Worth bugger all here, that's for sure."

This enjoyable friendly banter went on for the whole time they waited in the queue, and also while the three of them rode the monorail together (there was no aurora that day – too cloudy and the machine had a fault anyway). But afterwards Dave Vinsky was pained by a lingering thought. Lying beside Shehalagh in their mid-price Glasgow hotel bed he asked his snoring wife, "Do you think he's maybe right? Do you think the Burrows don't exist?"

This was still far from the minds of Professor Vanguard Pym and his assistant Sally who showed up at Annie Thromnick's bed next morning to hear the rest of her story, after they told her about the gig at the Comedy Library.

Annie rested on the ledge for several hours, puzzling over the easily legible health warning on her CaveBix packet that she'd somehow never noticed before. At some moments it became easier to read, then harder, then easier again.

"Were you squeezing your eyeballs?" asked Phoebe Signorelli who'd arrived late.

Annie explained that the inexplicable phosphorescence was changing colour, passing through shades of lime, mustard, topaz, burgundy. This really confused Phoebe who soon went away again. Annie was a bit freaked too, she lay on the ledge wondering if the nausea she felt was a result of psychedelic illumination or CaveBix. In the end she tried to stand up, but her head immediately throbbed, her heart raced, she lost her balance. "Everything was spinning and I thought, this is it, Annie, you're going to fall over the side and die."

"And did you?"

"I threw myself down onto the ledge."

"That was sensible."

But the ledge felt different this time, and the colours all around her were creating mental confusion. "I vomited."

Professor Vanguard Pym called for the nurse to sort it out, then realised Annie was referring to what happened in the plughole. "You threw up?"

"No," said Annie. "I vomited. But it didn't come up, or spew down."

Phoebe had only just come back into the room but went straight back out again.

"You see, there was no up or down. It was like gravity had cancelled itself out or something."

"So where did the vomit go?"

It stayed, she declared, in the air, like a mushy ball of CaveBix.

"That's disgusting," said Sally.

"Fascinating!" the Professor exclaimed. "If there was no gravity then that can only mean you had reached the centre of the Earth."

"Not in a day, though," said Annie.

"I suppose not."

Dave Vinsky went to work as usual as Security Consultant at BounceCorp, a leading blue-chip supplier of entrance control personnel, otherwise known as doormen. His task that day was to supervise a red-carpet event at the new Comedy Library, but as he waited for the electric limousine to emerge from Tunnel A52 and deposit its cargo of dignitaries he couldn't help asking himself: is any of this real? Did that lollipop man speak a profound truth when he had a go at me while we were overground? It ought to have been the holiday that felt illusory, a memory not too distant in time but so remote from normal life as to be like a dream. Yet it was superficial

Scotland that seemed authentic to him now, the Burrows he had been in all his life that felt insubstantial. The limousine arrived and Dave Vinsky leapt instinctively into action like the trained professional his social network profile said he was. In other words he snapped out of it.

Professor Vanguard Pym considered the possibility that Annie Thromnick had abseiled to the centre of the Earth using mainly her teeth. "You're right it's impossible."

"I did vomit, though. And it stayed floating in the air..."

"Like a glitterball above a dancefloor."

"Not really."

"It's a nicer image though."

"Finally I got to my feet and it felt weird, not having any gravity, no up or down."

"How about sideways?"

"I suppose I still had that."

"Then why didn't you just turn yourself in that direction instead? Better than nothing, surely?"

"You had to be there, Professor. What with all the strange lights and the ball of vomit..."

"You mean glitterball."

Phoebe came in eating a ham and cheese baguette. "Are you still on about eyeballs?"

"Glitter," the Professor corrected. "It seems there's one at the centre of the Earth."

Annie continued a story whose truth only Dave Vinsky might fathom, though he wasn't there, he was walking his Alsatian dog. "I stumbled a bit," she said, "then realised I could walk along the side of the plughole which was no longer a wall but instead a floor."

"Couldn't you propel yourself through the tube like the astroscots did?" Phoebe asked, but the Professor silenced her, not wishing to bring up the subject of the space station.

"I tried but it didn't work," said Annie. "The plughole had a kind of stickiness, I don't know how. Magnetism or something. I made my way along this glowing pipe until I realised that the colours weren't changing any more, the light was fading."

"At this point was it mustard or lime?" the professor inquired.

"Mustard," said Phoebe, who thought he was asking about her baguette.

"Then it went totally dark and the gravity switched itself back on, I had to grab for the sides and it was fifty-fifty whether I ended up the right way round, otherwise I was going down head-first and I was finished."

"So which was it?"

Dave Vinsky came home with the dog whose sad eyes followed him to the living room where Vinsky sat in the armchair and for the first time in his life thought, what if I ended it all? Would anyone even really care? The dog stood in front of him like she knew.

"We have to go back there," Professor Vanguard Pym declared.

"How the blazes are you going to climb down the plughole?" Annie asked.

"What I mean is, you've got to go back there."

But it had taken Annie a day and a half to climb out again, plus the half day she'd spent beforehand trying to figure out which way up she was. Annie was in no mood to repeat the experience. "It's hell, professor."

"That's a religious view; you're not allowed to express it in a public health facility."

"I meant metaphorically."

"Like squeezing your eyeballs?" Phoebe suggested.

"No, that was an analogy."

Dave Vinsky got up from his armchair, took hold of the dog's collar and led her to the back door. The garden was a mess; Shehalagh had been on at him ever since they moved in, about getting rid of those big stalagmites she kept tripping over whenever she went to hang out the washing. Vinsky encouraged the dog to go into the garden, usually she liked it but the animal seemed reluctant this time, unwilling to part from her master. Eventually Dave just had to push the door closed on the poor mutt who whimpered for a bit then accepted exile, tail drooping and head hung low, going to mope beside the shed. Dave put on his coat, went to the front and out, walking briskly along the access passage towards his destination. He passed The Pre-Cambrian Experience, heard the distant sounds of fairground rides and pounding music and screaming, laughing people. Took him twenty minutes to get all the way along the fence, then a stretch of rubble with not another soul in sight, until eventually he reached the place he was aiming for, a ring of darkness surrounded by the empty cheerfulness of advertising hoardings.

Dave Vinsky stood at the edge of the plughole, exactly like so many others had done before, and would do after him. We all have our moment, he told himself, then it's over and might as well not have happened. History's meant to be the thread of significance that makes everything worthwhile: the memory of your kids if you have any, or your friends or the people you loved, or who knows, maybe you do some little heroic thing that gets noticed, some special act that's worth mentioning over a pint. And history is vertical – being up to date, maybe going down in it. Life yearns for the horizontal Now. But the deeper you go, the smaller it gets. That's the wonder of it, Dave Vinsky thought, the wonder of anything, falling through nothing into nowhere. The Burrows have never existed, nor the Overland that claims ownership of it.

Professor Vanguard Pym rolled in his sleep, woke and felt Phoebe's breath on his cheek. He thought he heard a noise outside, a dog perhaps? A scream?

Ian Seggie rises early and checks his diving suit. The guide at Mary King's Close puts on her seventeenth-century costume, ready for another day's imagined heritage. In his secret bunker, the Secretary of State presides over rehearsal for a make-believe war and for every pit village a new day's honest hardship begins. In a cave, Ninian prays.

Our forebears chose to dig.

Scenes from the Word-Camera

The principle of operation of the word-camera lacks the geometrical simplicity of its optical counterpart; nevertheless it is not difficult to account for the manner in which objects presented before its lens are converted by the machine into descriptive text. A device which can interpret in words the world it sees; give a printed account of the items and events to which it is exposed, and moreover of the patterns which exist between these events, the interconnections by which the world is made a coherent whole. This is the function and unique ability of the word-camera.

Why was it not invented sooner? With any novel creation, one should question not only the existence of the necessary technology, but also of some need or will which might inspire the appropriate direction of that knowledge. The ancients could for example have invented the gramophone (they had wax from beehives with which to make discs or cylinders, and could easily have fixed a needle onto the end of a cone in order to transfer sound onto the moving surface). The ancients, however, did not make such a device. What purpose might it have served them? And the creation of the word-camera was held up not by technological inadequacy, but rather by mankind's long (and ultimately unrewarding) obsession with the visible.

The earliest attempts to put such a mechanism into effect (as first performed in those pioneering days many years ago) produced in the main results which were fragmentary, hesitant, incomplete; the manufactured texts being only the most fleeting description of the scenes and images recorded. These efforts, though they may seem crude by modern standards, nevertheless retain the power to move by their very simplicity. Such brief passages, produced by the most basic means, generally give only a vague sense of the things being recorded. An open window, with light streaming in (poorly described, the long exposure still being insufficient for a full account to be imprinted); or the movement of a figure across a room (blurred and indiscernible in the account, details omitted for want of finer resolution). Those early word-images usually amount to little more than the barest catalogue of whatever items happened to be in view, and yet they fascinate us because they give a record of things which might otherwise have been missed. They offer something coherent from an age that seems in other respects fragmented. No other medium could ever have this potential to preserve not only the appearance of the world but also its inner being.

Once they had progressed beyond catching a mere sentence or two of the world they saw, the more sophisticated word-cameras were used to note word portraits which could fill pages; whole autobiographies were constructed by early word-photographers who would sit themselves before the scrutiny of their own lens. Yet the verbose, sepia prose of these portraits often seeks to hide as much as it reveals. We see their subjects as they wanted to be known, and we are left to guess what they were really like. What thoughts, deeds, actions were kept carefully hidden from the word-camera? And what modifications may have been made to the text after printing?

It was with the development of improved word-lenses, and in particular the style filter, that the word-camera could become a truly creative medium. That all literary style is really a kind of selection, a form of negation; this was a crucial and far-reaching discovery. By then it seemed already that writing (at least as the term had previously been understood) was a dead art. A generation of poets, novelists and journalists found their precious skills to be redundant, usurped by the effortless perfection and infinite versatility of a machine that could record seamless text in an instant. No need now for the on-the-spot reporter, interpreting the muddle of world events between endless cigarettes and cups of coffee. The machine could be aimed, the button pressed, and the result put straight into mass circulation. And no need now for the expensive labour of the lonely fiction writer, when an entire story could be created in an instant, just by going for a walk with a word-camera and taking a few shots of whatever interesting scene might be chanced upon.

The reaction of those outmoded, unwanted litterateurs was inevitable. After losing the argument that the output of the word-camera somehow lacked soul, they were forced to retreat into a kind of writing that was abstract, irrational and wholly divorced from the reality which the word-camera captured with an ease they could only envy: the apt phrase invariably found with careless abandon, the most surprising trick of language brought forth simply by an accident of circumstance. Like any revolution, the age of the word-camera has had its casualties; though even now they refuse to lie down and die, as the nostalgic Campaign for Real Literature testifies.

The rapid pace at which the technology of word-photography has progressed still shows no sign of abating, and new applications are constantly being created. Modern word-cameras are not only capable of interpreting the world in whatever language or style may be desired, but also to a limit of detail that seems potentially unbounded. Whereas a landscape could provoke from the earliest machines a mere paragraph or two of description, today's ultra-modern devices can find within a drop of water whole volumes of analysis, commentary and speculation. Ideas previously undreamed of, observations quite beyond the power of human thought: all can now be made manifest by the constantly deepening verbal scrutiny of the word lens.

With the aid of microscopy and quickening shutter speeds, it is becoming possible to find out what happens during the briefest moments of time, and at the smallest scales. Already an entire encyclopaedia can be written about a single dust mote (its appearance, motion, qualities and attributes, and all the many ways in which it can be considered part of the universe). How much more might remain to be said, once even greater resolving powers can be attained? Single atoms will soon, we are told, be capable of inspection and description; their flickering quantum world made explicable and rendered in anything from the driest prose to the very richest poetry.

Whether there can be any end to this progression – some necessary limit to the wealth of verbalisation – is a matter on which philosophers are divided. Is it possible that a full account of the world could be given in a finite number of words (in which case, how close are we to achieving this task?); or is it the case that any object (a broom for example, leaning against a wall) would require an endless stream of words in order to be done full justice? That the universe might be finitely and fully describable suggests to some an obnoxious limitation, perhaps offending that last vestige of primitive superstition – the belief in the unknowable – which will never be erased from the human mind. And yet a universe inherently infinite in richness is one immediately fraught with paradox. Would, for example, a complete description of an object include in turn an account of all its possible descriptions? Or even the impossible ones? On the other hand, it may be that one can only describe the world down to some particular limit of detail, beyond which there lies nothing but a grainy, indeterminate region of existence where all things become indistinguishable: a primordial soup confounding any further expression or elucidation.

Such questions, if they are answerable at all (or even well posed) may find their solution in the future work of word photographers. For the time being we may only note that this, along with all other observations made here, is but a single example (defined by careful control of length, style and content settings) of the sort of text which may result when one word-camera is pointed at another, and made to construct some comment on what it sees.

The Last Midgie on Earth

I was on a gap year before beginning my degree in celebrity studies; I packed a few clothes, beach-wear, my battered old guitar, and flew to Scotland where I'd never been but had often dreamed of. I'd seen a picture in a book when I was a kid; long sandy beach, waves breaking gently, one or two bathers. This was Scotland: a peaceful, unhurried place where life was easy. There was that movie about the guys who ran a little tavern, they'd sit around staring at blue sky from under their broad hats; dreaming, philosophising, falling in love. Sure, I wanted some of that northern bliss, being able to stay outside nearly all of the day and never burning too much, even with only low-factor protection. I wanted to strum my guitar and hear cicadas chirping, watch pelicans alight on shore-side gantries.

I decided I'd get myself to an island called A-Ran, heard it was good for full-moon parties. First ride I hitched was in a sugar-truck, couldn't believe they still ran those things, must have been a hundred years old. Driver was called Dizzee and smelled of bacon, took one look at me, heard my accent and said, "Welcome tae God's own country." I liked that. They're such religious people.

Dizzee had this little thing hanging inside the cab of the sugar-truck dangling over the control board, not much bigger than my thumb, kind of a geodesic shape with black pentagons on it so I figured it must be like an icon or something. He said it was called a football: you touch it for luck. Dizzee told me about his two wives and six kids; he was about seventy, I think, though it was impossible to guess his age, the climate's easy on these people, they pick fruit the whole year round. Dizzee was delivering a consignment of kyleberries and not in any hurry. The spoiled ones had been juiced to power his truck.

"Where I come from, they banned these things a long time ago," I told him.

"It's these things gied us a' the life we got now," he said.

"How's that?"

"Carbon."

He told me this long and important story I forget, too busy looking through the cracked side window at the scenery slipping past. Whitewashed houses with their windows flung open to greet the balmy air; old ladies on rickety chairs gossiping cheerfully outside brightly painted front doors. A tavern whose sheltered terrace seemed an island of calm within calm.

Something else went by. "What's that?" I asked.

"Grass."

"What for?"

"Football. Needs a lot of watering though."

I twisted to watch the retreating rectangle of yellow-green and thought of all the holy services that must go on there, people on their knees bowing east or west or whatever they do, wearing their traditional tartan bonnets.

"You a student?" he asked.

"Sure."

"How come you're on your ain?"

I had to think about it. "Better travelling alone."

His stubbly chin curved into a wry smile. "Just you and your guitar, eh? That's nice. Expect you're looking for some female company, though. Not that I'm presuming, mind."

I felt embarrassed but reminded myself these are passionate people, open-hearted, frank. They live outdoors, baring their skin to the not-too-hostile sun. I'd even heard they made love on their roof terraces. Well, it was in that movie.

"So what's your place like, son? For girls, I mean."

I told him how we all mostly have to stay covered up so it's sometimes hard to tell the difference.

"Aye, I've heard about that. Suppose it could add to the excitement though."

I thought of telling him about Twenty-Seven, my girlfriend.

I could show him the picture on my foil, the one she zoned. I thought of the voice of her text and wondered if we'd ever get to meet each other in ambient space, wondered what it must be like to live wholly in flesh and blood, like these people, not digitally enhanced. My world was artificial and theirs was real. While I thought all this, Dizzee kept talking.

"Stanley Baxter... Robert Burns." He was giving me a history lesson. "Fafnir Trolsdottir... Manjit Raj." I don't think I'd heard of any of them but I could see that Dizzee took it all very seriously. Mostly they were poets, philosophers, revolutionaries, I think. Also one or two chefs.

"I saw the movie about those guys opening a tavern," I said.

He glanced at me with playful scorn, then indulgent pity. "Aye, that. It was okay, I suppose. But the Chinese always get Scotland wrong."

Dizzee drove me to a town called Krankie where our routes diverged. He dropped me at the town square, place like something from a story-book, a real open-air paved area with a fountain in the middle and short-sleeved people strolling. There were tottering infants, geriatrics walking arm-in-arm, and wherever I looked my eyes couldn't help falling on the slim, gently tanned legs of tall, exotic girls.

"Giesa a chune then."

I turned and saw one standing right next to me, less than an arm's-length away. I instinctively backed off and put my hand over my mouth.

"Ah'll no bite ye!"

I reminded myself I wasn't in the Dome now: there were no viruses to worry about here, only food poisoning and malaria if I didn't maintain standard precautions. She nodded at the guitar neck protruding behind my shoulder.

"Ur ye gonnae play that thing or is it just for show?"

I pulled it round in front of me and strummed a chord. "I need to tune it..."

"Aw, don't be shy. Bet you're dead good."

Her voice – strange and melodious – was like primal music, wholly natural and infinitely mysterious. She was pretty as a ripe tomato. I played "Peace Song of the United Workers".

"No bad, that. Catchy." She maybe said it as a way of making me stop. "I'm March."

"Hello, March."

"You'll never guess what month ma burthday's in."

"Won't I?"

"Wannae meet ma pals?" She pointed to a cafe terrace at the other side of the square where a large group sat round two or three tables, everyone gesticulating and talking at once, way they do. I followed her there, a couple of them looking round when we arrived and March introduced me. "This is.... whiss yer name?"

"Kalo"

"This is Carlo and he's gonnae play a chune for us."

A few more broke away from their conversations, sipping chilled bubblegum lattes while I began reprising "Peace Song of the United Workers".

A dark-skinned girl asked, "Zat a hit where you come frae?"

I nodded.

"Know any we'd know?"

She suggested a few titles that must have been religious songs. Seems they do a lot of singing at the football.

"Moan an sit here wi me," she ordered, but March wasn't having it.

"He's mine!" she laughed.

I'd been in Krankie all of ten minutes and here were two

beautiful girls fighting over me. I wish Twenty-Seven could see this, I said to myself. Wish everyone in the Dome could see. In the end I sat between them, once some people had swapped places to accommodate. The other girl was called Purple; she pointed to a muscly guy with a bandana at the far end of the group and said he was her boyfriend; I didn't catch his name but he smiled hello. Purple said he was a health consultant in the evenings and a gym instructor by day. I'd thought all these people were farmers and fishermen or tourist industry workers but I suppose you've got to have other jobs to make an economy work. They all kept talking about money.

"Thing is," Purple explained, "we're a poor country, backward, been like that for decades, centuries, whitever. So we've got tae work hard if we're gonnae catch up wi the likes o yous."

March agreed. "Postcolonic, that's whit we are."

Purple told me about her cousin who emigrated. "He wis in that dome o yours, cleaning supervisor, fourteen-hour shifts every day, made a packet, sent it all back here tae his family. Now they've got a big place on A-Ran."

"I'm heading there."

"Y'are? Look him up – ah'll gie you his contact."

"You mean it?"

"Seriously. Tell him ah sent ye."

"You're not just saying it? Where I come from, when you give someone a contact and tell them to get in touch, you don't really expect them to show up at your door."

"Aye, well, we're different. Here you go." She brought out her device and flashed the details to mine, then scrolled up a picture of her cousin's island home. "Look at that, no bad, eh?" A sprawling villa with an arcaded portico. "They've got horses and everything. He's loaded."

"All from working as a cleaning supervisor in the Dome?"

"Och no, it's from the business he started efter he came back."

March butted in. "He's a gangster."

"No he's no!" They both laughed but I couldn't tell how close the joke was to the truth: in this country everything's done with bribes and kickbacks, that was what I'd heard. It was in that movie. Only way they could open the tavern was by settling things with the local mob.

"How ye getting to A-Ran?" March asked.

"Hitching."

"On a copter? Jetfoil?"

"Could always swim there," Purple chuckled.

"Ma dad knows this skipper," said March. "He'll gie ye a lift."

A few texts were enough to settle it, though not on the sugar-boat she'd thought, instead a hoverboard taking oranges and a few tourists later that day. There was space for me too if I didn't mind standing.

"You're all such kind people," I said. The hours slipped like sand.

It worked out exactly as March promised: the hoverboard was bumpy but it felt good to be so close to the gentle sea, watching endless whitecaps and the occasional rise of dolphins. One kid swore she saw a flying fish while her mother unwrapped sandwiches in the salty air whose tang on my parched lips was like a kiss. A-Ran rose through heat haze but by the time we shored, the sun had dipped behind mountains and a welcome coolness had arrived. At the quayside I stopped to look at a shrine to a famous ancient poet called C John Taylor who summed up the spiritual effect of so much natural beauty in a verse I can't remember except for the last line: "It's nice to be nice".

There was an old woman in a bikini with a beach towel round her waist, plump and sun-tanned, dark glasses perched on her head. I showed her the house I was looking for on my foilscreen and she recognised it at once, nodding with appreciation. "The big fella, eh?" Everyone on the island knew Purple's cousin. "Moan and ah'll show ye." She led me along the esplanade, sandals flapping on the warm asphalt, and when eventually she paused I thought it was to admire the pelican we saw squatting on a capstan being fed sardines from a bucket by two small children. In fact she wanted to point out the hilltop overlooking the sea where the villa stood. "Ten minute walk," she informed me, and in her bluntness I noticed for the first time the pride that for these Scottish people lies just beneath the simple friendliness. It made me suddenly aware that she was old enough to be my grandmother yet was wearing what in the Dome would not even count as undergarments.

Time means nothing to them: the ten-minute walk was more like twenty. But eventually I reached the villa, looking like the image I had of it except for a new extension on one side. Fixed to the gate was a neatly made sign: *Big Fella*.

I walked up the path and rang the bell; a dog barked inside, nobody came. I rang again and the barking was joined by gruff shouts; I saw through the frosted door-pane a large approaching figure and when he opened I found myself looking at Big Fella himself, unshaved, in a string vest and with a drink tin in his hand. He stared suspiciously while I explained myself, but as soon as I mentioned Purple he smiled broadly and welcomed me inside, taking me to a spacious marble-floored room hung with abstract oil paintings. He said they were by his wife. The Scots are highly artistic people.

In the Dome you only ever make contact by appointment

but straight away this man was treating me like part of the family, inviting me to sit down, wanting to know all about me and about the Dome he hadn't been to in years, asking when I'd be going back, and if I wouldn't mind taking a package for him as long as it wasn't too much trouble.

"What sort of business do you do, Mr Fella?"

Import and export, he told me.

"Anything in particular?"

"This'n'that."

I began staring at the large canvas hanging behind him, a lot of dark blue with streaks of red that looked like they might be part of someone's anatomy. It made me think of those beaches I'd heard of where they don't even wear swim-suits, only sun-cream.

"Fancy a beer, son?"

I didn't know what he meant at first, then worked out he was offering me the same kind of traditional beverage that was in his hand. He went to fetch me one and I looked at more of the paintings. They all had those splodges and swirls that seemed vaguely rude. Big Fella's wife was obviously very talented.

He came back and handed me a chilled tin but it was such an old-fashioned kind I didn't even know how to open it. He helped me crack the lid and a button of foam spat out.

"Cheers, pal."

"Thank you, sir." It tasted disgusting, like mouldy bread. I guessed they didn't put sweeteners in their drinks because they needed all the sugar for their transportation vehicles. "You mentioned a parcel..."

"It's nothing, son. Friend of mine's needing some medicine, that's all." There were rules and regulations, apparently, stupid laws that meant he couldn't post it. "Like the pictures, eh?

That wee one there's a cracker."

"Is your wife a professional?"

"Ye could say that."

I sipped the beer as slowly and politely as I could, wondering what it was made from. In the movie they only ever drank stuff called wine that was really grape juice, they pressed it themselves from the fruit of their own vines. But the Chinese, I'd since discovered, always get Scotland wrong. In reality those grapes would more likely power a smoke-belching hoverboard. Beer must be a way of recycling bakery by-products. Might even have some kind of religious significance.

Big Fella told me he was a collector, pointed to a cabinet in a corner of the room and we went to look at what was inside: old coins and credit cards, a printed circuit, a bag made of polythene. His home was stylishly uncluttered; but a few ancient objects, carefully placed and thoughtfully displayed, created an air of taste and beauty. He showed me an antique device called an iPod, with parts a person would put inside their ears. Something to do with telepathy or mood control, I think, and although it obviously no longer worked, he still wanted me to try. I thought of all the infectious agents that could have accumulated on those porous buds over the years and politely said no. In another part of the room stood an archaic microwave oven that still pinged, and near it on a plinth I saw Big Fella's most precious relic, a glass box whose tiny occupant was held on a gold pin I could barely bring into focus beneath my eyes. Big Fella supplied a magnifying glass. It was, he said, the last midgie on Earth.

"Ye'll be stopping wi us after the party won't you?"

I hadn't known about it, but Big Fella said there was a full moon: I was in luck. He insisted I stay. That was one thing the movie certainly got right: the kindness and generosity of these people.

"Nother beer?"

I'd drunk hardly any; Big Fella suggested I might like to try a different beverage and brought out something called whisky. It looked promising because the measure he poured was a lot less than what was in my beer tin, though when I tasted it I could see why. I believe they make it by steeping chillies in oil for several years. Big Fella suggested adding water and in this way I was able to drink quite a lot, being thirsty from the long day's heat.

I started to feel giddy. Perhaps I'd picked up something blown from those ear buds because really I wasn't right at all though I didn't want to say anything to Big Fella who was being so friendly. What happened during the next few hours is not completely clear. At some point his wife Angelica arrived, blonde and beautiful and many years younger than Big Fella. She wanted to hear me play guitar so I suppose I must have sung "Peace Song of the United Workers" while she sketched my portrait in charcoals. When she was done she turned her drawing board and showed me what she had seen: a pile of geometric shapes in need of shaking. I think the next thing that happened was she started taking off some of her clothes.

Suddenly there were other people, many of them, and we were all on the beach standing naked beneath the bright round moon. There was some woman doing a lot of shouting who taught degree courses in shamanic drumming. And we burned a dead dog, or perhaps I only imagined that part. Well, here I was in the land of love and peace, the place I'd come in search of, even better than the movie about the guys opening a tavern. Everybody gets Scotland wrong, they think of beaches and hydrosurfing and don't realise it's a state of mind, it's about having the freedom to discover who you really are. Big Fella took me to one side and started explaining about the parcel, only some white powder in a little plastic bag for his sick friend, though on account of those stupid rules and regulations I'd need to hide it in an unusual place if that was okay, not the sort of place I'd ever thought of putting anything at all but a natural pocket of sorts, I suppose. And I said sure, no problem, because Scotland is a land of spiritual freedom and in Scotland nobody says no to anything, only an everlasting yes, in fact they were all shouting it in unison while that woman was banging away at her drum: "Yea! Yea! Yea!". But Big Fella must have detected a flicker of doubt because he said to me, are you really sure? You won't go telling anyone? He got Mrs Fella to contribute to the discussion and she was pretty persuasive. And all the time I kept hearing the shouts of the revellers, seeing their beautiful moonlit bodies. Never anything like that in the movie, I can tell you.

A very long time ago, maybe hundreds or thousands of years, I don't know exactly, midgies were these creatures that gave you plague and made Scotland a miserable unhappy place of war and famine. Kind of a symbol you could say, symbol of a nation that was sick and needed healing. But now the midgies were gone, and here were all these joyful, welcoming people, cured and free, and it was places like my own that were sick: the Dome, with its endless artificial daylight and sanitised air. "You need tae live a little," Big Fella advised. And you know, that is so profound. It's like in Scotland everyone's a philosopher, everyone's a poet. So let's do it, I thought. Let's live a little. Because when you really get down to it, it's nice to be nice.

That Place next to the Bread Shop

So there I was just coming out of Littlewoods when I bumped into Betty and she said to me Oh heavens Agnes! and she looked so pale like she'd seen a ghost and I said Betty you look like you've just seen a ghost and she says to me I just have that's what she said I just have.

She said she was coming out of Marks and Spencer when she saw old Bob Docherty you know old sour faced Bob with the pipe and she says hello Bob you're looking all dressed up today are you going anywhere special? Anywhere special she says to him and old Bob says oh aye Betty I'm going somewhere very special today and she says where's that Bob and he says with a smile on his face for a change I'm going to that place next to the bread shop and then off he goes round the corner.

That place next to the bread shop he said and Betty says to me she thought that's funny I don't know any place next to the bread shop he must be going off his head and she just carried on and forgot all about it but then later on she came round past the bread shop and thought to herself the old devil there was him smiling when he was going to a funeral because that's what's next to the bread shop it's the Co-op funeral parlour and she said to me she thought I wonder who's died now so she went over to see if she could find out who old Bob was done up for seeing as he doesn't have many friends.

So Betty goes inside a bit sheepish to try and find out if it's anyone she knows and there she was standing outside Littlewoods telling me all this and she says to me who do you think it was that they said had died and I said don't tell me

Betty it was old Bob Docherty and you'd just seen his ghost and she says no Agnes no it wasn't old Bob and that's why I'm so surprised because they said the one that died was you.

Impossible Tales

1

"Harry Blue, freelance philosopher."

"Good morning, Mr Blue," the young-sounding woman at the other end of the line greeted me. "I'm Lucy Gamble, project developer at Klein Torus plc. I'm calling to see if you can help us with an issue that's come up."

I don't usually handle commercial contracts, preferring to offer my philosophical services to ordinary members of the public whose existential problems have been left unresolved by religion, art, long walks or recreational drugs. "Have you tried Cogito?" I suggested.

Cogito, a consultancy division of the university, are the acknowledged experts in handling places like Klein Torus plc, whose board reaches crisis one day as someone interrupts a meeting to ask, "Why are we all doing this?" Around a highly polished table of stainless steel and veneered particleboard, men and women lift their eyes from the balance sheets and departmental reports spread before them to search instead each other's face and their own troubled hearts until an answer to the novel conundrum is quickly offered: they're here to earn money to support themselves and their families. "Yes," says one; "but why here? Why this?" A call to Cogito is then rewarded by a visit from a consultant who carries out a philosophical audit of the company's metaphysical, moral and ethical condition. Employees are interviewed, plant and machinery examined, coffee consumed. Some companies, subjected to the wise scrutiny of experienced auditors, are found not to exist at all, in anything other than a notional sense. More commonly, after a series of briefing sessions for senior personnel in which everyone hangs their jacket on the back of their stackable chair then stares at a flipchart for two and a half hours (with refreshment break), the auditor is able to draw up an Action Plan, headed by a Mission Statement which says in effect: "We're here to make money to support ourselves and our families." The auditor then departs, leaving a bill for some three to five thousand pounds.

"We've tried Cogito previously," said Lucy Gamble. "It didn't work."

I doubted I could be of any greater benefit. My clients are typically individuals who have grown tired of aromatherapy, astrology, the football field or pub. I tell them I can offer no answers, only new ways of framing the questions, and I give them the opportunity to terminate proceedings immediately at no charge. Those who opt to continue might then ask, "What is the meaning of life?", to which I would respond that it depends what you mean by life. And what you mean by mean, come to that. An hour later we agree a treatment plan and I give them a prescription which they take to the local library, this being the only place where anyone seeking to understand life should go. The "real world" (whatever that is) can only serve as a distraction; it's the problem, not the solution. Though now I'm in danger of sounding like the people from Cogito.

Lucy explained, "We're trying to work out if something can be in two different places at the same time."

So at least the problem was an interesting one; certainly more compelling than the way it had arisen in relation to monetising multiple downloads of digital content, or something like that. "My honest recommendation would be a twenty-day course of Leibniz," I informed her. "Though a quick chat might be sufficient to set your mind at ease."

The basic question, I soothingly elucidated, is how to define uniqueness. If all things are made of identical atoms, as Democritus proposed, then the only difference between one atom and another is location in space.

"I see," she said, evidently jotting things down on her notepad while the endless chatter and buzz of a thriving office unwound itself in an invisible background.

"Later, Duns Scotus," I continued, "was interested in the essential is-ness of things; what the Cogito people usually call quiddity, or what-ness, though it's also known as haecceity, which means this-ness."

"Okay, is-ness... what-ness... this-ness," she mumbled, scribbling. "How about where-ness and why-ness?"

"I could explain it all much more fully in a formal consultation."

"Never mind," she said. "How do I get hold of this Leibniz you mentioned?"

"He died in 1716," I told her. "His contemporaries thought him ridiculous because he wore a big black wig and outrageous clothes. And I suspect that after the end of our conversation this is the only thing you'll ever remember about poor Leibniz."

"Possibly," she said.

"But as a further piece of free information for your company, let me explain that Leibniz believed the universe to be made not of matter and space, but of 'monads', little minds which collectively constitute all possible worlds; and among these worlds is one we call real, though it has no more substance than a ghost or shadow."

She'd stopped writing. "Now you're freaking me out."

I added that Leibniz proposed a vast library with himself as curator, and a secret encyclopaedia – written by himself in symbolic numerical code – as its greatest asset. Lucy interrupted to remind me that all she wanted to know was whether something can be in two places at once. I told her about the Moslowski-Carlson thought experiment.

One day, I said, a machine is invented that duplicates matter. Put an apple in and you get two identical apples out. Moslowski and Carlson ask us to consider whether this second apple would be different from the first in anything other than position.

An immediate objection put forward by Hepple was that the MC machine (as it's now known in the trade) would violate the conservation of mass-energy. There's only so much stuff in the universe and you can't make a new apple out of thin air. Moslowski and Carlson petulantly retorted that the duplicate apple is fashioned from energy supplied by several nuclear power stations. The lights of ten cities flicker every time a single fruit is made. It's inefficient, but hey, it works.

"Hang on," said Lucy. "Is this for real? Has somebody made this machine?"

"It only exists in one of Leibniz's possible worlds," I reassured her. "And even that is questionable because the acrimonious debate between Dr Hepple and Professors Moslowski and Carslon – which almost turned to physical violence at a conference in France – centred on whether the machine would be a logical possibility as opposed to a purely technical one."

I could tell that Lucy had other calls to make, but anyone who phones a freelance philosopher looking for advice should be prepared for a long conversation. So I described how, in a Paris restaurant one evening following a symposium on "Quantum Ontology", the debate between the three experts continued. Colin Hepple, over a glass of red wine, argued that the MC machine would contravene the second law of thermodynamics, which states that the entropy or disorder of the universe can only increase. A large enough machine could recycle the universe itself, he declared, re-shaping dissipated energy into an endless cosmos of, let us say, beautifully sculpted porcelain figurines like the ones on a nearby shelf. Moslowski and Carlson, who were sharing an introductory salad, said that now he was being plain silly.

At this point Lucy, who was clearly quite bright given the powerful position she evidently held in Klein Torus, said, "Are these philosophers for real?"

The dead ones, certainly, I replied. But as part of my professional code of ethics I often change the names of the living to protect myself from legal action by the likes of Hepple and his real-world avatar.

"I see," she said. "Can you spell avatar?"

Hepple's thermodynamic argument was, however, invalid; the MC machine lowers local entropy in the same way as a refrigerator, but there's an overall energy cost. Suffice it to say that by time the main course arrived and they'd all calmed down (having been asked to do so by the manager), Moslowski and Carlson had persuaded Hepple that what they'd really proposed was a matter transporter that doesn't destroy the original object it transports.

"Matter transporter," said Lucy. "Right."

Or rather, Moslowski continued, a matter projector. You see, I told her, Moslowski was still bewitched by Leibniz's notion that what we call reality is hardly more than a shadow. Try telling that to my wife, I added, and Lucy gave a quiet murmur of assent. But while Hepple examined the texture of his steak, and Moslowski and Carlson lovingly shared with one another some succulent cubes of pork, the blissful workings of their proposed device came more clearly to light. Consider a film projector that sends a flat, intangible picture of an apple onto a distant wall. The MC machine delivers, by contrast, a picture that is three dimensional, solid, and completely indistinguishable from the original.

When I first read about this in bed I was quite struck by the notion. "Imagine a three-dimensional projector," I said to Deborah who was trimming her toenails.

"A what?"

Hepple, washing the meat from between his teeth with mouthfuls of pinot noir, objected again, saying Moslowki and Carlson's matter replicator would involve instantaneous transfer of information, contrary to Einstein's theory of relativity. Moslowski and Carlson, who were both on white, retorted that when an apple is projected by the machine, the duplicate appears a fraction of a second later, the delay being the time it takes for information to travel at the speed of light from the original to the three-dimensional image. So the Moslowski-Carlson machine doesn't put the same thing in two different places at the same time, Lucy, I told her, but rather makes a distant copy representing the object at an earlier time. Their conclusion, as the waiter came to clear the table and eyed the three of them with the suspicion reserved by right-minded people for those who can get all worked up about matter transporters and logical conundrums is that you can't have the same thing in two places at once, but you could have multiple copies of an object at different times in its history.

"When are you going to get a proper job?" Deborah asked me as a clipping flew onto the page I was reading.

"I'm lost," said Lucy.

Perhaps I've always been too willing to let Cogito soak up the easy money: Lucy's comment tempted me to tout for serious business. "People in a state of spiritual confusion are precisely those I aim to help. Tell me, Lucy, are you really satisfied with life?"

She said it was only the obscurity of the story that confused her, and once I got to the end of it she would happily return to her important duties in the rewarding and infinitely meaningful environment of Klein Torus plc.

"Alright," I said. "But suppose you were given a chance to be duplicated by the MC machine. Would you dare?"

In fact, I told her, even as Moslowski and Carlson were studying the dessert menu and I was contemplating Deborah's toenails, the machine was growing in size. Not only an apple or a person but a whole planet could be projected, or indeed a solar system. Perhaps it was simply the thought of the *crème brûlée* that over-excited them, but Moslowski and Carlson were prepared to envisage an orbital version of their creation which by means of elaborate gravitational lensing and esoteric quantum effects would be able to duplicate our whole planetary system in some far-flung corner of the night sky. Hepple subsequently said that by this stage he had his head in his hands and was shaking it slowly. Strangely enough, Deborah did exactly the same thing when I told her.

The machine, I continued, is now pointing slightly to the

left of anomalous binary star Korr-Helgason 45C, where the rotational energy of a black hole will enable our Earth and all its contents to be projected and reassembled. Aloft in its lonely geostationary orbit, the machine whirrs into action.

"Eh?" said Lucy. I have found, over the course of my career, that an elliptical and somewhat rhetorical manner is often the way to get ahead in freelance philosophy.

Thirty-three years, I told her, pass by. This is the time it takes for Earth's quantum image to fly through space and arrive at Korr-Helgason 45C, where a silvery apparition solidifies one afternoon into a perfect copy of our world, the sun, and all the other planets. I asked her, "How old are you, Lucy?"

"Twenty-nine."

Thirty-three years from now, I explained, on a duplicate Earth in another star system, 29-year-old Lucy will be having precisely this telephone conversation with a second Harry Blue. "Here on Earth you will be sixty-two years old and I might no longer be around."

"Weird shit," she said.

Well it certainly gave me pause for thought as I lay in bed listening to the click and snap of Deborah's nail scissors. And meanwhile the MC-machine is continuously transmitting Earth and its contents to the vicinity of anomalous binary Korr-Helgason 45C, where the duplicate world amounts (the notion is at once fantastic and grotesque) to a tangible film-show for the benefit of its oblivious duplicate inhabitants. People complain about late-running trains, I told Lucy, but that's nothing compared to the thirty-three-year gap between Earth and Korr-Helgason 45C. Still, the duplicate Earthlings don't mind because they don't know they're only projections of a world that's already moved on a generation. So when duplicate Lucy picks up the phone and dials the number she's found on her duplicate computer screen after searching for "philosophical services", she thinks the cause of this action is her own free will, influenced by a request from her line manager who's drinking duplicate coffee and picking his duplicate nose. But really, I explained, the actions of the other Lucy are dictated entirely by the invisible quantum signals emanating from a far-off planet – Earth – on which the original Lucy has now retired and is taking evening classes in watercolour painting.

"Do I have children?" she asked anxiously.

"One of each," I reassured her.

When Moslowski and Carlson hit on this idea they embraced vigorously. Somehow, Hepple felt, it only seemed to confirm and reinforce their absurd devotion. He told the waiter he'd have the *terrine au chocolat*.

"I had no idea people like you existed," Lucy told me abruptly.

As for Moslowski and Carlson, they were soon whispering to each other with rising excitement that their strange new machine offered the infinite multiplication of a perverse form of immortality. Hearing this, Hepple nearly choked on his chocolate terrine. His laughter sent brown globules across the tablecloth, much to the distress of his fastidiously clean companions, and even more to the annoyance of the hovering waiter who'd already warned these troublemakers to keep their voices down.

One day, though, there's a technical problem. The orbital MC machine has developed an irritating click in its gyroscopic axial compensators (due to the negligence of contractors who mistakenly thought the measurements in the plans were Imperial rather than metric), and this click in turn provokes excess strain on the quantum-gravitational defocuser. Basically the machine's knackered.

"Oh dear," I thought to myself as Deborah switched off the light.

Moslowski and Carlson wondered what would happen if the machine were to stop transmitting. Would duplicate Lucy – right in the middle of a conversation with Harry Blue, duplicate freelance philosopher – suddenly disappear from existence, along with the rest of her world? No, I told her; the signals that give life to her replica would still be in transit, and she would not die for another thirty-three years. But then?

Disturbed perhaps by the insurance implications, Moslowski and Carlson both got up to go to the toilet. Hepple had no idea what went on during their five-minute absence, but when they returned they announced that the orbital MC machine had been redesigned.

"Sit down and eat your *crème brûlée*," Hepple gruffly told them. They'd ordered one helping, two spoons, and there was a brown globule on top that had come from Hepple's mouth. Everybody pretended not to notice.

The new MC machine is equipped with something called the NDFSD (or "nid-for-sid", as it has come to be called in literary and philosophical circles), which stands for "non-deterministic fail-safe device". Now if the power cuts out – due to an industrial dispute, let's say – the duplicate world will not be doomed to vanish. Instead it will keep existing but will no longer be connected in any way with events on Earth.

Hepple was outraged. "This is merely special pleading!" he said, tearing at his napkin. I imagined it while the bedside light was off and Deborah was already snoring.

On the contrary, Moslowski and Carlson protested. The vanishing of duplicate Earth would be exactly the kind of mass-energy non-conservation that had earlier so infuriated Hepple;

their new proposal was physically reasonable. Hepple was having none of it. "Stop this nonsense!" he snarled; which was almost exactly what Deborah had told me a little earlier. But by now Lucy had received more than enough free information and it was time for me to try and reach a conclusion, though I've found that in the business of freelance philosophy this is always the hardest part.

Once constructed, I told her, the MC machine would project our world across the cosmos. Wherever conditions allowed, the emanating rays would make, like shadows of falling sunbeams, a new copy of Earth in exactly the form it took at the moment of transmission. Thereafter, these many worlds would proceed independently, according to their own whims and contingencies. Thirty-three years from now, for instance, the duplicate Lucy near Korr-Helgason 45C is free to hang up the phone and walk out of her job, even though her progenitor failed to do so. The universe, if big enough, could eventually contain our every possible world.

I realised this made as little impact on Lucy as it had done on my wife who in the darkness of our bedroom surprised me by suddenly saying something in her sleep, incomprehensible though possibly not insignificant.

Moslowski and Carlson were getting up to leave. Hepple, angered not only by their smart-arsed continental sophistry but even more so by their presumption that he would foot the entire dinner bill for the three of them and claim it on his own expenses, said that he had never heard of anything quite so ridiculous as their supposed "thought experiment". The waiter stood silently in attendance while credit cards were brought out. Then Moslowski said to Carlson: "How can we be sure that what we shall henceforth call the MC machine has not already been made by creatures in some distant galaxy, of whose remote and forgotten past we ourselves are no more than the palest and most distorted image?"

They understood then the dread import of Leibniz's observation that the world is but a shadow; and this was the realisation that had occurred to me, lying awake in bed while Deborah resumed snoring. I said to Lucy, "Ask your boss to consider the possibility that the true Earth vanished millions of years ago in another galaxy, and that Klein Torus only appeared here in the last half hour when a quantum beam accidentally interacted with some supernova dust left lying around, just as Klein Torus will appear again and again elsewhere until the end of time."

"I'll do that," she promised, and hung up, having received at least a tenner's worth of free philosophy. Perhaps Deborah's right, there's a fundamental flaw in my business model. She was soundly asleep again so I switched on the light to do some more reading.

2

Nearing the end of its life, the Fidel now caught less exo-plankton than ever. Barron and his wife were ronked in the vacuum shipment area, Timman was browsing a metatext, while the Chicken Sisters dreamily pursued another game of Wobble™ Ball.

Blown on the cosmic rays of stellar wind, exoplankton is now known to be a major component of the total mass of the universe, someone once said. Microscopic, unicellular, and metabolising motes of distant starlight at a slow rate of centuries, exoplankton spawned the first life on Earth, on Mars, and doubtless on a thousand other worlds whose creatures owe their existence and descent to the abundant celestial flotsam that went unnoticed for so long, someone else said while Timman turned up the deci-level of his metatext.

He was sitting in the observation bubble idly playing with himself by the light of a floating torch that spun slowly and precessed its cool light over his loose hyperwear and angry fingers. By mutual agreement of the entire Family, sex of any kind had been banished to the ObsoBub, following the entrapment of loose juices – weightless specks of gum – in the microwave oven's cooling fan. Timman blamed the Chicken Sisters but still ate his korfl well warmed.

Vast, tenuous and almost invisible, the scum of exoplankton was once seen as a new galactic continent, magnificent and limitless. Jubilant faces in press conferences known from school lessons called it the greatest discovery in human history. Yes, there was life in space after all; not ancient fossils but viable organisms whose precursor RNA indicated them to be our own cosmic ancestors, and those of our extinct Martian bacterial cousins.

History, as far as the Chicken Sisters were concerned, is a lot less interesting than Wobble™ Ball. Why should they care about a story made up by other people, they once told Timman, colliding in laughter then floating to opposite ends of the empty hold they'd embellished with the chevrons of an Olympic-sized Wobble™ court. What are you doing in this Family anyway, one of them asked him, hurling the Wobble™ to its target.

Now stand we, press conferencers misquoted, like proud Columbus; or like watchers of the sky, as new planets swim into our ken. One kid learned it by heart and grew up to be an accountant. Timman did a school project like everybody else; last time he saw his mother she still had the rimp though no longer owned a machine that could play it. The shiny tablet was in a box along with his first tooth, a broken toy and other valueless treasures. Please son, she said to him, don't get mixed up in this exo stuff. Don't waste your life. Look what it did to your dad.

Unfortunately at this point Timman came and sent an unanticipated thread of zero-gravity ejaculate that wormed and twisted onto the clear dome of the ObsoBub.

Remember to clean up, Tim, he heard, as Chicken One, having been watching him on her palmview exactly as he guessed, interrupted the metatext. Her words juxtaposed curiously with those of the voicewire above his brow: Nor Earth nor Heaven hath its secret corners; for the eye of God, though it peer through greatest darkness, perceiveth all matter.

"Is Barron with you?" Timman asked her.

"He's ronked out," said Chicken One. "That last gram of exo we caught must've had too much lith. By the way, Tim," she added, "Who were you thinking about this time? Was it me?"

Timman didn't care to admit that his act had been one of boredom and frustration rather than desire, and that the only secret corner of his mind had at the time been carelessly filled with thoughts of schooldays, his mother and an Elizabethan author.

"Actually I was thinking of your sister," said Timman.

"She's here right now," was the reply. "She's practising her triple Wobble™. Every time she does the under-arm Sardovski her butt ripples like a fish tank."

Chicken Two giggled her way into Timman's metatext. "Don't listen to her!" she complained. "We aren't Wobbling™ at all. As it happens, I'm in the bedroom shooting some very clean ex."

"Hoy, that's my ex!" screamed Chicken One, causing Timman to reduce the volume. "Sun-cunt!"

"It's my own snack," Two drawled. "Been saving it since Beacon Five."

Then at last another voice. A growl they all knew; an animal waking itself up, looking for the sky and finding only the mournful, familiar entombment of the vacuum shipment area. Carl Barron.

"Fucking Jesus fuck!"

"Snap it, Carl." Barron's wife had woken too, and soothed her husband from post-ronk dystopia as best she could.

"Timman's been janking without a condom again," Chicken One announced to the entire Family.

"It's allowed in the ObsoBub," Timman insisted, turning up his metatext once more for the benefit of his companions.

Man hath his dominions; yet all are laid waste. Roots and dregs alone command his spirits.

"Fuck you, Timman," Carl Barron snarled.

"Snap it, love."

"Fuck you too," he told his wife.

Another female voice joined them. It was Cuff, the only person on board the space trawler Fidel who had been doing anything useful during the preceding half hour. "Ex ahead! A big trace! I think this could be a whole fucking spawnfield!"

Cheers, oaths and a weightless many-personed scramble through the tubes and passages of the dying Fidel, then a congregation of starved ex-heads in the control room of the ship, gazing as one at the tracer ray.

We have detected a cloud, says a voice on a useless rimp in Mrs Timman's cardboard box, that lies beyond the orbit of Neptune, and whose absorption spectrum indicates the presence of protein molecules. The Chickens were never interested in the history bit, but wars were fought for this, Timman once pleaded. Hoy, they said, as long as we know where our next shot is coming from we couldn't give a geck.

Not acres, but gold alone hath turn'd the heads of Columbus or Cortez.

And we believe, furthermore, that these proteins could only be the products of living processes. Trans-Neptunian Cloud 85b contains animate creatures.

Mrs Timman had listened patiently while her young son displayed the history of exoplankton he'd compressed. The long years following initial discovery, when robotic missions had journeyed to the cloud and its companions in order to confirm what everyone already knew well enough to find remote and tedious, except in the metaphorical sense to which all history ultimately rises if it is to be remembered at all. There are little bugs in space, that's all. They photosynthesise starlight and receive in one million years no more energy than a blade of grass can catch in a single cloudy morning. They are so simple as to be negligible were they not instead ubiquitous; our own progenitors by an accident, some say, of comet-fall upon Earth's barren surface. Mrs Timman was so proud of her son's work.

The initial sample, his eight-year-old commentary had announced to her, was brought back by the Babuk mission, named (archive dub) after a New Guinean deity responsible for sowing humanity's first crops.

Ladies and gentlemen, having succeeded in cultivating exoplankton under laboratory micro-gravity conditions, and having established its effect on the mammalian telomere, we can now present to you what may ultimately prove to be the greatest breakthrough in the history of medicine... (Fast forward) of exoplankton, administered properly, can increase rodent lifetimes by up to eight hundred per cent. In human terms, this may offer us the ability to live a thousand years.

Nothing is immortal, sayeth the wise, save immortality itself.

At the control panel, Barron watched while Cuff selected wavelengths.

"It looks a good crop," Cuff confirmed.

"But is it spiked?" Chicken Two wondered.

They didn't want any more lithium in their veins, especially given the effect it had on Barron. "Just give us the fucking co-ordinates," he grunted at Cuff who was smoothly enacting pre-catch procedure. Somehow Cuff was never ronked, no matter how much ex she dabbed.

The Chickens were spasmodic with excitement. Chick Two, mildly high, was humming the theme to *Arse Biscuit 15*, tunelessly and without rhythm. Timman saw she had a feed wire in her ear. She might as well not be here.

The last time he saw his mother, Mrs Timman reminded him of his school project. He knew all about ex and what it did to his dad. That stuff was perfectly healthy as long as it was done by qualified doctors. It was what kept them all alive. You're only eight now, she said, but one day you'll be five hundred and eight and you'll still need your health.

He knew it all when he made the rimp, wise and dutiful child, repeating the solemn message proclaimed by the centrally planned "Kick Ex" campaigns. Into his credit-winning school project, part of the government metatext had been carefully spliced by his teacher Mrs Quine. Some people are in a nightclub, drinking narcotane mixers from polyplas vacuum-injected designer bottles. A stranger nudges one of them; a good-looking girl is led from the dance floor, out to the darkened street behind the club. There among the litter and the smell of piss (dubbed from some wildlife documentary) a dealer crouches over a portable centrifuge.

"Normally eighty-five a gram," he says. "But sheck us twenty and I'll rack you a snort."

She looks pretty and intelligent; the sort young Timman hoped might bear his children. "I thought this stuff could only live in zero grav," she says.

"Don't believe anything scientists tell you. They're only in it for the money."

In the government-sponsored omnidram the centrifuge is seen shuddering to a fatal halt. A glowing drop appears in a thin tube, held up to the scrutiny of a violet streetlight and the girl's tempted face.

"It only takes a moment," says the expert, who, within the caverns of an infra-link, shows children how exoplankton looks through a neutrino microscope. Carefully processed, it provides a possibility of endless life. Contaminated with oxygen, it forms an addictive hallucinogen with the power to destroy the human immune system.

"Baby lick my keyhole," Chicken Two offered, murmuring the *Arse Biscuit* theme as Cuff prolonged the ambient four-vectors with respect to Limit Trace 2163, the presumed mother-lode of local exoplankton with a terrestrial street value, enforcement would probably estimate, of several billion. If the pharmaceutical companies had got here first, Barron would at this stage have reasoned in saner days, they'd only have scooped it up and sold it at even greater profit, providing centuries of life to the inhabitants of popular retirement countries like Benin or Scotia. A simple bargain, then. You go for decades of legal mediocrity, channelling all your inherited wealth and share dividends into regular shots of Exelon delivered by white-coated professionals in free-fall. Or

else pay far less for a life of boundless pleasure that reaches a natural end before a century.

That was how Barron used to argue the case, the way he talked to Timman when they first met. Barron didn't look like the piss-stained dealer in the government ads, more like a shabby poet or the leader of some as-yet unfounded political movement. His wife even changed her name to be more like him: instead of Carl and Sonia they were Carl and Carla. When Timman was introduced to her, in the flat she and Barron shared with the Chicken Sisters, it was like talking to a female version of Carl. She came out with exactly the same arguments and comparisons, though somehow from Carla's mouth they were less convincing.

The pharms were selling off their old trawlers and didn't care who bought them or why, as long as competition didn't become too fierce. Already many of the major dealing circuits had gone over to dedicated trawlers, making robot retrievers a thing of the past. The pharms were ditching crewed vessels because of the health risks and insurance implications, leaving viable machines and empty skies for entrepreneurs like Carl, said Carla.

That was about a hundred years ago. Since then the Family had shipped enough ex to send half a continent to immortality or oblivion. They'd been chased by scouts, tangled with other circuits and shot a steady thousandth of a per cent of centrifuged catchload into their veins, balanced by an equally steady hundredth of a per cent unoxidised that kept them alive despite the crumbling of their immune systems. They were facades, killed and cured by habit, who spent most of the day masturbating or getting ronked or playing Wobble™ Ball. They'd forgotten how to like or hate each other, or how to think, or why they were here, it had all been so long. They didn't even know for sure where they were in the universe. The

Oort Cloud had briefly crossed their attention not long after their flight began; with it had passed all Earthly jurisdiction. Like the exoplankton itself, their only reason for existing was to carry on whatever it was they were meant to be doing. And all they were meant to do, it seemed, was exist.

"There's the catch," Cuff affirmed, gliding her wrist over the spectral integrator. They would all go home one day and be rich. Yes, that was the plan.

Ladies and gentlemen, we can announce the greatest discovery in human history. Space is a drug worth zillions. And it's all ours.

It was some months before they engaged with the alleged spawnfield. In that time Chicken One finally perfected the Petrov manoeuvre in Wobble™ Ball, Cuff resumed watercolour painting and Timman left countless tiny stains on the window of the ObsoBub. With each slow increase of the angular diameter of Limit Trace 2163, Carl Barron grew ever more pessimistic about its worth. Its spectrum had revealed it to be a non-stellar object harbouring vaporous proteins, but the usual accompanying molecular cloud that would provide the exoplankton's source of nutrition was absent, prompting Cuff to wonder if they had discovered a phenomenon in which science might be interested were its arid fingers able to probe this uncharted region where only greed and addiction had chanced to intrude.

Timman was on court watching the naked oscillating buttocks of Chicken Number Two when the news came. Two was reaching for a semi-returned Malko, extending her prod to maximum allowed extent (according to Olympic rules of an earlier century), flailing and scissoring her weightless legs into a pudendal vignette that briefly aroused Timman's ancient desire until a voice arrived and interrupted.

Andrew Crumey

"I've resolved the trace," Cuff sadly intoned. "I'm sorry, guys. It's only a planetoid."

Chicken Two abandoned the Malko and crashed forlornly into the steady-bars at court end. Chick One clenched her teeth, looked brow-wards to a place she once called "up" and cursed silently at first, then, already drained, shook her fists and moaned "cunt" before retreating into sobs. Timman sent the Wobble™ spinning in illegal retrograde motion then departed for the ObsoBub.

It was a fucking planet. No ronk-rich cloud of spawning ex freshly minted on the hub of a rotating GMC. No joyful sessions of mutual shooting, snorting, sniffing and patching; no games of straw exchange or pass the bunny. No shoal to swell the hold and send them homewards across unmeasured parsecs towards an Earth they had no confidence of ever finding. Instead they had discovered a large rocky sphere computed to be in orbit around a sickly star of no conceivable interest. This planet had complex life on it, betrayed by the filtration and analysis of starlight refracted into Fidel's prismatic eye by the atmosphere the little world sustained. The feeble signals Fidel still received from its own home planet were at least thirty years out of date by the crew's dull reckoning, and nobody could recall any news item ever announcing the discovery of complex creatures on another world, in which case the Family had made history. Yet none but a scientist at a press conference could show any enthusiasm for the possibility that a rock in space harboured yeast or worms. If we can't inject it, as Barron would once have said, we're not cooking.

Just two more months, Cuff reasoned, would place them in orbit round this ronkless little world of nothing, somewhere in the quiet suburbs of what the sky's cartographers once named anomalous binary Korr-Helgason 45C.

3

On afternoons like this it's often my habit to meet Richard Sand in Cafe Mozart, where waitresses wearing the smocks and pinafores of imagined eighteenth-century dairymaids gaze insolently while serving you a Mozart Mocha or Figaro Melange, and you can experience the fake history of a non-existent empire for the price of an ice cream.

While Dr Sand was describing a new flavour he thought I might find exciting, the time approached for me to introduce the photographs I'd received that morning in a brown envelope. The pictures had been subjected to some judicious cropping but the message was clear enough. Black and white, though not as grainy as I would have expected under the circumstances, they showed my wife Deborah in a variety of positions I never would have thought humanly possible, anatomy not having been among the subjects of which I have made myself a diligent student in the course of my career as freelance philosopher. The envelope had entered my hitherto tranquil life surreptitiously, by way of the doormat, and I can only say that I'm very glad I had chosen the privacy of the toilet as the place in which Deborah's white flesh and her companion's formidable physique (greyer in tone, and dramatically shadowed) should have burst into the pine-scented light of day.

Arriving at Cafe Mozart some hours later, I looked through the plate-glass windows and saw in front of one of the tables a waitress's theatrically-clad rump in mid-serve. Straightening herself and moving away, she revealed to me a cream-topped Viennois in a tall porcelain cup before the figure of Dr Sand, who asked me how I was as soon as I stepped inside to join him. Fine, I said, but unfortunately my fears about my wife have been confirmed. I think you'd better tell me about it, said Dr Sand; sit down and I'll buy you an ice cream. That's a good idea, I said, the matter having thus been decided for me by Dr Sand's kind offer, though all my worries were now replaced by the difficult question of deciding which flavour to try. A degree of adventurousness with regard to desserts is one of my characteristic traits, but Coconut Explosion or Pineapple Rapture seemed a little too flippant under the circumstances. A smartly dressed man who had come in after me was already placing his order with the waitress at a nearby table, which only added to my feeling of urgency. I'll have chocolate, I said abruptly, it now being time for me to bring the troubling evidence from my briefcase.

Dr Sand however paid no attention to the large brown envelope I had deposited on the table, perhaps out of customary tact, and instead attempted to describe the new flavour he'd mentioned, called simply Pleasure, until the waitress came back within range and approached at my friend's bidding. Her difficulty in carrying her eighteenth-century costume with ease suggested her employment here to be of recent origin.

"A chocolate ice cream for my companion, please," Dr Sand requested.

"We've got Midnight Rhapsody, Chocolate Chip and Belgian White Chocolate." This statement of fact was delivered with the marmoreal tenor of a railway announcement.

"Which would you prefer?" Dr Sand said, turning to me.

"Actually in my present condition the choice is a matter of profound indifference. I leave it to you."

"What's Midnight Rhapsody?" he asked her.

"It's basically just chocolate."

"Then I think we'll settle for that one, thank you Remora."

He had read the name on the mandatory badge pinned incongruously to her dirndl bodice, and she left us without another word. "How appropriate," he then said.

"What do you mean?"

"I don't suppose she's aware of it, but her name is Latin for 'delay'."

Nevertheless she returned soon enough with a precious and tastefully embellished serving of Midnight Rhapsody. I removed the envelope from the table while she placed the dish before me.

"I'd better not get any chocolate ice cream on this," I explained, lifting the envelope to my chest.

"I suppose not," she agreed.

"You see, it contains some photographs of my wife in a very compromising situation. Several situations, actually. And chocolate ice cream can be quite detrimental to photographic paper." The smartly dressed man at the neighbouring table appeared to take note of this, even though it was only a pastry he was about to consume, and without any documents that might suffer damage from falling flakes.

Remora nodded sympathetically and left us while Dr Sand watched her retreating form. "Now," he said, "Tell me about Deborah. No, don't show me the photographs. At least, not yet. Simply tell me everything I need to know."

"I don't think you really need to know anything," I said, putting the envelope safely on my lap and taking up my spoon. "Knowledge of the matter, in your case, would constitute a recreational activity rather than a necessity. And I believe this ice cream has come straight from the freezer."

"Would you prefer another kind?" asked Dr Sand.

I shook my head. "The air will soon soften it. In any case I'm too distraught to worry about the texture of some frozen milk, eggs and sugar."

"I can see that," said Dr Sand, "Though I think you'll find that the ice cream is made with vegetable oils, skimmed milk, a little gelatine perhaps."

"Do you really think so?" I asked incredulously.

"I'd be willing to put money on it," said Dr Sand, and he called the waitress back to ask her. She listened to his enquiry with patience and concern, her eyes hardly leaving the brown envelope which by now I had removed from my lap and put on a corner of the table which I felt confident would remain free from contamination by ice cream.

"No," Remora was saying, "no animal fats."

"What about milk and eggs?" I proposed.

"Alright, I suppose milk and eggs are technically animal fat, but you know what I mean."

"Skimmed milk?" Dr Sand pursued.

"Well, maybe" the waitress conceded.

"And powdered egg?" was my contribution. In my mind, dark suspicions multiplied.

"Powdered?" she asked. "How do you powder an egg?"

"You dry it first," said the smartly dressed man at the next table.

"Look, what is this?" the waitress pleaded.

"Miss, could I see the manager?" the man retorted.

Remora appeared confused, an uncertain compass needle swinging amid fluctuating magnetic fields. She looked at me, at Dr Sand, at the man at the next table. At me again, and finally at the envelope.

"This strudel is stale, miss," said our neighbour. "Could I see the manager please?"

"Certainly sir," she said curtly. "I'll fetch her straight away."

307

"Well then," said Dr Sand, once this scene had concluded itself. "Are you going to tell me about Deborah?"

I passed the brown envelope to Dr Sand, who opened it then studied the photographs of my wife and her friend while my ice cream attempted to thaw. Despite his distance, the man at the other table also had a tolerably good view of the pictures, though I refrained from suggesting to Dr Sand that he pass them to him for clearer inspection.

"I do like Cafe Mozart," I observed, as Dr Sand went through the series of photographs for a fourth time. Deborah's affair was perhaps after all, as Dr Sand suggested, somehow inevitable, our lives being not unlike the dollop of whipped cream atop his Viennois, patterned with an apparent complexity beyond comprehension yet issuing deterministically from the nozzle of a can with a single easy squirt. At least I think that was the gist of what he said before Remora arrived at the neighbouring table accompanied by her superior, an older woman.

"What's the problem?" the manageress asked, courteously but in a manner suggesting readiness for a fight.

"This strudel is stale," the disgruntled customer reasserted.

"I can assure you that all our food is fresh, sir." Her arms were folded.

"I can assure you this isn't," said the man, opting for a more relaxed and asymmetric posture.

Dr Sand, possibly in order to refresh his memory, deviated from the sequence he'd been following and went back unexpectedly to the third photograph, showing Deborah's participation in an activity which looked particularly strenuous, and this caused Remora and her superior to be momentarily distracted from the pastry debate. The manageress, her attention engaged by the photograph held like a preserved butterfly in Dr Sand's scrupulous grip while upon his other hand his Viennois cooled slowly in its cup, now seemed less interested in a dubious strudel than in my wife's over-exposed buttocks.

"Quite honestly, madam, it's stale," the man at the next table reiterated.

"Oh, alright," said the manageress with complete indifference, her gaze adjusting only to the extent needed for her eyes to move from Deborah's thighs to her lover's chest, which in its dramatic contrasts of grey-tones was reminiscent, to me at least, of a postcard I once received from Mount Rushmore. In fact I thought I could almost discern, in the flexing, sweat-moistened pectorals, the profile of Thomas Jefferson.

"Would you like anything else instead?" asked the manageress, her question addressed to the man at the next table, though by now she too seemed to have discovered Jefferson's proud demeanour.

"No thanks," he said. "Just give me the bill for the coffee."

This was Remora's job, and a nod from the manageress sent her to carry it out. The manageress followed, then Dr Sand said to our neighbour, "You appear to be good at handling awkward interpersonal situations. Why don't you come and join us?"

He replied that he would be delighted, but first we must excuse him. He went to settle his bill, then confidently walked towards the well-hidden toilets which most customers can locate only after a member of staff has indicated them loudly and dramatically for the benefit of everybody else in the room.

"Do you know who he is?" said Dr Sand, still examining the photographs.

"I've no idea, though his ease in finding the gents would indicate he's either a regular or a psychic."

"No, not him," said Dr Sand. "I mean this gentleman seen

here penetrating your wife."

"Oh, no," I said. "I've no idea who he is, nor can I under-stand why he and Deborah should have chosen to engage in this sordid business, other than for the most obvious and banal of reasons."

Dr Sand commented that the couple must have been aware of the presence of the photographer. If the matter had been of any interest to us we might have asked ourselves who this photographer could have been, or what his motives were in taking the pictures and delivering them to my house.

"Perhaps they were intended for Deborah, not for you," said Dr Sand, who had noticed that the envelope was unmarked. I was more concerned with my frozen ice cream, which I had begun to attack with the provided long-handled spoon in the manner of an arctic explorer. An explorer, that is, of a region that is very small and dark brown in colour.

"What do you intend to do about this?" asked Dr Sand.

"I shall just have to let it melt naturally," I conceded.

Ignoring this, Dr Sand added, "A minor but not wholly insignificant point which I can't resist raising is that the woman's face is not clearly visible in any of the photographs. Even in the best view that we get of her head, her hair hangs across much of her profile, and her cheek is considerably distorted by the swollen object in her mouth. How can you be sure that this is Deborah?"

"I would recognise her toenails anywhere," I said. "She is my wife, after all."

"Quite," said Dr Sand apologetically. "And you have no idea who her companion might be?"

I told him I believed he bore some resemblance to a fellow who sometimes reads the weather on television late at night; but Dr Sand pointed out that as with Deborah's case, his body was better represented in the photographs than his face, so that there was little chance of identifying him with any certainty except perhaps by way of a line-up in a Turkish bath. Actually the only resemblance to the weatherman was the configuration in one photograph of an outstretched arm that seemed to be offering manual stimulation to an area of particularly sensitive nerve endings but could as easily have been indicating a high pressure region off the west coast of Ireland.

"I think you should forget all about this," said Dr Sand, returning the photographs to their envelope. "You have far more important things to do than worry about people's private lives, least of all your wife's." He is well acquainted with my disdain of anecdote, contingency and biography in general. Our new friend returned and Dr Sand expressed sympathy for his strudel distress.

"It's nothing," he replied as he sat down with us. "These things happen all the time in my line of work."

"And what line is that?" I inquired while continuing to chip at my ice cream.

"I'm with a major food company," he informed us, introducing himself with a handshake as Angus Crone.

"What sort of major foods do you manufacture, Mr Crone?" I asked him, to which he responded with a gentle laugh of a confident, professional kind.

"Our interests are very diverse," he said.

"Ours likewise," observed Dr Sand. "I'm a writer, translator and psychotherapist. Harry is a freelance philosopher."

"Then I'll know who to come to if I ever need that sort of help," Crone said pleasantly. He asked Dr Sand about his writing, prompting my friend to begin describing a project already familiar to me: his new translation of Alfredo Galli's *Racconti Impossibili* or "Impossible Tales".

Galli, Dr Sand explained, pioneered a technique variously called oneirism, narcology or hypnographia, inspired by the way in which images of reality appear to us in transformed or permuted forms in our dreams. Galli's experiments in dreaming were extensive (he was, according to one source, "a lazy sod") and his sleep studies led him to develop theories about writing, translating and psychotherapy: areas of interest exactly coincident with Dr Sand's. In fact I've sometimes wondered if Galli ever really existed, or whether instead my friend simply made him up as a necessary though hitherto strangely absent element of human existence.

"Dreaming is a process of juxtaposition and substitution," Dr Sand said while I made gradual headway with Midnight Rhapsody. Mr Crone noticed my patient endeavour.

"We're launching a product that'll make problems like yours a thing of the past. Room-temperature ice cream."

"I beg your pardon?"

"An end to overchill," Mr Crone grandly declared. "It has a melting point of thirty-three point five degrees Celsius, so doesn't usually have to be kept in a fridge, yet melts instantly in the mouth."

Dr Sand said this sounded like ordinary chocolate, or even butter.

"But here's the clever part," Mr Crone continued. "It has an extremely high latent heat of fusion, far higher than ordinary domestic refrigerant and also rather more palatable. The result is something that tastes frozen because of the sudden cooling effect it has on your mouth. I've tried it and believe me it works. Retailers can throw away their expensive freezer units. Consumers will love the flexibility and convenience."

"But what does it taste like?" I asked him.

"Oh, you get used to it."

Alfredo Galli's greatest project, Dr Sand resumed, was to be the embodiment of his literary theory. "A conventional novel or story collection is a sequence of parts in some predetermined order. We could of course read them any way we like: often I start a book at the end and follow the narrative in reverse, which I'm sure is an improvement in about fifty per cent of cases. But no matter which permutation we choose, it remains a sequence. Like, say, a pile of photographs." My eyes fell momentarily on the brown envelope still resting a safe distance from my slowly thawing ice cream, and when I raised them I saw that Mr Crone's had been similarly directed. "Suppose however," Dr Sand continued, "that the photographs are arranged in a grid; a rectangle four pictures wide and three deep."

"There aren't that many, are there?" I said, trying to imagine if twelve images of the weatherman with my wife could really have sustained my interest while I hid at home in the loo inspecting them.

"It was a hypothetical figure," said Dr Sand.

"Unlike my thirty-three point five degrees Celsius," Crone beamed, probably wishing to make some claim about the superiority of industrial chemistry over experimental fiction which Dr Sand nevertheless ignored, determined to pursue his argument.

"Let us go further and imagine a three-dimensional array of photographs."

"Arranged with the help of shelves," I suggested, since I already knew where all of this was going. The three of us by now could picture something like an IKEA bookcase on each of whose adjustable levels lay a rectangle of grainy images, possibly of a sexually explicit nature though to other eyes they might look like automatic shots from an underwater camera in

313

Loch Ness.

I said, "What we're really talking about is neo-Hegelian idealism. Very popular in Cambridge in the late nineteenth century."

"Along with cricket and homosexuality," Crone chummily presumed and was again ignored.

"The shelves and photographs are what philosophers such as Bradley termed the Absolute." No harm, I thought, in fishing for some consultancy work in major foods. "Bradley's a real philosopher, incidentally, by which I mean a dead one. He said that our experience of time is a path through the Absolute; a succession of images picked from the shelves. We could of course select a path in any number of ways; one of the mysteries that Bradley could never quite figure out is why we all seem to agree pretty well on the order that gets chosen. But he did wonder if, for every one of us, there is a sort of anti-person who is making their own selection in reverse order, inhabiting an anti-universe. Reading the Absolute back-to-front, so to speak."

Crone gave a facial expression I've seen many times in my career as freelance philosopher, conveying utter bewilderment. "You make a living from this?"

"Alfredo Galli," Dr Sand persisted, "wanted to create his own literary Absolute, a matrix of compositional elements through which numerous paths could be conceived, each a possible book with its own multiplicity of readings."

"Time is an appearance, not a reality," I added. "That's the thrust of Bradley's argument."

"Pardon me," Crone interrupted, "are we discussing the philosopher or the novelist?"

"Neither," said Dr Sand. "Or rather both, in their mutual contradiction."

"My friend is a lover of paradox, Mr Crone. I'm sure he'll be an avid consumer of room-temperature ice cream. The question is, if time is an appearance rather than reality, then what is 'now'?"

Mr Crone glanced at the watch gleaming expensively on his wrist, perhaps by way of giving an answer mutely analogous to his thirty-three point five degrees Celsius, or else to see if he needed to be somewhere else.

"For a long time I used to go to bed early," Dr Sand quoted. "Is 'now' the moment when the words were written, or when they're read, or all those moments when the writer or any other 'I' used to go to bed? When is the 'now' of a story?" Dr Sand's remark would indeed become prophetic in the light of subsequent events, but meanwhile he continued to describe Galli's project, crucial to which was the requirement that any path through the matrix of narrative possibilities should be a story not only scandalously disjointed but also inherently inconsistent: an appearance betraying its own unreality. "His collection of impossible tales was itself an impossibility. Even if he had spent less time in bed and more time writing."

"Yet you're translating it," Crone reminded him, as if any of us needed reminding.

"A book was published under Galli's name by a small press in Milan; something implausibly purporting to have been inspired by it was subsequently promulgated by a charlatan called Nick Jones."

"They have history," I explained to Crone in a half-whisper; then in sesqui-whisper mouthed: *Fragments of Sand*.

"If the Milanese volume has any claim to authenticity," Dr Sand continued, "it is but one path through a labyrinth only imagination can reconstruct."

"Like trying to visualise a pot from fragments," I said.

"Or a tree from its shadow." I'd heard many analogies over many Mozart Mochas and knew that Dr Sand would next say something about Galli's theory of translation; or rather, his idea that any two texts can be considered translations of each other within some hypothetical language pair.

"For example, there is a system where *sono andato a letto presto* translates into *I've been going to bed early*, but there exists another where it becomes *photograph of Deborah*." I gave a cough and Dr Sand politely offered a different example. "Or let's say, *nel mezzo del cammin di nostra vita* could accurately be rendered, *he do the police in different voices*."

"It sounds," said Mr Crone, "as if you're free to translate this book any way you choose."

"The canvas may be blank but the paints are of certain colour," Dr Sand said gnomically.

"And what if you mix them?" Crone suggested.

Undeterred, Dr Sand spoke of what he considered to be the key to the portal to the lobby of his endeavour: a piece that by Galli's own account was itself a reworking of Leopardi's *"L'infinito"*.

"A poem about looking over a hedge," I explained. In Sand's version it was to be called "The Unending": a story where the one rule is that there must be no mention of hedges.

"Harder than you might think," said Sand. "In fact I've been quite stuck on it. In the mean time Harry has been inspecting some of my other drafts."

"They're my current bedtime reading," I told Crone. "I'm particularly enjoying a sequence in what might be called a science-fiction mode, throwing us from an academic conference into a space adventure. It gave me a few ideas that I shared with a client who called asking for philosophical assistance."

Mr Crone glanced again at his watch, at the envelope, and at my diminishing ice cream before meeting my gaze in a manner that almost betrayed a flicker of contempt. "I wish you both luck," he said with room-temperature frigidity.

Remora joined us again. "Would you care for anything else?" she recited swiftly.

"Nothing for me," I said, pushing aside my bowl to indicate I'd had enough Midnight Rhapsody, then returning the envelope to my briefcase. "I ought to go now." The sense of termination was unanimous. Dr Sand asked for the bill.

"But tell me," he said to her, "How did you come to acquire your unusual name?"

She blushed. "It's a long story."

"My favourite kind; short ones can be so over-rated."

"It's a kind of fish," she explained. "My mother was a marine biologist." She left us to ponder the fact along with the curl of paper deposited on a small plastic dish bearing Mozart's eternal face.

"Her story was a short one after all," said Dr Sand. "And indeed over-rated." He lifted the bill and told me he'd settle it after visiting the gents. "Meanwhile goodbye to both of you."

Mr Crone held the door for me as we exited together. "Harry," he said earnestly when we were outside. "I'd like to make a business proposition." It seemed he had, after all, become aware of the importance of philosophy in the world of major foods.

"When would be a good time to discuss this further?" I asked.

"How about now? In fact, if you're free, I'd like to show you our office, introduce you to the team. My car is just around the corner."

If I were a smarter businessman I would have declined,

offering the excuse of some other pressing engagement, and would have made an appointment for which I could have been better prepared. But the truth was that I was only going to walk home, hope for a call from some retired schoolteacher worried about the afterlife, and look at those photographs again. So I accompanied Crone to his silver-grey Mercedes, registration ACR 0NE, and settled into its luxurious interior whose fresh-smelling leather was in better condition than the briefcase on my lap.

"It's a ten-minute drive," he said, swiping a touchpad on the steering column as we set off and filling the air between us with bland rock music. I wondered if it was a way of indicating conversation to be unnecessary, but then he asked me how I knew Dr Sand, how well and for how long; matters of no possible relevance to whatever commercial transaction we might be about to undertake. "Do you travel far in your line of work?"

"Philosophers don't get out much. And when they do it's usually in the Kantian manner, strictly timetabled and of short distance."

"I see, you operate out of a home office. You have a family?"

"Deborah and I have been blessed with no offspring."

Glancing at Crone beside me I could see him nodding slowly, thoughtfully. "What does Deborah do?"

"I don't really know. I could tell you her job title and the name of her employer, and I have a fairly good idea of her salary; but how she passes the day, in specific detail, is as much a mystery to me as I suspect the question would be to most spouses. I expect she reads and responds to lots of emails, chats to a few colleagues, ignores some others, takes a phone call or two. Are you married, Mr Crone?"

"Yes."

That was all he appeared willing to say on the subject. We reached a roundabout junction at the edge of town where the exit options included Magnesia Business Park, Superstore and All Other Routes. It was the latter Crone chose, a direction that took us past landscaped parkland disguising former mine workings. The rock music, identified on the dashboard display as *Lenny Kravitz: "Fly Away"*, was now serving its function of replacing superfluous communication, so I opened my briefcase and brought out some pages to read.

I was ronked in the Wobble™ court when Timman told it on the metaphone, he was saying like, it's Earth, it's fucking Earth out there, and we'd come back, that last hyperzip we trucked when we were all chasing the bunny on F deck and the tite rode us, and here we were again, catch-hold damn half empty, scarce a drop more ex to yield than when we were blowing round the Royce Belt those years back. What you've missed? The fuck! All those deccs of Timman hamming in the ObsoBub and Barron bursting his head at us about how much we were going to make when we came home, all those trillions we'd score, fat fucking chance mister! We'd been washed home on a freak gravity wave, some fucking black pulsar'd snorted us up on our own fucking doorstep.

I was zipped, mighty weight. Cuff says, should as well spec it. The fuck, I tell her, what you want spec our own damn planet for? Let's get the hell out of here before the pledge are on our scut. No, says Cuff, something up with the master scan. The fuck I care? She says, look at this, the mass spec says they're choking on CFCs down there, ozone's down, CO2's through the roof. Hasn't been so bad since the twenty-first century, she says, the fuck I care, I tell her. So they've snorked themselves up their own assholes – you think any of this matters a snake to us, Miss Straight-A Tighthole? No need for that, Chicken

One, she says to me. Point is, either we've wound up at some new kind of theme planet or else we hit a wormhole and missed the show through being too ronked to notice. What you got down there is Earth circa 2020. Everything checks out, even the zorny RF broadcasts we're stranding.

Yeah, the fuck I worry. Miss Nipple's all tuned about it – how do we get back to the fucking ex grounds, that's what I want to know. How do we get back where our half-empty catch-hold is worth a shine-eyed fuck? Hoy, Miss Cuff, any idea what the street value of exoplankton is, circa 2020?

They might like it if they tried it, says Timman on the metaphone.

Looking up I saw we were now passing rural woodland. The navigation screen showed we were heading nowhere in particular and had been driving for more than ten minutes. Mr Crone was apparently lost in space as well as thought. But then he spoke. "I know everything," he said quietly.

"I beg your pardon?" My reply was motivated not by any impairment of audibility due to the continuing rock music (otherwise how could I have quoted him?) but because his claim to omniscience was questionable *a priori*.

"I'm talking about Deborah," he said.

"A very limited sub-species of 'everything'."

"You know exactly what I mean."

"Be careful not to steer us from metaphysics towards linguistic philosophy."

He suddenly slowed, turned left and brought us to a halt. "You're the one who should be careful, Harry."

We stared at each other in a condition of mutual aporia. The rock music, louder now the engine was silenced, only added to the intellectual discomfort.

"Let's get out of the car, Harry."

"Are we allowed to park here?"

"Just get out."

Opening my door and exiting with my briefcase I saw a sign pointing towards a picnic area somewhere further along the forest road at whose mouth Mr Crone was apparently determined to leave his vehicle, though we risked impeding any heavy agricultural traffic that might wish to pass, for example if logging operations should happen to be in progress. "Are you sure this is a good idea, Mr Crone?"

"I know what I'm doing. Now walk."

Perhaps on a previous visit he'd found inadequate parking facilities at the picnic area, which was why he wished us to do this last part on foot. At least that's what I think I thought at the time; though my inferences, as I was soon to discover, stemmed from false premises. "Is there a toilet at the picnic spot? I really should have gone in Cafe Mozart."

"We won't be having any picnic. This way, Harry."

A rough footpath sloping gently up into the forest was the direction he wished us to take. The only way his office and team might be found at the end of that poor track, I reasoned, was if they inhabited a treehouse. I had begun to realise that I was in an unusual, possibly even disconcerting situation, and though the earthy path was dry and smooth I wished I could have been warned to bring more appropriate footwear. Eventually we arrived at an escarpment overlooking a densely thicketed stream some twenty feet below us, whose evocative trickle added to my discomfort.

"Stop here," he said behind me while I gazed at the overgrown gorge.

"I could find a better place to relieve myself..."

"Open the briefcase."

"Good heavens, you want me to do it in there?"

"You know what I want."

I turned and saw that Mr Crone was holding an aerosol can in one hand and a long-bladed knife in the other. This struck me as quite ominous.

"Give me what's in your briefcase and then let's forget the whole thing."

At last I understood. He was not after all an executive with a major food company. His story of room-temperature ice-cream was a deceit, even the staleness of his strudel that had led to our introduction was undoubtedly fake, if only we had heeded the manageress who honestly insisted on the freshness of her produce. No, Mr Crone was not interested in food but must instead be one of those people Dr Sand had sometimes warned me about: rival translators determined to pre-empt his edition of the *Racconti Impossibili* with their own versions, even if it meant stealing his work. Crone wanted me to hand over the pages of Sand's typescript.

"You won't have them," I insisted.

"When you and Sand were looking at them in the cafe, what did you tell him?"

"Only that they're sure to attract a great deal of public interest."

"I won't let you blackmail me, Harry. Hand them over right now or I swear I'll hurt you."

Despite the loyalty I felt to my friend Dr Sand, and to literature in general, I was persuaded by the glint of the knife and the threat of the aerosol I took to be some noxious or poisonous substance. I opened my case, brought out the wad of pages and thrust them in my outstretched arm towards him.

"Not that, you idiot. I mean the photographs."

He then went into a sordid explanation of events that was precisely the kind of exposition Dr Sand has told me he mostly tries to avoid, though some have called it the essential basis of Galli's style.

"So you're actually a weatherman, Mr Crone? I'm sure I've never seen you on television."

"When I received the pictures I thought it was only Deborah playing games. I put them back through her door – your door – after she'd texted saying you were out and she'd be back first."

The details were tediously specific and my outstretched arm was tiring. "But who made the snaps, and where?"

"Are you telling me it wasn't you? Why would Deborah...? My God, I bet it's those bastards at Häagen-Dazs." As if gripped by the horror of his insight he gazed past me, his face expressing sudden amazement. "What the fuck is that?"

From behind me came a sound like an aircraft, very low and fast, a screech and blast that shook us off our feet. The pages flew from my hand, blown by a powerful gust that peppered me with grit. I found myself tumbling, rolling down the bank towards the stream, and in a final moment of consciousness I saw the white pages swirling, twisting like gulls above. I thought to myself: you're about to die, Harry Blue, and then you'll no longer be a freelance philosopher but a real one. It was quite a happy thought.

4

Bad court, I'm telling you. Caught a wormhole and gone back in time? The fuck! Cuff had her specs wrong again, that's all. I say we take her down. Dump the Fidel in the first lot we find, grab ourselves another crate and strike out.

– Oh, and you think we get ourselves a craft on planet Earth circa 2020, Chicken One? says Carla. What, you're gunna hyperzip the fucking Space Shuttle, zattit?

– Theme-world, time-warp, who gives, zip-brain? Let's ditch and snatch. Like the old days.

– Yeah, the old days, Two says. Moment of nostalgia, false optimism, etc. The fuck.

We conference. It takes a while. About a week in fact with a lot of blaring in between. Then something hit us, bit of unscooped booster apparently. What a shazzle.

I was with Two on the Wobble™ court when it happened. Only about to execute trilateral Mishkov, too, my best in years. Then fa-lang, biggest lurch you ever saw this side of Denmark, as they say.

– The fuck was that?

– N17 impact, announces oh-so-clever Timman, suddenly gone into professional astronaut mode.

– The fuck's an N17, jerk-czar?

– This is no theme-world, folks. That's real space-junk out there, unfiltered, like you learned about in school. And we caught a bit of it. Sorry babes, the catch-hold's spiked.

Spiked! It was one nightfuck upon another.

– Means we're going to lose the tank, Tim.

Right, he says. If we don't go down straightway we lose every nano of ex we didn't already fuge.

No conference necessary. Toil it down there, boy, and never mind the lights. We didn't care where we dropped, could be the ranging sea for all we screwed. Only get the Fidel low enough for atmospheric to hold back whatever ex was still there, all spoiled and messed, shit, it made you cry to think of.

– Way, says Cuff, it'll still do for party mixers.

– The fuck, Miss Tittybrain.

First thing I do when we split, I kill her.

So we go pure vert, bad descent and black out. I wake first

with my head spinning and stare at the others as they slowly get their shit back, except Carla who'll need med whenever anyone can give. I'm lying over a locker door and my voice comes out a croak. Let's get the hell away before the scouts show, I offer. Cuff groans back, we're gravved.

She was right, of course. We're zero-g babes, no muscles to deal with full Earth gravity. Could hardly lift my fucking arm less stand. Felt like a heap of nydersecks had fallen on me. Turning my head I could see an emergency hatch auto-hinging, light blinding me. The blazing sun. Hadn't seen that in a long time. Barron trying to drag himself with his hands, legs pushing a bit, sliding. I copy, even lifting my head's a torture at first. Stay you don't break nothing, says Sis, we're too low-calc for this ride, don't wanna cruise with a snapped leg.

But the bone-salve musta been working, cause after Barron passed round the flex shots he reached and snatched, we struck A1, on our knees first then getting up like biscuit roaches, Timman first to stand, grunting to the hatch and looking outside, me behind him. We were in a forest, took some trees down.

– What we guide in on? pokes Tim.

Cuff, rubbing back and trying to straighten, says all expertisian: Tracker beam, must be a beacon some place.

Beacon? says I to Cuff Brains. The fuck's a beacon doing on Earth circa 2020? I say it with gravitational irony. This is no fucking time-loop, Cuff, I tell her. Not if there was a beak to pull us down. We're on home planet, my old cunt-blossom.

Can it, says Barron who's tending to his unconscious wife while we stare through the open hatchway and inhale the air, smells of chlorophyll like a museum. Carla's gonna be fine, he says. Musta been an energy source some place brought us down so hard.

Well I don't fucking see it out there, says I, clambering awkwardly like I've been pumped full of mangonile as I decraft. Breeze blowing, real nitrox. Real sun. I call back inside: Hoy, who the fuck ever said this was Korr-Helgason 45C?

– I tell you it damn was, Cuff re-says.

The fuck, bitch, I iterate back. We're home.

They conference briefly. They don't follow it, but the beam and the RF signals and the spec traces and all the rest make Tim announce that this whole sweet fucking air I'm breathing has to be some kind of illusion.

– This is not Earth, he jerks. This place cannot be real. We've been brought down by a selectron beam thirty-three light years from Earth.

Screw you, I sing, snorting pollen on the passing current. Brown dirt and leaves beneath my lead-heavy feet. Could almost kiss the ground if I thought I'd be able to stand again. One step at a time, trying to get round the craft and see what's on the other side. Only more trees, real ones like in old pictures.

Timman follows. Let's hike, I call to him. He says don't Chick, like he's worried he'd piss his pants. He says, this isn't Earth, can't be. This place is not real. It's dangerful.

Gradually he gets to realising. The tank rup incrafted some oxidised catch. We're hallucinating says Tim, collective exavation. If we all lie down inside it'll trans in a while and we can get the hell on.

Exavation my tit, I tell him, this is no ex-dream. I know the diff tween exworld and fucking reality.

– Not in the dose we musta hyped, he says. We're in exoland, Chick One, he says.

– Vac it, jerk-mouth, I snort back. I'm still trying to get

round the craft, beached like a fuged Wobble™ with a broken cell grip. Hoy, I snipe, there's sumth on farside.

– Get back in the craft, says Timman, you're exing and unsafe. We'll come out of this and then we can solve. Chick, man, we're still in orbit, still going round an anomalous binary getting spiked with cosmo-rays and leaking ex, can't you accept the plain truth?

By now, handle-barring the warm craft while my legs prod the earth and I get myself round to view, I can see the swathe of trees we brought down while in the further distance there's movement, a human figure across the clearing, man kinda staggering towards us. Oh my cornea, I say with a whistle and call back to the others, babies you ought to see this.

Tim's come look, dragging himself round the craft. Chick, he says, get back inside and lie down. I'll give you a shot of gravy until the exavation passes. Oh shit...

He's seen too. Man getting closer and I'm wondering if he's gonna try bust us for squashing his day.

– Let's go parse him, I say.

– No way, says Tim. This is not real, Chick. It's dangerful to try and behave rationally during collective exavation. We need to rest until our synapses clear.

Tim's starting to get on my crotch. Fuckit I've had more exavations than he's had one-man grunts in the ObsoBub. I know reality and this place is real. So we came down on a particle beam into a theme-world? The fuck why not? It's a free ticket and I wanna see it. Now I'm limping over there and Tim's on the move after me. The man has stopped and watches us hobble to him like he doesn't know what to do.

Hoy there, I shout as we approach, what's your space? He's all muddy in his old-world torn costume like he's an actor in a histodram or a tour guide who lost his party. He motions like he wants to fucking shake hands.

My name is Harry Blue and I'm a freelance philosopher.

– Did he say he's called Hari Bo?

Are you sure you're allowed to land here?

– Chick let's leave this alone.

I wonder if I'm dreaming this in an ambulance on the way to hospital?

I say eat your own truth. You want mine, I vouch some weird event vac-warped us down and gozzle knows whatsome else. Our hold's vented enough ex to trans the entire fucking planet ten times over so what we think about it is, to be pale, slightly administrative. We're in a floating world, boys.

Was I ever real?

He crumples like his outfit and collapses on the dirt. I say we take him back to the Fidel.

– Why the fuck?

– The fuck why not? Cummon Tim, if this'll all go away when you wake you can do whatever the dick you like with him.

A glimmer in Timman's eye. Might be fun.

We drag the chole across ground and find Cuff vexed at the hatchway shouting we need to lift out of here. Her theory is gravitationally induced time loop and I tell her to switch off before I crane her. We incraft and pressurate. Barron takes a look at our trophy and without a flicker responds in parity with what I guess is Timman's whim. Hoy, one hundred years in a small craft with the same friends and you've got it pent up, no matter how much ex you've shipped. Hari Bo could be useful, everyone agrees. Cuff does a full medic on him, calls him clean.

Soon we're up. Whole exploit took less time than one of Tim's ObsoBub enclosures. We're orbiting and this is happening, man, I keep telling him. Barron agrees. We've found some fucking duplicate Earth, can't figure out how it happened, but it's down there, completely real-unreal. Billions of fake people with fake lives, Hari Bo is one of them. Could farm the fuckers if only we had a market.

In following days Tim and Cuff do some research when they're not playing with our sleeping pet who's kept under with gravy shots. Even Chick Two feels the benefit. As for Tim and Cuff, they come up with a story from the archives saying that before the 2025 high-energy test ban treaty there was a fear that particle accelerator experiments on Earth might cause some space vac rift that Tim understands but I don't. They were going to try and make a coms network with superheavy entanglement until experts called it off realising they might destroy the planet, but what if somebody really did it after all, says Tim to me and Two while she's sitting on the pet as it's her turn on the rota. What if the experiment happened in secret and nobody knew? And it caused a vacuum phase transition says Cuff, so the real Earth was destroyed but sent quantum waves across the universe making shadow worlds wherever conditions were right.

That's fine says Two, so this bitch has no identity and civil rights. Makes me all the happier about what we're doing.

Sure, says Cuff. But remember, the test ban happened a few hundred years ago. The true Earth disappeared long before any of us got born. We're duplicates too.

– So none of this is real?

Or all equally, she says. Us, the craft, the pet's world. Hari Bo comes from a different copy of Earth, that's all. There must be star systems with other translations too.

As time passed I came to realise that catching the pet made the Family dynamic go nonlinear. Tim and Cuff often in the

ObsoBub together yielding tokens. Barron near invisible, coming from his kennel only when it was his shift on Hari. Eventually I said to Two, this craft is not what it used to be.

Two agreed. Since the pet, we weren't even lobbing Wobble™ no more. And we'd lost our entire fucking catch, all drained onto that shadow Earth below where the shadow people were drinking it in their water, breathing it in their air and getting their shadow brains slowly ronked, the precious bastards. Wonder how it woulda worked out if those dumb scientists all those centuries ago had never destroyed the real Earth in the first place with their damn particle accelerator.

But hoy, who gives? I say to Two one orbit, let's ditch the pet.

– The fuck you're launching?

I say, the pet's spoiled everything. And I don't like having shadow matter in my hutch, it ain't right.

Two can't fathom the subtleties but we resolve nevertheless. Drop down and ditch him somewhere then evacuate while the others are asleep. We can tell them he went in the macerator by mistake.

Two says, why not just do that? Chop the squawk to ambient.

But no, I want Hari to go back to his little duplicate world where he belongs. Reminds me of a story mother used to tell us about a kid and a catfish. I say to Two, let's dip.

So I'm singing it, that's what we did. When the rest were on gravy to salve their ex-lag. Lowered on manual and freed the puppy. Barron tipped the lance when he checked. Said we should fetch another, maybe a squad. Cuff and Timman didn't care, their only worry was if the waste outlet was blocked of tissue after we macerated the bitch by mistake. No problem.

I could give you a conference about this but I'll zip to

closure. We couldn't stay there, not with an empty catch hold. If we want to live we need more ex but all our stash was now oxidised and diluted round the entire atmosphere of shadow Earth below. So we decoupled from anomalous binary Korr-Helgason 45C, left the blinkers to sort themselves out if they can. Crazy world they've got themselves now, with all that bad ex leaking into their brains, but I guess the multiverse must be full of impossible tales like that. This one's ended till we hit the next spawning ground. Farewell Hari Bo. Goodnight Dr Sand.

The Unending

It was during a thaw that I was born. An unexpected breath of warmth had entered the leafless world; birds and old ladies noticed it first, the snow was sinking and receding, retreating from lost territory like Father's hairline. In the garden, a mound appeared; a gentle white hump in the melting landscape, barely discernible at first, but as the days passed and the white burden relentlessly diminished it became distinct, unmistakeable. Every morning, through the thick green pane of the kitchen window, Mother observed its progress while Father, in silence, watched Mother.

Eventually it parted, the last cap of snow upon the little rise in the garden, and the swollen earth was revealed, hard and frigid yet forced up by unseen pressure from beneath. Still the hump grew, slow as the endless season, until one morning at the window Mother fainted: the soil had cracked. A few days later, when she dared look out again, she saw the tiny bowed head of a child pushing up from the ground, blue with cold, the face frozen in folds.

Father went and fetched the large shovel. He pushed its flat blade down on four sides of me, digging carefully to avoid the roots, and raised me from the ground, carrying me inside, still encased in a chilled block of clay that he placed on a board in the pantry, where cheese was stored, and where the temperature, he said gravely, was just right, being insufficient to provoke the sudden shock of melting that might have killed me. Two days more my mother had to wait before declaring that the time had come for my entry into the world. The soil was pulled away from me: with hands, with teaspoons; scraped and wiped from me; worked from between my fingers and toes; teased from my navel with a clothes peg, from my nails with a toothbrush. Finally I was taken to the sink to be washed with soap and warm water. At the first splash I coughed, cried, drew breath, and my life began.

It was all so different then. Days were shorter, the winter constant and serene. Even the snow was otherwise; I think they made it from paper. In the street, like twigs on a stream, people met and spoke in soft voices, unwilling to disturb the perfection of silence. Tradition did not exist, because everything was tradition. Stories did not exist, because everything was true. Yes, the days were certainly shorter, impossible to measure now or confirm but also unnecessary, because memory proves everything. In fact I know that the sun was mounted on a great iron wheel of constant rotation, and on the stillest days, coming across the bare fields and dulled only by the intermittent calling of hooded crows, you could hear its turning, the low rumble of its great untiring axle. I think there was someone who oiled it, perhaps a team.

Going out each day into the cold, we were instructed first to take our medicine, standing in line with the porcelain obedience of dolls. Onto our projecting tongues a drop of Father's bronze-tinted spirit would be poured judiciously from a spoon; to each of us a single splash, sharp as cut-glass, an explosion of head-filling warmth to counterbalance the sublime unending frost. Alcohol, I maintain, like all else, was in those days other, better, more fulfilling, in fact not entirely as liquid as it subsequently became with the descent of time. I think Father may have found a way of freezing it. You could do that then.

I miss that precious spirit as much as I miss the long and carefree nights when we would play without fear or worry, never even stopping to consider what we silently assumed, that nothing in our world would ever cease, that nothing need be measured except by administering adults who rationed life only so as not to spoil us with it. We thought the last of the rime would never go, the crystal never shatter.

See there, Father would say, his outstretched limb combing the black sky and picking out, like a nit, the sparkle of a star. That, he would tell us, is where the ice comes from, where everything comes from, the frozen water of life. It's only because there are so many of them that we never notice. And to instruct us he took the cardboard tube in which his medicine bottle was stored – the bottle our daily doses could never empty or even noticeably deplete – and removing cap and base provided a tunnel to our view, a channel to the clockwork sky. See, he said – aiming the tube at a star and thereby isolating it for each child's eye in succession – see its glitter and it will make you tingle. It was true; the drop of light, concentrated by steady vision, was as warming as liquor. They made stars properly then, without plastic. Father said that not so far away was a place where the most enormous cardboard tube had been constructed, housed in a splendid birch-wood dome, so that hundreds of people at a time could see the sky's bewildering chaos cleansed, purified, distilled; the vatted stars made single.

But they had to be careful about how many people they let in at a time, because there was only so much wisdom to go round. Even then, I had the dimmest intimation that the world is not infinite, its bounty not unlimited.

Most of all I remember the coldest days when Mother would send me to fetch fire. Hunting for money; she'd always try the old teapot first, usually empty; then we would all run our hands behind cushions, look under rugs until eventually a few worn coins would be found and Mother would sit me down to fasten my leather boots. She would wrap a long scarf around my neck and pull my coat tight, then I would march stiffly in my thick clothing into the snow-filled street.

The fire seller's patch was a corner not far away where he would stand, tall and thin faced, every day and night, with the little bottles of fire glowing on a bandolier across his chest. He always demanded too high a price, and I always had to haggle him down to what we both knew to be the correct one, then he would unhook a bottle and I would feel in my hand its solemn weight; I would watch through the thick glass the dancing flames inside. On the label, in big letters: *NOT TO BE OPENED BY CHILDREN*.

Carrying it home safe in my grip, I would tread with a mixture of pride and fear. What if I should slip in the snow, and the bottle were to break? Then home again; the hearth prepared, my sisters crowding round as Mother took the bottle, ordering us to keep back in case anything went wrong, and she would stoop beside the fireplace with the precious flask held level in her hand. Slowly, carefully, she would unscrew the lid, and out would trickle a single golden bud of fire, its scent exactly like our medicine, gathering and swelling on the lip then falling into the dark nest of coal and waste papers.

At first nothing, as if perhaps it had died, and we would wait a moment holding our breath until there it was again, leaping out from its hiding place and skipping around the tinder, leaving flames wherever it touched, and soon it would all be going, a regular fire, you could feel the warmth starting and my sisters' faces would be red and smiling with delight, and Mother would take the bottle and put it in a special cupboard high on the wall, the only one in the house you could lock, and I would look up at that cupboard and long – how foolishly I would long – for the day when I would be tall enough to reach it.

Acknowledgment

Different versions of some parts of this book appeared previously in:

Magnetic North (edited by Claire Malcolm); *So, What Kept You?* (edited by Margaret Wilkinson); *NW15* (edited by Bernardine Evaristo and Maggie Gee); *Headshook* (edited by Stuart Kelly); *The Seven Wonders of Scotland* (edited by Gerry Hassan); *Gutter 9* (edited by Helen Sedgwick, Colin Begg and Adrian Searle); The Herald; Radio 4.

Praise for Andrew Crumey

Music, in a Foreign Language

Music, in a Foreign Language won *The Saltire Best First Book Award* and launched the literary career of one of the UK's cleverest and most original post-modern novelists.

'*Music, in a Foreign Language* used the brilliant conceit of a Britain just emerging from 40 years of polite Stalinism as a platform for some glittering intellectual fireworks.'
Boyd Tonkin in The New Statesman

'The strikingly inventive structure of this novel allows the author to explore the similarities between fictions and history. At any point, there are infinite possibilities for the way the story, a life, or the history of the world might progress. The whole work is enjoyably unpredictable, and poses profound questions about the issues of motivation, choice and morality.'
The Sunday Times

'A writer more interested in inheriting the mantle of Perec and Kundera than Amis and Drabble. Like much of the most interesting British fiction around at the moment, Music, in a Foreign Language is being published in paperback by a small independent publishing house, giving hope that a tentative but long overdue counter-attack is being mounted on the indelible conservatism of the modern English novel. With this novel he has begun his own small stand against cultural mediocrity, and to set himself up, like his hero, as "a refugee from drabness. From tinned peas, and rain".'   Jonathan Coe in *The Guardian*

'Watch Andrew Crumey, whose very different *Music, in a Foreign Language* handled real intricacies of time and ideas with astonishing maturity in a haunting, low-key up-date of 1984.'   Douglas Gifford in *The Scotsman's Books of the Year*

'Italo Calvino's fragmented narrative springs to mind when reading this story that twists history and alternative destinies. In a marvellously inventive tale, the narrator, living in a totalitarian Britain, has been writing a novel about a man and woman who meet on a train and begin an affair, but he is distracted by possible outcomes and erotic fantasies. Crumey's glorious imagination is complemented by a skill that manages to sustain the structure.'   *The Herald*

£7.99   ISBN   78 1873982 11 2   243p   B. Format

Pfitz

'Rreinnstadt is a place which exists nowhere – the conception of an 18th century prince who devotes his time, and that of his subjects, to laying down on paper the architecture and street-plans of this great, yet illusory city. Its inhabitants must also be devised: artists and authors, their fictional lives and works, all concocted by different departments. When Schenck, a worker in the Cartography Office, discovers the "existence" of Pfitz, a manservant visiting Rreinnstadt, he sets about illicitly recreating Pfitz's life. Crumey is a daring writer: using the stuff of fairy tales, he ponders the difference between fact and fiction, weaving together philosophy and fantasy to create a magical, witty novel.'   *The Sunday Times*

'*Pfitz* is a surprisingly warm and likeable book, a combination of intellectual high-wire act and good traditional storytelling with a population of lovers and madmen we do care about, despite their advertised fictionality. Certainly, Crumey's narrative gymnastics have not affected his ability to create strong, fleshy characters, and none more fleshy, more fleshly, than Frau Luppen, Schenck's middle-aged landlady, a great blown rose of a woman who expresses her affection for her lodger by feeding him bowls of inedible stew.'
Andrew Miller in *The New York Times*

'Built out of fantasy, Andrew Crumey's novel stands, like the monumental museum at the centre of its imaginary city, as an edifice of erudition.'
Andrea Ashworth in *The Times Literary Supplement*

'*Pfitz* manifests the same healthy disdain for realism that made his first novel, *Music, in a Foreign Language*, such a pleasant surprise. His borrowings from Borges, Calvino and Pavic are here just as shameless. But at this rate Crumey may yet become a hero to fans of the postmodern Euro-novel who wonder why we Brits seldom produce a homegrown variety.'

Jonathan Coe in *The Guardian*

'In the manner of Flann O'Brien's classic *At Swim-Two-Birds*, *Pfitz* is a hilariously mind-boggling story within a story within a story, all of whose characters eventually intrude on one another as plot lines converge. SF fans will want to join the literati in laughing over former theoretical physicist Crumey's brainy romp.'

Ray Olson in *Booklist*

£8.99   ISBN   78 1 909232 80 8   164p   B. Format

D'Alembert's Principle

'Wonderfully diverting and stimulating entertainment. Cunningly structured and as satisfying as an intricate piece of clockwork, it plays with narrative, revels in ideas and succeeds in being both fey and sharp, detached and compassionate.'
David Coward in *The Times Literary Supplement*

'It is a prolonged attack on reductive thought, on any one way of seeing the world. Like quantum physics, the novel wants to offer the reader possibilities. It is very post-modern. The book also sets the taste by which it should be judged. Like Crumey's giant astronomical clock, marking time of the universe, his ambitious novel works. It doesn't stop ticking.'
Alice Thompson in *The Scotsman*

'Crumey does produce excellent post-modernist novels, each as concentric and cunning as the others. This is a triptych starting with D'Alembert penning his imagined memoirs. The literary equivalent of an Escher, the story has no identifiable end or beginning. Clever, entertaining, engaging.'
Lucy Atkins in *The Guardian*

'Swift, who relished every storyteller's ruse and mocked the pomp of scholarship, would have enjoyed the Scottish writer Andrew Crumey.'   Boyd Tonkin in *The New Statesman*

£7.99   ISBN 978 1 873982 32 7   203p   B. Format

Mr Mee

'Clever, puckish, and artfully complicated... [Crumey's book] raises seductive questions about the nature of experience... Fans of Tom Stoppard and Michael Frayn will relish this novel's puzzles and paradoxes, its unfolding and ingenious designs... Jaunty and sometimes enjoyably silly... Crumey is a confident narrator, and his book has a heart as well as a brain. It is not only an intellectual treat but a moving meditation on aspiration and desire.'

Hilary Mantel in *The New York Times*

'The book is fabulous stuff: erudite but not patronising, elegantly and simply written, jumping ambitiously across the centuries with a good dash of down-to-earth entertainment. More than once, Crumey makes his reader pause, rest the book in his lap, and acknowledge that life is really quite extraordinary. He deserves to be better known.' *The Times*

'Andrew Crumey's new novel rolls up a suggestively tangled mishmash of literary theory, quantum physics and bogus Enlightenment philosophy into an engaging whimsical narrative.' Sam Leith in *The Guardian*

'An intellectual romp... Crumey has spun a delightful brain-tickler of a novel that undermines its own pretensions, a subversion that is in fact at the heart of the book's very real debate over the power of literature to redeem or corrupt or do anything at all.' Maureen Shelly in *Time Out*

'Crumey tells [his] tale with elegance and humor, and in rich detail. His immense talent reveals itself most potently in his ability to find remarkable connections in otherwise disparate intellectual concepts conceived over the course of several centuries, and then to turn those connections into a coherent and lively story... The many surprises and twists [in this book] provide a rare and spectacular reading experience... *Mr. Mee* is a challenging book, but it's one to savour.'

Andrew C. Ervin in *The Washington Post Book World*

'In short – it's fabulous. This is a novel which deserves to break its author through, if ever I read one... *Mr Mee* had me helpless with laughter.'   Jonathan Coe

£9.99   ISBN 978 1 909232 94 5   344p   B. Format

Mobius Dick

'I have a weakness for Andrew Crumey's novels. I call it a weakness because I've noticed that, when reading them in waiting rooms or on trains, people look up angrily whenever I laugh. There's much to laugh at in *Mobius Dick*. Like a magical conjuror, Crumey keeps all manner of subjects – chaos and coincidence, quantum mechanics, psychoanalysis, technology, telepathy and much else – whirling amazingly in the air.'

Michael Holroyd in *The New Statesmen's Books of the Year*

'In *Mobius Dick*, the narrative becomes a series of coincidences that we interpret as we wish, and all things are real only insofar as we want to see them that way. Under the skin of this teasing lurks a concern for the reputation of artists, and the role of chance in building the career of great musicians and writers. If Brahms had been ugly, would he have stayed playing the piano in a brothel? If *Buddenbrooks* had sold poorly, would Thomas Mann ever have been heard of at all? Andrew Crumey's work has been highly praised and not widely enough read for too long. In all the possible futures that exist for this intelligent, witty and accomplished writer, a wider readership should be more than just a matter of chance.'

James Wood in *The London Magazine*

'When the physicist John Ringer receives an anonymous text message saying "Call me: H", he thinks it could be from his former lover... What follows is a playful piece of scientific and literary conjuring, with Schrödinger, Schumann and Melville all folded into three increasingly bizarre interlocking narratives. The central plot hangs on a quantum computer buried deep under a Scottish mental hospital that Ringer fears might just produce "the biggest bang in 14 million years" – or, worse, entangle our reality with other possible realities, turning "the planet, perhaps the very cosmos itself, into a joke, which God alone might laugh at". The author has a PhD in theoretical physics, so you feel you're in safe hands, even as he leads you on a merry dance through the madder fringes of scientific conjecture. I'm not sure my grip on non-collapsible wave functions was any firmer by the end of the novel, but it was certainly a stimulating ride.'

Jonathan Gibbin *The Daily Telegraph*

'Ingenious is far too pallid a term of praise for this cunningly contrived entertainment, which may sound ponderous in outline but is actually a breeze, by turns slyly comic and oddly melancholy. For most readers, the soundness of its science will be of small consequence; as fiction it is solid plutonium, and unflaggingly enjoyable.'

Kevin Jackson in *The Sunday Times*

'Andrew Crumey manages to make complex ideas seem simple, and he has that commodity so rare among sci-fi writers – a sense of humour. He has already won critical acclaim for his earlier novels and deserves a wider readership. This novel combines the intellectual parlour games of David Lodge with the unnerving prescient vision of JG Ballard.'

Sebastien Shakespeare in *The Literary Review*

£9.99 ISBN 978 1 909232 93 8 312p B. Format

Sputnik Caledonia

'*Sputnik Caledonia* is a wildly imaginative novel, but it's engaging too, the early chapters of Robbie in a recognisable early-1970s Scotland sustaining our interest through all the twists it takes later on. And although Crumey doesn't tie up all his loose ends in a conventional manner, within the bounds of the book's own internal logic, all its pieces fit neatly together. It's an exciting novel, experimenting with quantum realities without sacrificing the essential emotional core of a work of fiction.'
Alastair Mabbott in *The Herald*

'This is a surprisingly moving novel about the impersonal forces – be they political, quantum, temporal or otherwise – that can threaten or shatter the bonds of love, and of family life. Never has astrophysics seemed so touching and funny.'
Sinclair McKay in *The Daily Telegraph*

'You are invited to use your own brain to grasp the links between Goethe and science, the circular thinking of Kant and the inward gravity of black holes, and come out with your own answers, your own universe. There are echoes, here, of Alasdair Gray's *Lanark*: echoes, oddly enough, of Jonathan Coe's *What a Carve Up!* In a way, none of it should work but it does, gloriously. There is some beautiful writing, and quiet fun. Along the way one gets to learn a surprising amount about the historical, near-poetic links between hard science and philosophy. At the end, however, two aspects linger; the deftly drawn parallel world, a real haunting triumph, and the very real, very human, quietly tragic tale, only properly there at the very end, of a good if misguided man, father Joe, given up on competing global philosophies but struggling with something far harder, harder than Einstein or Goethe: to cope, simply, with the loss of his wee boy.'

Euan Ferguson in The Observer

'An ingenious blend of philosophy, physics and fantasy... immensely stimulating and entertaining.'

The Sunday Telegraph

'The chirpily surreal title of this novel sums up Andrew Crumey's work, which sites itself at a risky double intersection between physics and comedy, sci-fi and serious contemporary fiction.'

M. John Harrison in The Times Literary Supplement

'...the sweep and scope of *Sputnik Caledonia* should leave you breathless with admiration: not only do we learn, as we often have from Crumey's novels before, but we also laugh, a lot. The final revelation on which the novel ends is both emotionally powerful and intensely satisfying. *Sputnik Caledonia* is a quantum leap forward for the Scottish novel.'

David Stenhouse in Scotland on Sunday

£9.99   ISBN 978 1 910213 13 1   553p   B. Format

The Secret Knowledge

'In 1913 Yvette stands in the Paris sunshine, gazing at a fairground wheel and waiting for composer Pierre to greet her with what she hopes will be a marriage proposal – but fears will be something darker. Their rendezvous ends with a bang that propels Crumey's seventh novel past Walter Benjamin, Theodor Adorno, civil unrest and war and into the present day, where troubled pianist David Conroy and his student Paige come across the dark symphony Pierre was writing before his tryst with Yvette. Various men – some charming, some threatening, none entirely trustworthy – seek Pierre's notes, and as Conroy retreats into paranoia and Paige dreams of fame, another conflagration looms. With its enthusiasm for secret societies and acts that echo through time, *The Secret Knowledge* mines the fruitful ground between *Cloud Atlas* and Foucault's *Pendulum*. Some scenes – a febrile union meeting, a loaded meeting between rival pianists – are wonderful.'

James Smart in *The Guardian*

'Andrew Crumey writes big fiction about big ideas; his previous novels confidently discuss the work of real-life thinkers such as Schrödinger or Goethe, and his latest is no exception... the book is an extraordinarily clever enterprise that repays close reading.'   *Gutter Magazine*

'Crumey takes on the complex and thorny subjects of parallel universes, Schrödinger's cat, and the plight of philosopher Walter Benjamin in this intelligent work of speculative fiction. The narrative pivots back and forth among various times and locales, including the present day; Paris in 1913, home of rising composer Pierre Klauer and his fiancée, Yvette; Scotland in 1919; and Spain in 1940. When Pierre is shot and apparently killed, Yvette honours his last wish and, with the help of a stranger, Louis Carreau, reclaims his unpublished score from his parents' house. Pierre then appears to resurface in Scotland several years later as a factory worker. Whether he lived or died – or both – is the question, as modern-day pianist David Conroy, his career on the wane, ponders if a rediscovered Klauer score might be the answer to all his problems. The philosophical questions the book raises are clever and insightful.'   *Publishers Weekly*

'...one of the most interesting books I've read this year. I recommend it, as a head-turning sort of philosophical fiction that's rarely done, and even more rarely done so well.'
John Self in *Asylum*

'Andrew Crumey's seventh novel finds the author up to his old tricks. Crumey begins his story in Paris in 1913, a date perhaps chosen for its significance both to modern music (the premiere of *The Rite of Spring*) and quantum theory (the Bohr model of the atom). A young composer at a peak moment – out at a fair with his fiancée on his arm and his first major work locked away back home – suddenly vanishes, only to pop up again six years later as a political agitator in Scotland. As Crumey's readers will immediately recognize, we have entered one of his mirrored boxes of many worlds. Pierre Klauer, a Schrödinger's cat writ large, is simultaneously dead in Paris and alive on Clydeside.'
Paul Griffiths in *The Times Literary Supplement*

£9.99   ISBN 9781 909232 45 7   237p   B. Format